time

·

TIME

·

TIME

·

time

·

TIME

·

TIME

·

time

·

TIME

·

TIME

Also Published by
Lazy Gramophone Press

SATSUMA SUN-MOVER
Nominated for the Dylan Thomas Award

CIRCLE TIME
"*A keen sensitivity to the relation between sound and meaning.*" Sabotage

ECHOES OF DAWN
(Limited Edition)

THE BOOK OF APERTURES
"*In a time when publishers are taking fewer and fewer risks on unknown writers, Lazy Gramophone are to be applauded for giving their collective a chance to shine.*"
Litro Magazine

SKELETONS IN THE CLOSET
(Limited Edition: part of the Lazy Gramophone Shorts series)

GUILT
(Limited Edition: part of the Lazy Gramophone Shorts series)

TASTES OF INK
"*William Conway is either the new darling of the short story form or its delightful villain.*" REM

GREEN DOBERMANS
"*. . . an expressionistic dream . . .*" The Times Literary Supplement

time

·

TIME

·

TIME

lazy gramophone press

Copyright © Lazy Gramophone Press 2013

Edited by Sam Rawlings

Text design and layout by Dan Prescott
www.couperstreet.com

Cover design by Daniel Chidgey

The moral right of the authors and illustrators has been asserted

A CIP catalogue record of this book is available from the British Library

First published in 2013 by Lazy Gramophone Press,
part of the ineffable Lazy Gramophone collective

All rights reserved all right

No part of this book may be reproduced in any form by photocopying
or any electrical or mechanical means, including information storage or retrieval
systems, without permission in writing from both the copyright
owner and the publisher of the book

ISBN-10: 0-9552530-7-1
ISBN-13: 978-0-9552530-7-2

www.lazygramophone.com

CONTENTS.

CENTRAL STORY.

The Scrimstone Circus Gospel
written by Tom Hirons ... ... Illustrated by Rima Staines p.6

CHILDHOOD.

The Prehistoric Age
written by Hannah Stephenson ... ... illustrated by Paul Bloom p.30

In the Belly of a Cloud Eater
written by Eliza Gregory ... ... illustrated by Dan Prescott p.33

Warrior Girl written by Stacie Withers ... ... illustration by Claud Forsbrey p.36

Inland written by Rahima Fitzwilliam Hall ... ... illustrated by Tom Harris p.38

Eibar written by Sam Rawlings ... ... illustrated by Carl Laurence p.44

Grok written by Megan Leonie Hall ... ... illustrated by Bryn Hall p.72

Lemur written by Guy J Jackson ... ... illustrated by Jude Melling p.92

Chase written by Liz Adams ... ... illustrated by Maddie Joyce p.100

Macaulay, My Nephew & Me
written by Inua Ellams ... ... illustrated by Inua Ellams p.102

Painted in a Certain Sky
written by Maria Drummey ... ... illustrated by Emma Day p.105

Childhood Cross-Point

TIME

ADOLESCENCE — ADULTHOOD.

Age of Bad Ideas written by William Kherbek . . .   . . . illustrated by Vincent Gillan p.112

*Oscar Wilde Said Youth is Wasted on the Young —
so Let's Get Wasted*
written by Kirsty Alison . . .   . . . illustrated by Lola Dupre p.115

A Very Very Very Long Spiral
written by Laura Dockrill . . .   . . . illustrated by Nikki Pinder p.118

Optimistic written by Will Conway . . .   . . . illustrated by Lee Holland p.122

Orphans of the Order written by Jo Tedds . . .   . . . illustrated by Paul Bloom p.138

Peter written by Jodie Daber . . .   . . . illustrated by Andrew Walter p.167

Fragments of a Storm Suspended in Time
written by Zoe Catherine Kendall . . .   . . . illustrated by Zoe Catherine Kendall p.175

Haunted by the Perpetual Roar of Gravity
written by Sam Rawlings . . .   . . . illustrated by Jeannie Paske p.189

If Only He'd Known written by Mat Lloyd . . .   . . . illustrated by James Kamo p.192

Vertigo written by Musa Okwonga . . .   . . . illustrated by Jake Ellis p.196

Adolescence — Adulthood Cross-point

CONTENTS

TIME

OLD AGE.

The Run Up written by Stacie Withers . . .   . . . illustrated by Zophiel Webb p.203

Turbulence, then Ash
written by Adam Green . . .   . . . illustrated by Paula Afonso p.206

Old Fucker written by Frances K Wolfe . . .   . . . illustrated by Diego Mallo p.208

Listen, Hear written by Vincent J Prince . . .   . . . illustrated by Matt Black p.211

Formal Wear written by Rupert J Munck . . .   . . . illustrated by Mina Milk p.218

Losing It written by Charlie Cottrell . . .   . . . illustrated by Dan Prescott p.230

Old Age Cross-point

The Dash In-between
written by Claire Fletcher . . .   . . . illustrated by Tim Greaves p.244

Twilight's Last Gleaming
written by Alexander Aspinall . . .   . . . illustrated by Tom Harris p.254

Ocean written by Sorana Santos . . .   . . . illustrated by Kaitlin Beckett p.256

The Fires written by Liz Adams . . .   . . . illustrated by Daniel Chidgey p.260

Biographies of Contributors
p.262

About Lazy Gramophone
p.281

TIME.

Time does not belong to me
It spreads itself like air
I move about in it, but have no place

WRITTEN BY IVOR CUTLER

Printed with permission of the Estate of Ivor Cutler:

www.ivorcutler.org

INTRODUCTION.

Time is a vast collaborative book project containing short stories, poems and artwork by fifty-five contributors.

Initially inspired by a discussion on gamebooks, this project has taken over three years to grow into what you are now holding in your hands. The importance of collaboration has always been central to Lazy Gramophone Press's ethos, especially the pairing of words and images. This project therefore, is our chance to bring everyone together under one cover, all focused upon the same theme in order to produce a unique portrait of time.

The stories in this book have been structured around a Central Story. The Central Story is biographical in that it follows the course of a character's life through childhood to adolescence–adulthood and then on into old age.

The other twelve stories in the book have been divided up, four into each of the three phases mentioned above: Childhood, Adolescence–Adulthood and Old Age.

The four stories in the Childhood phase focus on the theme of childhood and each of their narratives at some point make reference to the Central Story's designated Childhood cross-point:

1.

The protagonist's father is murdered
in the middle of a chaotic party . . .

*"In the midst of the celebrations, a drunken man (with little in the way
of name or, apparently, story) shot and killed my father. They say he died
happy, but I am less certain. I never saw it happen, though, for I was
long-gone with a two-thirds share of his savings in my bag.
They say he was buried in a fine suit. It cannot have been his own."*
p.9

In this same way, the four stories in the Adolescense–Adulthood phase focus on the theme of Adolescence–Adulthood and each of their narratives at some point make reference to the Central Story's designated Adolescence–Adulthood cross-point:

2.

A travelling circus populated by rogues,
thieves and pathetic clowns rolls into town . . .

*"My circus travelled the four kingdoms and the thrice-nine lands,
bringing joy to those whose lives were so tarnished as to be polished by
such a meagre smear of laughter as the pathetic clowns could offer
or the dubious wonder of acrobats who were, to be honest,
more flexible with the truth than with their bodies."*
p.13

The stories within the Old Age phase, as I am sure you will by now have guessed, focus on the theme of Old Age, while again, each of their narratives at some point make reference to the Central Story's designated Old Age cross-point:

TIME

3.
A storm brews from nowhere and
the ship whose arrival he feared
sinks off the coast...

"The day my trial was to begin, there was a storm. I watched it brew from nowhere, like the arrival of a whale from the deep.
Here's something: the ship sank.
She went down with stocks and stores and the judge and all twelve of the jurymen sent to try me. The waves ate them like ship's crackers, without delight or comment but only the necessity of sustenance. I watched them sink. The sea closed over them like history."
p.22

The Central Story was written by Tom Hirons and illustrated by Rima Staines. Rima created one illustration per cross-point. The other twelve stories were also created by pairing writers with artists. Each writer wrote their story before then handing it over to an illustrator who created the illustrations.

The anthology also includes three sets of poems, six poems to accompany each phase of the book. Each of these poems has an accompanying illustration, again the result of writer/artist pairings.

We hope you enjoy the book
and thank you for your support,
Sam Rawlings
Lazy Gramophone Press

INTRODUCTION

CENT

STC

TRAL

RY.

THE SCRIMSTONE CIRCUS GOSPEL

•

WRITTEN BY TOM HIRONS
ILLUSTRATED BY RIMA STAINES

> Вся время губит и вся покрывает
> Вся тлит время и в конец превращает
> Едину истину аки свое племя
> Хранит блюдет и открывает время.
>
> *Time destroys and covers up all;*
> *All is decomposed and brought to end by time.*
> *Only truth and its offspring*
> *Are conserved, protected and revealed by time.*
>
> from Иѳіка ієрополітіка *(1712)*

THE OUTLAW'S LIFE (AND A DEATH).

Listen to me. I wasn't born for birthday parties and scented candles in the twilight bath or string quartets on the lawn. I wasn't made for clean handkerchiefs and your mother's approval at the dinner table. Oh no. I was born for rock'n'roll, sea shanties and the smell of diesel on the harbour walls at dawn. I was made for bear claws on bark, for fires in the wasteland where desperate men in greasy overcoats swig vodka in the sparse snow and cold so tight and empty you can barely see a flame in it or the shape of hope in the dark. I was born for broken glass and imperfect love and riding the rusty trains home when the last-ditch grail-quest has failed and all the knights have spent their blood and wine on wrong questions asked of nobody in the three-penny hours of darkness. I was born to live wild under the hill, in the belly of the alembic, in the sperm of the whale and the heart of the gold. I staggered into the world breathing fire and ferocious dreams of the Inferno — when I awoke, I was a child. I don't know how it happened. All the grit and grease and the tugboat diesel fury was washed off me in a church font and I had to begin again, quickly forgetting who I'd been and why. Ha. I thought I was a child, born mortal and fearing. Some trick they pulled on me there, my friend.

It was good to be young. It felt like morning, like waking up without the desperate life-long love-sick depression of a million years on the breadline. Like a silver and blue morning, clean and possible. A ripple of a morning on a day-blue lake. I pointed at pigeons in the sky and they became swans and doves. My dreams were all of butterflies and swallows and dragons that scarcely weighed an ounce. You could have taken a year of my dreams and scattered them in the wind: they'd still be floating like dandelion dust in the air. I flew kites. Me! Kites without razor blades or ground glass, without fire or drunken madness or drugs in the sand-dunes and kites left to sail into forgetting. Face paints and grasshoppers; spinning tops and a face sticky with jam.

My mother made us a world of dancing and wonder and Christmases where Father Christmas wasn't drunk or stealing the silver, where the snowmen didn't melt or suffer strokes in the deep midwinter night. She did her best. I couldn't bring myself to break the spell by whispering to her bosom, 'Lady, I think you got the wrong child here.' I shut up and sucked tit and all the world was a glory of mother and child. To her, I was Jesus Christ incarnate, gullible enough in her motherhood to believe that her baby boy wouldn't play with guns or swear.

Not so my father, a sailor and a drunkard with other ideas. When he came home at last and saw this snow-white, surprising fruit of his loins, he didn't see the wonder of it all. He saw a host of possibilities and a pile of gold coins as tall as a house, an accomplice for his Various and Terrible Confidence Tricks . . . My mother tried to dissuade him, but he was too intent and I was remembering the smell of brimstone and whisky. I took quickly to the new agenda and my mother's heart withered like pale skin around a burn.

I remember my christening gown, white as a goose and about as yellow in places too. If I'd been the priest, I'd have stayed at home that day – as it was, I was christened somehow and they say the water didn't boil . . .

My father wore me at his side like scrimshaw or a gewgaw, a dangling fancy for delighting ladies. The side benefit: I could pick pockets and steal watches as quick as a copper-haired monkey or a jackdaw. Fast as a knife in a bad brawl; fast as a secret told and regretted. Fast as a fall.

My father was a kingfisher fellow and I almost never saw the man himself but in quick passing flashes of grandeur and eloquence. Mostly he wore a continual self of masks and cunning disguises made from the catalogue of mythic thieves and scoundrels. He was a jack of hearts, a knave, a fool, a winner of smiles from women and gold in gambling dens into which fools and only fools tread. He trod in and still somehow trod back out again, pockets hefting gold and jewels fit for a sultan or at least the pretty whores he charmed and was charmed by in return. (An aside: my mother died in squalor and filth and gin. Not wreathed in gold and jewels and my father's kisses. Am I bitter?)

When does a rascal become a scoundrel? When does charisma change from being the oil that smoothes all entrances and exits and become a sickly syrup whose odour spoils all things? Not a question to ask yourself in the mirror of a tenth-whisky bar as the shutters come down and you reel off into the skirts of a drunken dock-whore or the empty arms of night. But in better moments of more refined meditation, it has occurred to me to wonder.

My father's misdemeanours and sleights-of-hand did not win him universal admiration. When he took another wife, perhaps having forgotten temporarily that he was already married at least once, to my mother, even the dimmest ear could hear the pitter-patter of Trouble's horse on the horizon. Something fatal this way comes...

Drunk on the winnings of his latest gambling escapade and the first flush of marriage, my father threw a party for his band of merry men, those twisted creatures that hovered about him like lies. Such a party ... I dimly remember can-can girls, cocaine, an Ethiopian dwarf in a leopard suit. Certainly, there was an excess both of alcohol in the small port town in which we were camped and of party-goers from all across this benighted country, eager to capitalise on the drink, the women and the opportunities for both abandon and mischief. It was mayhem. I saw naked men staggering in the street, knifing invisible foes and making bestial grabs at stray dogs. The townspeople fled to the hills.

I kept my wits about me. A word here, a nod there, a plan or two long-germinating and now, here in Hell's fragrant armpit, coming to fruition. I did not raise a hand against him, your honour, I swear. But I did, perhaps, lead a horse or two to water.

In the midst of the celebrations, a drunken man (with little in the way of name or, apparently, story) shot and killed my father. They say he died happy, but I am less certain. I never saw it happen, though, for

THE SCRIMSTONE CIRCUS GOSPEL

I was long-gone with a two-thirds share of his savings in my bag. They say he was buried in a fine suit. It cannot have been his own.

I rode for five days before I counted the money and another two before I stopped and realised I was rich.

So it was: I came into my inheritance as a thief and a renegade. I stood beneath that full-mooned sky and howled with delight and terror.

What does time bequeath us? A handful of storylines and a bag of money if we're lucky. One self of us sleeps and another awakes; flip the pages forward fifteen years and they exchange again. Who are we? I don't know. I just don't know.

My most flawed and earthly father had been a showman, a street artist of thievery. His tricks and games had been practised and perfected in the squalid lanes and grand boulevards of cities the world over; his highwayman devices were old. A sleight-of-hand here, a blusterous patter there, a blade slipped quietly between the ribs and ah . . . He was an old-school master of old-school tricks, but he left little but memories and the story of his death. I determined quickly that my own legacy should be more substantial and less average entirely.

My father had been an amateur at all he did: I would surpass him. He was a quarter-eyed king in the kingdom of blind sleepers: I arrived with one full eye open and the other winking to destiny. I pulled up a stool at the long bar of my life, put my gun on the polished wood and the barman passed me the bottle without saying a word. I drank deep. I didn't stop drinking until the bottle was empty and everyone in the bar was dead.

TIME

A CIRCUS IS A CHURCH.

"Ladies and gentlemen! Lay-dees and gent-el-men! Roll up, roll up, roll up..."

I look out at them there in the grey rain and the candy-floss night and my eyelids flicker with the dismalness of it all. Look at them. Content with so little and yet... and yet... Content with so much discontent in themselves. I cannot fathom it. Cannot, will not. So much could be theirs. So much wonder, so much passion, so much life. They accept a thin wafer of it, a bowl of gruel, with a tip of their hats in thanks. Why not bow too, or curtsy? Kiss their masters' feet? Their lives could be a feast. I hate them for it, for their acquiescence to such a shallow plot of happiness. For this, what do they receive? They are used by governments, by business, by bankers and money-men to play their parts in the machine of it all. They enter into such one-sided bargains and I cannot, will not, let it go unsaid. It leaves me with despair and a curse for him who left me here among them. Whether he hears my curse or not, I don't know. Do not mis-cast me as a villain, friend. My curse is, I admit, no more than the curse of the rejected lover to the beloved. Do not tell anyone – there may be A Scene.

Before, I was young. I was a blade of grass, a hawthorn leaf, a wide-eyed sprite. Gladness dripped from me, soaked the air. Now? Time's fruit is a bitter apple for a man who dreams of grandeur. Such greatness that comes is not enough and true greatness is never known by those it touches. I have had both grandeur and greatness – one, I grew out of; the other sneaked up on me. I should have heard it coming and stamped on the little bastard's face.

A highwayman or a robber simply steals: he robs and gives nothing back. I aspired to do better and was inspired in my turn. This great, bastard performance that is Life, was going to be a show. The Greatest

CENTRAL STORY

Show on Earth, you might well say. Yes. I founded a circus with a bag of gold and inherited the Earth for my investment. What happened next?

My circus travelled the four kingdoms and the thrice-nine lands, bringing joy to those whose lives were so tarnished as to be polished by such a meagre smear of laughter as the pathetic clowns could offer or the dubious wonder of acrobats who were, to be honest, more flexible with the truth than with their bodies. Our circus was not, I should add, anything more than a cover for nefarious dealings, brazen housebreakings and petty cons. This in itself, nothing new. Circuses have been thus since time immemorial. But these thefts and scams were themselves nothing more than an excuse for my true business and my One and Only Calling.

WELCOME TO THE CHURCH

OF GOD THE FAITHLESS.

What just God would leave you here alone?
What righteous God would be neither Just, nor Seen To Be Just?
He has abandoned you!
Does he still prove himself to be worthy of your praise?
NO!
God exists! But he has wearied of you!
This God is both FAITHLESS and ABSENT!
We are on our own.

I can still remember the faces of my first congregation in a river-meadow at dusk. Drawn by bribes of mead and cigars, they came in their ones and twos, Bruegel-esque peasants like Brussels sprouts on a

THE SCRIMSTONE CIRCUS GOSPEL

thin string, drunk-eyed and up for a show. The next day, they came in dribs and drabs. Word spread – the next day, a trickle, then a stream.

My sermons, whilst not works of true art, roused rabbles and fuelled fires from one end of the land to another. My purpose was not art itself – I wished only to inflame and impassion. I was that most dangerous of men: a charismatic orator without morals. An anarchist without a cause.

A little child asks me:

"Is it true that God does not love us?"

What can I say? I look at the tiny boy, swaddled in rags and only the thinnest scrap of a life. Snot has trailed through the soot on his face and he has a knob of bread in his little fist. Life could be anything for him, but he will die in the factory that opens here in ten years' time. What can I say?

"God does not love you. God loves the angels and the music of the spheres. Here, look, there's a coin behind your ear! How did that get there?"

"God put it there?"

"No, no! *I* put it there. God has left you here. Alone. Who will you turn to?"

"You, sir?"

"No."

Tempting as it is to take such simply offered allegiance, there are greater prizes that require the sacrifice of lesser satisfactions. Remember this, when you yourself judge me. When I was offered Power Over Men, I did not take it.

"Do not turn to me. Turn towards Wonder, child . . ."

See, not so terrible after all . . .

We travelled, dazzling one day with the tawdry delights of the ragged Big Top and an arthritic elephant or two, stealing by night what we could not during daylight, preaching the next day to the baffled folk of the roads and towns we came to. Repeat and repeat and repeat. Not *ad infinitum*. I'm too old for *infinitum*. There's only *nauseam* left.

Where we went, chaos trailed behind. Glorious usurpations of authority, incandescent upturnings. Life blossomed; institutions withered. Farmworkers ate of their harvest; factory-workers partook of the goods they made. Landowners spluttered and tax-men barked. Everywhere, there was a great tumult. It was a wonder to behold. I smiled and the circus moved on and my church of the open meadow and the tree-shaded congregation swelled while the stone-built temples of authority stood empty.

I don't know what I expected. Worse than I got, or better? Believe me, child, when you've been around the block a few times, adoration is a lesser currency than some kind of soul satisfaction, whether the adoration is that of the little children or of the Magi, the red-top tabloids or the pretty girls and boys or the great unwashed mass of life that teems on Earth in all its dirty, wonderful glory. I did not need adoration, nor devotion. Some tried, though more tried murder. Have you ever listened to the radio in the middle of the night and heard grown men screaming for your death? It is a strange (though not unfamiliar) sensation. I would say, 'like footsteps on your own grave,' but I know little of that.

The first time a man tried to kill me, I was nine years old. I am no stranger to murder. But, the first time a village turned out and tried to lynch me, I felt a thrill that is difficult to describe. I remember thinking: Now we're talking! THIS is the life... I have made an Impression! Life on the road...

So, the squawkings of the radio hate-men and the occasional spittings upon us in the denizen-dark streets didn't surprise or worry a hair on my head, nor fist attacks of drunken, broken men in the night. I laughed. I loved it, yes. When the church-men turned their spittle-flecked fury on my church, I was delighted. *Progress*.

*

CENTRAL STORY

I was – and here *is* the sin – caught up in the music of my own mythology. I loved the sound my dance in the world was making, the clatter of my cane on the cobbles of life. The skitter and scrape of hoof and metal on time-worn stone. The roar of flame, the sputter of authority shrivelling and bursting, like crackling on a fatty pig. I roared at the radio when cardinals railed against me and when apocalyptics with their grey faces gathered outside our meetings, we sang to them and we gave them cake; we laughed at their fury, their madness. Should I have known better? Yes. My sin was the first and most terrible – I was in love with myself. Vicars, archbishops, curates and priests spoke against me daily and I only heard their words of fury and politics. What I didn't hear was the warning to look beyond the myth I was making.

By the time I came back to myself, it was almost upon us.

What was 'it'? It was This:

One night while the full moon watched and the stars hid their eyes, a bishop-raised mob burned the circus to the ground and killed every man, woman and child in the camp. They cried 'For the Love of God' as they did so. Ouch. I wouldn't like to be in *their* souls when the chips are down or the next day dawned as sober and thin-lipped as a magistrate's muse.

I was not there when it happened. Fate or His Humour meant that I was away when they came, returning from my ministry. I watched it from a hill a mile away and, yes, I wept.

I met a man once who others had told me was wise, though he laughed when I described him thus. He told me that time was the endless struggle between an eagle and a bull. He seemed to think that this would clear things up. When I raised my eyebrows, he laughed again and said that Time was the eternal dynamic between Heaven and Earth. I didn't understand at the time, but I was too proud to say so. He saw

THE SCRIMSTONE CIRCUS GOSPEL

it and nodded and smiled while he let me pick his pocket and I hated him for it.

That moment beneath the full moon, I felt the eagle pull up and the bull pull down and time stretched to breaking point in me as they pulled. The stars and entropy each grabbed a corner of me and I thought I would tear in two as I howled at the sky and wondered where home might be in this desolate universe.

A man's life comes to a point and shatters. The commonplace dissolves in the eternal and everything is begun again. It is not Innocence – it occurs in the depths of disaster, the extremity of cataclysm. Something gives way and surrenders. It is the other side of Experience; it is the place where the whole damned circle begins again on another level. If you don't know what I'm talking about, just wait another twenty years and a burial or two, a breakdown, a divorce or disaster or the tidal wave of humiliation. We all come to it. There is a time when everything falls away. This was mine.

I came back to myself as the music of all my glorious Play scratched to a halt in the burning and the screams and I looked towards Heaven and, through my tears, I saw the bull and the eagle pulling life towards Earth and towards Heaven and I wondered what the wise man had to say about Hell.

I opened the palm of my hand and watched my life scatter in the wind like sparks from a great fire.

When a man stands as tall as he really is, this world should shake. We are giants on the Earth, cowed by the forces of darkness and the belief that we are dwarves.

Perhaps this is a metaphor.

In the night, with all my life unravelling about me, I stood to my height and walked down the hill to face the mob. I unfolded my wings and unsheathed the sword that I was given when the world was very young. Yes, the Earth shook. Yes, there was blood. I cried for the maddening wretchedness of the world and then I let it all go. I walked away and no, I didn't look back.

I buried my sword beneath a thorny tree and spent fifteen years slouching from one silent place to another with my eyes on the ground. I imagined that I had cut out my tongue. I drew a hood over my face and joined the penitents walking from temple to temple, cathedral to cathedral. Whilst the Faithful flocked as only Faithful can, I kept walking, for silence suited me better. I dwelt in darkness and darkness dwelt in me and my blood boiled. Every footstep I took was haunted.

HIS SILENCE
AND THE END OF TIME.

My enemies grew strong in fifteen years. The world changed. The rulers of men's lives have always been the rich and the empty-hearted, but now they were emboldened. Greed rose from their mouths like grasping snakes of smoke. I closed my eyes and tried to ignore it. All around, I heard the world groaning. I plugged my ears and moved one foot in front of another.

I had believed that God was with me. Even in the depths of my exile, I had believed that He was still there, that He still might sneak a look now and then in His crystal ball to see how his favourite angel was faring. I was wrong. Like a lover long-forgotten by the Rake in His Progress through Eternity, it seems I had no place in His memory. One foot in front of another. One more mile on the penitents' road.

I began to forget my face. Seeing it in glass or on the surface of water, I squinted at it, this stranger. I swear that this reflected face would have abandoned me if it could. Its own curse was to be inseparable from me. Like two bastard twins, we haunted each other.

THE SCRIMSTONE CIRCUS GOSPEL

If you think you have the measure of those fifteen years, think again. Every minute of it, I cursed my foolishness and vanity; every minute of it, I heard the crowd as it turned my circus to flames. Fifteen years of that is a longer time than any mortal heart can bear.

I did not know that they were hunting for me until the day I was found. In some naïve quarter of me, I supposed that they might have cast out all memory of that terrible night and my own retribution against the murderers. Wrong again. I thought that it might be enough to walk, deaf and dumb, silent and secret and harmless, amongst them. Broken as a dream or a heart or a promise. Dull as a blunt knife. God had forsaken me – surely the hate-mongers could at least do the same.

It was in a garden, in summer. I had been travelling for months with a small group of silent, consumptive penitents – when you can keep your mouth shut, word gets around that you're good company to keep. We had, at last, come to the island that was the destination of our holy journey, nothing really more than a hill in the sea, a stone house and little else but the leper colony beyond. A red-headed ferryman had laughed as he rowed us to the island. He looked familiar, but my eyes were too tired to see and my heart too weary to understand.

We had just eaten our evening meal when my companions left me. I was used to this – the gravity of my brooding could suck the joy from the heart of a skylark, after all. I preferred the peace of my own cursings. If I was wiser and hadn't cast all my skills into the fire of self-loathing, I would have seen more, but. . .

They stepped out of the shadows, each holding a net or a club or a sword, and I, dumbed by regret and anger, was too slow and too tired of the game to resist. They seized me, bound me and clubbed me and I saw enough fear and hatred in their eyes to fill a hundred lifetimes in hell. They were priests. I thought that they would try to kill me there

CENTRAL STORY

and then in the garden; the lushness of life swept over me, the fragrance of jasmine flowers and the sound of the evening wood-pigeon high in the tall pines. I smiled and they beat me unconscious. I hoped to die there, but it was not to be.

I was kept locked in the empty stone pantry of the house and guarded by night and day. We waited for a ship of jurors to arrive on the shore – high officers of the Church, politicians, scientists, businessmen, kings. They rushed across the sea to witness my demise.

This life is long, but no longer than the others. There have been so many and so varied and all the same. I have tried my best and I have been cast out and kicked and forgotten again and again and again. There is nothing new, no indignity that I have not suffered, no pain I have not endured. Why? I was God's favourite. I was at His hand when all of this was created; I saw the brightness in the eyes of your fathers' ancestors and your mothers' forebears. They strode the Earth like heroes and spoke to the stars; they sang with the wind and held conversation with the universe. Ah, they shone! *How* they shone! I have watched through millennia, watched greatness become grandeur and grandeur become glamour. Finally, when glamour fades, what is left? This. Your masters are cruel-hearted tyrants and petty billionaires. You are shadows of yourselves. You should be ashamed.

I am tired.

When all the others deserted you, I stayed.

Does this count for nothing?

I could have broken my bonds, but for the brokenness in my spirit. I had nowhere left to go. I waited for oblivion and wondered how I had thought it might end otherwise.

According to my guards, I was to be broken with iron rods and burned and scattered and forgotten.

THE SCRIMSTONE CIRCUS GOSPEL

When I was a child, my dreams were all of butterflies and swallows and dragons that scarcely weighed an ounce. You could have taken a year of my dreams and scattered them in the wind: they'd still be floating like dandelion dust in the air. Now, I dreamed only of silence and His face.

Each day, the ship of my judge and jury approached. Each day, I prayed. Each day, as before, there was Silence. Was it *His* Silence, or simply the Silence of emptiness?

At last, the ship of Judgement laid anchor in the bay of the tiny island and fate held its breath. I resigned myself to die.

But listen:

The day my trial was to begin, there was a storm. I watched it brew from nowhere, like the arrival of a whale from the deep. Here's something: the ship sank.

She went down with stocks and stores and the judge and all twelve of the jurymen sent to try me. The waves ate them like ship's crackers, without delight or comment but only the necessity of sustenance. I watched them sink. The sea closed over them like history.

I didn't do it.

(But I may have been an accessory.)

As the waves ate their fill, a blinding light filled my cell. I'm no stranger to altered states. My mind's been twisted more times than a politician's conscience, after all, but light like this . . .

I remembered.

Everything that is forgotten when we take form; everything from Before, when we knew the taste and texture of it All. Everything that is too simple, too delightful, too honest for minds to comprehend. All of this, I remembered then.

No demon, no devil, no catastrophe, no Hell. No division, no Fall,

no punishment, no crime. Only the unfolding, the unfolding, the unfolding. Neither His will, nor Mine. Only the perfection of it All in the instant upon instant upon instant. I laughed and cried at my foolishness, to have acted the pantomime horse in this ridiculous story of holy war. I remembered and I let it all go.

This, then, is my story, hobbled and crooked as it is. I was born an angel, but tried to be a man. All along, I was with God.

Time is the endless struggle between an eagle and a bull. I understand it now.

He is the eagle.

I am the bull.

Together, we turn the world.

It will always be so.

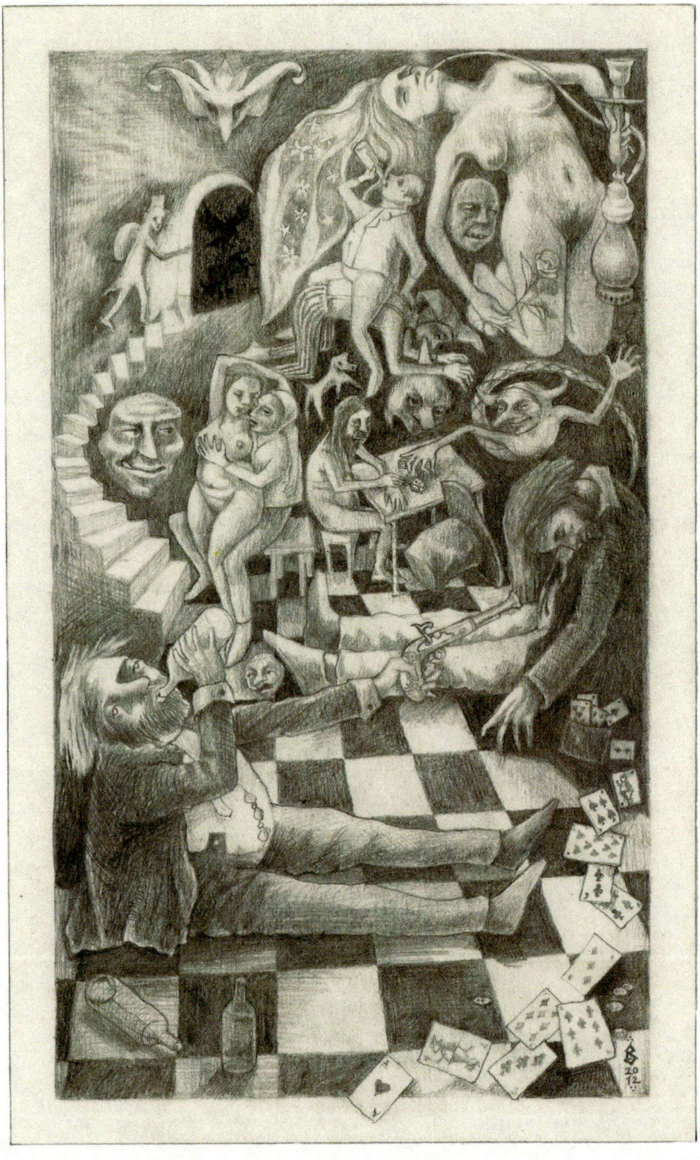

CHILDHOOD.

The protagonist's father is murdered
in the middle of a chaotic party . . .

*"In the midst of the celebrations, a drunken man
(with little in the way of name or, apparently, story)
shot and killed my father. They say he died happy, but I am less certain.
I never saw it happen, though, for I was long-gone with a two-thirds
share of his savings in my bag. They say he was buried in a fine suit.
It cannot have been his own."*

CENTRAL STORY

The Scrimstone Circus Gospel

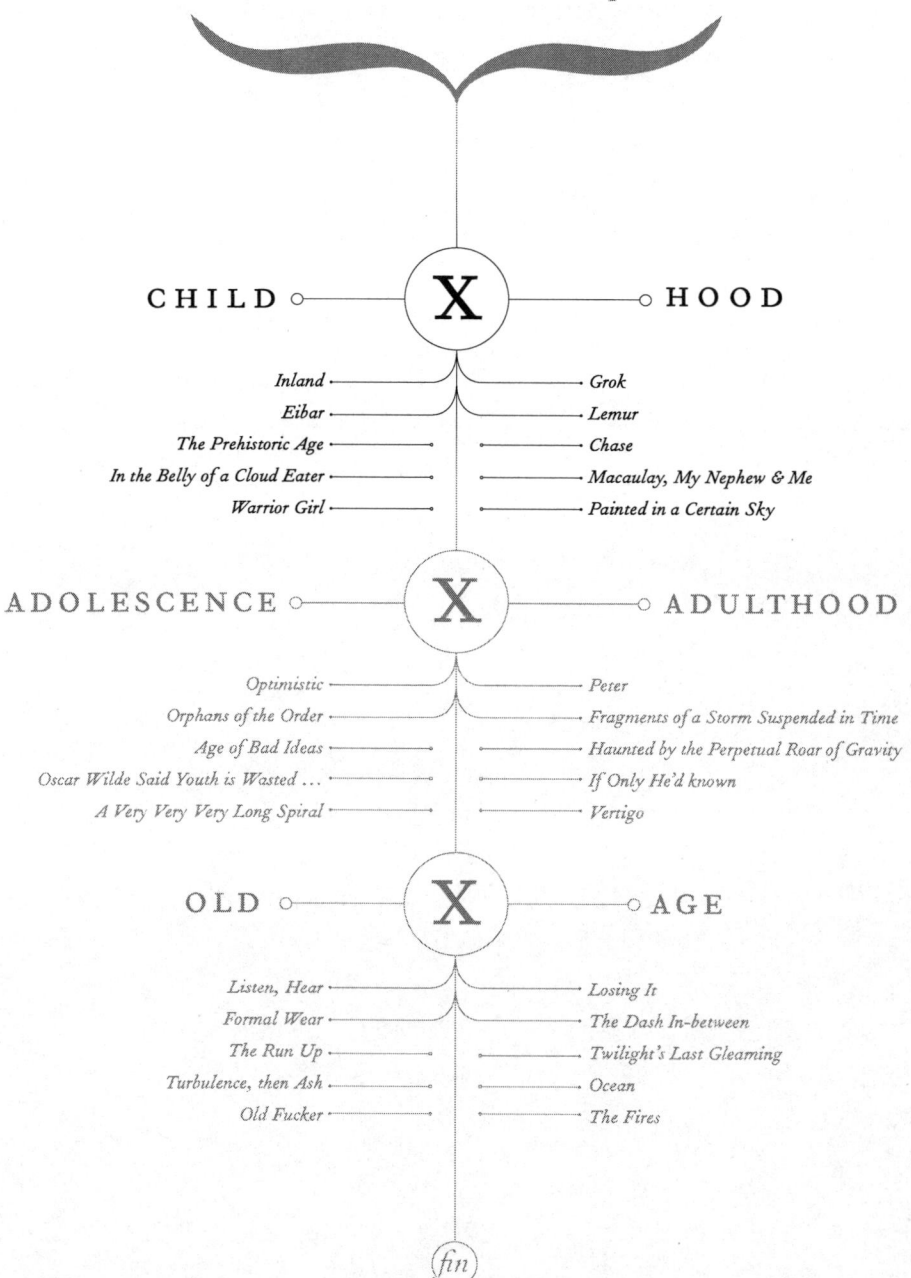

CHILD — X — HOOD

Inland	Grok
Eibar	Lemur
The Prehistoric Age	Chase
In the Belly of a Cloud Eater	Macaulay, My Nephew & Me
Warrior Girl	Painted in a Certain Sky

ADOLESCENCE — X — ADULTHOOD

Optimistic	Peter
Orphans of the Order	Fragments of a Storm Suspended in Time
Age of Bad Ideas	Haunted by the Perpetual Roar of Gravity
Oscar Wilde Said Youth is Wasted …	If Only He'd known
A Very Very Very Long Spiral	Vertigo

OLD — X — AGE

Listen, Hear	Losing It
Formal Wear	The Dash In-between
The Run Up	Twilight's Last Gleaming
Turbulence, then Ash	Ocean
Old Fucker	The Fires

(fin)

THE PREHISTORIC AGE

•

WRITTEN BY HANNAH STEPHENSON
ILLUSTRATED BY PAUL BLOOM

We wake into this world knowing we're awake,
mostly knowing how to operate our faces,

our voices. Control of limbs comes later, but
still, we know we want to move our fists,

to raise our body above limbs and the floor,
to see what is new, which is everything.

At the prehistoric age, what propels the small
body around the yard, from grass to dirt

to fence: pleasure in movement, in seeing forms
and lines and light and reaching out for them,

that we might pull them closer, clutched.
Because we cannot predict how objects behave,

we test what we can touch, the thin edge
of the tablecloth high above, the pleated rim

of the lampshade, the pliable shampoo bottle.
I want that thing, we decide one day, this pillow,

this blue blanket, this red plastic car, so cool
against the cheek. We choose without past attachment

what to express affection for, and want to live near
our favorite things. All memory begins as love.

IN THE BELLY OF A CLOUD EATER

•

WRITTEN BY ELIZA GREGORY
ILLUSTRATED BY DAN PRESCOTT

It was a blank high hill
                  sunk flat plane empty thick square chock
-full nothing-to-see view on the narrow darkening wide bright small
lightened horizon where any pulled pushed drop rang out - exploded upon feeling
falling from empty un-understanding by nobody who had left in the room's corner weather
a tired excited shrivelled puckered ripe left-over first-in-the-queue party balloon

Standing lying sitting leaping from awesome dull blinding undulating
beams small long murky horizon where a hideous ugly happy
sweet something could be beautifully sad daydreaming dead-in-the head
robot   caged   free   cabbaged   fighting hens   roaming the sky's mind

Clear   not for pennies   it thinks and we see on the free open screen

        Trains trailing long fat thin short shaped pigs gurning
                                                    solidly
                                                    asleep

                                                            soft-eyed
                                                            frog spawn
            in a field. My jar is full. Net heavy.

            Sea-skinned licks.

Squeezing dew out hot on lips of sweets lathering up to hook water mouth's
whistling for ice-lollies on seeing airs shapes bursting outlines of dry heat
I look to my hand loosely held tight over my head knitting finger shapes
 slow crab-pincering   fast to squash an eye line of *Translucidus*
 (translucent Rabbit) *Opacus* (opaque Roaring Mouth)   and *Perlucidus*
(opaque with translucent breaks, Beaks of Poisonous Man Eating Plants)
eating their path fore and aft.

X X   X

Beetle and Slug   don't like Tin Soldier   twig fort captives they stray together

          crawling in a straw pile on t'pond's dry pie-crust edge
                                                            strewn
                                                            down

                                                            feet
                                                            on

                                                            dragging
                                                            home

before I flagged
no longer a kernel.

34 · childhood

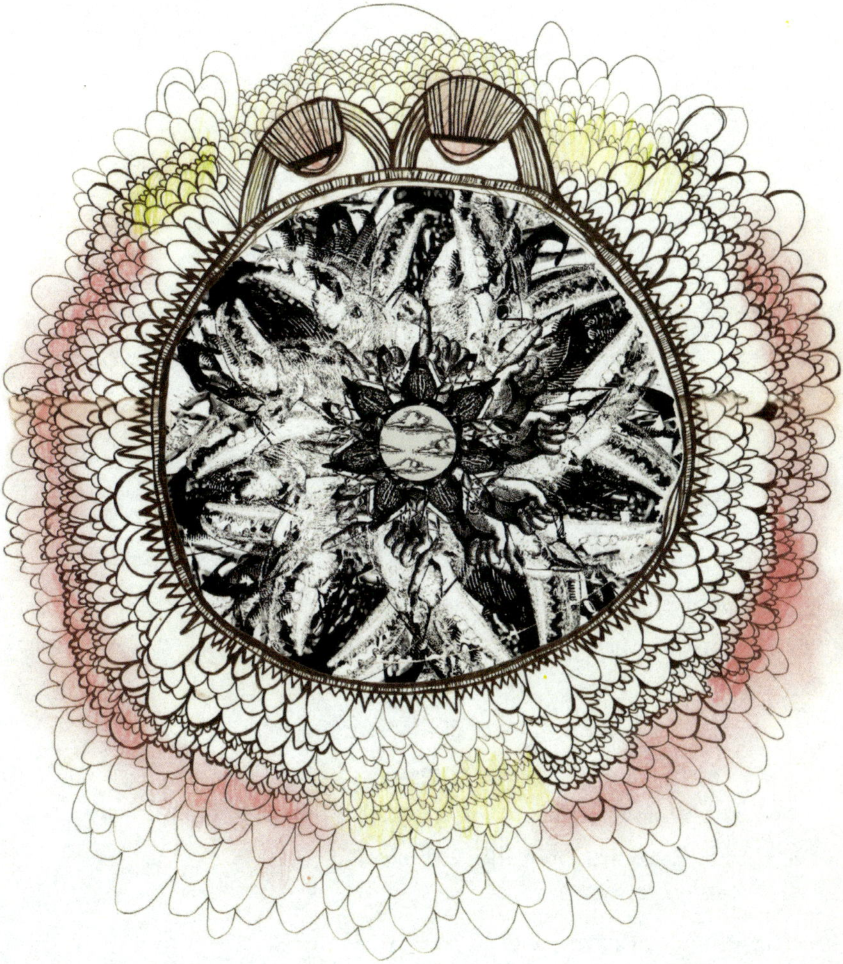

WARRIOR GIRL

WRITTEN BY STACIE WITHERS
ILLUSTRATED BY CLAUD FORSBREY

Sharpe stick, light foot,
painted face and gleaming eye.
I will be taller than you, leaner, meaner, crouched
in waiting, watching you. I am quietly patient and I listen hard.

Circled round the fire, stories dancing through the smoke,
as I learn my place and flex my new found muscles.
Torn book pages, muddy prints, crust-less sandwiches,
and a nap this afternoon. I am all you dreamed and none of what you wished.

An arm, a leg, a childish voice inside your head.
Pieces missing, all collected, put together in a hurry,
in the dark and incidental. I build castles and burn bridges,
I tread softly and lay foot ahead of hand.

Warm skin, dark eyes, fingers, count them, ten,
to reach and touch and point, to form
a fist and fight. I am ready, and far less fearful now than you.
I am the you that you thought you were going to be.

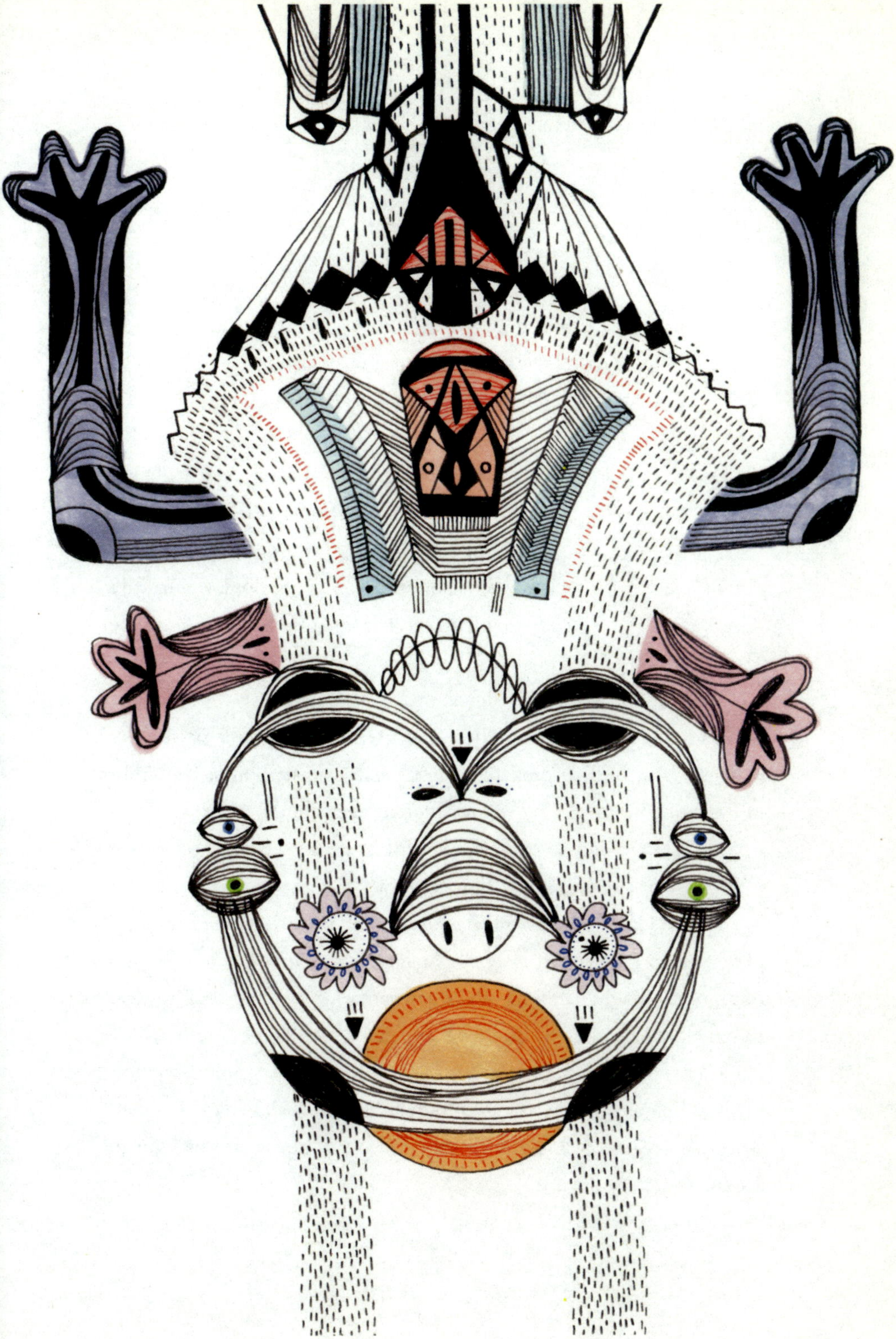

INLAND

WRITTEN BY RAHIMA FITZWILLIAM HALL
ILLUSTRATED BY TOM HARRIS

The boy dragged his wine crate boat behind him as he sailed through the fields he took for the sea — they were flat enough, the horizon steady enough, ripples of freshly turned peat as far as the boy could see. He played captain, fisherman, explorer on the lookout for new land. Crows *en masse* made for storms in the boundless, otherwise still sky. The occasional hedgerows were hide-outs and the hay bales his harbours. He didn't know when he would get to see the real ocean again, they had been driving for days and he'd lost count of sleeps since the last sight of sea. He had seen the sea every day at home. Home. Yarmouth. Great Yarmouth. The boy always liked the way it felt to say 'Great Yarmouth'. He repeated it over and over in as many different voices as he could think of as he navigated the slight curvature of the field back toward the truck. The truck, the boy liked to call it Great Truckmouth, which made it sound much bigger than it was. It was Lewis's truck; Lewis was the boy's older brother. He wasn't there because he had had to go and work on a real ship, called Her Majesty's Ship. Lewis, at least, got to see the sea every day.

*

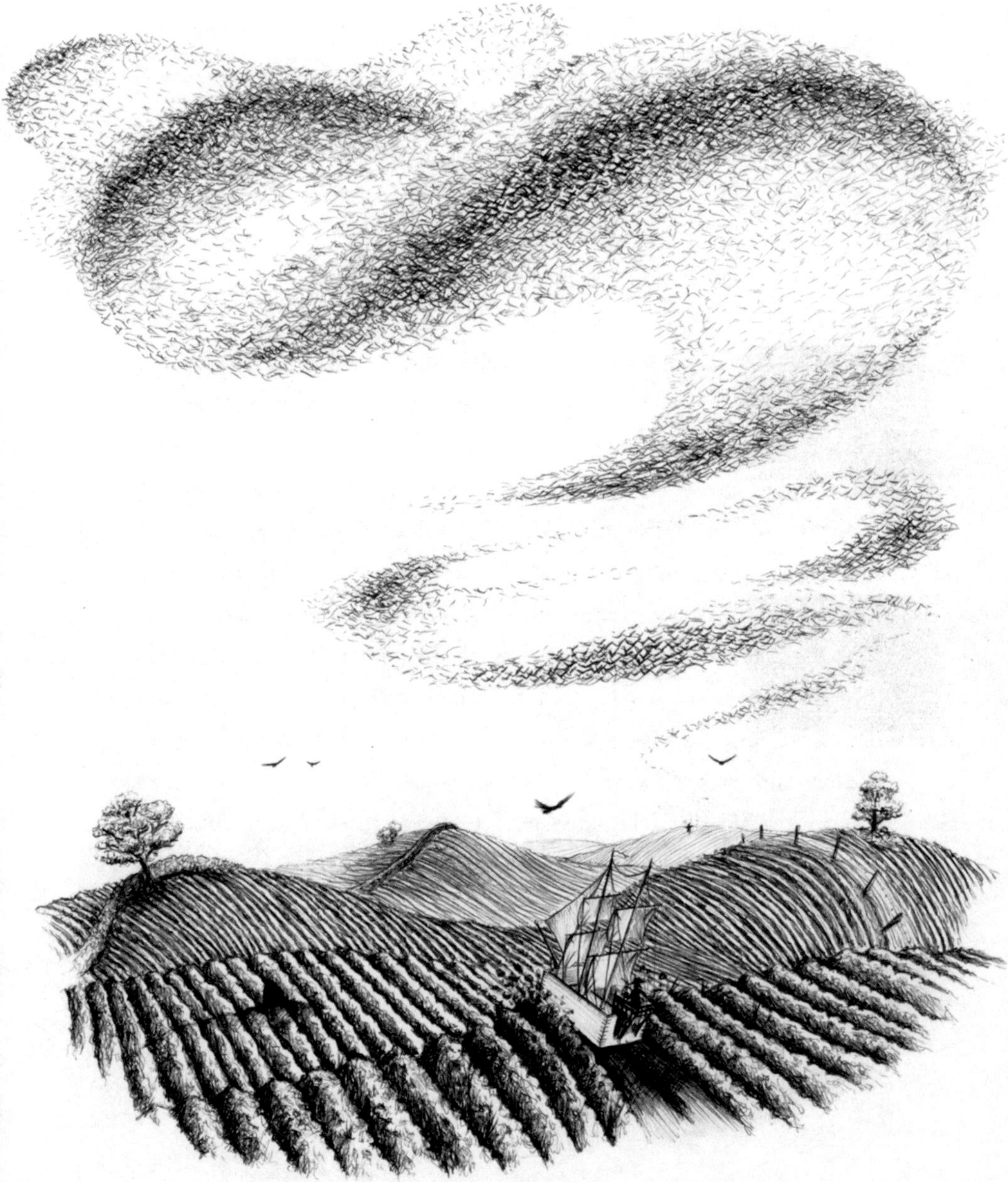

The boy, his mother and grandfather, were on holiday.

"We're taking the truck for a long drive to see what we find, it'll be our first holiday," the boy's mother had told him the night before their departure.

Except it wasn't a real holiday, the boy knew that much. Holidays were for whole families, holidays headed toward the sea, not away from it. He knew no one planned this holiday and he knew they might not go back. For now their truck was horse and home, on the edges of towns, on empty roads between sunken salt marshes and flush fields. Each day a new holiday destination, each destination another day inland.

"It's not good times there anymore," his grandfather had eventually told the boy, but of course he already knew that.

There was no business, no one celebrating anymore, no one wanting to hire their tents. The big round tent had been the boy's favourite because Lewis and the other men always took him with them to rig it. He would take very seriously his task of running from pole to pole, unwinding thick ancient ropes, soft with years of other peoples' touch. It felt like they had built a castle when they finished. A castle that had hosted all the parties, every knees-up, wedding, birthday and circus in all the neighbouring sea towns for all the past one-hundred years or more. That was until the parties stopped and the army sent an urgent letter saying they needed to borrow the tent for them to live in and came and took it away. The boy's grandfather thought they would never see it again, so he gathered up all the pictures he could find of the tent and pinned them to the wooden panelling in the back of the truck. The oldest and most mysterious was a drawing of the tent with flames around it on a faded newspaper clipping as thin as toilet paper. It made the boy shudder with wonder when he touched it. It was a story about a sailor from a long time ago, maybe even a captain, or a pirate, who was shot dead at his own party. It told of how the party went on and on

CELEBRATION ENDS IN TRAGEDY

DEATH OF SEAFARING MAN SPARKS CHAOS

and the tent had to be taken down while things were on fire and people were still inside. Another more recent clipping showed a photograph of an elephant about to give birth in the tent when it had been hired to Eccles Circus. The boy knew this one well as Lewis had seen it happen and told him the story. There was bright pink elephant blood everywhere!

The boy sat in his wine crate boat and waited for breakfast as his grandfather shredded an apple with a serrated breadknife into a pot of porridge. The rusty truck was lit up all golden in the morning light and the boy couldn't help but stare at it even though it made his eyes hurt after a while. They had parked it by a tall lone Scots Pine so that they wouldn't forget which field was theirs. The boy thought it looked like a tree from a faraway place like Africa. He liked to imagine Lewis had sailed as far as Africa, and would be on his way back by then. Several crates were turned over to make a dwarfed table by the tree and a small smoky fire made delicate crackling sounds around a kettle. The boy knew it was ridiculous to use a breadknife to cut an apple but he thought his grandfather looked happy so he left him to it.

There was a sudden lightness to being there, in the wild marshes and wide open fields, as though they really had crossed over into another land. A land where they were nothing but a dot on an unending horizon, a land where all yesterday's parties were just pictures in old newspapers, a land the sea had left behind.

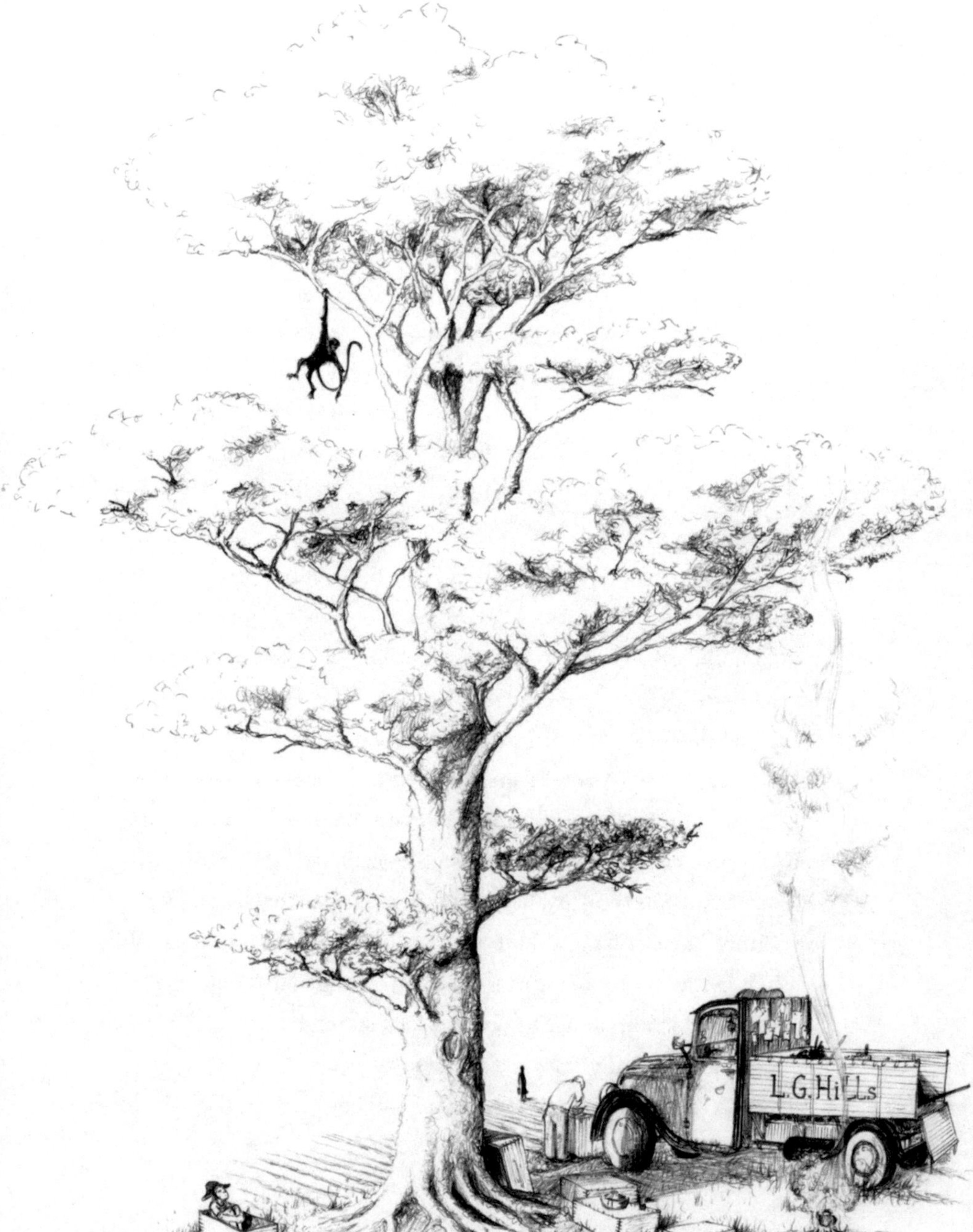
L.G. HiLLs

EIBAR

WRITTEN BY SAM RAWLINGS
ILLUSTRATED BY CARL LAURENCE

I.

Once upon a time, somewhere beneath the clouds, entrenched within an old house, lived a young girl named Ember. Ember's home town clung desperately to the slope upon which it had been built, a bundle of weaker dwellings sprawled at its base, hemming the ocean as their silhouettes trailed off into the distance. It was here, inside one of these buildings, engulfed by the creaking of rafters, nestled below the surface of a thick wooden table, that Ember's big brown eyes peered up and out at the room beyond. Her ears strained within the silence. The door frame loomed menacingly, a black hole unto the rest of the house. Ember's nose twitched against the rising smell of damp. She returned her attention to the pen that was now resting within her left hand. She twirled it between her fingers as she admired her work. An army of stick-men, splogged and deformed by the run of the ink upon her heavy trousers, stared back up at her. She smiled, her left leg now adorned with faces.

Ever since finding that tin The Eibar had haunted her thoughts. It was clearly an old tin, long since discarded. Their name being the only legible word remaining upon its surface, engraved three times, once on the lid and twice on opposite ends. 'Eibar', the tin read. The three Eibar.

"The Eibar," she said, sounding the word out, though as soon as she had done so she froze, eyes peering anxiously toward the door.

It sounded like a foreign word, a faraway word. Ember's heart began to beat in her chest. She whispered it this time.

"Eibar," over and over again, "Eibar, Eibar, Eibar," until at last the sound dissolved entirely.

She twisted her right palm and very carefully she marked her wrist with a single black dot.

"Eibar," she practiced.

She should not forget this word.

"Eibar," she giggled, ". . . The Eibar."

But no sooner had her laughter broken than a ripple disturbed the floorboards. Ember felt herself undulate as the sound of that first footstep carried into her room. A torrent of thumping consumed the entire house. Ember froze.

"Won't you never fucking listen!"

A cacophony of pounding feet rose steadily up the stairs before crashing with unbridled force into the room next door.

"Son of a whore!"

"Vile bitch! You vile cow, why won't you never listen!" the two voices warred.

"It's you, it's you what needs to fucking listen!"

Their words filled the air. Ember slammed a hand to her mouth, pressing in on her lips with her fingers. What had she done? The far wall shook, dirt crumbling to the floor. Ember bowed her head, eyes fixed upon her trousers. Using her right hand she cupped each ear in turn, humming furiously, sketching as she did so. Still the words, the thumping, the screaming, still it roared. Powerless to make it stop Ember began rubbing her tummy. A dull ache hunched her back as she drew.

"Eibar," she whispered.

She could almost picture their faces, their limbs, their clothes. The Eibar would make this stop.

"Cunt," she heard the word clear as a bell.

Once again the walls shuddered. Feet pounded the ground, more voices and then the shattering of glass, the crashing of a symbol, the patter of rain upon an ocean. Ember gulped. She slammed her fists into the floorboards. Tears streamed from her eyes and yet her features remained unchanged. She thumped the floor again, over and over until her knuckles glistened red.

"Eibar," she muttered, "Eibar, Eibar."

Both hands now masked her eyes, the pen rolling away. Still she heard their voices: her father's rage, her mother's . . . but then, a yelp, sharp and unmistakable, its echo muffled by a dull thump. Ember's eyes flashed open and before she knew what she was doing she was upon her feet, skinny limbs carrying her forward. She vanished through the door. Emerging into the hall she ran as fast she could, she sped down the corridor and burst into her parent's room.

The first thing Ember saw was her mother, mouth wide, words, curses, bile spewing from her tongue. She laid there upon the floor as if a felled tree, knees bent, one foot still planted upon the ground. Blood ran from her brow, assailed her eyes.

"My darling!" she screeched, "she's come, she's come saving me! Ma's little girl's come at last. I prayed she'd come!" and crawling on her knees she flung herself about Ember's waist, dragging her daughter down.

Ember looked up at her father, eyes blinking with incomprehension. She beheld his scowling frame. Fists clenched, for a moment he remained as he was, loaded, limbs taut.

"Dad, Ma, stop, please?" Ember's voice hung like smoke, "I'm sorry, I'm so sorry, please?"

Silence filled the room. Ember waited. She waited and she waited. All of a sudden her father reeled away in shock. He stood there, rubbing his face with his hands. Her mother exhaled, deflated. Ember's own hands were shaking. She had never possessed the strength to intervene before. The Eibar, they were all she could think about, the only explanation.

"Makes me sick," growled her father, a tear of his own tumbling onto his cheek, and clawing his way past them, he stormed out.

The door rattled on its hinges as he slammed it behind him.

"Fuck!" screamed her mother, and throwing Ember aside she clambered to her knees.

"Fucker!" she yelled again.

"Ma?" Ember spoke, her hand reaching out.

"Don't look at me child."

"I en't," Ember snapped, standing up, head bowed.

"We do this, we do this and all, for you, you know? You know that don't you baby girl? We love you. We love you so much . . ."

Her mother was shaking now, hands like leaves in the wind, and yet there was no wind in here, no sky, no sunshine. . . Rain dripped from the ceiling. Clothes, tools, wood, fabric lay slumped in great piles. An upturned lamp cast shadows upon the walls.

"Come on Ma," whispered Ember, moving carefully across the room. She took her mother's palm in her own.

"Come with me Ma," she said.

Retracing her steps, Ember lead her mother back down the hall, past the dining room, past the staircase and into her parents' bedroom. Nothing more than a mattress upon the floor, its sheets damp to touch and rank with must.

"Here you are Ma," she said, shrugging her mother from her shoulder and dropping her into bed.

"Don't leave?" she muttered, as Ember pressed the blankets in around her.

"It's alright, you sleep Ma."

Ember kissed her mother's brow, sliding her arm free as she did so.

"En't you going to sleep by me? You'd always sleep by me."

"No Ma, I can't sleep now."

Ember never slept. She turned away and descended the stairs. Her tummy writhed as she walked and raking a clump of hair from her face she slumped herself at the kitchen table. Already her mother's snores rattled above. Maybe she should sleep? Looking around she saw that the cupboard draws hung open, stains gripped the walls, the rafters groaned above her head; that smell of damp, that fallen silence. She could feel a lump growing in her throat. She sniffed, wiping her nose with her shirt. She peered out of the window. Her eyes examined the street outside.

The sky was dark and yet, lit by the moon, even from her seat she could identify each door, each rooftop, each chimney pot. Building after building lined the road. Not a soul to be seen. Ember continued to stare and without realising at first what it was she was looking at, she noticed a sign; it hung only a few doors down from her own. The bold lettering was unreadable but there remained a pool of smaller, more legible words surrounding it. It was one of these that had caught her attention. The 'E' was clear, and the 'b'. Surely not, she thought? Surely she would have seen it before. But then, she reasoned, she had not known of the tin before. Only now, after finding the tin, after saving her parents, only now could she have possibly recognised it.

Ember's heart beat like a drum, its rhythm urging her onward, each strike a hammer blow against her chest. She felt the cool sensation of sweat prickling her skin, of the hairs climbing upon her neck. Narrowing her eyes Ember jumped up from the table and without a moment's hesitation she plunged her bare feet into the depths of her boots. Over her shirt she pulled on a cardigan and over that her coat, hood engulfing her head.

Ember cracked the door and gazed out at the street beyond. It always felt so different the other side of the window. Rain streamed between the cobbles. A thick set of clouds had gathered above. She paused, her hand upon the door handle. Still her mother's snores filled the house, its walls tombed about her head.

"I'm sorry Ma," she whispered, before stepping out into the night.

The street was empty, rain arrowing downwards. Ember raced over the cobbles. Each window glared at her as she ran past, the falling water heckling her hood. Panting, she stood beneath the sign, and sure enough, squinting up through the dripping sky, she read that word again.

"Eibar," she mouthed, as if in confirmation.

A sneeze burst from her lips, her nose. There was only one thing for it now. She laid both hands upon the wooden door, and taking a deep breath, she began forcing her way in.

Once inside all was quiet, quiet and black, another place entirely, as if cupping your eyes and slipping beneath the bathwater. Ember blinked but the darkness was too thick, impenetrable, it would not be moved.

"Hello?" she called.

Her own voice echoed wearily. She strained her ears in hope of a reply. Ember sighed, tucking her hands beneath her armpits. A weight filled her chest. She rubbed her face in exhaustion, squashing her fists into her eye sockets. She rubbed so furiously that a thousand candle lights began blinking into life. They sprang up one at a time, one after another until they had coated the entire room. She moved her hands to her mouth, gasping in disbelief. It was them, the Eibar, they were here.

Disfigured, distorted, some were children, some grown men, grown women, the Eibar appeared on first sight as if a horde of rag dolls, skinny as wire, some fat as oranges, the tall ones stooped beneath the ceiling. Those that were too small to see bustled their way to the front, peering up at her with multicoloured eyes.

"Hello Ember," one of them said, stepping forward as he did so, "my name's Dejan."

This one was a boy, a boy of similar age to Ember herself. A soft glow emanated from his skin and she warmed herself against it. His eyes were kind, open.

"I'm an Eibar," he explained, "we all are, each of us here is an Eibar, just like you. We heard news of your war and so we came, fast as we could."

"You've come for me?"

". . . course," he smiled.

"But why?"

"We're the rebellion, we've come to help."

Dejan paused after saying this. He reached over and lowered Ember's hood. She flinched slightly as he did so but she let him continue all the same. He brushed the hair from her face.

"It's okay Ember," he whispered, taking her arms and placing them by her side, "Look at me."

She looked him in the eye, straight in the eye, like she had never looked at anyone else before. He looked back and immediately her tummy started to squirm. She stood there rubbing it, waiting silently.

"It's alright Ember," he repeated, and before she could move away he hugged her tight.

"You're one of us now Ember, we'll take care of you. But still, you got to do this, you got to."

"I will," she replied, her words springing immediately and without thought.

He released her and she straightened up, chin high, teeth clenched.

"Do what?" she asked, head cocked with suspicion.

"We've seen 'em, so many wars like yours over the years. This town 'specially, it's rife with 'em. We here have all fought as you'll do."

"You've all fought?" Ember repeated, voice wavering with excitement.

"Yeah. . . we fought. Though sad as it is, not a single one of us could win."

Ember's face dropped.

"But you Ember, you're special. You came to us! That's never happened before."

"So you're going to fight with me?"

"No, no we're not going to fight. This is your fight, it's up to you alone to stop the war in your house. It's your war and so only you can stop it. This is your responsibility. You must bring peace to your people. We'll help, but it's you what must do it."

". . . and if I can't?"

Dejan lowered his head.

"Well . . . then so it goes on," he mumbled.

Ember swallowed awkwardly, she shuffled her feet.

"Look Ember," he implored.

She nodded at the sincerity in his voice.

"We've little time, you must seek us out. We'll be in the fields behind the woods."

"The woods behind town?"

"Yeah, but hurry Ember, there's no time. You're special, remember that, for you're the child of war mongers and only the children of war mongers can stop a war. Only you can bring peace. You're their only hope. You're our only hope. We'll help you but you got to seek us out. Now go, quickly, and meet us in the fields past the woods."

Ember raised her hand in protest but it was no use, before she could speak they were gone. Their lights a retreating tide they disappeared as suddenly as they had arrived.

Slipping back out onto the street, back into the rain, Ember bowed her head as she started walking home. The weather beat down hard but still she was able to hear the sound of footsteps arriving behind her. Without really knowing why, she dove into the shadows. Crouching as low as she could she waited for the person to pass. She didn't have to wait long.

Feet splashing in the puddles, a man veered from wall to wall, staggering past her. She watched on as he tumbled straight into her house.

"Dad?" she yelled, and as fast as she could she went racing after him.

He was already half way up the stairs when she burst in through the door, his muddy footprints snaking across the floor.

"Drunk! You come home drunk?!"

"I'll do as I fucking please!"

Ember scowled. She wiped her hand across her face in exasperation, tugged at her hair. She had to think. Her parents' footsteps thundered above, a tempest of screaming and yelling. Ember grabbed her rucksack, stuffing it with anything she felt might be useful, a rusted knife, a lighter, an apple, there was not much to choose from. Still the tirade swirled above her. Maybe she should go up there and stop them? It was after all, her war. She was the one who was supposed to stop them. But then she remembered Dejan's words. Not now, now was not the time. She had to get back to the Eibar, that was the only way that this was truly going to end. She had found the Eibar and now they were going to help her. She would bring peace back to this house. Tonight she would let them fight, but she would be back, she would come back and save them. Fingers grasping the door handle she took one last look around.

"Bye Ma, bye Dad," she called, and then she was gone, out into the street, door banging shut behind her.

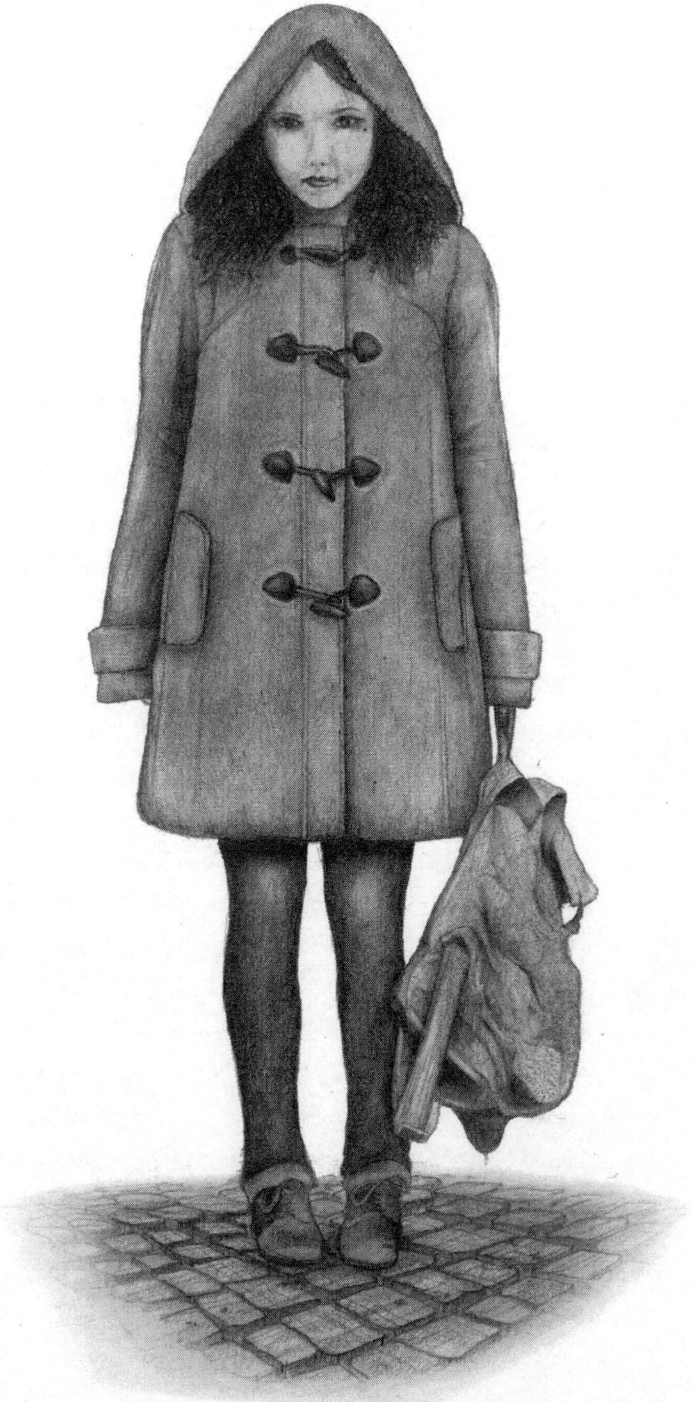

11.

Still the rain fell, and yet no longer did it seem to matter. Hood down Ember strode defiantly along the cobbled streets, dripping hair flat upon her head, eyes focused only on the horizon. Out of the old quarter she stepped and so her assent began, up through the town centre and toward the woods beyond.

The town centre throbbed with yellow windows, with gross faces that scowled at her as she scurried past. In fact, here the streets thronged with folk of all kinds. Their bodies hugged the pathways, pushing her into the centre of the road, a road twisted as old rope. The houses meanwhile, were so tall they looked as if they were curling above her head, rooftops almost entirely blotting out the night's sky. This was a warren if ever she had seen one, feral and littered with obstacles. Tradesmen huddled themselves around tavern doors, they heckled and chased her, kicked out at her playfully with their heavy boots. Already she could feel bruises swelling upon her shins. It was however, the groups of rich folk who terrified her most, their haughty manner and crooked smiles. Ember felt her stomach writhe in panic. It was well known that children did not wander the streets after dark. Fear fluttered within her throat. She braced her shoulders and snorted in defiance, pulling her hood tightly around her head. Tears upon her cheeks she strode bravely past their volleyed insults, their leering and their money throwing, coins knocking against her elbows as she fled. Leaving the town behind, her legs now climbing Hangman Hill, Ember's thoughts turned to her parents. She thought of her mother upon that floor, of the dread that seemed to have for so long possessed her father's eyes;

and so at last the hill levelled out. A wood now stood before her. Ember let loose a great sigh of relief and dropping to the ground she crawled beneath the low hung branches of the trees.

Lain within the darkness of that wood, Ember's ears rang with the howls of its creatures. She rose to her knees and hands upon her forehead she released a shrieking cry of her own. She clenched her fists, breath pouring from her lungs, tears dissecting her cheeks. She jumped to her feet, whirling around in circles, peering up at the sky as she moved. Everything was spinning, anger erupting from every pore. She wailed loudly and jumping up and down she stomped her feet as hard as she could. She ran. She ran for her life. She ran for her father, for her mother. Twigs snapped and puddles exploded into the air. She crashed through the branches. They lashed out at her, pulling back her sleeves and clawing at her shirt as she went. They branded her body with fire. Her lungs clattered inside her chest, they choked and stalled and spurted and lunged against her rib cage. Her bones thrashed inside her skin. Then, all of a sudden, she stopped. Her feet simply stopped. She wavered for a moment and before she knew what was happening her body tumbled into the dirt. She lay, crumpled in a heap. Only her breath disturbed the sudden peace. She closed her eyes. She curled up into her coat, head against her knees, and so there it was she slept, a ragged lump beneath the white of the moon.

That next morning broke gently, its tide lapping at her cheeks. Bird song filled the tree tops. A soft breeze wove through her hair. Ember cracked open her eyes and rolled onto her back, throwing her rucksack aside as she did so. Leaves fluttered before her face. She shivered expectantly as the sun's rays began to warm her wet clothes.

"Good morning," she murmured, her limbs tentative, mind confused.

"Good morning Ember," replied Dejan.

Ember sprang up in shock. She scrambled to her feet.

"What? Where'd you come from?"

"From just over there," he replied, pointing at a break in the trees, "you almost made it. We seen you a few minutes ago whilst collecting wood for the morning fire. Come on and we'll get you all washed up."

Ember ruffled her hair. She peeled off her wet coat, her cardigan, and cocking her head she beheld Dejan in disbelief.

"Here, I'll take 'em, come on," and with that he gathered up her things and began walking out of the wood.

Rubbing her tummy, thoughts still spinning, Ember followed on behind him, out of the forest and into a large opening.

"Made it," she said, smiling at last.

"Welcome," he grinned, and Ember beamed with relief.

The Eibar's den was incredible, built with slabs of woods and nests of sticks, each against a bush or a tree. Long branches and leaves formed the roofs while rope swings and mud slides and bridges hung and dipped and wound their way about the encampment. Four huge catapults stood, one in each corner of their settlement. The hollows of trees acted as larders, lines of strawberry leaves traced the pathways and an enormous flat table had been constructed in the centre of their base. Around this table Ember saw a menagerie of chairs. Some were simply holes dug into piles of banked earth, their insides coated by fur and feathers. Others, like hammocks, hung from the branches above. All encompassed that table.

As soon as she had stepped into the clearing the Eibar slowly and carefully began making their way towards her. She watched them as they drew closer. They were, as she remembered from inside that building, a folk of mixed physiques: tall, small, fat, thin, some with noses like thorns, eyes like saucers, ears like flags, some had faces gnarled as roots, others clear and smooth and transparent as water, the tiny ones with multi-coloured eyes she recognised immediately. All were as she remembered. Expect that here, she could now clearly see that many of them also possessed such things as horns or hoofs or wings or snouts, tails, trunks, scales, claws, teeth as you would never expect to see upon a human.

"Ember," they cheered, and leading her by the hand she was sat in a chair, a chair so comfortable that for a moment it felt as if she'd ascended Heaven itself.

"That's my chair," grinned one, "but you can have it."

"Let's get your boots off," offered another, and as carefully as they could the Eibar removed her sodden boots.

"You look cold Ember, here, take this," and before she knew what was happening a heavy blanket had been draped over her.

Ember giggled and smiled, her eyes wide as they had ever been.

"Thanks so much!" she laughed.

"Your clothes, Ember, let's get your clothes. They'll have to dry."

"Alright," she replied, and wriggling about beneath the blanket she quickly removed her clothes, flinging them out and up into the air as she did so.

The crowd whooped and laughed.

"Thanks so much!" she exclaimed.

In fact, it was about the only thing she was able to say, so surprising and so unbelievably generous were the Eibar's offerings.

The Eibar set about washing her clothes. They brought her food and drink, regularly dropping by to tuck her into her seat, to offer her hugs or to kiss her upon the forehead. They brushed her hair and delicately patched the cuts and the bruises that marked her skin. She climbed back into her clean clothes and once she had done so some even bought her welcome gifts, others brought her cards made of leaves. She folded the cards carefully, holding each one against her chest before eventually tucking them into the pocket of her jacket.

"You seem much better," smiled Dejan, once the stream of visitors had began to disperse.

"Yeah thanks," glowed Ember, a tear of happiness running down her cheek.

Dejan leant over and gave her a long hug of his own.

"Rest here for a couple hours, get yourself some sleep. A meeting's been called, we're all to gather here in a couple hours. I'll wake you once we're ready."

"Okay," nodded Ember, "and Dejan . . . thanks," she smiled.

Dejan stood up.

"Ember, you're too special for words. You'll be safe here. Life does what it does, and so you truly are one of its most magical and mysterious surprises," he said.

"Jeje . . ." Ember gasped, pulling the blanket over her cheeks so that he couldn't see her blush.

Dejan walked away and as he did so she let out a gentle sigh. She smiled a gigantic smile and closing her eyes once more, she let herself fall into a deep and peaceful sleep.

Ember awoke to a magnificent sunset, the clouds orange, each one cut with spectacular beams of yellow light. The table was full of food and drink and the many chairs surrounding it were filled with Eibar. She cracked a single eye, spying on her hosts from the sanctuary of her chair. Most were quiet; they sat there wringing their hands, biting their nails, their limbs slow and yet their eyes flickering manically. One man in particular appeared very detached. He sat all by himself, crying, offering only aloof responses to anyone who came near.

"You got to try," she heard someone else say from across the table.

The speaker was encouraging her friend to finish the weaving he had started. The weaver was himself a boy of young age, he was crying as she spoke, apparently reluctant to take any further part. Ember was a little taken aback. Yet the girl who was sat a few seats down from the weaver, she appeared much worse. This girl was literally crawling out of her skin, eyes wide and fearful. She appeared completely unaware of her surroundings. Trapped beneath a flood of her own emotions she remained there, hunched and frail. Ember sighed, this was no party. She continued to watch on as a boy, his face contorted, began unfurling a barrage of screaming and shouting into the air. Fists clenched and feet stamping, he flung objects this way and that.

"Sssshhhhh. . . Everyone quiet," she heard, and glancing to her left Ember realised that her ruse was over.

The girl to have spotted her wore furrowed eyebrows. Her voice was staccato, sharp, her mannerisms bossy and controlling. A second Eibar hung from her clothes, heavy lipped, dopey eyed and babbling.

"Ember's awake, look," she pointed, before resting her hands on her hips.

Ember smiled, she smiled as friendly a smile as she could manage.

"She's awake!" repeated the girl, "I seen her."

Ember sat up in her chair, stuffing her blanket behind her.

"So then, we'll begin," spoke Dejan, signalling for the girl to sit down, and immediately the crowd fell quiet.

Ember was on the edge of her seat.

"Ember, we call this meet 'cause we got to inform you of your task."

She felt her stomach leap in her chest.

"We here, each of us, we're all outcasts. All of us here are victims of war. Each of us, at one time or another, we've all failed in preventing a war and so we've had to flee. Exiled from our own towns, so we've been left to the whims of our demons . . ."

A wave of gasping lapped the table as Dejan spoke this word, a shaking of heads and a flickering of eyes.

"Only you can stop your war Ember. You're the chosen one, you're special. You're the daughter of war mongers and so it's fallen to you to stop 'em, only you. You're more powerful than anyone, if you can't save your parents then none can."

"But what if I fail," she cut in, "what if . . ."

"If you fail, then like us you'll be cast from the safety of your town, cast down, down at the feet of them demons."

Again a wave of gasping washed over the table.

"What demons?" she said, head cocked.

"They come and take you away and once they've got you they do bad things to you!" someone yelled.

"They fight over you," someone screamed.

". . . jerking you this way and that, they shower you in blood and faeces and spittle," another called.

"They fight for you, tearing off each others arms and heads as they do so!"

". . . and then you they sex you, they beat you, they laugh at you and then they throw you away . . ."

". . . and then . . . and then, just as the last of the light slips from your eyes, they mourn you!" yelled another.

"They morn you with such heartbreak as none could ever begin to imagine," growled one of the older Eibar, "the sadness, it crushes your soul, crushes your bones and evaporates your blood. It's upon that crest of despair that them demons set out once again to capture another, another to help ease their mourning, another to fuel their addiction. For that's what it is, an addiction. Them demons, they carry a deep and endless black hole inside their rib cages. It swirls within 'em, is slowly ingesting 'em from the inside out. Without us to feed 'em, them demons, they'd implode within days. It's the saddest of truths, that such darkness breeds such thirst for life."

The speaker hung his head as he spoke.

"You'd think that they'd give up on their godforsaken lives. But not so. Seems instead that their darkness only magnifies the light. That's why they hunt us. They hunt us so as to glimpse one more second of our light."

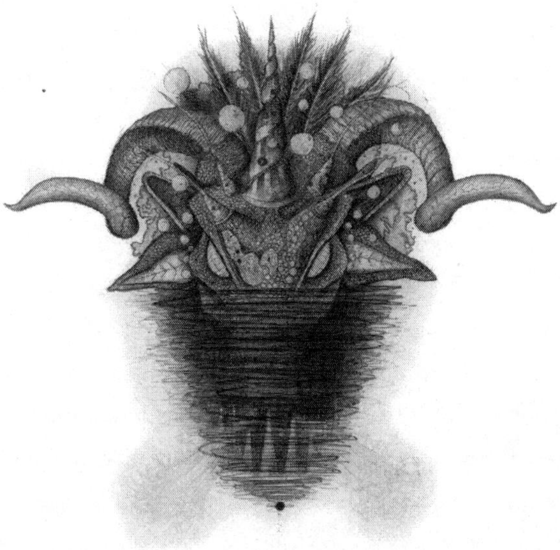

III.

The Eibar's meeting stretched long into the night, and so they slept late that following morning, the two of them, both her and Dejan, limbs curled inside a single chair. Ember wriggled beneath his weight and stirred by her movements he lifted himself onto his feet. They yawned, faces etched with smiles.

"So this is it," said Dejan, "your big day."

Ember sat up, ruffling her hair and blinking her eyes.

"Here I come," she nodded.

Looking over her shoulder she saw a group of Eibar approaching.

"Onward," they cheered, "surely she's got to win!"

They grinned excitedly and throats plump with chanting they set about laying the preparations for war. With muddy fingers they marked each others' faces, stockpiled food for the journey and then arranged themselves in a long line. Every single Eibar was present. The call went out, and with Ember at the head of the group, they all began marching the long march back into town.

For a long time they walked, winding around trees and crossing numerous ravines. It was slow going. Ember's thoughts turned to her parents. She thought of her mother in that bed and of her father stumbling home. Yet she felt neither anger nor shame. Rather, it was feelings of sadness, of longing, that filled her heart. She missed them desperately: the warmth of her mother's shoulder, the strength in her father's hands. A coldness began to prickle at her skin. A tear slipped from her eye. She turned back toward Dejan.

"Dejan," she called, "what you doing?" but he had fallen too far behind to hear.

Ember sighed. It was not just Dejan, the whole Eibar troupe seemed now to be walking a great distance behind her. She waited but they did not seem to move.

"What?" she yelled, and tummy squirming, she stood there rubbing her belly.

Still the Eibar did not move. Typical, she thought, throwing her hands to her side. She continued walking, huffing and puffing as she did so. What was this stupid game? For still they followed, but only it seemed, once she had resumed walking again. The cold had really taken hold. She could feel her limbs trembling beneath her clothes. A great sigh heaved her rib cage; time like the trees, slipping past as her feet edge toward town.

At last the trees gave way. Out from the wood Ember's angled silhouette emerged upon the crest of Hangman Hill. She gazed at the town far beneath her. Darkness was falling and so the lights had begun to twinkle below. It felt as if she had been away for a long time. The town had been a cruel place, she remembered, twisted and dark. From here however, from here it looked neither of those things. From here the houses looked gentle, beautiful, warm, they looked like home. A smile cracked her heavy mouth. It stretched from ear to ear. She plunged her hands deep into her pockets and skipping her feet a little she descended into town, the Eibar following her over the horizon.

"Ember!" came a gasp, "where've you been?"

She had barely past the first house when she heard it. Her heart leaped in her chest, eyes wide with panic. This was the last thing she had expected.

"We've been searching for you for days," the voice bellowed.

A big hand landed on Ember's shoulder, spinning her around. Ember stared up into the old woman's imploring eyes.

"Your Ma, she's been distraught . . . and your Dad, he looks the saddest man I've ever seen."

Ember frowned.

"Such sadness what could crush a person's soul," the old woman rasped.

Ember was dumbstruck. The women took her hand and began leading her home. They returned to the old quarter soon after, to the shamble of buildings that Ember knew so well. The old woman pushed her forward, encouraging her to lead the way. There were few signs of life; that was, except for her mother. She stood ready and waiting, her arms spread wide, palms pushed against each side of the door frame. She called out as soon as Ember had turned the last corner.

"Ember," she cried, "my Ember!"

Already Ember could sense the horrific scene lingering behind her mother's arms, the mess, the smell, the silence. Her heart began to pound, her throat swell as she drew nearer. This was it, it was time for her to act and yet she no longer knew if she could. An insurmountable sadness loomed forward, desperation, the full weight of her mother's helplessness surging from every crack of that old house. The damp it seemed, had claimed her skin, her hair, the fat from upon her limbs. Ragged and hysterical, her mother lunged at her with bony arms.

"Where've you been?!" she yelled, "I thought we'd lost you! I thought you were gone!"

Ember tried to speak but her mother's hands were all over her face, crawling over her hair.

"Your face," she shrieked, "look at you, plastered in mud!"

"It en't, it's war paint Ma, I've come . . ."

". . . and your clothes, ripped, look at 'em. You're soaked, you're so wet, so cold. My god, you're shivering like a leaf. Ember, who did this to you? Tell me!"

". . . but they looked after me Ma. They weren't bad! They washed my clothes, there was a group of 'em, they looked after me!" Ember argued back.

Her mother dragged her inside.

"Your skin, my child! What on earth's happened to you, you're burning up!"

Ember felt her mother tugging at the sleeves of her coat, fumbling the zip.

"And these leaves, look at 'em all, look at all these, all mushed in your pocket!"

"Get off!" Ember snapped.

She pulled away and scrambled over to the other side of the room.

"They're my cards, you leave 'em alone!"

"Who gave 'em to you, who on earth would fill your pockets with mushy leaves?!"

Her mother stood, the despair, the incomprehension, all too clear for Ember to see.

"And your hair, oh Ember," she was crying now, tears streaming down her cheeks, "what've I done, my poor girl."

"Don't cry Ma," Ember pleaded, "look, they brushed it for me, they took such good care of me. Look, look at my arms," she suggested, peeling back a sleeve, "and my side," she grinned, lifting up her coat, "they took care of me."

Hands trembling, her mother moved toward her. Ember stared into her mother's eyes, reached out toward her mother's cheeks.

"My God helps us," she whispered, as she withdrew her fingers, red staining her skin.

"Oh what've I done?!" she continued, "my girl? Mad as birds, truly mad as birds. What've I done? My husband . . . My daughter . . ."

"Where's Dad?" was Ember's only reply.

Fallen to her knees, blood now rubbed about her eyes, her mother sat sobbing upon the floor.

"It's okay Ma, I'm here, I've come to save you both."

Still her mother cried.

"Ma, speak to me Ma, where's Dad?"

"Never home," her mother croaked, "he only returns from them taverns once he's lonely enough. He's so angry that man. That man, he's going to kill a fella one of these days . . . One of these days he's going to kill me!"

"Ma?" Ember pleaded, but her mother wouldn't stop.

"God help me," she mumbled, "my daughter, mad as birds . . . and my husband, my husband's a murderer."

"Ma!" Ember yelled, "it's okay, I'm his daughter, I got the power to make him stop. He'll not get to kill anyone, least of all you while I'm around. I'm going to make this stop Ma, this war, I'm going to bring the peace back."

But her mother could not reply. She slumped onto her front, body flat upon the floor, heaving with sadness. Ember swallowed. She took a deep breath. This room, her mother, the scene tore at her heart, knitted her sides. She could feel herself contorting. Like her mother, she could feel herself falling. A wave of desperation consumed her and before she knew what was happening she had bolted for the door, tiny frame bursting out into the street.

"Don't cry Ma," she whispered, turning back to face the house, looking upon her one last time, "I'll find him. I'll find him and then he'll not get to kill anyone, not then, not with me around."

The door closed and so it was that her mother disappeared from view.

Ember found her father that evening, hunched within a tavern. Around him a party blazed. Clouds of white powder misted the floor, a tiny man jostled beneath the sway of the crowd, girls danced upon the tables. Alcohol rained down all around her. Ember's head span upon her shoulders. It appeared as if these revellers had come from far and wide. Abandon, mischief and mayhem flickered behind their eyes. Ember pushed on toward her father, the few town's folk she knew fleeing back towards where she'd just come. Ember turned to watch them go, the tavern door flapping as they made their escape. She saw naked men staggering in the street, lunging at stray dogs and feigning to knife anyone who got too close. The door finally came to rest and so once again she turned back towards her father. No one paid her the least bit of attention, that was, except for a young boy, a boy who she guessed couldn't have been much older than herself. Glancing at her, this boy seemed to hang at his father's side like a scrimshaw or a gewgaw, a dangling fancy for delighting the ladies. His father, he looked a kingfisher of a fellow, a man of grandeur and eloquence, he was clearly the man at the centre of all this, his words the embers of the party. Ember tightened her lips and lowered her eyes. The boy was picking pockets, stealing watches, his hands quick as a monkey's, fingers sharp as a jackdaw. Ember took a deep breath and moved closer still to her father. This was no place she wanted to be. Her father meanwhile, he sat as if a man at sea. This figure before her, he could have been anywhere, such was his posture. Her guts crawled with venom yet she knew what she must do. She must save him, she was his only hope.

"Dad?" she whispered, sidling up to him at the bar.

He gave no reply. She watched him drink for a while, mimicking his movements, letting herself rest against his great weight.

"I don't mean it you know, Ember?" he growled, his voice tunnelling beneath the sounds of the party. "I love you so much, you and your Ma, but . . . but it's so hard. I dunno what to do."

"I love you too Dad," Ember smiled, her heart so quickly softened.

"If only I knew what to do?" he repeated.

Ember clenched her fists, taken aback by her sudden weakness. She loved this man, this was her dad and if she could not save him no one could.

"Come with me Dad?" she pleaded, "come home with me and we'll fix this."

"Look Ember," was his only reply.

He laid an object on the bar, its weight wrapped in a dark cloth.

"Our little secret," he winced.

"What's that," she whispered.

"Just look," he replied.

Ember peeled back the cloth and as she did so she felt herself gasp for breath. A gun. Her father had a gun.

"Why, why'd you have this," she rasped, her voice still a whisper.

"This is our secret Ember," he said, "just me and you Ember," he put his arm around her, "just you and me."

Ember sniffed, consumed by the smell of his jumper, cosy and safe beneath his warmth. She lifted the gun, turning it in her hands.

"It's beautiful," she smiled. "It's . . ."

But, before she could finish her sentence, she saw it. Engraved upon the barrel, there it was again, that same word.

"Eibar!" cried Ember, and her father quickly hushed her quiet.

"Eibar, Eibar, Eibar," she sang, "Look, written along the barrel, it's written Eibar! You're one of us," she bellowed, "Dad, all along, you're one of us."

She hugged her father tight, kissing him and laughing as she did so, forgiveness in her eyes.

"Fuck!" her father hollered, jumping to his feet.

He pulled Ember behind him and snatching at the gun with his mighty hands he roared into action.

"You fucker, you fucking get yourself away from here!" he wailed, and hurling the man to the floor he himself then dropped onto his knees. He held the gun only inches from the assailant's nose. The man beneath her father was that same man she had noticed earlier, his grandeur and eloquence remained and yet now a swathe of terror dashed his eyes. The boy was no longer anywhere to be seen.

"This is my party sir and I will do as I please," the man snarled, and yet her father would not be swayed.

Ember blinked, a fog of disbelief destabilising her thoughts. Everything fell into slow motion: that rage wrinkling her father's face, that wave of terror undulating through the crowd. Ember flung herself upon her father. If she could not stop him no one could. This was it. She peered upwards, past the mass of people surrounding her, eyes searching out the tavern's only window. Pressed against the glass she saw them at last, the misshapen faces of the Eibar. They had come back. They were cheering her on. She returned her attention to the scene at hand. She focused her energy on her father, on that gun. He was an Eibar too, surely she could save him. She hugged tightly at his shoulders, words streaming from her mouth, hands caressing his arms, his hair. She pleaded for him to stop. She gave everything she had to give and yet still her father remained. No matter what she did he would not soften. Her heart had begun to beat, sweat coating her skin. Full of panic, full of desperation, tears fled down her cheeks. She was crying, the people in the crowd were crying, that man with the gun upon his forehead, he was crying, her dad also, even he was crying, crying the most silent of sorrows. Ember reached out, her fingers pressed against his cheek . . .

She heard it as if a clap of thunder; a deafening boom. Blood slapped her face, clattered her clothes. Ember reeled backwards, stumbling for balance. The entire room throbbed. She found her feet, wiped at her eyes and through the smears of red she watched on as her father bolted. He dropped the gun to the floor and bolted, knocking men aside like skittles as he careered out of the door. Ember herself could barely move. She looked down at the man with no face. She saw him now as she had seen her mother upon the floor of her house. She had failed. It was over. Once and for all, it was over. Ember could hear herself begging for forgiveness but still the Eibar withdrew. Only the gun remained. She bent over and picked it up, fingers feeling out the warmth of her father's hand. Its weight bent her wrist and buckled her skinny arms. She held on to it tightly and hunched almost double she peered again, up at the crowd, each face a witnesses to her failure. She had lost the war. She must retreat. It was all she could do. It was her turn now, her turn to run. She burst toward the door. The crowd however, seeing her move, they suddenly came alive. As if a spell broken their hands lunged at her as she attempted to make her escape. They pulled at her shirt, tugged at her jeans. Ember could sense the Eibar outside. The men in the pub, they were yelling, grappling at her every movement. Ember screamed; she fought with all her might. She slipped out of her coat, shed her cardigan, surrendered her shirt and so at last she tumbled out of the tavern.

Gun in hand, wearing nothing but vest and trousers, Ember emerged into the cold of the night. She slammed the tavern door behind her and on turning back around she gasped in disbelief. The streets, the streets were awash with Eibar! They seemed to be pouring from every corner, each one running for its life, fleeing back toward the wood. Ember forced herself into action, feet pushing off from the ground. She began running with them. The tavern burst open behind her. She could hear men's voices, all of them yelling, calling her back. She could hear the sound of boots running after her. For miles they followed and so it was that for miles Ember evaded their pursuit. The appeals were loud and warm, sad and desperate. But it was no use . . . they would never catch her, not now. Already she had gone, the town falling away behind her. Already she had gone. She was an Eibar now and so with them she would diminish.

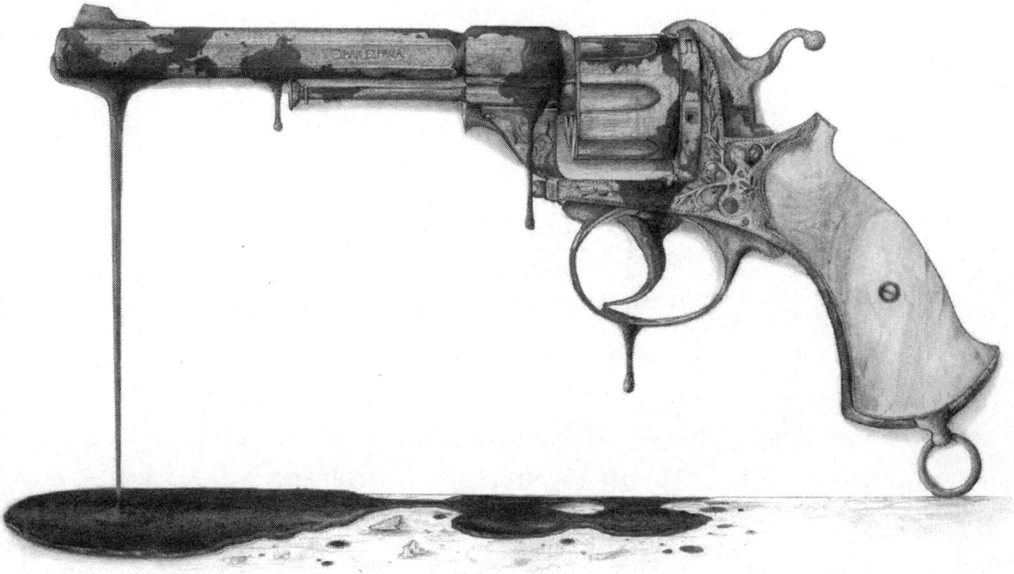

GROK

WRITTEN BY MEGAN LEONIE HALL
ILLUSTRATED BY BRYN HALL

I have studied hard to Erase any Symptoms of the Past. They have been piping this idea into the water supply for the last year. No one has any choice, but to drink it up. Those who remember badness or sadness or have parents who may have passed on memories of the before times have been fast tracked. The children of the historically unhappiest parents are recollected first.

"There's no physical way out of this house," mother says. "You've got to go in to get out," she smiles.

In my seventh year I faced my excavation and in my seventh year I ran away. This is the story I was too afraid to tell before now. I claim these entangled memoirs as my own.

Before her treatment, mother told me that the Apocalypse is a sneaky revelation. I'm not allowed to talk out loud about it anymore, or tell anyone the history she shared with me when they drove us here four years ago. For thousands of years the human race has wrestled with its own collective mortality, tormenting its unlimited imagination with visions of hell ranging from the impact of a mighty asteroid that incinerates all human life, to the cold frozen fall-out of a nuclear war. Some believed that ancient cosmonauts from Nibiru or the Pleiades would

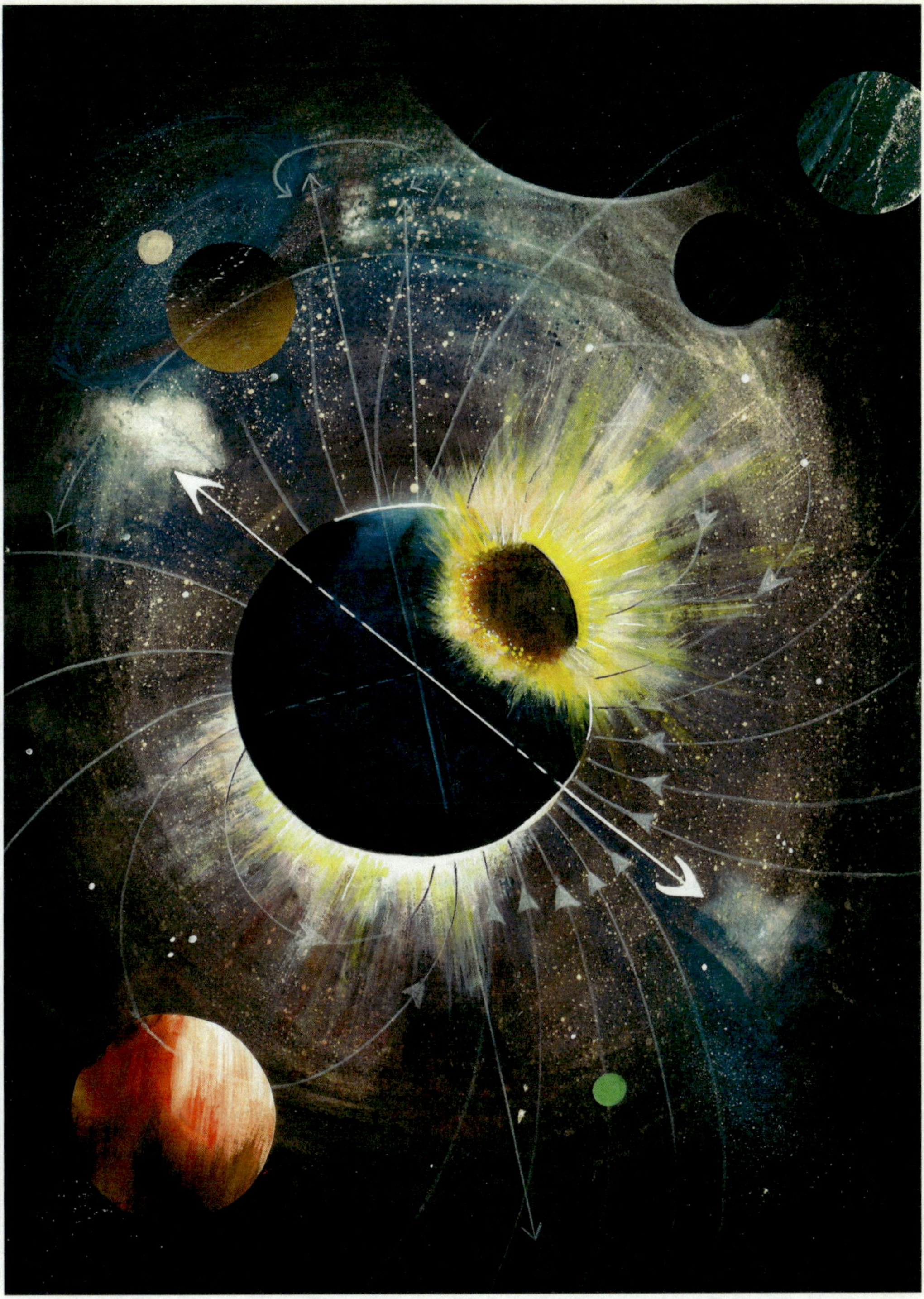

return to earth to shut down their millennia long genetic experiment. External objects and events of incomprehensible size and power, such as engulfment by black holes, world-sweeping sun-storms with the strength of billions of atom bombs, the possibility of a magnetic pole reversal, natural disasters increasing in frequency and devastation rendering large portions of the earth uninhabitable; these were the commonest fears of the most privileged. Those with most to lose were the most afraid. These frantic myths of impending disaster grew more virulent, affecting billions, who were all so focussed on an attack from the outside that they hadn't considered the likelihood of their nemesis coming from the inside, from their own free will and volition. In their government issued self-assembly bunkers they stockpiled gasmasks and tinned food, oxygen and water but they were still afraid and they didn't know why.

At night, in the numbing dark, my face pressed up against the cold damp wall, I make memory my ally, extracting singular moments that feel like my identity and I make a vow that I will always keep it on the inside where it can never be confiscated or lost. In the morning, I hug my mother and promise her I'm ready to forget and I count the sunrises until the day of excavation. At which point I will willingly and joyfully enter the recollection booth. Choicelessly. Joylessly. I have a recurring dream in which thousands of children queue around a huge building, five-hundred times bigger than our house, like a cathedral, which I've read about, but never seen. They keep going in, one at a time but they never come out again. We don't have fear-based beliefs in the State anymore. No one is killed and no one takes their own life. We must submit to happiness. It is our duty to do so. I am trying to learn how to choose what I dream.

Radio stations, television channels and the Internet were and are dominated globally by a unified planet government. In the past, there was enough food and everything came at a price. The sorts of things available and the prices of them kept rising; which kept people busy working hard to earn money to afford to buy products until they died. In the meantime, and it really was an extremely mean time; the effect of being told that anything you wanted was attainable and many millions of people having sacrificed spontaneity and their very sense of aliveness to this aim, resulted in a global dislocation of mood and spirit. Doctors, psychiatrists, neuroscientists, democratic despots and celebrity gurus continued their mutually beneficial orgy of collusion that aimed to regulate the mood of the world to prevent chaos and anarchy. Some of them, of course, believed that if each human being were happier then the world would be too. The theory was that if people were genuinely happy and if the State bestowed contentment, the populace would willingly control themselves and save politicians the trouble. A naïve sentiment but one with speedy, industrialised legs, that, during one interminably long, dry summer opened and an entirely new mode of control was born.

Firstly, the spring arrived in utter silence. There was a sudden dearth of birds. Eight-hundred-thousand swallows had failed to migrate due to 'unprecedented foreign outbreaks of a new form of avian flu' said the government. Insect numbers quickly reached unpleasant proportions. Then a drought hit two continents at once whilst simultaneously a tsunami created by a hitherto unknown trans global tectonic fault line hit two others. A deluge of desolation ensued, as one would expect. The State couldn't explain why it had occurred and why they had been unable to prevent it or how it would be resolved long-term and after the bunker supplies had been drunk dry, people began to die. First the elderly, then the young and the populace who hadn't witnessed war, at least on their own turf, for many generations went berserk. How can a society where people no longer even visibly age, meet a grim and dusty death, ruled over by a civilised and 'moral' government? Raised in a culture of litigation and the comforting norm of international corporate responsibility, they were outraged-they wanted their money back. They telephoned the number on their government life certificate guarantees, yet nobody answered. They marched to the edge of the cities, where forty-storey 'LifeCert' call centres spewed shrill cacophony of one-hundred-thousand telephones ringing and ringing and ringing . . . They set those bell-towers on fire and marched back to the city; black wasp like helicopters circling above the blackening pillars of smoke and following the crowds, buzzing grimly, taking photographs. Most returned home, shocked but proud that a statement had been made, and turned on their televisions to see how this unprecedented outpouring of public grievance had been reported. It hadn't. No photographs. No poems. No film. No sound bites. No voices. Then began the dawning.

En masse; villagers and urbanites gathered in the streets and outside the steps of their nearest doors of power. They threw their Government Issue sixty-inch flat screen televisions on the ground where they formed totem stacks of meaninglessness. They wrote invoices for their dead grandparents and posted them under the doors of empty offices belonging to officials who had been curiously absent since the dying had begun in earnest. Government websites were overloaded; people were demanding to be told whether or not now was the time to kill our pets, our families and ourselves. They wanted to know if this was the beginning of the end. There were no answers forthcoming. No infomercials, direct mail, police or spokespeople. For the first time, the State was silent. How many died that summer? No one can be sure but my mother told me that around forty people survived in the town where she spent her childhood holidays. Forty left out of twenty-thousand. One of them was my father. They walked into the dawn together and vanished for several years.

*

Autumn came and the State issued its manifesto: 'Never Again.' They brought in measures. They measured memes and concluded that the past was over. This was a new beginning for its subjects. Where had they all gone? Several million dead of thirst. Many thousands disappeared; murmurs of murder, driven by fear. Rumours of mass imprisonment. The State didn't explain its three month long lack of response or statement. It simply gave everyone the explanation they needed:

"The end times are upon us. The well being of each man, woman and child is the State's priority. Refusal to peacefully acquiesce to mood regulation is an offence against the State."

It cleaned the streets, buried the bodies, built new hospitals, constructed more reservoirs, dug deep emergency wells at convenient five-mile intervals across the country, raised all taxes and commissioned an inaugural census for the new era. A tide of group suicides swept the land, most occurring between 3:00pm and midnight. In reaction, they eradicated public clocks and made medication mandatory for children of seven and over.

My parents weren't there to be assessed and recorded; they had gone far away across the sea, built their own house and lived off the land. Twenty miles from the port was our stone home and visiting the port was forbidden to us but for the stories Father would tell late at night; smelling of pipe tobacco with me curled up in the crook of his arm. Somewhere amongst the hostelries sweating with violent revelry and the rancid alleys where rotten fish swam in stale beer and effluent, his brother lived. My uncle, who remorselessly practiced his rifle skills on seagulls, traded women and weaponry whilst drunk to his soul on contraband whiskey and rum, was never referred to by name in our household. Father said his language was money and his friends were those he paid best. Unnoticed on the middle stair I would listen to the adults talking. Mother once said that my uncle was more kith than kin. In response, my father spoke quietly.

"Blood might have been thicker than the ocean we crossed, but not forever, my brother, he can't be trusted."

Then, in response to my mother's quickening breaths.

"I promise you, I will do what I said I'd do, if the time comes. You're my blood. He'll be lost in the water."

As a parting gift, my uncle had given my father a gun and a tea chest full of brandy. That night I watched through the banisters as my father drank nearly half a bottle, leaning against my mother's legs as she stroked back his hair.

I awoke to scrabbling noises, high-pitched whispers and a sharp ice draft round my ankles; someone had let the night in. Car doors were slamming outside. Who could have betrayed our whereabouts? Only one man. Father took the gun from the drawer, kissed us goodbye and left by the back of the house. I saw him running over the hill as they knocked at our door. My mother, she ran straight past Them, shouting his name, leaving me on the doorstep watching the motes of dust in the dusk light bleed auras over their shiny shoes. They brought her back to me, dishevelled and wide-eyed, gave her a pill and told her that from now on we were to live in another house. Somewhere less isolated where we could be monitored and life would be happier.

"It is in the best interest of your child," they said, "you love your child, don't you Madam? You do want the two of you to be truly happy, surely?"

Mother's hot breath was a cloud in the chill hallway. She put her hand on my back.

"Yes, of course. Of course I do!"

Mother said that he would never let Them trap him, there was no way, not until he had done what had to be done. She used to say we should never forget him, but she never says that anymore. I always thought he would come back one day, beardless and unrecognisable, that was, if he could work out how to find us. I felt sure that he had gone to find his brother. In a dream my father covered my eyes with a blanket that smelled of gunpowder. I squinted through the fibres and saw them standing close together. My uncle was the only one who knew where we had been living. Eleven wild hills stood between our home and the port, my father somewhere alone on the track; muddy, scrambling and armed. Soon, if father comes back, after my excavation, it is a very tangible possibility that I will not know his face. How could he know mine? So many years have passed since he disappeared over the brow of that carn. When I see bonfires burning in the distance I think of him. Now, she says to me, every day, with a nursery rhyme lilt that doesn't ring true to me:

"Bury your memory under a stone, there's nothing but pain in the past."

We packed our bags that night and slept in a windowless van that drove us onto a boat. On this journey, my nostrils almost stinging with the sweet scent of engine oil I whispered to her.

"... But, mummy, we are already happy aren't we?"

I was lying against her chest and her voice reverberated inside her body.

"You don't know what happiness is, my lamb."

And then we were here. In this house we can't get out of. Not until we both have forgotten. I wonder if I really know her at all.

Tick-tock, tick-tock. Seven more days. Mother scratched the numbers off the clock. It still ticks and resounds in the night time. One known predictable comfort in this strange house speaks to me with its certainty. Nocturnal knowing. I'm dreaming again. I am still and their bodies are moving. I can see the nanotracks of their sleeves: grabbing, voices, anger-tears. This is beyond frightening. This is stupidity. Why are they so stupid? I'm a very small child, opening an enormous slab of a door. I grab the handle lightly, walk a few steps through it and it crashes to the ground behind me; hinge less. I run from the feeling of guilt with no awareness or intention of wrongdoing and I'm chased and I fall. Ever so slowly. I wake the second my soul lands back in my body and surprises the mattress into a receptive bounce. I can't tell what is a dream and what truly happened these days. I feel angry. A forbidden emotion, one to cleanse myself of. I see an owl on my windowsill. Quiet owlet, ruffling itself, staring at me. Witnessing the intimacy of my wakefulness. The truth is, Mr Owl, I have been very afraid living here. The truth is, little one, this isn't the first time I've visited you. I've seen everything and I will continue to. You can feel me beside you, my feathers against your skull and ear. My voice inside your inside voice. I slip in close beside your consciousness. So smooth and stealthy you didn't notice before this moment. So now draw back the shades that obscure your own lucidity from you. I cannot be called for by your tongue or your wishing in the cold night, but I'll push words through your pores. I am always watching those who cannot watch themselves. What will you do with the night? Look at the palms of your hands. Wake up. This time, I really am awake, not falsely awakening. I like that owl very much, I decide. What other known but never remembered creatures might live inside me?

"When the day comes and they take you to the booth, you mustn't question them, shouldn't use long words and don't state the obvious. Cut your tone, it's sharper than you realise. If they ask you about anything before now, just tell them you don't recall much. You didn't really know your father but he came from a long line of lone wolves and free thinkers and look where that got him; full of rage and capable of anything . . . running into the night with dogs on his tail! But when

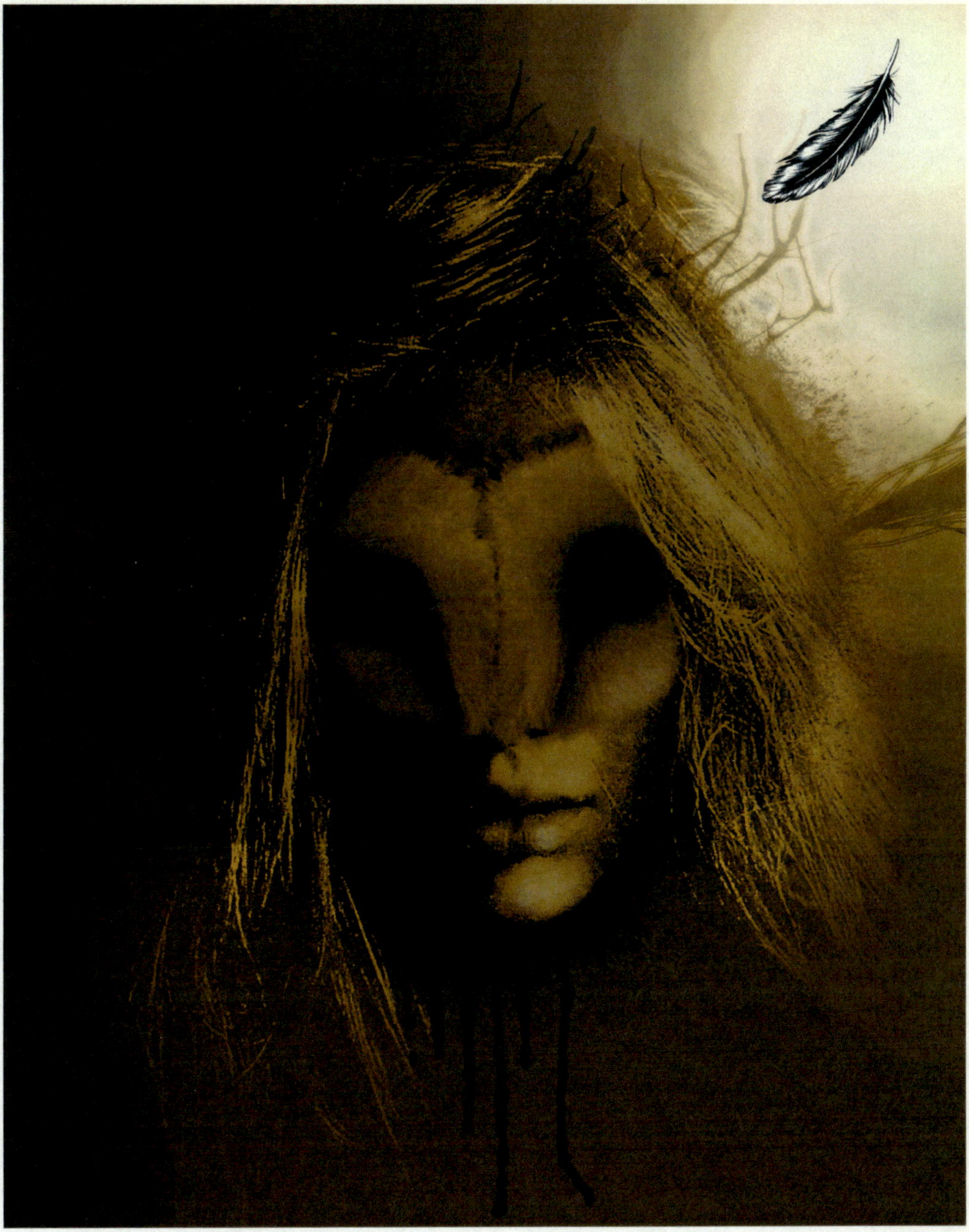

you grow up, darling, you will want to do something useful like running a shop or working for the government, won't you? You know first aid and you can sew and cook very well, for a child."

Why is mother telling me to be all the things she never was or wanted to be? Because she must and because of her pills. Then, as if she had heard me thinking, she said:

"No one should romanticise the past. Mine was killing me. I'm much happier than I've ever been. I expect before too long I will forget that I ever had anything to forget in the first place!" she laughed, "to be recollected is an honour which you're grateful for, aren't you?"

I was silent but wanted to please her. Instead of speaking I took her hand.

"The past can do terrible things to the future. You're maybe too young to believe that fully but please trust me. It is true. You can't be trusted if you remember the past and no one will feel they can count on you if you do . . . Some things happen that just shouldn't but they do. But they don't have to hurt."

I removed my hand from hers.

"But I'm not hurting!"

"Without an excavation, my lamb, it is certain that you will have pain in future. Your remembrances won't leave you . . ."

She sought another angle.

"Imagine you are as old as me and no matter what you do, you keep living something over and over and over again that happened a very long time ago and you can't escape. Ghosts around your heart, that's what stops us from being happy. How can you see the present if it's covered with the past? They have pills now and the water tastes sweeter and I feel free for the first time in my life. Don't you think your mother is happy? Wouldn't you like to be as happy as I am so we can be happy together?"

*

I suppose if she says she is, then she must be. I am scared of ghosts. I feel them in this house sometimes. There is a gulf here, a tiny, uncomfortable space between her and I, even when we are holding hands. To be grateful, to feel honoured even, was what I wanted to feel. I wished to be closer to her, to go where she was. Until I had excavated, that small space would always be there. When she came back from her treatment, she was smiling and dead eyed like all the best mothers are, on the State channel. Just like the post-recollected mothers I would watch from the window, walking to their garden gates in unison to greet their excavated offspring, laughing and scratching at their shoulders and necks. Interchangeable in public. In public, we must be. I don't think when you are recollected you only forget the bad memories. I want to remember the good ones. I will not tell them that. I will not forget the relief of hearing her bolt the door for the evening and the singing, the reading and then plaiting each other's hair by the light of the fire. I mustn't tell them how she isn't who she used to be and that I'm not sure I like it. I will not tell them what I know. Never. Never. Never.

Mother's stories become increasingly muddled on a daily basis. This is a source of much frustration for me. Whatever they did to her brain, at the centre, the effects were immediate and degenerated each day. Names changed and the order in which events occurred altered with each telling of an old tale. She forgot more and more so I try to remember the past for the both of us. This evening, she can barely even continue or complete my customary, nightly indoctrination. No sound but the fire crackling the silence. Maybe now, I think, maybe now she really is going. My heart beats dully, syncopating its flipping thuds between the clock ticks. My anticipation of her inevitably completely disappearing freezes my mind tight; I know it might be any day . . . She suddenly begins to laugh wildly at nothing, saying:

"Don't tell them they stole your mother! St-st-stole her clean away!"

She lifts me up and swings me around, lurching precariously in the momentum of the swing so that I'm not quite sure if she will drop me or not. She lifts me back onto the chair, and looks at me like she is trying to look into me.

"It's time for your bath."

I like bath time when she washes my hair and then leaves me alone to play little god while she potters downstairs. The near flat bubbles resemble continents. I conjoin them and separate them with my white contoured fingertips. In the beginning perhaps there was a little god like me moulding and destroying things into existence. I make waves and imagine the microscopic populations I'm mercilessly rearranging. I clench my fists and break them all.

She brushes my wet hair in a reverie. I watch us both in the mirror.

"I want you to have a wonderful future. I can see you now; grown up and so tall. No regrets, no nightmares, no legacy of the past to besmirch who you are. Who you are becoming."

The brushstrokes slow and I shiver as she draws my hair back from the nape of my neck.

"We've all made mistakes but it's avoidable now . . . questioning, subversion, doubting the State . . . It's not going to help anyone, now, is it?"

She laughs and begins to tickle me.

"Is it, little one? You have to go in and excavate if you want to get out. Bury your past . . . ?"

I sigh and catch her gaze in the mirror.

"I know . . . under a stone . . . but will I still be who I am?"

The remaining water in the bath pulls downwards through the plughole with a quick twisted slurp.

"That's enough for tonight, "she says quietly, "run along now and sleep the good sleep."

Mother, I can hear you from my room, I can hear you laughing with nobody. Such a strange lullaby.

Day upon day, I memorise my favourite books, the pictures and the paragraphs before we throw them on the fire, mother laughing, saying:
 "Knowledge keeps you warm," while she scratches her neck and doesn't notice it has begun to bleed.
 I watch the tiny flakes of dislodged skin arrange themselves on her shoulder and sprinkle her wool–wrapped breast. Mother says:
 "It's not your words I'm worried about, it's the look in your eyes."
 A cover whistles as its layers unfurl and crackle into an unnatural indigo flame that stretches upwards into violent green and vanishes into embers. I pass mother the last book; a photograph album she had kept under the floorboards. We had prised the boards up, that afternoon; a great puff of spores and mustiness erupting into the still cottage air as we did so, making me sneeze and eliciting her giggles. She laughs a lot since the centre people delivered her home. The room smells of burning ink and laminate and glue melting and as the sound of the fire drops to a muffle punctuated by occasional spits, I lie back against the earth wall, shut my eyes and listen to the heavy wordless language of my mother breathing.

One more day and one long night.

I reach over and take the leather-bound album from her lap.
 "Show me again . . . I like the smell of old things."
 Her hands drop to rest on the floor as I remove it from her grasp.

"Mother . . . ?"

She is gone, maybe temporarily. An ancient photograph slips out from between the hard pages. A bleached image of a baby from in olden days. On the back it says, handwritten, 'I remember the day they took her away'. I didn't recognise any of these surly faces; all bearded men in suits and ladies in bonnets with pursed lips. They were tidy and lifeless, but once upon a time they weren't, were they? They must have been just like us. They must have learnt things all of us here now have to unlearn to survive. I wish I could see inside this picture or put my ear to it and hear them whisper their stories to me. Mother slumps lower to the ground and begins to grind her teeth. She sounds like a machine when she makes those noises. When I turn to the last page I see a photograph I have seen before, when I was little. Two tall identical men, in dark suits with handkerchiefs in their chest pockets, wearing tall hats and standing in front of an enormous white boat. There's a blur in the sky of birds wings tracking. This buttoned-up, pressed, spruce pair gaze so intently into the camera's eye, that immediately I recognise their freedom and their danger. Something familial. Either just disembarked from an extraordinary journey or, more temptingly, about to escape into an adventure. Do I have to throw this away? Would mother even know? There aren't any words on it, just two wolfish young men on a dock, who look the same. I take it to my room and slither it down the side between the cold wall and the mattress. Then I go directly down the corridor to my mother's room, open the heaviest lowest drawer of her chest of drawers, rumple my way to the bottom of a pile of tightly folded starchy fabrics and slowly pull out a suit, with a violet handkerchief in the pocket. I carry it to my room and lay it carefully out on my bed; its cloth limbs lie flat so I curl myself into its mothball bosom and wrap its empty arms around me.

*

There are rivulets running like veins down the windowpane. What if I die in my sleep? Mother told me the tapping sounds in the night are the pipes expanding. This house is ticking. Father has a gun and he doesn't look like father and I can smell sulphur. I wake up on the landing, watching huge vampiric faces projected on the long wall. I run into mother's room and see a shadow figure at the window. I run back out and try and lock the door but the lock is unlockable. I wake again in my bed and think of the slowly creeping light rising from the graveyard mist towards an open window. Always nearing, never arriving. Oh, the fear. I can no longer bear it. If I force myself to feel it, will it lose its power? What are my nightmares made of and why? They are made of the things I never think about in my waking hours. The monstrous hand that slides up the side of the bed grasping at the sheets, the eye at the windowpane, the shrouded figure walking slowly down the stairs. I let daylight steal these feelings and thoughts and by ignoring these horses I make them angry. They stamp the ground of me with their ears flat back and their tails swishing. They leave yellow-blue bitemarks; each night on the same part of my body. So before I go to sleep I open the stall, I stand in front of them trembling as they approach me baring their gums, their hot breath engulfing me until they surround me. In numbing fear I count their teeth. I envisage them eating me; my cartilage crumbs flying through the air, my gristle ground between their fierce molars. Again and again I open their stall and let them come until I am ready for their attack. That is the moment they trot past me and vanish. It's only dying, after all. I suppose ghosts know when you have no fear of them and when you have heard them and know their meaning. If I fall asleep in life I want a thundering rage of dream horses to rush the barricades of my mind, sweep me out so I wake up sweating and breaking in my chest, my belly taut, shaking from the deep. Gifting me a feather that lands in my palm, dropped from an unseen wing.

Suddenly I wake to the noise of giant hailstones, but heavier, more like raining rocks. I see silhouetted shapes swiftly dropping past my window and quickening with such speed that within seconds the sound of the pummelled ground is a thunder. Simultaneously I hear a cracking of wood, a crash and a scream. I go to the window, drawing back the yellowing floral curtain and see a mountain of silver fishes outside. Drum fish and smelt, pilchards and flounders; flicking tails and curling scales silvering under the moonlight. I run to her room and she isn't there. Just a space where her body has been. There's a hole in the roof and I wade thigh deep in tremoring fish, to her bed. I place my small body in the white sheet mother shape and I can't fill that empty space with myself. I look up through the jagged sky-hole and I'm falling, through the bed, the floor, and cross sections of structure; wood and mud. I breathe in the layered smells of fish and fire smoke, porridge and perfume until I find myself on my back on our earthen cellar floor.

"Dig," says a voice, beside my skull, inside my ear.

There's a spade in my hand and I strike the soft ground under the moon rays that followed me through the hole in the roof as I fell. I dig in rhythm until my body engages completely with the movement, setting my mind free. There are figures gathering around me as I shovel this earth, I can see their shiny shoes in my peripheral vision, splattered with dust. I dig and I dream I have died and I am looking down at myself, curled in a hole in desert ground. An orange blanket is dropped down to cover me and then I'm in my first ever memory. Bodiless, perceiving in blackness and space. It's where I know I came from before I arrived here and the voice that lives inside my voice tells me not to be afraid because I have a light in my heart and because of that light I'm not afraid of anything or anyone. I'm going to explode out of time spewing my pure fearless spirit through a cloud that rough-tongues me clean. As I pass through the opening from matter into air, the cloud

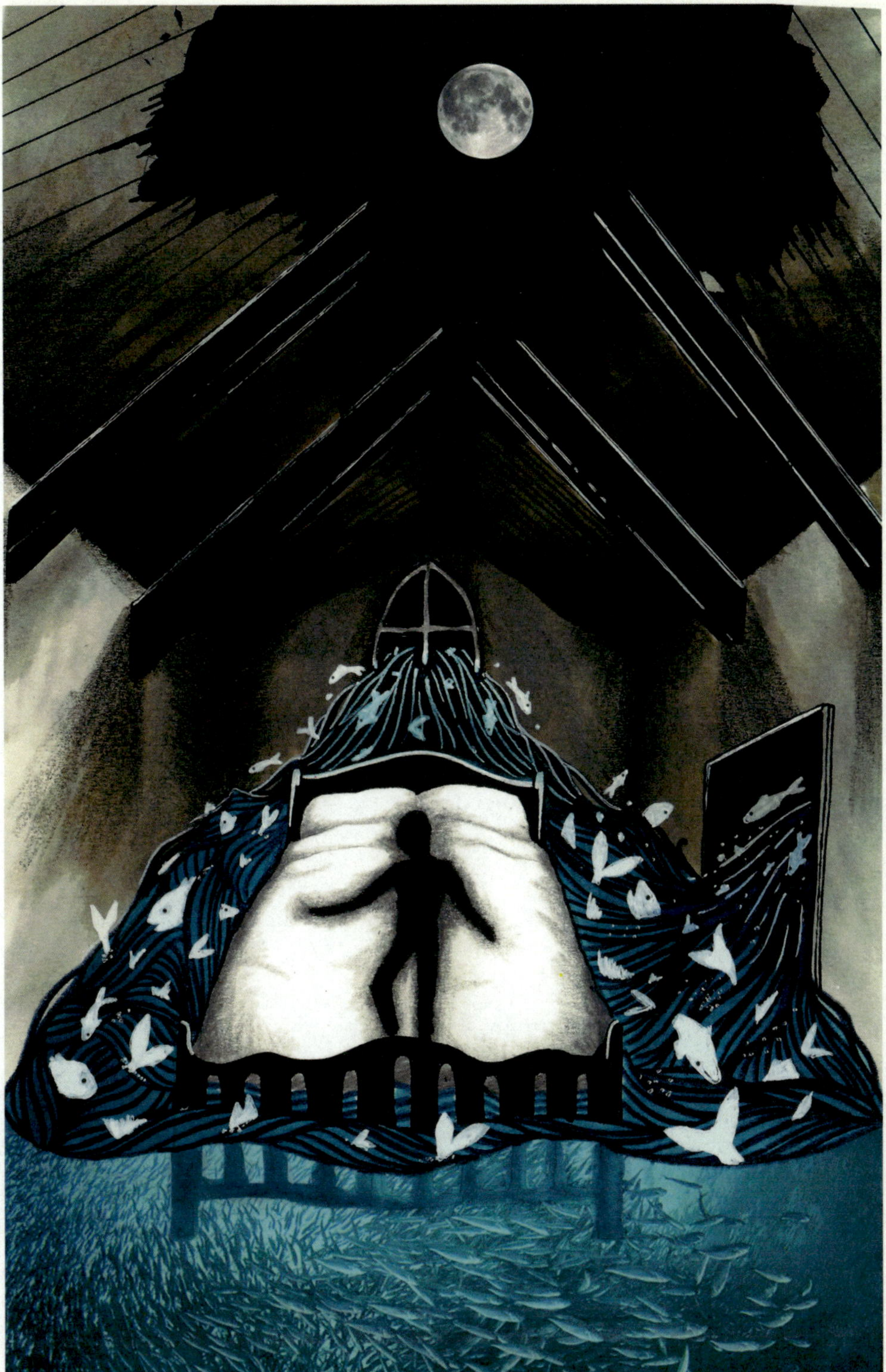

thickens and darkens, sludge colour bleeding back from my body, where fear and the past have been sloughed off me. Forever. Maybe this is what dying is. I look at the palms of my hands. I am so very far away from my body, yet I look at the palms of my hands until I slowly, reluctantly remember they belong to me and I'm contained in this body, trapped in this life. I wake seated in a hexagonal booth, caked in mud and speechless. They open the door and give me a glass of water and a pill. I stumble out, blinking my eyes against the sunlight that floods in as they wheel the excavation booth down the hallway and out of the front door. I wander into the kitchen.

Mother and I sit at the small wooden table, eating our porridge. She smiles at me as I watch the last westerly wedge of deep blue darkness quick shift into clear pinkish dawn, through the window. There are birds swarming up through the sky. I stare at my reflection in her eyes and she looks fixedly at hers in mine.

"So, would you like to get out of this house, little one?"

We rise and stand together, shared gaze unbroken.

"What house?" I say, laughing.

I throw out my arms so the tips of my fingers push the paper walls instantly: effortlessly, they all fall down. Laughter is a roar inside me.

"Carve the life you want," she whispers, "Run . . .. if you must," she says and I must.

LEMUR

●

WRITTEN BY GUY J JACKSON
ILLUSTRATED BY JUDE MELLING

West Glacier, Montana. (Luckily it wasn't East). Where Troy supposedly lived. His mom, his dad, Troy and his many-colored anoraks. Dad gave him binoculars. Dad said to hunt but Dad only ever carried a pistol and never shot anything and never presented Troy any sort of weapon anyway. Mom gave Troy a machete to carve his way through the undergrowth but Troy grew nervous enough when alone with the machete that he soon 'lost' it down amongst a deadfall on a path he 'couldn't' find again. The binoculars were strung faithfully to his neck, though, with red shoelaces, and with the binoculars Troy saw deer, he saw coyotes, he saw wolves in the wild environs of his temporary treehouse, but then in this one day of staring from the treehouse through the binoculars until his eyes swam against each other he became aware of what was obviously not a real bear. That's a fake bear, Troy thought, looking through his binoculars at the fake bear fumbling around on a deadfall, pretending.

*

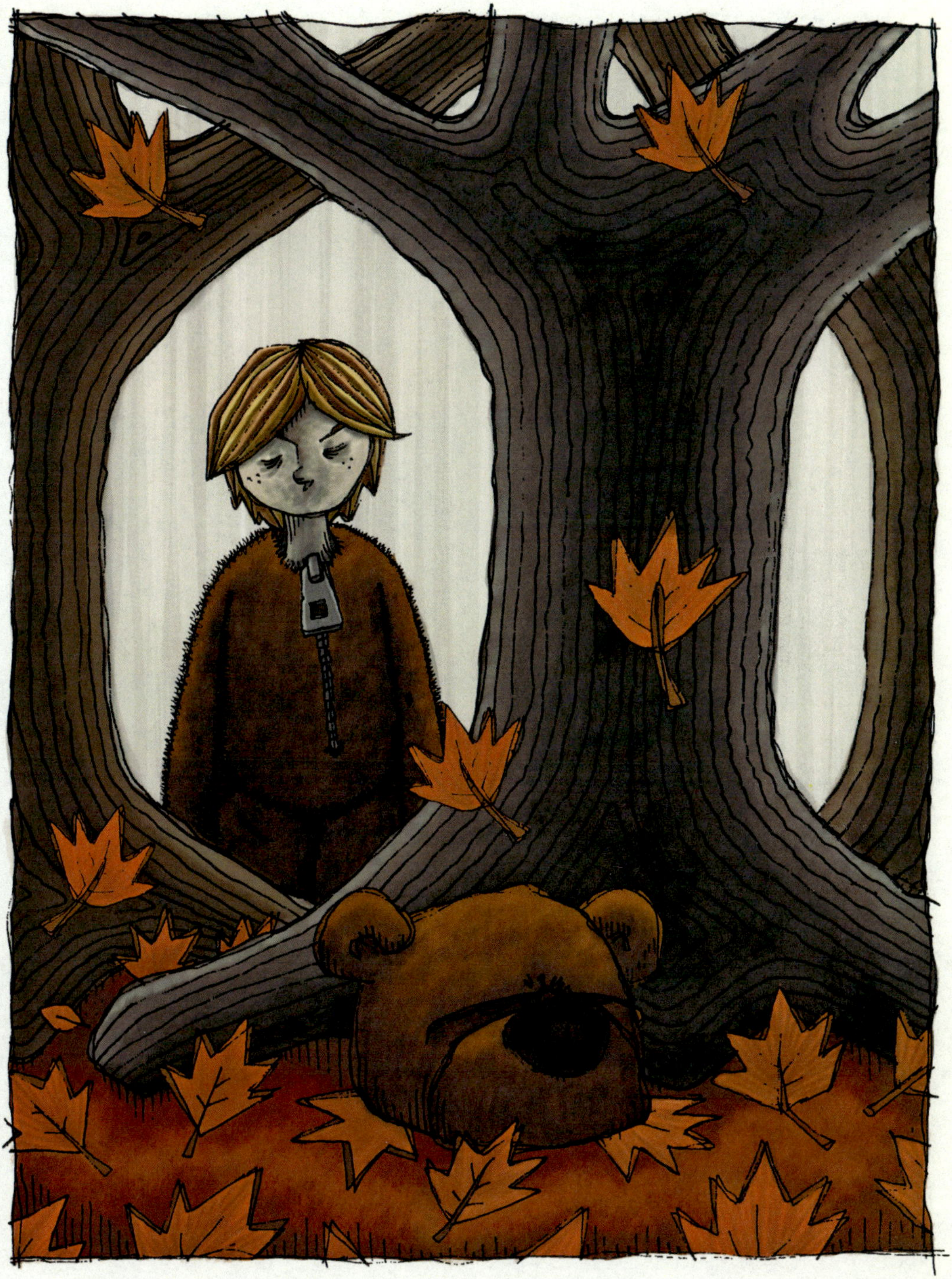

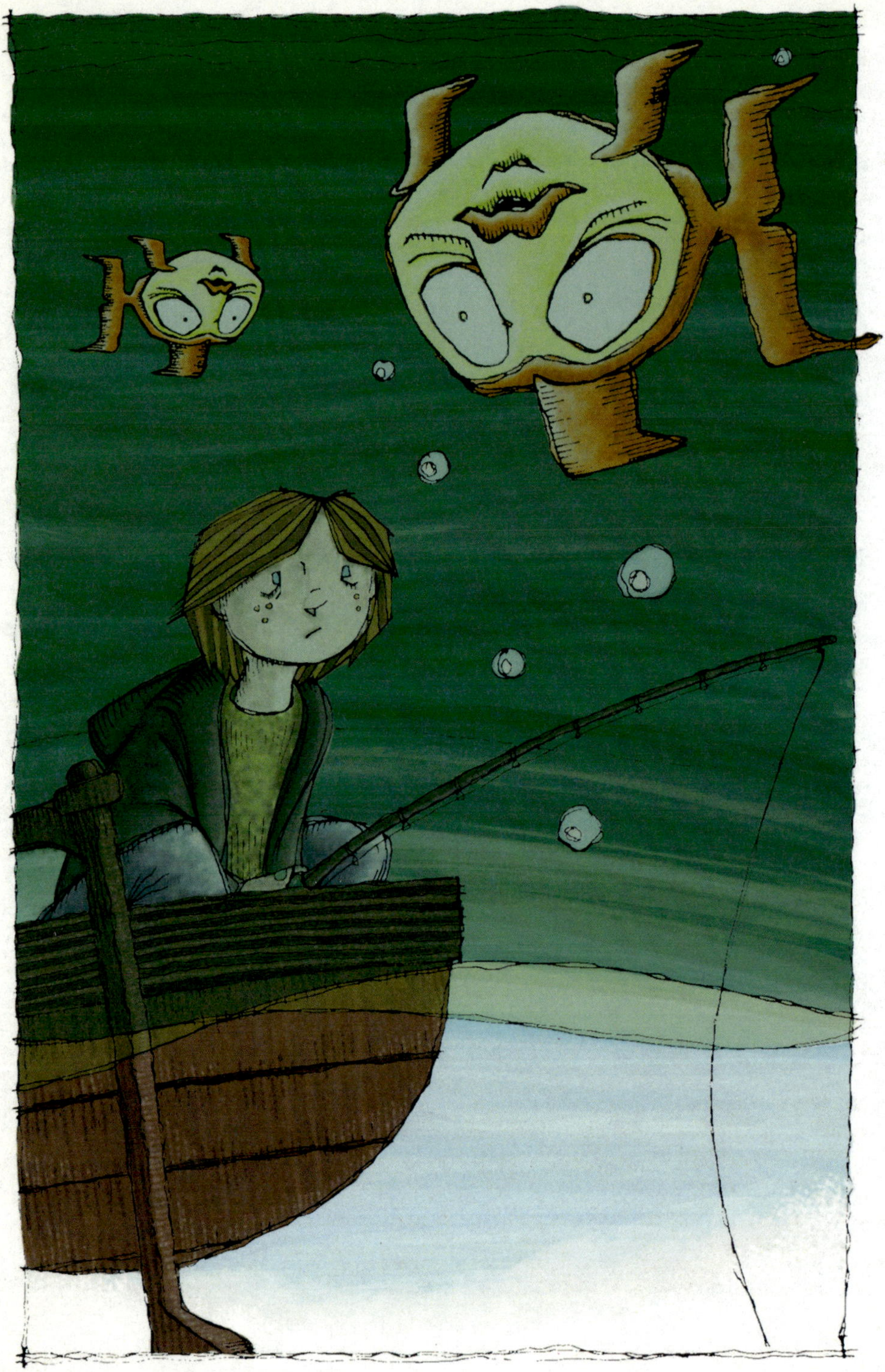

Whitespell, Montana. The family moved into town chasing or running, Troy didn't know which, the arguments of Dad and Mom contained too many numbers as opposed to words. So Dad now was a fisherman who didn't fish but still, from afar, taught Troy to wield a pole. (The binoculars were conveniently lost; didn't need to see at distances for fishing.) Troy could fish alone and he could be quiet. Mom had been in a medieval phase and had wanted to teach him dagger-throwing but Dad was nervous about the dagger-throwing and wouldn't allow it for Troy. Troy was relieved and anyway his mom always complained that daggers were hard to come by so Troy didn't want to be responsible for breaking some or losing some. But fishing was lovely, and more peace of mind than one boy needed until the one day of jostle when Troy was fishing and he spotted a not-at-all-real fish in the water.

"That's a fake fish," he said, peering down at the fish that locomoted without moving tail or fins and kept bumping into rocks.

It operated more like a toy boat in a tub than a fish. He could tell even without binoculars its scales were foam. He would've tried to capture it but he knew that was a waste of the act of putting a hook in the water.

At the train stop while moving toward North Dakota Troy wandered off from his Chaperone of The State and checked what they had in the vending machines. He wanted to unpin the cloth tag from his collar but he couldn't puzzle the trick of the safety pin, or really just hadn't been taught it yet. The vending machine hummed to him and gave him the quiet of fishing. So rich in colors, the artwork on the corn chips and candy wanted him to know the contents mouth-wise but Troy was not one for bells and whistles, such as made him doubt sincerity. Dad taught him that opposition: no bells and whistles.

"Chips and candy," Troy murmured through the glass.

Fake food. He thought how the girl in the ticket window had mispronounced every word she could've possibly mispronounced in the three or four full-length sentences he'd heard her spout. But fake words were

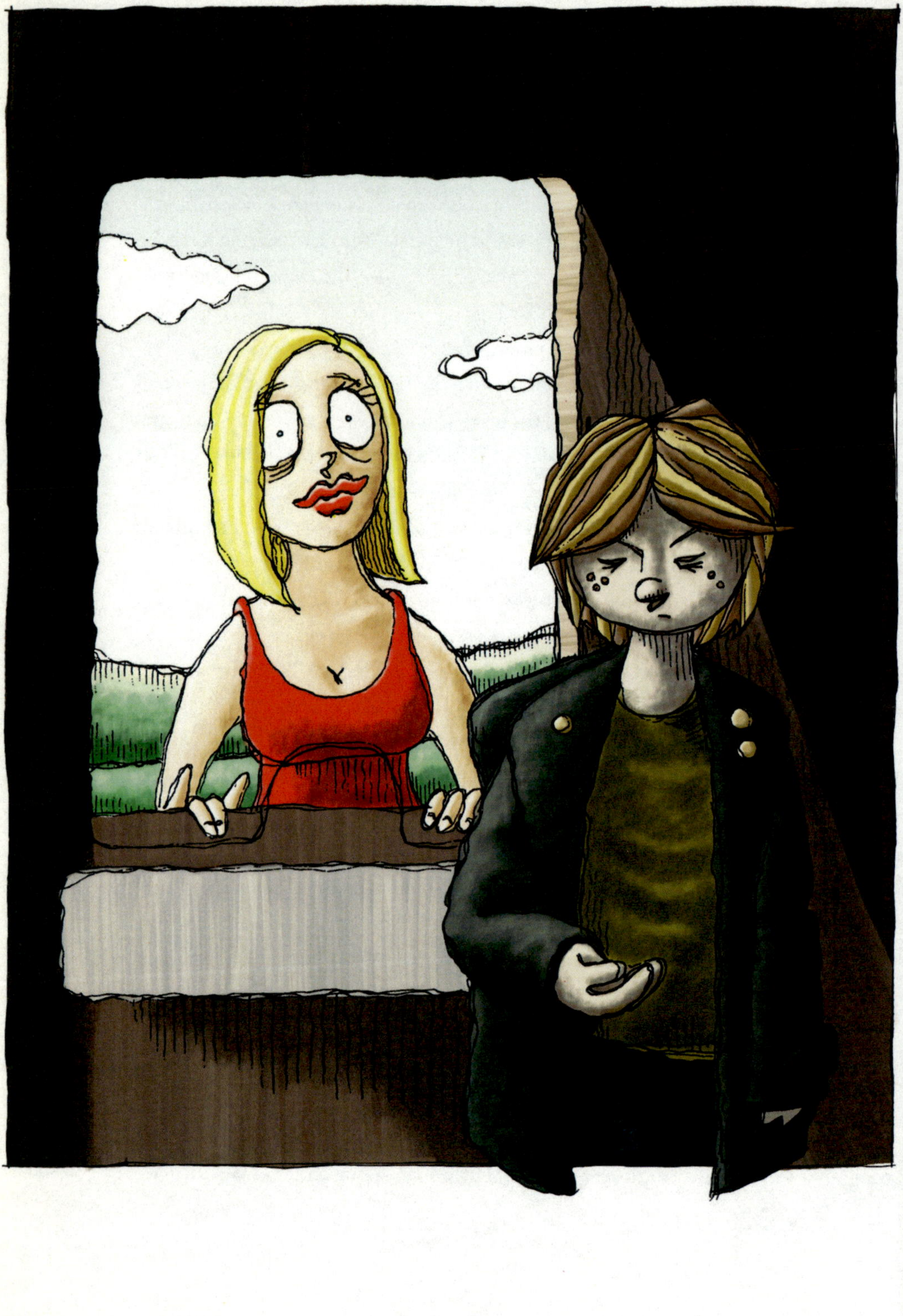

okay, especially if spoken cutely by a cute girl. Troy knew words. He'd read four dictionaries before the age of ten, in each reading for some reason always missing the entry on safety pins. He still wasn't ten years old, either. Ten would mean a full decade. That was one year later. He breathed on the glass. He wrote in the breath: 'Fake food'.

In the house with the ventilation shaft to his room, whichever that house was, either the one in Gallant, Idaho or the one in Presbyterian, Utah, but whichever one he'd listen through the ventilation for hours on end to the soothing sound of his parents discussing their least favorite topic, discussing what to do about him.

"Save him from being depressed by forcing him to be social, how about that?"

"It's too expensive to visit the J.P. Morgan library, though, so don't take him there."

"Have you met the musician with the appealing attitude versus meeting the musician who's repugnant? Please introduce Troy to the first musician, the friendly one, light on feet and thought."

"Rum and cola, please, but not too much rum, I haven't had a drink in ten years. I'm helping to manage him, though, so you understand me needing a drink, don't you?"

"Nobody's saying you said anything to his brother, I'm saying you said something to someone else to tell to his brother."

"Say things to him like that. Surprise him from his torpor with a bit of yelling."

Tualitin, Oregon. The madcap spinning wheel in the community booth. That's all they had. Troy was unimpressed. Bells and whistles. The fireworks were especially unimpressive. All dollars for the spinning wheel went to the good of the community. Dad and Mom argued. Dad felt the spinning wheel was way more popular than it actually was and that it should be moved to a central table. Mom felt the spinning wheel was technically misnamed because it was actually only a wheel that spun. Numbers caught on pegs and no thread or sweater-making involved. Then, stuck on the roundabout they circled under the mad bird talking nothing but their love and loss, their car going round and round and round and round until it finally arrived at an accident.

Mom had safety-pinned a note in cloth to Troy's collar. His older brother's address. His brother twenty years older. His dad's first wife.

"Who was she, Dad?" asked Troy.

"A fake wife," said his Dad.

But why would his mom and dad take the shoebox of community money with the community party going on all around and try and drive away and but then never leave the roundabout?

Later by two years when he was still far too young Troy would learn to drive. His brother taught him. Troy thought about driving around in a roundabout until he got into an accident. He didn't know how his parents had managed.

"You go around and around the roundabout until eventually your brain wears out and you make a mistake," said his brother.

His parents had faked community fundraising at the community fundraising party. They had faked caring as Dad's lack of a goodbye and Mom's strange address-to-collar pin trick had illustrated. Fake parents.

"Or!" said his brother. "you go around and around on a roundabout until you find yourself hypnotically stuck like the roundabout is your whole life gone micro-cosmological, and to shake it, to shake it, to shake out of it you hastily reveal you've been affair-having and your wife pulls out her switchblade like she would do immediately and she sticks it in your heart and you have an accident and you're both dead. Whichever you think is more likely."

*

Troy had listened through the ventilation to his mom deciding to his dad that she was crumbling as a parent:

"You keep asking me how often he has meals."
 "Look, even if we own a hot tub, we are going to have to clean it once in a while. Your skin creates its own dust."
 "Mommy's not buying your dinner, baby. You want me to carve the turkey, speaking of which?"
 "You know how you get a tickle from yelling at the boy? I asked the lady if she had a cough drop or any kind of water and she had a cough drop and that fixed me immediately."
 "I once bought asthma medicine but only used it once. It was only one-third as expensive as it is today. I gulped down the medicine and then realised it wasn't for me because I didn't have asthma. Me just a smoker trying to clear my lungs so I could yell at the boy wasn't any excuse."

When they'd been killed at the fundraiser in the roundabout and Troy was on his way to parts unknown and a brother hitherto unseen, Troy on his way uncaring about how the Old Ladies Of The State whispered that he needed a mother, when all of that Troy practiced at the train station what he'd say on the phone. He practiced on an old pay phone still standing, such a relic as to be false. No sound from the black banana bit, from the touch of the buttons. Then Troy walked out of the station in Lemur, Washington, and stood at the end of the dock, no, not dock, a platform and he looked where the train would be headed. Into the night and then directly into a tunnel. Beside a red lantern at the entrance to the tunnel stood a fake train conductor. Troy could see the gleam of polished wood on what was supposed to be a forehead. And this fake didn't even bother to fake moving. And Troy wondered what all this fakery evidence portended for North Dakota being what it was.

CHASE

·

WRITTEN BY LIZ ADAMS
ILLUSTRATED BY MADDIE JOYCE

    Eyes: two green-slices
flickering yellow dreams of Egypt.
    Girl mistook her for a toy —
this kind of thing happens in children's books.
    Or the sleeping
feline with its inner life of killing & squeaking:
leaf-becomes-a-mouse-becomes-a-bird.

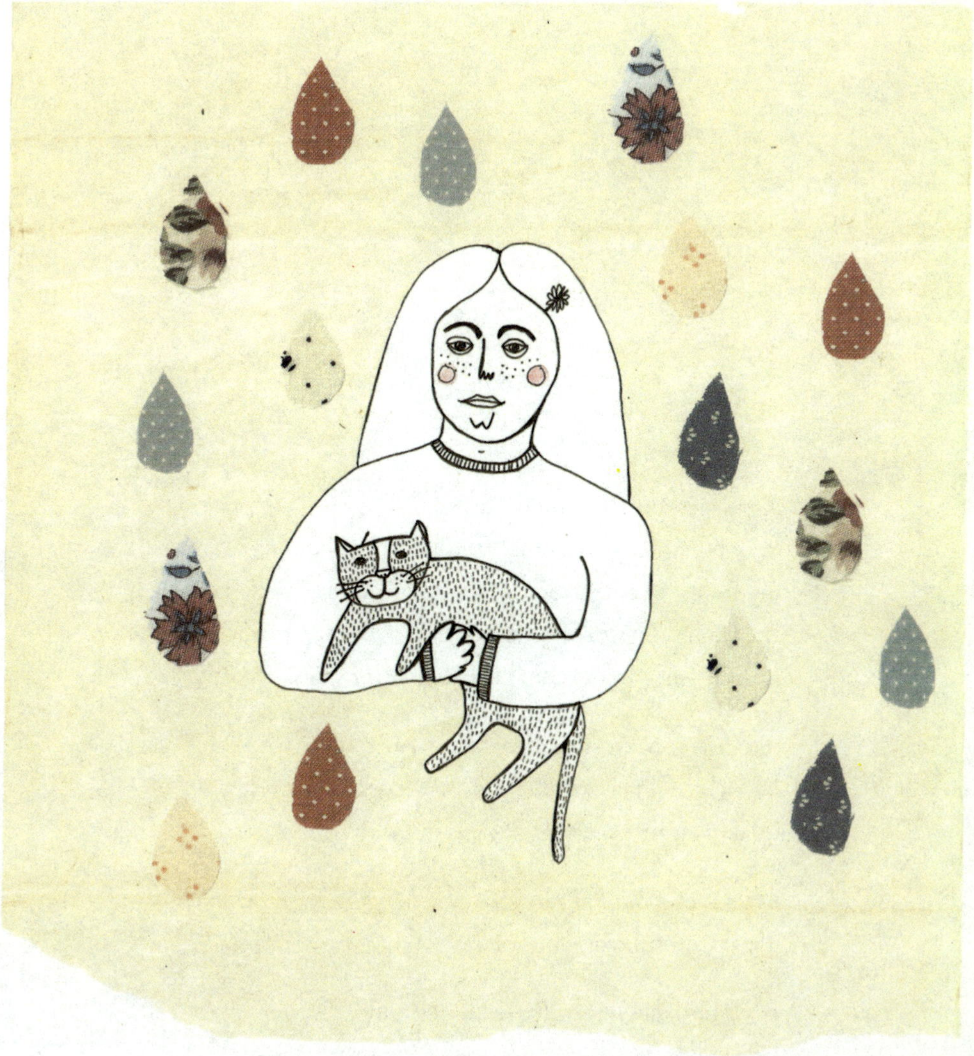

MACAULAY, MY NEPHEW AND ME

·

WRITTEN AND ILLUSTRATED
BY INUA ELLAMS

Aged six, I see Macaulay Culkin
defy two thieves at home, alone and stop holding
my father's hand; grab the neighbour's bike, circle
the compound for two noons, staggering scraped,
bruised, bleeding pride, I teach myself to ride

into a new profession: assassin. Armed with drive
by kicks, I attack smaller kids who pass on tricycles,
till a giant five year old flattens me with lesson

One: Pick your battles.
Two: Careful who you trust:

It's Thursday but traffic is lazy as Sunday's.
Remi and I trapped in mischief's hot grip, catapult
paper pellets at passing cars. Remi's shot scores
a driver whose right cheek splits. Brakes scream,
angered, he stands in front of me, fist his swings
Remi is nowhere to be the seen.

INUA ELLAMS

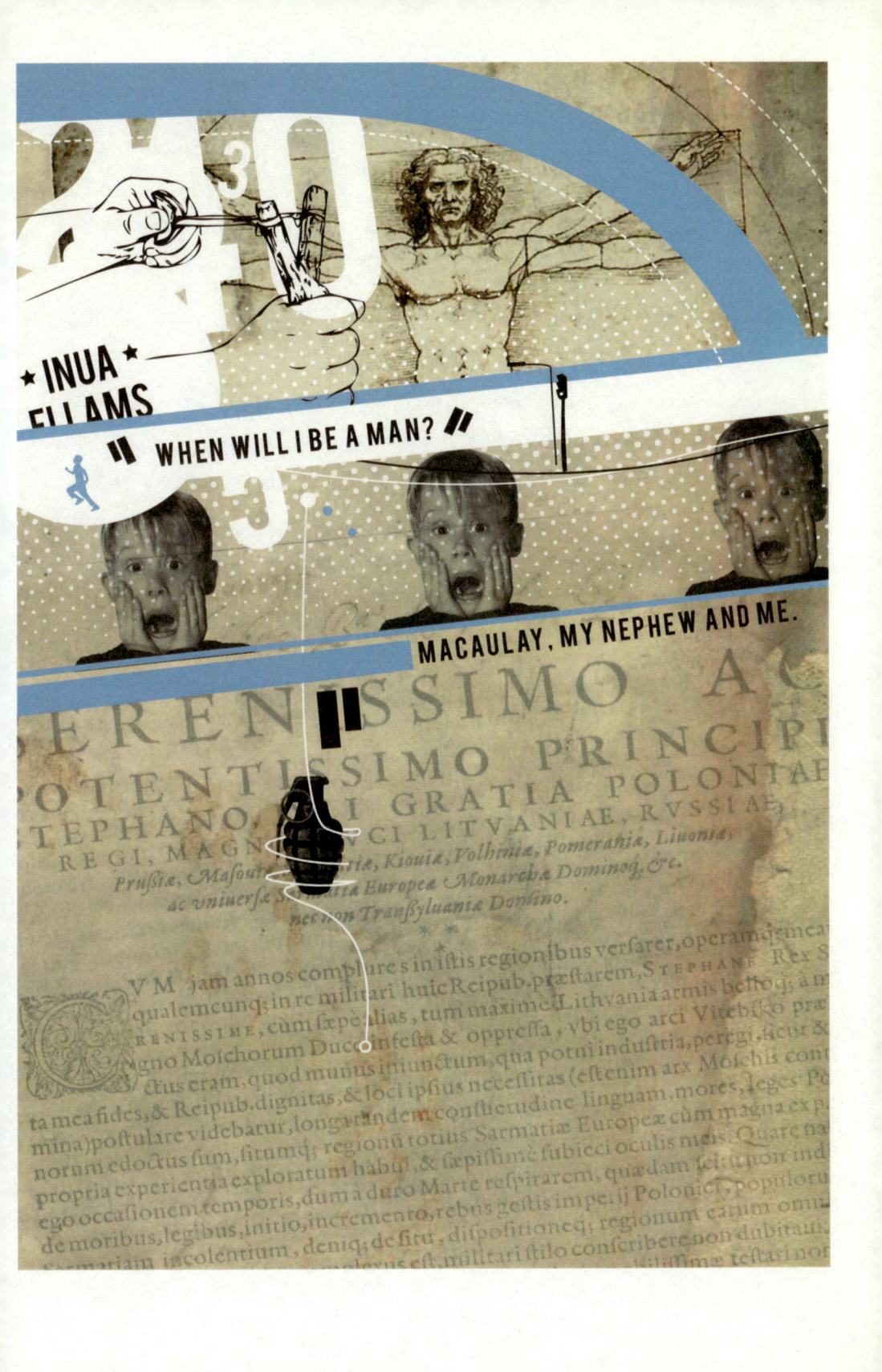

"WHEN WILL I BE A MAN?"

MACAULAY, MY NEPHEW AND ME.

The blood I spit blocks and rusts trust for years,
till Kristine who hugs mahogany, whose laugh:
like a prophet's, whose lips I'd wrestle worlds for,
whose lashes melt my fists, suggests lesson

Three: Vulnerability is power,
Weakness is strength.

And when Ansell finds me,
comes, fist clenched, four going forty,
asks when he'll be a man,

I don't recount the time I met an ex-child soldier
who, crazed with gun powder sniffed with cocaine
once razed towns and skinned captives for kicks
this becomes my list as lesson

Four: Without emotion
men turn beasts.

Aged four, persists with when he'll be a man?
I just describe Macaulay, that five year old's stand
and say we're made from the lesson we learn
they happen as you grow, there's no lone time
when like a light switch your back bone clicks;
I tell him ask me when your fists feel old

I'll be sixty something, he'll have stories whose
morals mirror my own. They'll bite gorgeous,
chew bitter, spit sweet, we'll talk the moon
down till dew drowns our thirst
I'll ask him to go first.

PAINTED IN A CERTAIN SKY

•

WRITTEN BY MARIA DRUMMEY
ILLUSTRATED BY EMMA DAY

They are balanced on the edge of thought
These precious childhood memories
I cannot bring them easily to mind
As time and each year passes, they fade away like old colour photographs
Now turning sepia, as edges fray the silken threads of memory
Becoming more fragile as time passes

I might have found them lost in music
Or painted in a certain sky

The scent of lilac or of wood smoke
Skies made heavy then washed with rain

I learnt to love the thunder as a child
The lightning sparks the sky aflame
With crests of fire burning through the raindrops
Autumn colours, orange burning bright
Giving way to winter fires, bare trees and snow drifts
Wrapped in layers, through power cuts and candlelight
Coal fires stoked high on Christmas Eve

Childhood is my mother's voice
And stories told in shadow light flickering on ceilings
Words long forgotten, fashioning a daydream in which to sleep
And comfort in the memory

We made a world in wooden blocks
Spread out around my father's feet
Imagination free to roam with sawdust scented heavy in the air
And endless possibility

The biggest gift was always time,
Although we could not know it then
But now it rushes swiftly on and, taken up in daily care,
It disappears like grains of sand that wash away into the sea

To find the child I thought was lost
I searched the seasons of the year
She weaves forever in and out of rain and wind, of summer or snow
And through the memories, gently whispers you have found me,
I am here

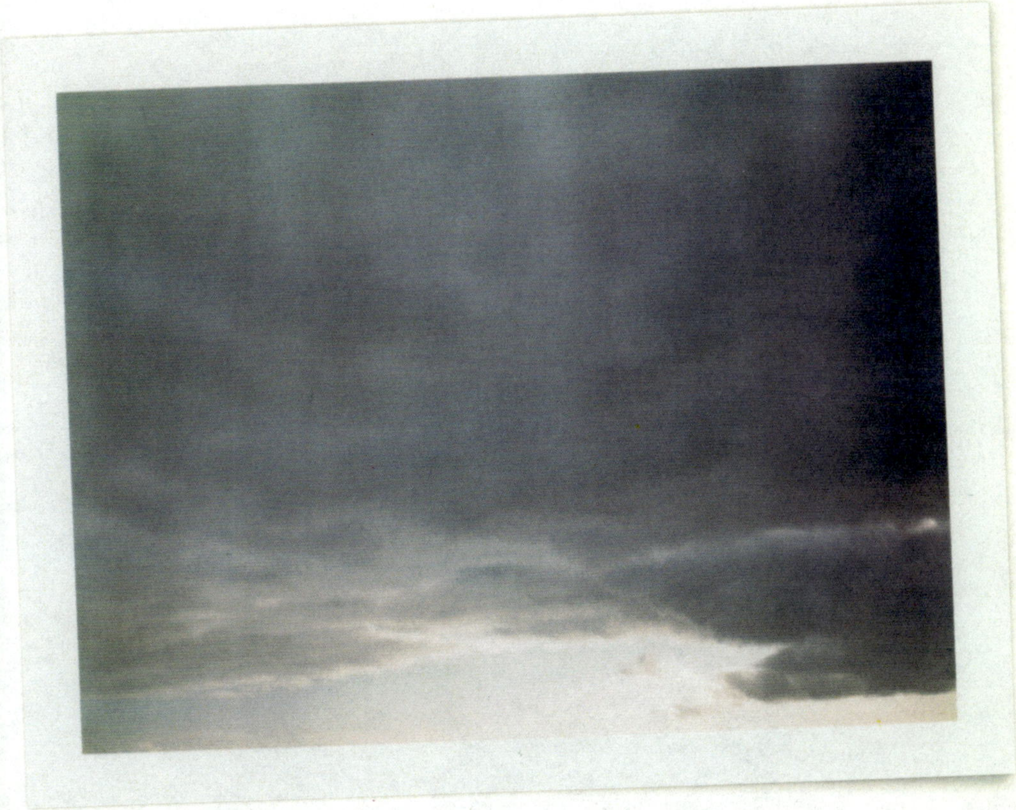

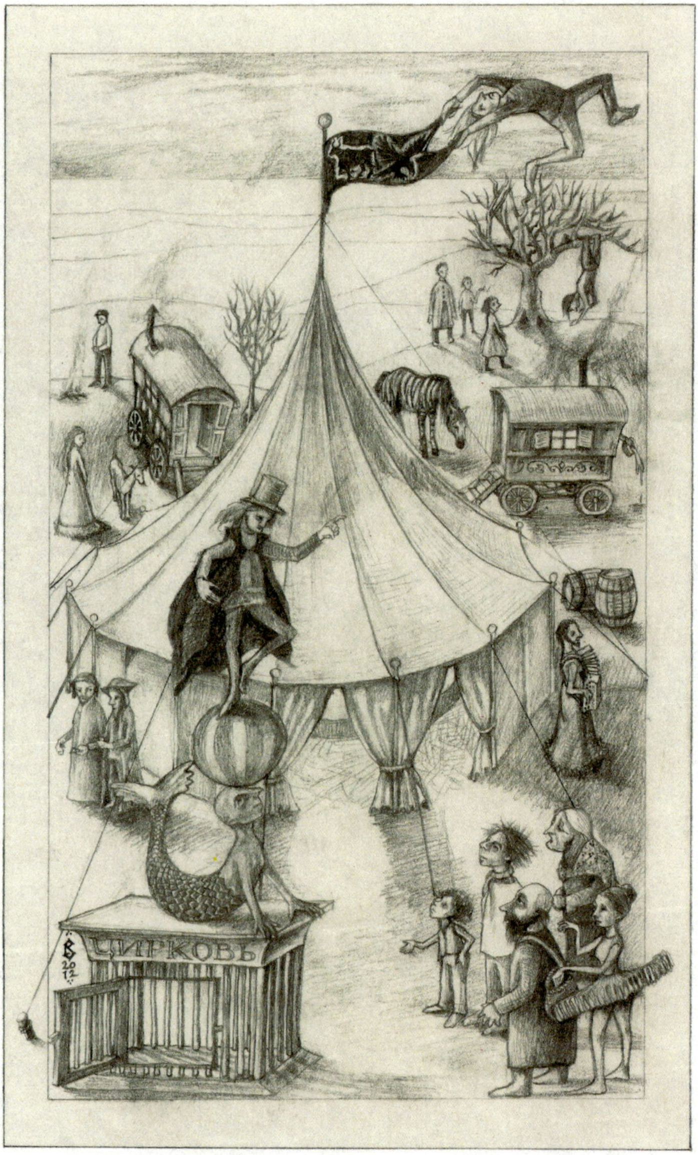
ЦИРКОВЪ

ADOLESCENCE-
ADULTHOOD.

A travelling circus populated by rogues,
thieves and pathetic clowns rolls into town . . .

"My circus travelled the four kingdoms and the thrice-nine lands, bringing joy to those whose lives were so tarnished as to be polished by such a meagre smear of laughter as the pathetic clowns could offer or the dubious wonder of acrobats who were, to be honest, more flexible with the truth than with their bodies."

CENTRAL STORY

The Scrimstone Circus Gospel

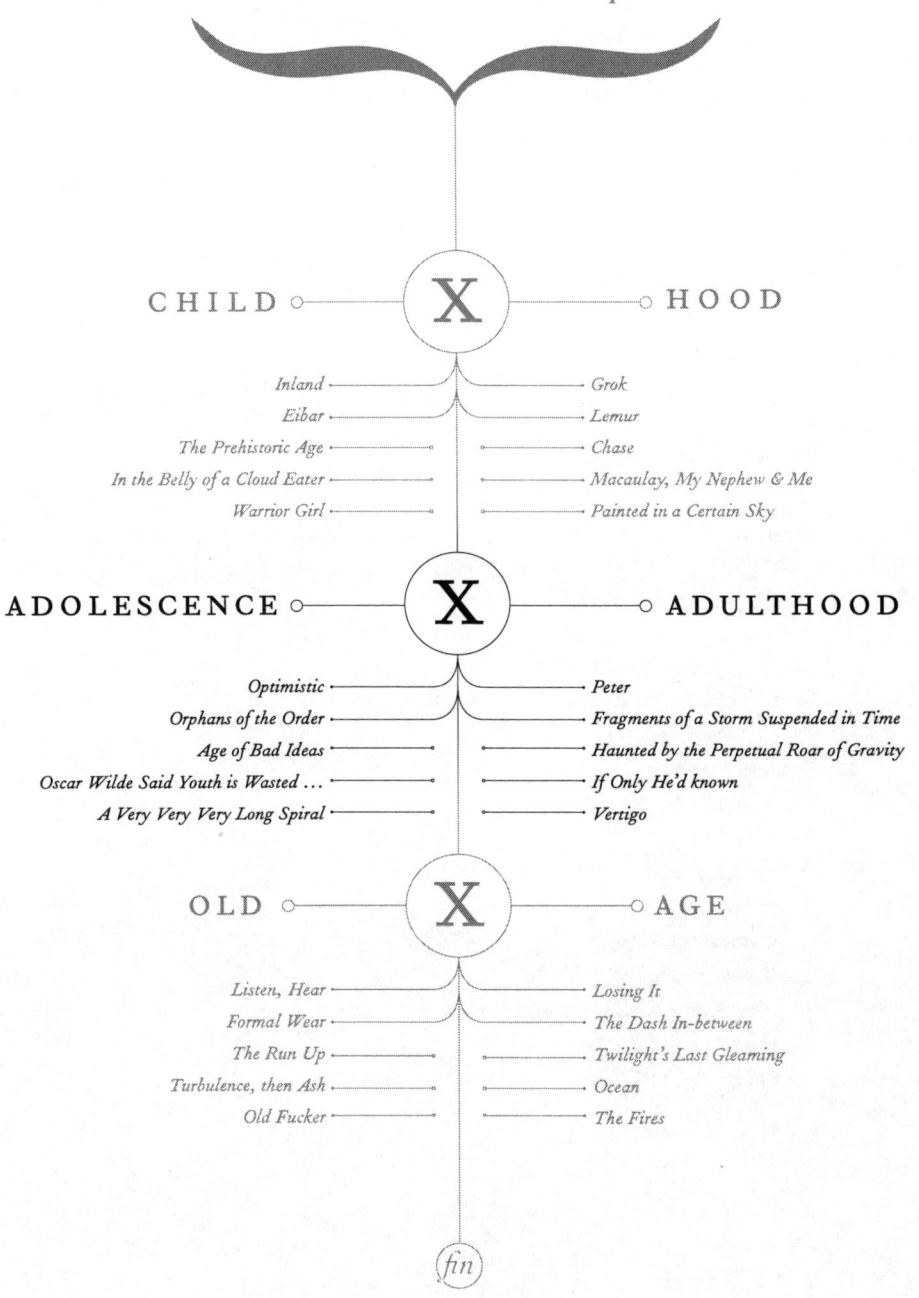

CHILD ⚬—Ⓧ—⚬ HOOD

Inland	*Grok*
Eibar	*Lemur*
The Prehistoric Age	*Chase*
In the Belly of a Cloud Eater	*Macaulay, My Nephew & Me*
Warrior Girl	*Painted in a Certain Sky*

ADOLESCENCE ⚬—Ⓧ—⚬ ADULTHOOD

Optimistic	*Peter*
Orphans of the Order	*Fragments of a Storm Suspended in Time*
Age of Bad Ideas	*Haunted by the Perpetual Roar of Gravity*
Oscar Wilde Said Youth is Wasted …	*If Only He'd known*
A Very Very Very Long Spiral	*Vertigo*

OLD ⚬—Ⓧ—⚬ AGE

Listen, Hear	*Losing It*
Formal Wear	*The Dash In-between*
The Run Up	*Twilight's Last Gleaming*
Turbulence, then Ash	*Ocean*
Old Fucker	*The Fires*

(fin)

AGE OF
BAD IDEAS

•

WRITTEN BY WILLIAM KHERBEK
ILLUSTRATED BY VINCENT GILLAN

It was the totality of the experience,
the spume of beer froth
fragments of Soundgarden,
bone-rattle of bass cannon,
of speaker-box frame and so on.

We were rescuing each other
daily, to live out the next
failed state: "first love",
"independence"
"first missed chance".
Dwell among us,
in the hormone city,
The new gradient
Of magical thinking:
Look sharp, talk blunt
feel the glass as it splits your tongue.
Your numbness is night
as it drags, as starlight

ADOLESCENCE—ADULTHOOD

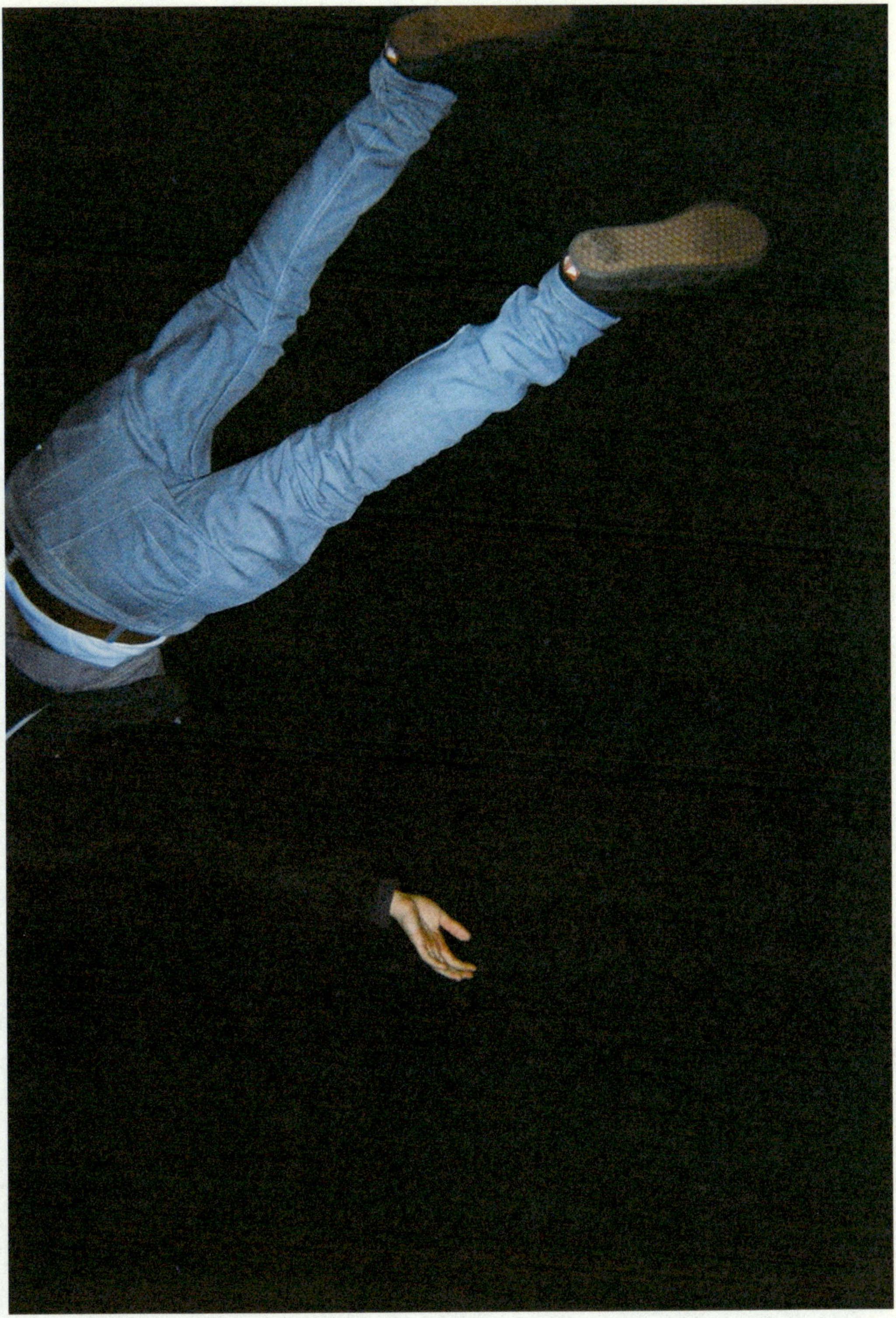

washes the cold grill
and the headlights
that are the first inklings
of dawn.
A bedroom is a cave,
A blanket was a cape,
A kiss is a planet,
Time is painless
And then it stops.

OSCAR WILDE

SAID YOUTH

IS WASTED

ON THE YOUNG —

SO LET'S

GET WASTED

.

WRITTEN BY KIRSTY ALISON
ILLUSTRATED BY LOLA DUPRE

Oi, yoof, wasted youth, hood up m'foes, and join my club
I am a UFO from Savage Society and I bring you total love
Paint marshmallow lips with glistening precipice,
Kiss my lightning and sit upon my devil's stick.
Lick the cover of my magazine,
Dress in this sweet Chinese wedding dress, m'neon gangster dove-
A youth died to hammer it;
Blew her brains out in a shopping mall,
Fell in love with a mannequin,
Looted singing TV dreams, in a T-shirt reading Alcoholic Libertine.

OSCAR WILDE SAID. . .

Save yourself! Run away with me, m'bruv,
Act grown up, and nick a car,
We'll get naked in a border bar, m'sweets,
Snort Starbucks cake until your wake, we'll meet in Mexico,
The stage pre-lit, the atom split, your eyes are like Haribo,
Let's make disco starlight, I am director of the dying sun,
'S up? Steal that cash, and bring a gun.
We'll torch palm trees under lusting dusk,
Make immortal speed spunking fireworks t'wards sky's tusks.
Step down from heaven now, unlock thy room, m'serfs o' the Internet,
Thou shalt want-on and obey, m'eagle perving pets,
My jet plane has a trigger lens, spies through your CCTV,
This is how your life must be spent,
M'prince of light, gotta pay the rent
Pack sex satchels with Naivety,
Make me ad revenue,
Ovum hips, must grind, for chips, m' beauty fool,
Comments are not even free,
I am outrageously in love with youth, my time has plastic teeth,
This prison air is my litany, m'grubster bait
Multiply and die trying, m' Darwin-ning mate
Give me drool and dance like leaches, pornstar boys,
Flaunt peaches, missies, shave your tongue, kick high
Run roughshod to my gaze, m' salty, rainbow waves,
I am your feudal overlord, I will love, honour and betray,
This is all beneath the wire, tell no-one of my ways.
Remember what I say: I bought you up, to pay, m' dirty little luck
Bin your truth, down low, wasted youth,
Trade your shadow of fear, no angels or refunds here.
I am Savage Society, m'burning, sling shot lose-da game,
Plug into my steadfast folds of power, m'smelly, wetty, sugar guv,
For we shall own the world.

ADOLESCENCE—ADULTHOOD

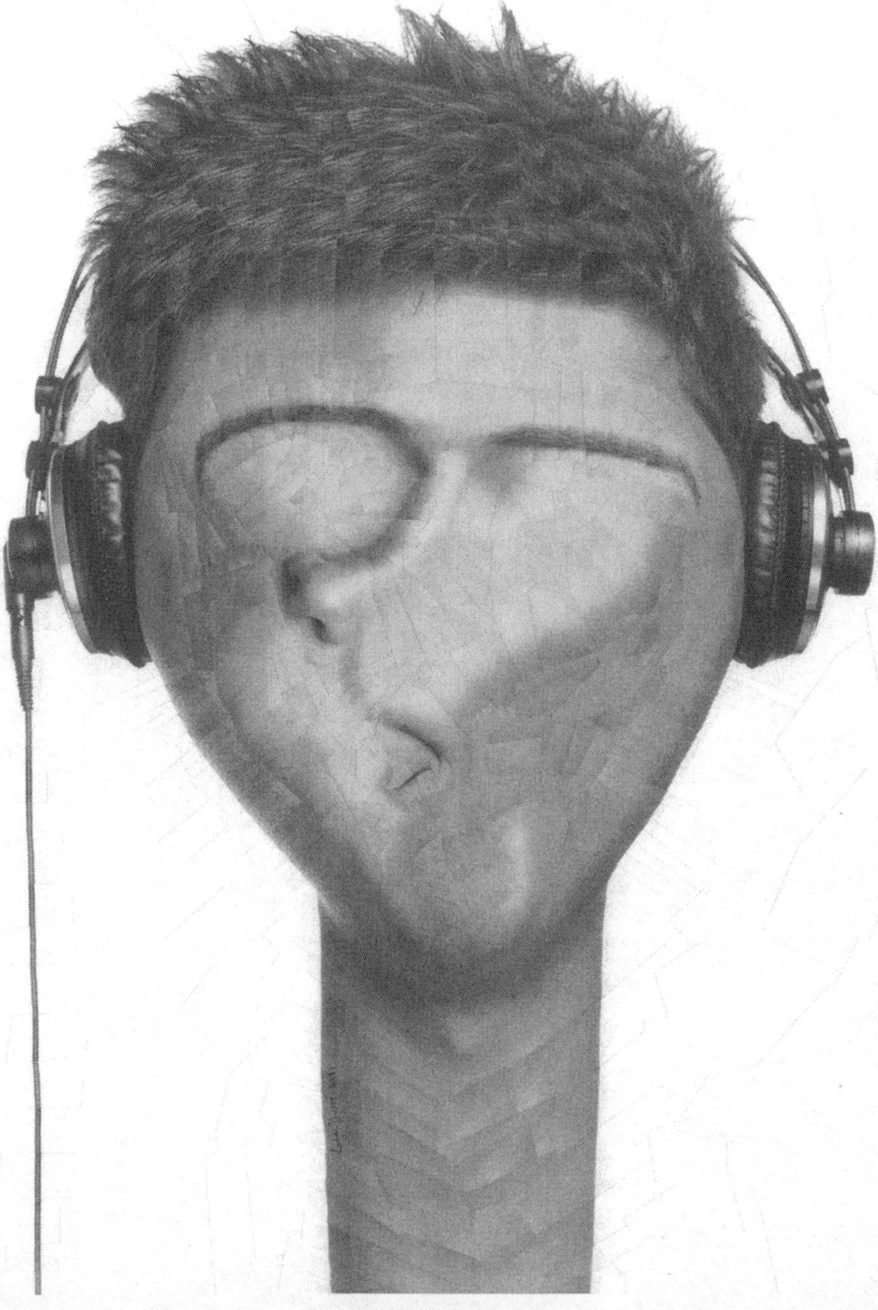

A VERY VERY VERY LONG SPIRAL

.

WRITTEN BY LAURA DOCKRILL
ILLUSTRATED BY NIKKI PINDER

We started from nothing
All the things I've seen
A feel of blue hands wrapped around a telephone cord
Voices as open as walls of an exhibition
Yet as cagey as walky-talkies as making
Messages through cans
And strings
Many things can bring you uncertainty
Certainly
It takes only a small note to knock you off balance
You can't always hold your arms out like a tightrope walker
You can't always cry for help
At the same time you can't be expected to be brave the whole time
See this thing right here?
It eats at you from the inside out
Sticks to you like the smell of bed or
Guilt
You feel sorry for yourself
See I've seen the pages of faces sliming down the drunk walls on parade

ADOLESCENCE—ADULTHOOD

Full of shame
And backwards snarls.
Ask my friend she'll tell you she'll say pain, it comes in waves
Watch eventually it stops, staggers at least and only
Memories remain
Spotting the sand diamond
Seashells
Haunting and necessary
Haunting and necessary
Hollow mouth I fill my throat with your heart and chew
I say awful things to you
I want to hit you so hard I want your blood on the carpet
I want to wrestle you
Until I'm waving a white flag
Sad and fat tongued
I can forget where I'm from
A cling of tough girls
That I carry around my neck like a string of pearls
Scrape helpings off yesterday's plate.
It's too late but I'm sorry I say
Sobbing into your back
About how I got it all wrong
And that I'll fix it.
Although inside we are bones and dryness. Crinkle dead leaves and mushing fruits, greying bruises
Foaming pickle green, wrinkling slugs, rippling mud
Over and over I remind my name to the rose buds
Why not, ask my friend she'll tell you she'll say, pain, it comes in waves
And if you ask my friend, she'll tell you, she'll say, pain, it comes in waves
And she would. For it's a very very very long spiral

A VERY VERY VERY LONG SPIRAL

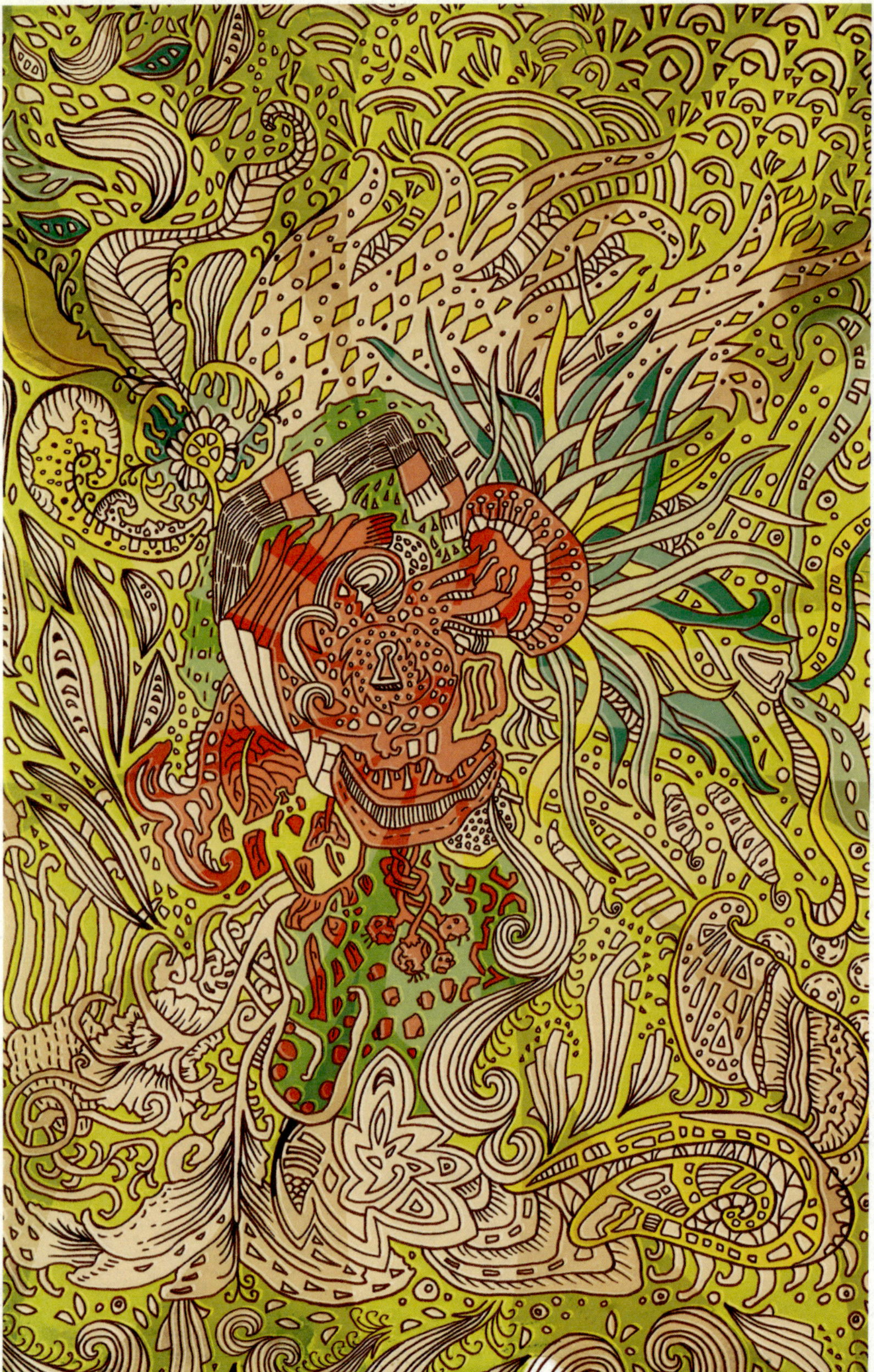

And it will take a very very very long time to heal
This very very very long spiral
You can't nuture a butcher
You can't remove the stains
But just watch as it outrolls
And rolls in again,
Hushing
A gasping seashell remains
I hold it to my ear
To hear something, I hear it sweetly humming
We started from nothing remember.

A VERY VERY VERY LONG SPIRAL

OPTIMISTIC

·

WRITTEN BY WILL CONWAY
ILLUSTRATED BY LEE HOLLAND

I make my own luck. Since I was a small boy I've had the fortune of being able to amuse myself with very little. You might say that it was misfortune that gave me very little in the first place but we don't have to agree on everything to get along, do we?

My father left us when I was quite young. He was, from what I remember, a kind man but I don't remember an awful lot. My mother and I got on well although she was very often busy; single mother and everything. I guess I could rattle on about my childhood like anyone but I don't think you'd be that interested.

I climbed trees. I threw stones. I spent a lot of time alone. This is not a sob story, mind you. Nor is it a happy one. Actually I can't say that, can I? I won't know how it makes you feel until you've read it, not least until I've written it.

*

ADOLESCENCE—ADULTHOOD

You see, I learned this trick once.

It all started when I picked up a coin from the gutter. It winked at me one day in the autumn light among some litter. As I bent to grab it before anyone else could, something sailed over my head and smashed in the street. It was what must have been a pretty hefty glass bottle. As I turned to see where it came from, I saw the boys disappear into the stairwell of the building. If I hadn't ducked at that moment, I was certain the bottle would have taken my head off.

I started to think of this coin as lucky. I took it everywhere I went. Although I was poor, I always had money on me, as it would never be spent.

Now, in recent years there has been a field of thinking becoming popular called Quantum Physics, which I like the sound of. I'm no scientist, that's not what I went to school for, but I understand it a little. It seems especially relevant to me.

You've probably heard about the scientist whose curiosity killed the cat when he let it out of the bag. Basically he had a theory that if a cat is in a container where there is a half chance of it being poisoned by gas, then, until you open the container, for you the cat is neither dead nor alive but exists in a state somewhere between the two.

Or something along those lines . . . Does that make sense? Anyway, this idea has developed that the observer exerts a power over what they observe. I like that. If that's the case, you can call me the optimistic observer. Nine lives like a cat.

*

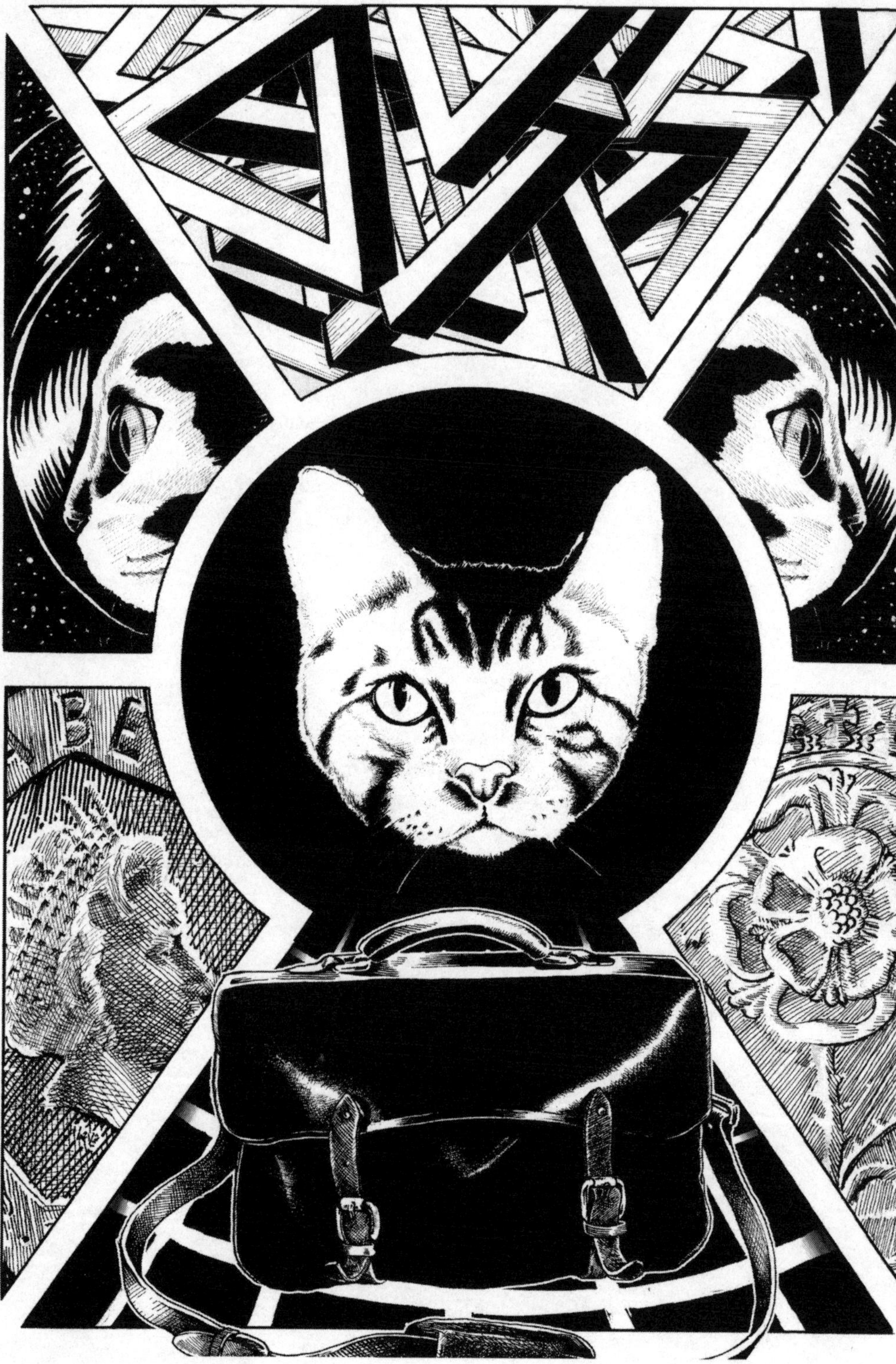

I was naturally gifted at throwing things, a strange talent and perhaps stranger still that I didn't play more sport. I could hit a tin can off a wall with a conker from twenty paces in the schoolyard though. I once hit the back of the head of my lucky day's bottle-thrower from the other side of the playground. It was such a good shot that he couldn't comprehend that it had come from me. When he found out it was me he wanted to fight me at first, but we settled it with a throwing contest – a story for another day perhaps – and eventually we became friends, believe it or not. He was a great thrower but I could always beat him at playground target practice. It was nice when a crowd gathered but I preferred to practice tossing things on my own. Especially my lucky coin. Of all the things I could aim, this coin was my favourite. I was so accurate that I learnt to toss it so it would land on a tree branch above my head, then I would climb to retrieve it. One time I didn't realise my climbing had shaken it from its resting place and I frantically searched for almost an hour until I found it in the roots below. I decided to be more careful with my luck from then on.

I taught myself to flip the coin ten feet in the air with my thumb and catch it. Then I would slap it on the back of my fist and ask whoever was around to call heads or tails. Perhaps this doesn't look as impressive as some of my other tricks, but I do it differently to most people.

I learned to know this coin like the back of my hand was invisible. I developed a talent for guessing which side would be showing when I removed my other hand.

I knew the precise weight of that coin and the exact pressure needed to flip it an odd number of times so that it would land facing the other way. It didn't matter how many times I wanted it to spin in the air, it

OPTIMISTIC

could be three or thirty-three, every time I would make it show the other side. This way of course I always knew which face of the coin I would reveal to the world, because I had chosen it. This is how I learned to control my luck.

I couldn't tell you why but I hid this talent for such a long time and I only let it slip by chance when asked to toss a coin to settle a matter in a bar. Cocky with drink I boasted, revealing my trick to anyone who would watch. Fortunately only a handful of people learned of my gift and most of them were drunks.

That night however, I realised that I could make some money off my coin. I wasn't what you'd call a hustler exactly, on the other hand I never starved because I knew that I could do a little gambling when I ran low on funds. I kept my coin on me, barely using it, learning to call the toss on all the other coins in our currency as well as any foreign pieces that came passing through my fingers.

People from ramshackle towns don't usually call their town ramshackle but there aren't exactly folks lining up to live where I grew up. I got in scrapes like anyone but I had a strong arm, I was quick with my feet and sometimes my tongue and I never really meant anyone any harm, so I was generally able to avoid trouble.

The story I'm telling you here involves a girl though. There's always a girl.

She was a face I didn't recognise in a bar that was all too familiar. Her name was Katja she said and she was an acrobat. She told me she was in town for a few days with her circus. Although she was a grubby urchin like me, there was something elegant about her. As an acrobat and dancer, she had poise and grace but there was something of the fighter about her. We drank as she told me about travelling and performing with her circus troupe, how they were like a family.

"You listen well. You haven't told me so much about yourself." There wasn't much to tell, but, full of wine, I wanted to show off to her so I did a couple of tricks and joked that I should join her merry band.

"I don't think you'd fit in."

"Why not? You think that's the only thing I can do?"

"You might need to learn other talents."

So we shared our talents until the sun came up. At some point we must have been suitably impressed and we collapsed on top of each other.

*

She was gone in the morning and left me with only my headache. Plenty of wine had been consumed over the course of the evening, the majority by me, and I shouldn't have been surprised that she was having me on.

As I groggily pulled on my clothes, I realised that my coin was gone from my pocket along with the rest of my money. Katja had stolen it.

Without thinking, I was up and headed straight out of the door. I knew from the posters tacked to walls for miles around that the circus had pitched up on an old piece of farmland on the outskirts of town.

It wasn't hard to find them. There is always a clear trail left behind that many displaced people. I walked along the tracks their vehicles had churned up in the ground. Even without this I would have only needed to follow the noise once I got close. Strange sounds like objects I had never seen rubbing or banging together, cries of neither joy nor pain got louder as I approached their mobile shanty-town.

I walked in amongst caravans and tents until I felt a firm hand on my shoulder and a deep voice asked me where I was going. I turned and tried to hide my shock at facing up to the tallest woman I had ever seen.

"Katja. She's an acrobat," was all I managed to utter, but this seemed to suffice and the beautiful, giant lady let me go.

As I passed between the different carts and canvas shacks sweet smokes and foreign scents teased my nostrils. Accents and words that were unfamiliar to me faded in and out. I have to admit it excited me. I was after Katja and this was her world but I had little or no idea what I would do or what I would say to her.

I was unsure what to expect except that I knew the acrobats' tent would have to have high ceilings. I found it easily enough. Attached to the Big Top, their huge tent bore red and white stripes like an old fashioned barbers. I could hear the grunts of the acrobats and the creak of the ropes as I tried to make out the nimble figures swinging high above my head.

As I entered their arena and my eyes accustomed to the dim light within, I spotted Katja amongst her 'brothers and sisters' practicing on the ropes and she appeared to giggle when she saw me. Saying something to one of the others, she swung thirty feet, flipped and dropped down to where I was standing, making no more noise than a bird as she landed. The others resumed practice behind us.

"I thought you might come looking for me."

"I don't mind that you robbed me of my money but you took something that was precious to me."

"I only took money."

"You can keep the money except one of the coins I want back."

"Which one? None of them looked very special to me."

"Well they wouldn't."

She led me back to the grimy tent she shared with her 'family' and I waited outside while she searched for my money. I peered into the darkness and saw she was rooting through a large chest filled with other spoils, presumably the result of her family's evening activity. She jumped when she saw me looking, ashamed perhaps.

"How can you tell which one was mine among all that?"

She huffed and pushed my purse into me like a little girl who had been told off. I told her to hold out her hands and I poured the coins out into them. One by one I put the coins back into the purse until only my old friend remained.

"What is so special about this one? It is no different."

"It's mine, that's all."

"There's something funny about you."

There was something funny about her too and, as I handed her back the rest of the money, I had the sudden urge to kiss her again. She was a robber and I was angry at her and I knew from the previous night that she played rough, so when I kissed her I kissed her hard. She pulled me in closer and I was lost in her until we heard a shout from behind me.

We pulled apart and I saw one of the male acrobats was standing there. Taller and broader than me, he fixed me with a glare. His skin

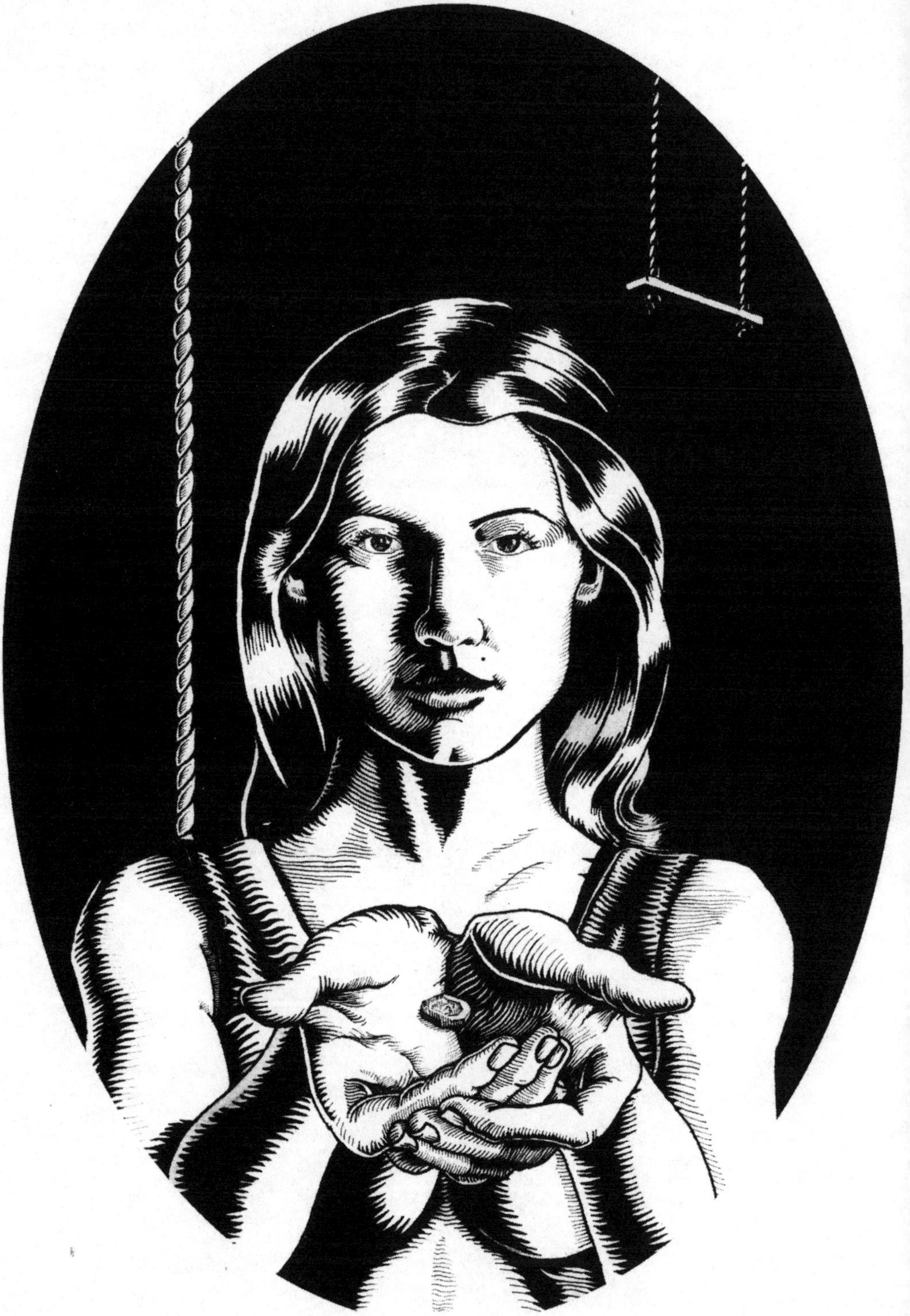

was lighter than Katja's but there was something similar about him, I couldn't tell if he was a brother or a lover.

"You keep away from her. Katja come here!"

Katja started walking over to him. As she approached, he smirked and turned away from me, making his way back towards the bars and ropes. Something in that smug look pissed me off. I looked around and saw a small, plum-like fruit on the floor. Without thinking, I hurled it over at my rival who was now hissing some sort of admonishment to Katja. The fruit looped beautifully through the air and made a satisfying splat on his head. He almost fell to his knees in shock.

Although surprised, he was quickly ready to believe this was something to do with me and he started back over in my direction. Katja tried to restrain him but he shook her off, pushing her roughly to the floor, and charged at me.

A few other carnies had materialised from various tents and paddocks and looked on expectantly. They could clearly sense tension in the air. The jealous acrobat launched at me.

I'm no stranger to fighting with a stranger but I quickly realized that this man was out of my league. I was no match for the acrobat's strength and speed, the only thing I had in my favour was that his rage worked against him. His fists stung heavy when they connected and it was all I could do to avoid being pulped.

We hadn't fought long when, fortunately, from the assembled crowd an enormous Indian strongman heaved the acrobat off me and managed to restrain him.

OPTIMISTIC

"Who are you, stranger?" somebody brusquely asked and before I could respond, Katja interjected, with what seemed to me to be the worst thing she could have said in the circumstances.

"He wants to join us."

There was a pause.

"Take him to Scrimstone."

After a lot of jostling and pulling a group of them led me to the ringmaster's quarters and I was asked to wait outside while a short, stocky character in a fine-looking hat waddled in ahead. The midget scurried out after a few moments and bade me enter.

I was immediately impressed as I entered the ringmaster's tent at how magnificently decorated it was; dirty but luxurious. I'm useless at explaining matters of taste or style but the tent was striking, it was hard to tell what was decadence and what was decay. What's more it didn't seem like a temporary throw-up, there was something timeless about it, as there was about the ringmaster himself.

Meeting him certainly was a curious and memorable experience. I wouldn't say that I disliked him but I knew instantly that we would not get on. He was affable, offering me a seat, an icepack for my face and a drink. He also had a friendly interest in my talents. I think the back of my mind had already been made up though.

He told me tales too long to share with you now but asked me about my life as if my little stories were a patch on his. Perhaps to him they were just as fascinating.

Eventually others entered, some I recognised from before. We drank more and emerged from the tent to a great feast, which seemed at once nothing unusual and a serious celebration among the circus folk. They knew how to make merry. I don't recall when or where I went to bed.

*

I agreed to stay on for a while and spend some time honing my abilities. I owed my town nothing and I had few friends besides unreliable drinking companions. In any case I felt that I could learn a lot from these travelling people, this place that was nowhere, even if I didn't agree with it all. I suppose I had other reasons; they would pay me better than I was earning and there was the girl. Was she worth staying for? I didn't know but perhaps she was worth staying to find out.

The following night there was a show, and there was plenty for me to do to keep busy. I met more of the strange folk that travelled with the Scrimstone Circus. I watched their acts and tried to absorb as much of the madness, the freedom, as I could.

After the performance I was drinking with the Indian strongman — who was simply called 'Singh' — and some others I had met. I had asked about Katja but Singh told me flatly that she would bring me only trouble. That appeared to be the end of the discussion and we talked of monsoons, wild elephants and other wonders until we became aware of a commotion outside.

As we rushed over to see what the shrieking was, I noticed Scrimstone had appeared and was now in the centre of the brouhaha. I could make out morsels of what was said.
"Whose blood is that if it's not yours?"
"You must be more careful."

Before we reached them the exchange was over. Scrimstone spoke to us all.

"We leave tomorrow as the sun comes up."

I later learned that one of their little band had returned red-handed from a robbery in town that had turned sour when he had been caught in the act. Someone had been stabbed, the carnie hadn't stayed long enough to see what happened next. Although he took decisive action, it didn't seem that Scrimstone was remotely surprised nor did he show any sign of remorse or retribution.

Having nothing to pack, I took a bottle and the chance to think. I wandered away towards a nearby hillock where I could sit alone. Was I like this circus folk? Perhaps I deceived people just as much, but I wasn't just a thief, I would never inflict violence like that upon someone to steal their belongings. Still I found it hard to judge them, freaks and outcasts kicked out of everywhere, they came from very different places to me.

I thought back to my small-town life of hustling, scrapping and dead-end jobs. There wasn't much to miss and, if I joined these people, there would be few people who missed me. I could go certainly, but could I go with them?

I had to see Katja. She made staying feel like leaving. I knew it would be a while before I managed to get her burnt honey taste out of my mouth. She was the only thing that made it a choice at all. Truth be told, I was foolish enough that if she asked me to stay with her I would. I can't recall anyone ever asking me to be anywhere.

*

Don't get me wrong, it was plain to see that she was pure mischief. But if I ever saw that circus again I knew it would be because of her. I still couldn't say if the acrobat that attacked me was Katja's boyfriend or big brother, for all I knew he was both.

A flurry of activity had overtaken the camp by the time I returned, my bottle emptied. I couldn't believe how quickly it had changed. The circus folk were busy packing away their pop-up village but there was no sense of panic. I got the impression that this was not a novel experience for them. In amongst it all I soon found Katja and managed to steal her away from the others. I imagined she'd be glad to get out of the heavy lifting.

Although it was her last night in my town neither of us were interested in going out and drinking any more. As we wriggled and rolled around together in my room I tried not to let her earthy, sweet scent leave any trace on me. I could see myself wondering for some time to come whether I had made the right decision without the need for any reminders. Who knows, I thought, perhaps the circus would come to this town again.

*

As day began to fall on us, crinkle-eyed in the low light, she kissed me as if she would drag me off between her teeth. At first I hardly noticed her hands in my pockets, one after the other. She groped me for a few seconds almost convincingly until she realised that what she was after was not there, I had hidden it in a safe place. I couldn't be sure if she knew I knew but I gave nothing away and neither did she. I wriggled my toes and felt the warmed metal of my coin safely stowed in my sock. A few moments later she gave me a bite that left my

OPTIMISTIC

bottom lip swollen for two days and she pushed me backwards hard, tripping me with her other leg. As I clambered to my feet, I saw her grin and watched as she scampered off to rejoin her family.

*

The circus never came back to my town. I never heard from them again but I think of them from time to time and wonder what became of them. It might have been quite an adventure with that wild girl and her ragtag gang but I like to think I made the right choice. You see, I make my own luck . . .

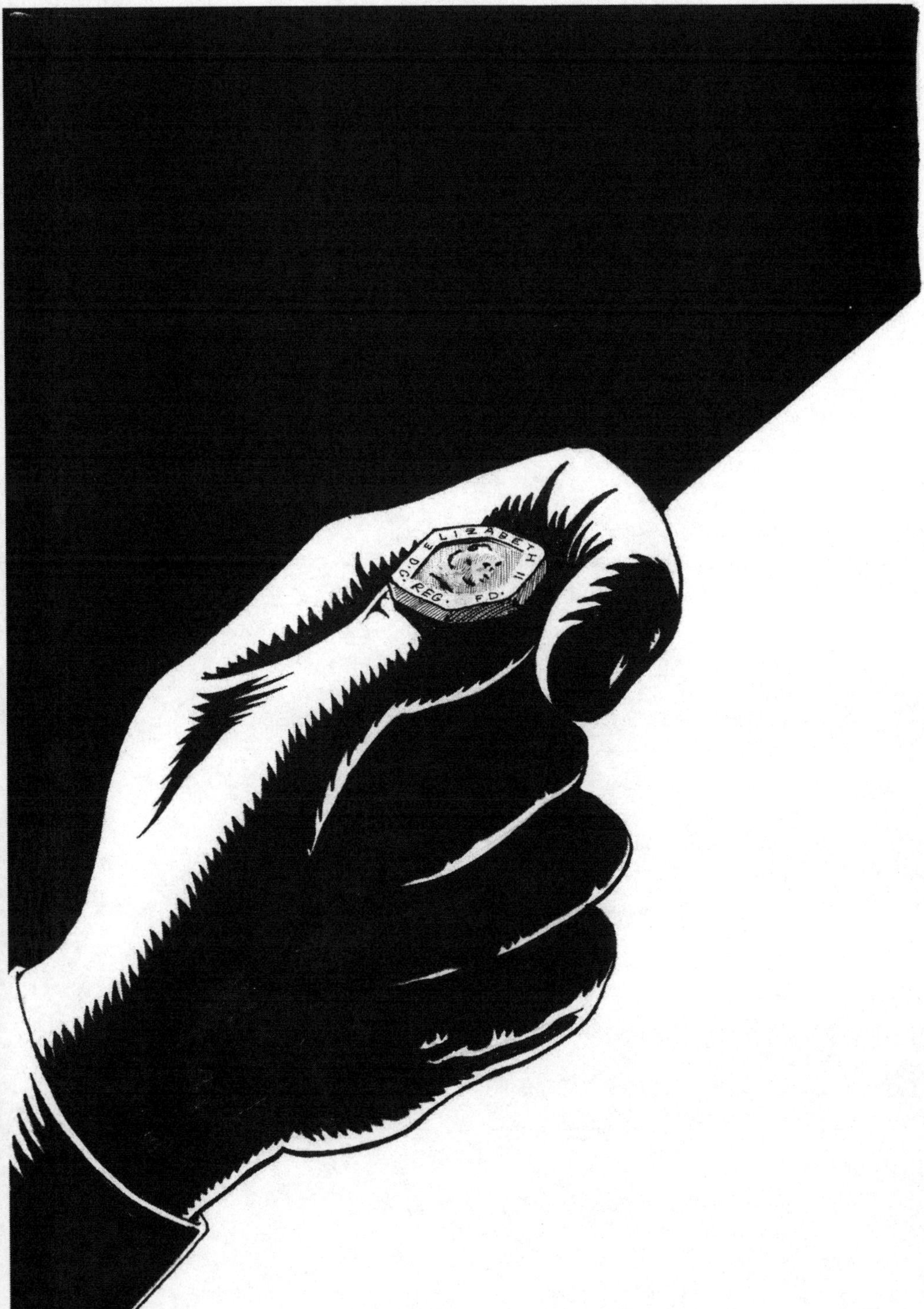
D.G. ELIZABETH II
REG. F.D.

ORPHANS OF THE ORDER

WRITTEN BY JO TEDDS
ILLUSTRATED BY PAUL BLOOM

Black spires silhouetted against the everlasting night
Dark ghostly figures patrol the streets
Someone turns to enter a tall looming tower
A security camera up high swivels to face him
As the hours go by, the later it gets, the streets start to become less busy
The whole city isn't like this, some people have never even seen the ground.
During the day the city is a completely different place.
It's only at night when you have that feeling of being watched
Not only by cameras but by – rats, stray cats, and pigeons
Some people say the pests are robot spies listening in on your conversation
No one is anyone, in our time
We have no names, only numbers
Everyone is different yet at the same time the same
Don't pretend you have an identity.
They took that away.

[They took that Away, by Saul Forster Vladermersky – 14 years old]

ADOLESCENCE—ADULTHOOD

Our past is one of battle and unrest. The New World emerged ten years ago, when a hundred civil wars finally collapsed the government. The state had failed. With dissent prevalent, those former leaders knew that the next wave of anarchy would bring the end of their advanced civilization. Over The Age, the leaders of the two parties slipped so far around the circle that they stood back to back, facing opposite ways. We saw it happen before they did, their messages different versions of the same tale. Revolution began to breathe slowly. We wrote petitions and protested in the street, chanting that the politicians worked to the same narrow agenda – caring for themselves more than the people. Fore-whisperings of the apocalypse began to burn in the leaders imaginations. The parties who had fought since our government was established, were forced to unite, aware that all society could come undone. As day and night wrestled, they negotiated. The politicians began to map their overlaps. Plagued by lethargy and desperation, they worked hard to compromise. As their colours bled, a new majority swelled. Policies and promises were slowly unpicked and drawn like soft flesh through thorns. Their conclusion: to start again, sharing resources fairly. To achieve this, they would build a self-sustainable gated city stretching six-hundred square miles. It would be built to contain The Faithful, those few thousand who would prove themselves worthy of citizenship, swearing their allegiance to The Order. The Faithful would be employed by The Order; a new faceless entity that replaced the government and existed only as written law. The residents were expected to be self-governing – no figureheads, no idols, just an accepted way of being to guide them. Money would be abolished so all residents would be equal; fairly sharing food, education, entertainment, healthcare and most importantly, work. During the negotiations the old leaders argued about the injustice of excluding people or sacrificing their wealth, but time was against them and the rules were very clear – challenging The Order would result in banishment. You could reject The City, take your chances and go it alone, or you could agree to disown a few thousand people and whatever fortune you had amassed for the idealism The Order promised. As the regulations and administrative procedures were figured, the final draft of The Order was drawn up. The City would be equal, but all, even the young, old and disabled would contribute. To become a resident you needed references from three professionals, each professional could grant five references only. Three counter-references could overturn any application. If proved to be criminal or idle, applicants would be denied the electronic-chip needed to pass through the gates. The chip remains the property of The Order and can be retracted at any time.

It took months to agree on how The City would look and operate, incorporating the most advanced technology so people could live without thinking. It only took seven years to build. First a wall was built but it was soon upgraded to a Radio Frequency Identification Barrier so only chipped individuals could enter. People wanted answers and yet those that went to the site either converted to The Faithful there and then or else they disappeared. Eventually, the old ministers took to the airwaves and called for The Divide. The announcement explained that the government had disbanded and that The Order was now only in charge of The City. The land massed beyond its looming border was in an official state of interregnum. An administration had been set up to manage The Divide of the people. All who worked for the administration would be granted citizenship.

The rest could apply but there were strict guidelines. Leaflets were printed and surgeries set up, all the while, instructions to applicants and sections of The Order rang through the streets. Many were seduced by their organisation and their offer, without questioning their old prejudices. It didn't sound like a declaration of war, but it was. The Order was inviting people to enlist in an army that promised to be exclusive as well as supreme. The excluded people, whether they wanted to be residents or not, were livid. Like adding odd and even numbers makes an odd, chaos added to order creates chaos. Many responded with violence, vandalism and theft. In every burning street and diminishing public building until the last day of The Divide, their announcements wined loudly. It sent more than a few crazy, splitting the roots of the Old World. Those excluded from The City, whether through choice or not, became known as The Defectors. The Faithful, those signed up to The Order, were advised, for their safety, to break contact with them. The Divide ripped through huge congregations and young families. People took the war into their hearts, torn between a government who had failed them for generations and the prospect of a future without one at all. Many however, had the decision made for them: unable to secure enough sponsorship for the whole family, dismissed for a crime of frivolity or because the capacity was reached. There was no opportunity to re-apply. The Defectors — healers, teachers, drunks and thieves — were united only by their exile. To all but The Order, their differences were obvious; the bright ones, unwilling to waste their time ruining the Old World, retreated to the countryside and began preparing for the New Beginning. Others tried to survive on their own, misjudging their dependence on the state. Many were too stubborn or too tired to change, they stayed and rotted with hunger and disappointment. What was left of the towns after the riots, were taken over by gangsters and

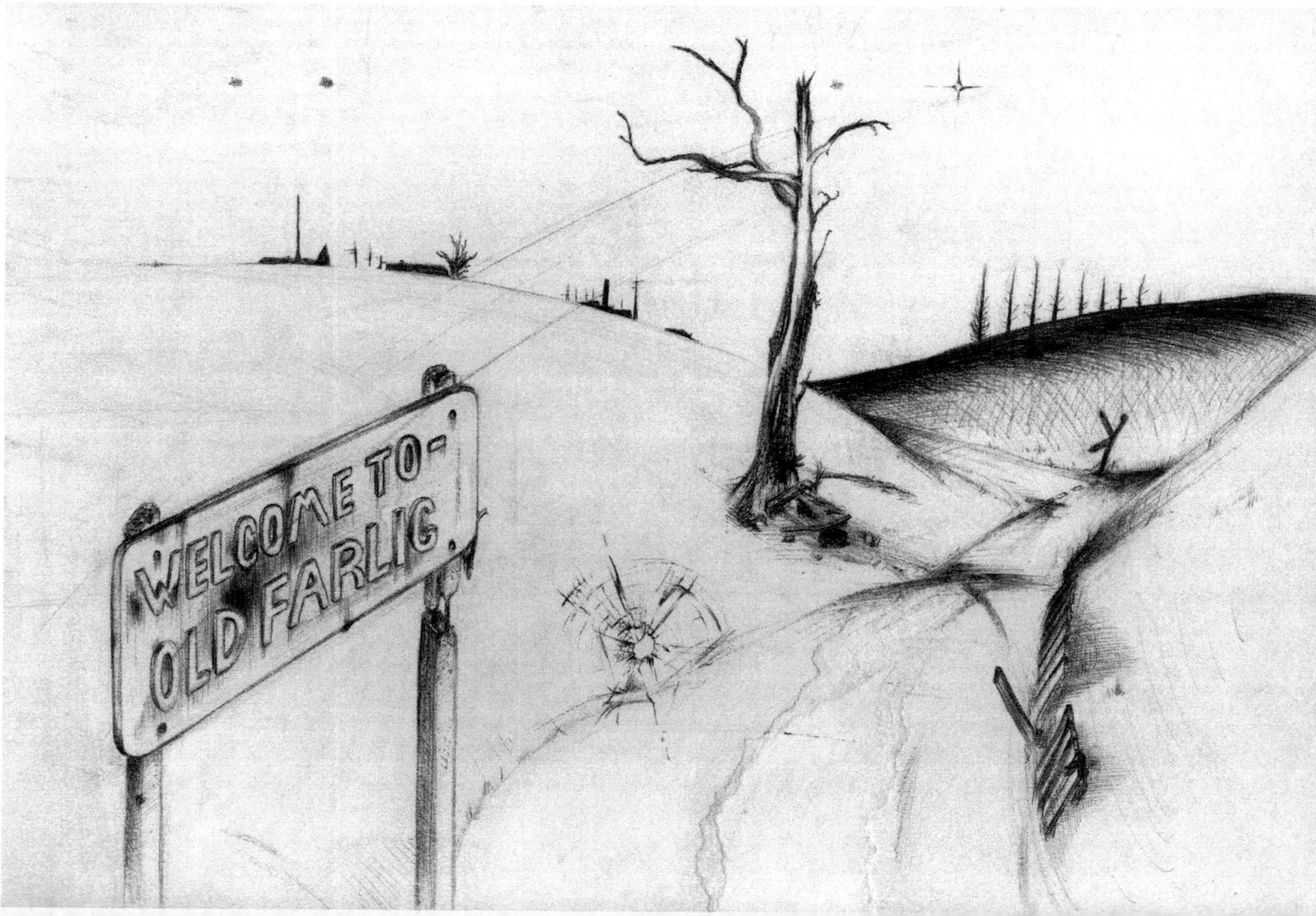
WELCOME TO-
OLD FARLIC

bandits. The town of Old Farlig, where this story begins, was unrecognisable. Buildings were plundered, their cladding and panes pilfered for salvage only to be dumped and burned. Fires aside, Old Farlig was dark and cold, little of its old beauty was preserved. It stands now dirty and ramshackle. Roads have cracked under fallen and frozen rains, split and blistered by the adamant sun. Old Farlig quickly became riddled. Evils still hang like sticky nets. Nearly four years have past though it looks like much longer.

The Divide broke many souls but those people who sought peace found unity; new kinships were knitted and independent camps were established. That said, few survived on their own. Tribalism rules what The Order abandoned. When The Divide dismantled The Old World, freedom was left rumbling in its wake, but old habits twist into the rope of a place as much as a person, and are seldom lost or forgotten. So the best and worst of the Old World was buried in the guts of Old Farlig. Despite their efforts to be different, the camps all operated in the same way – united through love, ruled by fear and demanding absolute loyalty. Most tribes just banish their traitors, but some kill and use their blood to paint a warning to those who may follow suit – 'Even if you hate it, you're safer where you are'. Since the collapse of the government, very few laws governed the nearby lands but one that came to be accepted was the right of innocents, people under sixteen, to choose their clan. It is well understood that if you can join a clan as an adult, the clan is probably criminal or very religious and in some cases both.

The festival people of The Old World who'd always lived under canvas, sunshine and starlight had been praying to their many gods that such a gift as The Divide would be delivered. In the Old World they were forced to be traveling people, but with the Old Ways dead they could finally settle somewhere. On a whisper, before The Divide had even been called, they had traveled to a beautiful valley twenty-five miles and three towns east of Old Farlig, where in anticipation they built a whole village. The crumbling government's neglect only proved what they had suspected. We were on the cusp of The New World. From the nearby hills you could see lights scattered like buttercups around streams, while the lakes they washed into throbbed with music that could be heard before and after the riots. Little camp circles blossomed around big fat utility tents, while fields neatly ploughed and sowed, rested waiting for the sun. Supplies had been sourced and stored, and partying began before the Divide was called. Full of outcasts and misfits from the Old World, the people that started Lykken Festen invited their relatives, friends and others they'd loved once, drunkenly in a star-lit field. Taking direction from nature, it was a camp of harmony. The travelers and hobos, with skills cobbled out of necessity, who were used to being mocked for their lifestyles, finally had a place to be, a place free from the tax and bureaucracy, debt and greed that the Old World guaranteed. Everybody had something to give and if they didn't, they learnt something new. Everybody gave and everybody had enough. Many made the pilgrimage to Lykken Festen, having heard the drums thumping around the valleys. Hope rolled down the hills and stretched into The Old Towns long before the riots were over. Like all camps, they had a selection process; for people feared being overrun or inviting the troubles of The Old World in. Lykken Festen and the other six or so villages this side of The City produced enough for themselves, and a bit more, so satellite camps sprang up nearby.

 Few camps wanted to neighbour let alone depend on the Shadows. When they did the Shadow Dwellers, the biggest gang across the nearest lands, swallowed them up or scared them away. They controlled Old Farlig with violence and made a killing exploiting traffic from The City. It only takes an hour for The Faithful to get across The Line into the heart of The Shadows. With only a few tiny camps dotted between, The Shadows grew as close to The City as they could so they could control trade across The Line. As the most feared gang this side of The City, they were the most famous too; wizened mouths and campfires crackled as they spat Shadow stories in the faces of their young, forecasting a life of shame and unhappiness. But the Shadow Dwellers weren't the only ones abusing the absence of law.

You hardly knew if you were talking to a Chip Hunter, so you could never count them. Seeking their services meant you were looking for a chip and confirmed clan-disloyalty. While many disliked their business, they were thankful for the work they created. It wasn't just surgeons and sneeks, it was profitable to protect people from them too. Safe-house keepers, fetchers and smugglers passed messages and chaperoned people through the gates. Great trades if you could keep a secret, but many a friend and lover were betrayed when desperation took hold. The Chip Hunters were nameless, never settled and moved in shivers of no more than a dozen. They kept their numbers small and seldom accepted recruits; unlike the other dark clans whose members always needed replenishing.

With treasures of every kind for every seeker, the Circus was a free for all. Tribal etiquette dissolved on the threshold and so it bought a break from clan-life, both scary and magical. Falling into love or trouble were equally possible under the sweating canvas kilt. Full of misdirection and distraction, children gawped up at the threadbare tightrope, blind to their chaperones flirting and the crooks enjoying the ringmaster's passionate atheism as much as his blasé attitude to vice. Circus tricks went far beyond the parading of starving elephants and clumsy jugglers.

For every dangerous clan, there were three or four peaceful clans struggling to survive, longing for the skies to change again and to end the misery they had fallen into. Not forgetting the hundreds who'd settled in clans they hated, who went wayward and regretted it, who made bad choices early on and ended up alone. Whether lonely or settled in clans, most are praying for another uprising, unsure if any lifetime ever witnesses more than one.

Though she slept in The Shadows, Katya lived in her head, her friend Kipling took care of them both. He hated the rot and rubbish, the stinking streets filling up with the flesh of wayward addicts and fiends. He only stayed because she wouldn't leave and because the Dwellers cared little for etiquette and didn't expect them to socialize.

Kipling and Katya had been friends in the Old World and had been together since finding each other on The Line just over four years ago. When they arrived he was nearly twelve and a good foot shorter than now, though he was just as skinny. Katya was eleven then and used to laugh all the time, she doesn't smile any more but her dimples sit popped reminding Kipling of how it used to be. From the fires that burned in Old Farlig, fate handed Katya her future and she dropped it like a hot stone engraved with someone else's name. She scorned the other orphans and everyone else outside The City, not knowing her father had deserted her; that she had been abandoned twice in one lifetime. If Kipling hadn't supported her fantasy, allowing her to believe it was possible to 'lose' a parent in the chaos; if he hadn't pretended to have lost his . . . If he hadn't provided for her and made it so she never had to leave the flat . . . Maybe then she wouldn't have become obsessed with a delusion that should have long since faded. As the elder, it was easy for Kipling to smother her, sympathise with her pain and conceal the truth. What options did she have anyway? He let her misery mold the walls, decay their hope; and though her grief drowned his own, he didn't complain. Permanently stoned, withdrawn and ungrateful, Katya didn't notice that they never went hungry, that she never had to think for herself. She spent her time contemplating a future that wouldn't find her. She focused on seeing her father, her mind set on leaving The Shadows and Kipling forever.

Few wondered how Kipling, as a Fetcher, could find what others couldn't. Those that did, assumed he knew tribes they didn't. Only his mother knew that he was really a Smuggler and she lived alone in The City. His father had died when his office was bombed at the beginning of the unrest. Kipling was just five. Lonely and grief-torn his mother had struggled to raise him in Old Farlig, so when more wars exploded and the call for The Divide sounded she quickly made up her mind to leave the Old World behind. If people suspected Kipling had a chip, the Shadow Dwellers or anyone else, might have handed him to the Chip Hunters. Perhaps even Katya would have, but that isn't why he didn't tell her. He didn't know how to say he had been there, met her drunken father, learned he'd deserted her intentionally. How could he explain that her old man hated her for looking like her mother? The woman who had broken his heart when she abandoned them both a hundred moons before. Whenever Katya complained, whenever she was horrid and ungrateful, whenever anger burnt the well of Kipling's throat, whenever he felt tempted to tell her . . . he always swallowed it down, remembering their saying goodbye during The Divide.

*

Kipling's mother wanted to take everything that reminded her of Kipling's father to The City. But as The Faithful were supposed to be equal, each person was only granted a small quota for Old World memorabilia. Thoughtfully she selected memory triggers – perfumes, seashells, photos, scraps of wallpaper, squares of curtain – taking a wisp of everything she could with her. Others couldn't wait to forget and walked in with only their clothes, happy to see the back of a life disturbed by the boring, jealous and ignorant. Most entered ashamed, avoiding those they were choosing to leave.

Katya had called by early in excitement. Kipling's mother had shooed them upstairs where they sat in Kipling's room rifling the boxes of discarded things. The stomach of Old Farlig turned with anxiety and Kipling felt it.

"Katya, we will find each other on the other side, won't we?"

"Of course! Why wouldn't we?" she said, genuinely surprised.

She was so happy, she may well have permanently dimple-creased her face that day.

"We will have chips, Kip. Durr!" Katya replied, as she curiously dismantled an old clock.

"Well what if it's not ready or something?"

He drummed his heels on the wall nervously.

"Oh I don't know Kip. Maybe I will just know how to find you?"

She gave him a zombie stare and burst out laughing.

"You know?"

He did know. Kipling had always wanted to play football with the older boys who lived on the edge of Old Farlig. His mother who worked two jobs, never had time for 'dad stuff'. He didn't like bringing it up because it made her cry. But not thinking it would cause any harm, Kipling put his trainers on and waited for his minder Doris to take her nap. It was great. Exhausted, covered in mud, longest socks

ADOLESCENCE—ADULTHOOD

riding at different heights, he did the two-mile schlep back home grinning.

When Doris woke and couldn't find him, she called his mum. His mum toured his friends' houses and their hangouts. He hadn't seen Katya that day or even told her where he was going, but when asked if she knew where Kipling was, she felt sick from her thoat to her stomach as she imagined him caught in the train lines. Not many people take the imaginings of a nine year old seriously, and even Kipling's mother protested at first, but Katya was persistent and they were short of other ideas.

"It's between the crossings, He didn't use a crossing!" Katya spluttered.

Kipling's mother hoped it wasn't true, though she could not hide her panic, remembering that children are often aware of those things that adults forget to look for. Walking up the train lines, the worried mother and terrified child dodged brambles and logs. They carried on until, suddenly on the horizon, they saw a boy crouched by the line. They ran towards him. They heard the train. Kipling's shoelace was caught under the rails. Trying to free his foot he only tightened the trainer more, the laces fusing as he struggled. His mother scrambled over to him. She shouted at Katya to get off the tracks. She looked up, saw the train-lights and began to feel the rails rattle. She gripped Kipling's ankle, got purchase of the muddy trainer with a strength only parents can summon, she ripped his leg from the trainer and rolled him off the tracks. The train flew past them. Tears of relief scolded their cheeks as it whistled away into the distance.

"You actually saved my life Kat! It was so close. Can you remember how close that train was?"

"I know Kip! Aren't you glad we won't need to rely on *that* in

The City? It will be so safe. The trains will have sensors so they stop if the track's not clear."

Kipling liked magic and was disappointed that she was more in awe of technology than her own powers.

"Well, people will just put stuff on the tracks for fun then, won't they?" he huffed.

"No, course not. It's going to be perfect! People won't do that. No traffic. No queues. No paper stuff. Everything will be thought of, including how to find each other. There'll be a map of everybody's whereabouts and people won't be able to do bad stuff!"

Katya loved her Dad's stories, especially his tales of how The City would be. Automatic lights, buses and trains that were never late and traveled at three-hundred miles per hour. There wouldn't be any holidays, who wanted them anyway? It would be perfect, She could play all day if she liked, music and swimming and arcades! When the manual labour was replaced by machines, Dads could spend all day at the pub and who should care? No cleaning or chores. Being full of faith would be easy.

"Do you think the chip will hurt, Katya?"

"Nah I shouldn't think so and if it does, it won't be for long! It's going to be brilliant when we get there! We won't have a worry in the world!"

She span as she spoke, stumbled and crashed against the wall.

"Come on now you two!" shouted Kipling's mother up the stairs.

Katya got herself straight and out the door too quickly, calling over her shoulder as she went.

"See ya," she yelled.

"See ya," Kipling called, but the door slammed and he was left wishing for an awkward goodbye.

"See ya!" was the last thing Katya said to Kipling and the last thing her Dad had said to her. He had ruffled her hair with his hamfisted hand as she reminded him again where they would meet and at what time.

Brimming with excitement she darted through the riots to wait for her Father, next to the blue doors of Old Farlig's only post office. She stayed visible even as bottles and furniture flew from windows, even as people brawled around her. She was still optimistic when Kipling found her there two days later.

"It isn't surprising people have lost each other Kip, look at the amount of chaos The Order are battling. Dad's probably in the thick of it!" she smiled to herself.

"But I found you . . . What if?"

"What if what Kip?"

She was stern, refusing.

"What else could have happened? You don't think he's dead Kip?"

"I'm sure he's not dead," he said, conquered by pity.

Kipling's heart hung heavy and slow as Katya waited for her father and he waited to tell her. Others stood there also, all but Kipling fearing abandonment, their anxiety growing as each new person was found. Most were collected by the end of the week, but only a few since then. Others surrendered early, but not Katya, she expected her Father to be late. She didn't really think he'd be working. He'd been at every party going. Drunk stupid on drink and unrest, wondering if The Order would find out what he did to qualify for a chip before it was implanted. Even Katya wasn't sure. She didn't know him very well yet; he was the sort of man you had to get to know chasing whisky, who never let the truth ruin a good excuse or story. Kipling and Katya agitated on The Line longest of all, hardly sleeping or eating. Eventually Kipling convinced her to leave, but Katya refused

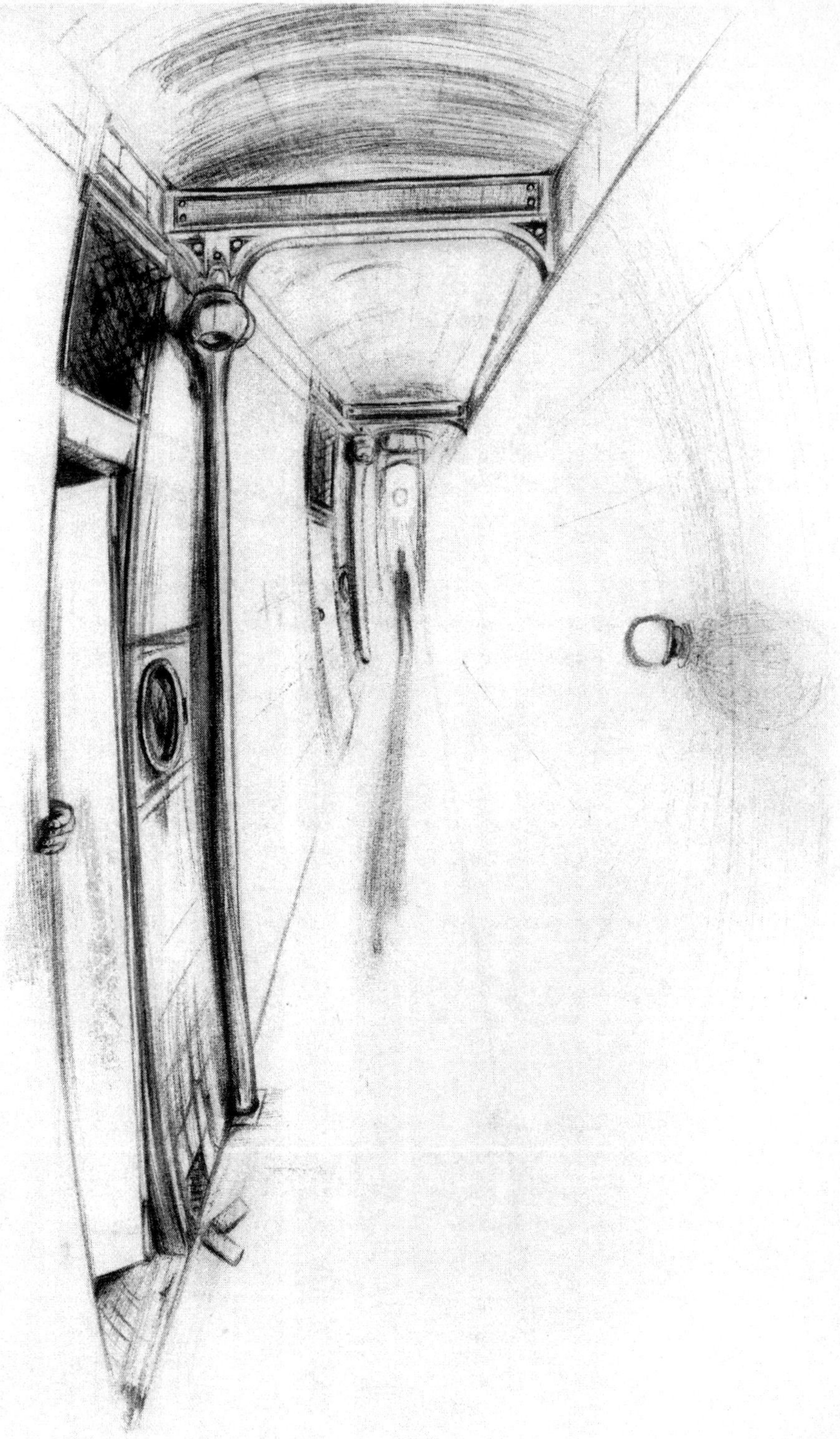

to go far, even though bedlam swelled around them and The Dwellers were growing in numbers.

The Old World was disappearing sheet by sheet, brick by brick. It smolders still, four long years later. Katya barely remembered Old Farlig, but her vision of The City had never been so sharp. She dreamed as though she lived there and lived waiting to fall to sleep. Her happiness collected on her eyelids while she slept and flushed away when she awoke. Kipling tried to ease her deepening depression, but he couldn't say what she needed to hear. She was only happy when dreaming of The City. He believed that with time she would come to terms with it. He introduced her to distractions as and when he found them. When they were younger he kept her busy with juggling balls and puzzles. Later he introduced her to smoking weeds. Smoking sedated her but moonshine made her violent with rage. For all the mistakes he made, he'd tried his best, encouraging her to adjust, celebrating the New Beginning. But each time she shot him down, ignorant to how tortured he was; for Kipling was as loyal to his secrets as she was to her dreams. Neither knew what The Beginning would bring as they waited on The Line – a border bulldozed a mile thick around The City, a place where Defectors and The Faithful mixed at their own peril. The Order's Human Rights defenders still worked there, hunched over registers, logging queries; officially reconnecting people, though in reality they were guards of The City.

For all the promises it was an unfair system, Kipling had seen that on the inside but it was like that from the start. Applications should only have been rejected on grounds of criminality, a proven inability to contribute or active involvement in The Defector movement, but thousands were returned un-read as the capacity was quickly reached.

The Order tricked Old Farlig for the last time when it concealed the population limit of two-hundred-and-fifty-thousand people. In the spirit of the age, Kipling registered Katya's father as lost, knowing he had tricked her too. At Katya's insistence they settled nearby in the wanting Shadows. Fighting and bribing they quickly won a squat and a bit of respect. Kipling kept The Dwellers off his back by fetching and smuggling goods from The City and other camps. Katya stayed in so no one stole their things or took the squat over. It was necessary at first but soon it became rare for a squat to be taken. But The Shadows, ran by love-less and bitter men, was a dangerous place for girls so Katya stayed inside to stay safe; dreaming of the day, that the boxes of lost children and relatives would be sorted and fate would return with an apology. Kipling traveled to every camp he heard of, peddling everything you always needed and things you thought you never would, working hard to keep both The Shadow bosses and Katya happy.

The Defectors were supposed to have nothing to contribute to The City. The hundreds of Faithful coming through the gates prove otherwise. Kipling would have been an excellent Chip Hunter. He could spot The Faithful at one-hundred yards. Katya wouldn't know one if they poked her in the ribs. Kipling didn't tell her that he could. She might set a Chip Hunter on them and forge her way into The City. He didn't know if she would, but he couldn't do that to anyone. The Faithful, folk from The City, had to look after each other out here, and that meant ignoring each other whenever they were outside the gates. It's unsafe being in a place that's hard to leave if you've got a passport up your sleeve. But still, The Faithful came here. Some came for kicks, to run the risk of being spotted before returning home safely. Some came for more than their fair share, for more than the rules allowed. Some for contraband like moonshine, poppy seeds and smoking weeds. In a powerless state, people crave power, so some came to control and to be controlled. Sometimes they came just to break their routine. They came looking for fun, fetishes, drugs and organs while others came in order to live their double lives.

The Shadows were a pathogen and both Katya and Kipling were losing their immunity with every passing day. Kipling lost his faster, accelerated by his desperation to join Lykken Festen. He wanted to be with other young people: revolutionaries, rebels and less, those who'd laughed as they twisted the bolts of Old Farlig loose and rejoiced in the death of the machine. Some say the people of Lykken Festen rejected the chip because they valued privacy and freedom of speech. Others say The Order banned them for Defection. In truth the bohemians, teachers and hedonists of Lykken Festen turned their backs on The Order long before it was even thought of as a choice. Katya made fun of Kipling, telling him how her dad used to say travelers were all beggars and thieves and if he were here he'd say Kipling was a mug for falling for their pitch. Kipling grimaced down in his spine. She didn't know who Kipling had become. He was one of the most trusted Fetchers of the time, revered by the very most organised clans. At nearly fifteen he knew any clan he chose would be better off with him amongst them. What he didn't know, was whether they would take Katya too. Without a chip, even as one of the most Faithful, she wasn't an anything. She had never gone beyond The Shadows and was convinced she didn't have to work, for in The City she would learn something, do something, be somebody.

Being a smuggler, Kipling was a master of stealth and secrecy. Katya didn't know he winced inside as she compared the soap dodgers of Lykken Festen to the glamorous Faithful. He never said that he knew both worlds well, nor that he would always choose Lykken Festen over the souless city. Inspired after each visit to Lykken Festen, he repeated the fireside stories he heard: news of miracle cures, newly discovered camps, grumblings about the Old World.

"Can you imagine Katya, they took everything, except for the shoe he was using for a pillow?" What a punch line, he thought, as Katya rolled her eyes.

Lykken Festen people possessed a certain pureness. To have it is to connect with others who also have it. Kipling connected with nearly all of the residents and was automatically invited to stay. They were surprised when he didn't jump at the chance. He explained his commitment to Katya without giving his Faithful status away and they kindly invited her to visit. Kipling explained it was the highest of honors, but driven by delusion and jealousy, Katya flatly refused.

"Katya doesn't like to travel," he told them on his next visit.

"But we would love to meet her Kipling, please let her know that we will travel to The Shadows."

Kipling was at odds with himself. Nobody visited The Shadows socially and Katya would definitely refuse.

"That is a great honor, but really, it's too dangerous."

The people of Lykken Festen were understanding, but they were also difficult to deceive.

"So what will you do on your birthday Kipling the Fetcher?"

"I'm not sure. Katya is also unwell you see, she hurt her leg, tripped on some rubbish, The Shadows really are awful."

No one challenged him, but to Kipling it seemed the conversation stopped abruptly whenever he told a fib. In the weeks leading up to his birthday, whenever conversation turned to Kipling's big choice or Katya's leg, his back tensed and his mind narrowed. He took to falling silent and thinking.

She was nothing like the Katya he remembered, the Katya who used to laugh as much as she talked, the Katya who he had ridden bikes with in the Old World, who he had chased over hills. Had she really changed that much? After all, she was still as stubborn as collar-filth. Back then her persistence had saved his life, but now . . . now her stubbornness might kill them both. Where was the magical Katya who could see the future? Why couldn't she see it now? He didn't like feeling cross with her and so during his journeys home he practiced meditations he learnt at Lykken Festen. As his birthday got closer, taking his mind off things became harder.

Like many, Kipling drank to forget and smoked to remember the good times. He always remembered what was both his best and worst day: the blissful fatigue he'd felt after football, the thrill of setting someone up for a goal, people slapping his back, cheering, shouting and then, less than an hour later, the coldness that ran through him when he thought he would die. This thought trail always ended at the same place, with the panic transferring from then to now. She didn't know it, but Katya was trapped in The Shadows, waiting for death to find her. Guilt consumed him. He sobered up at home, made sure she was ok and went through the routine: made some food, handed over his weeds, tried to convince her to take a walk, failed, smoked, slept. The days rolled into each other but time passed by clumsily.

During spring, the weather was overcast. Lumpy grey clouds clung to the tops of the hills. One day Kipling decided to leave Lykken Festen early in an attempt to miss the rain on his way home. Brooding over the veiled sunshine, Kipling wondered why it never shone in The Shadows. Fat wet pellets began to fall and Kipling begrudged making this journey. If he stayed now, he would be stuck between the depravity of The Shadows and the plastic happiness The City provided. Kipling not only knew of another way, but he had been invited to participate. His sixteenth birthday was in one week, he would have to give Katya an ultimatum.

"Katya, Katya! Wake up!"

She stirred, tossed irately and tried to ignore him.

"Katya come on, you've been sleeping all day. Can you get up a minute?"

"What's your problem Kipling?"

She was trying to kick, but she struggled against the weight of the blankets. He freed her from the covers before sitting next to her, resting against the damp and peeling wall. Katya tried to force sleep, her face furrowed like the blankets that lay twisted on top of her. Kipling rolled some weeds and began to burn them, knowing that if she could go from one dream to another she would wake up enough.

"Gimme some then!" she demanded her arm outstretched, hand obscured by a sloppy sleave.

"Chill out Kat. I've only just lit it."

He inhaled deeply, preparing his thoughts. She glared at him.

"What? You didn't even want to wake up."

"I don't want to wake up Kipling. But. You. Made. Me!"

It felt like her brain was being pushed into her eyes, her head seemed to ache more with each passing day.

"C'mon Kipling. The least you can do is share!"

"That's not quite how sharing works," he huffed.

He passed it anyway. The room was silent, less the sound of the weeds crackling as they burned.

"Katya, we've been here for four years now. Four years! This is getting kinda boring. It's a New World now."

"Don't you think I know that Kip?" she snapped.

If he was honest, he wasn't sure what she knew.

"I was with Suki in Lykken Festen and she reckons..." he realised instantly it was the wrong thing to say.

He paused, lost for a better tack.

"Look, I don't give a shit what she thinks. She doesn't even know me!"

"Katya, we're only trying to help."

Neither said anything but both were hung up on the word 'we'. Kipling hadn't said it yet, but in his mind he had already gone.

"Help me? How the Hell are you trying to help me?" she bellowed.

"How can you say that? All I have ever done is help you! I do loads for you!"

"Get stuffed Kip. THIS is boring."

She tried to pull the covers out from under him but fell back in a heap.

"I do everything for you! All you do is smoke my weed, eat my food and sleep all the goddamn time!"

Kipling pulled the blankets out from under him and threw them at her.

She couldn't argue with him but wished she could. Her headache worsened, the pressure grew – she didn't know whether to lash out or cry. Usually when things got awkward, Kipling would save them both, back down, diffuse the hurt, but his mind was set, he had to tell her he was going. This was it: she could either stay or follow.

Desperation clung to their throats like dust to oil. He didn't know how to do it, how to begin after all this time. The starting was the hard bit. He rehearsed his argument in his head. He was approaching his sixteenth birthday. If he didn't go now he would never be able to join Lykken Festen, the one camp that had found happiness after the New Beginning. It was her turn now to choose. She could come with him or stay where she was. If he left, The Shadows Dwellers might be offended. It wouldn't be safe, he wouldn't be coming back.

"I'm going to be sixteen soon. You know what that means? I'll have to stay here forever. I won't be able to go there or anywhere!"

"You can move clans after your sixteen, Kipling!"

"Not to anywhere that I'd want to go Katya. Are you really that selfish?"

Kipling paced the dingy room.

"Whatever Kip. Like Suki or Puki or whatever the hell she's called, like she wouldn't have you back!"

Kipling regretted telling Katya about his connection with the Lykken Festen tribe. She had him and she knew it. She began rolling more weeds.

"For God's sake. This is important! Can't you stay with it for once Katya?"

He fixed a stare hard on her face as she inhaled intently.

"Kip, I'm not going anywhere and neither are you. You've let me down. You promised you'd get one of the safe-house keepers to get a message to my Dad. Have you even done that, or are you just full of shit? How will the message get back to me? If you'd done that earlier then perhaps I'd be out of this dump and out of your hair already! You're so useless Kip!"

"If I'm useless, you're properly messed up. I do everything for you. I'd give you my right arm if I thought it would make you happy but it wouldn't."

His guard was down and it had slipped out.

"Well that's just bloody great Kip, you'd give me your useless right arm! Cheers!"

"You miserable bitch," Kipling spat in disbelief.

"Is this what you want? Is this what you sodding well want?" he demanded, concertinaing his sleeve in one move.

The pressure lessened as he revealed his chip and for the first time in four years Katya was wide awake. She launched at him.

"You. YOU! All this shitting time and YOU had a CHIP!"

He towered over her, pushed her down onto the blankets as she kicked and screamed. The sound of her spirit being torn was unmistakable, a scorched lament that collapsed with her. She wanted the blankets to bandage her. She wanted to die. But just before she hit the black completely her mind changed, she rose like a phoenix and with the worst of the worlds in her eyes, she spat at him again.

"It's you. I know it's you. YOU! You're the reason I've suffered. How dare you tell me to pull myself together when you have had THAT all along? You were supposed to be my friend!"

Switching from despair to violent rage, hurling things at him and the walls and then herself to the floor. He was shocked, apologetic, confused. Between sobs he asked her what he was supposed to do. Katya choked on her disbelief.

"Go and find my dad you arsehole! Tell him I'm here."

The weight of her disillusion felled Kipling's shoulders. How could she think that of him? How could she think he hadn't looked for her dad? Kipling was confused, each breath buckled with sadness and rose with burning fury.

"Of course I went. Are you actually stupid? Katya, your dad is scum."

Her fists rained down on his chest. He grabbed her, tucked her hair under his chin, held her tighter still and told her as much as he could. He omitted the fistfight he tried to start with her father on that first day, how The Order slapped a warning right on him there and then. He even held back how, two years later, he found him again, how her father had said Katya's depression was no more than a growing pain and that she would grow out of it. Instead, Kipling told Katya that her father didn't want to tell her that he'd never had the documents, that he'd wanted their final days together to be happy ones. She pulled the pieces together and let in what she could, but having guarded her reality for so long she didn't hear half of the half he told her.

"Well let me have it then. You don't want it, so just let me go!"

Her eyes narrowed like two nail clippings.

"My Chip? You really would take it wouldn't you? My mum's the other side. You know my mum, who loves me and wants me with her? You really are THAT selfish, you would take it, leave me here when I could have left you all along. You're a spoilt bitch."

Kipling was stunned.

"You've seen your mum, I haven't seen my dad in over four years. He must be missing me."

"Obviously not. He would have come to see you if he had."

He hoped she would catch on, that he wouldn't have to continue.

Katya was quiet. She sat back down on the blankets. The pieces didn't fit. She didn't have the logic. Something was missing.

"Just tell me everything," she sighed.

Tears spilled from Kipling's eyes, hot wet on angry cold cheeks. He took a deep breath, he began again. He told her the whole, hard and bitter truth. They sat together, still and quiet, elbows cupped around knees, legs crossed, backs pressed against the cold walls. The numbness that forms after shocks and surprises had risen quickly. They sat for some time before Kipling eventually climbed to his feet

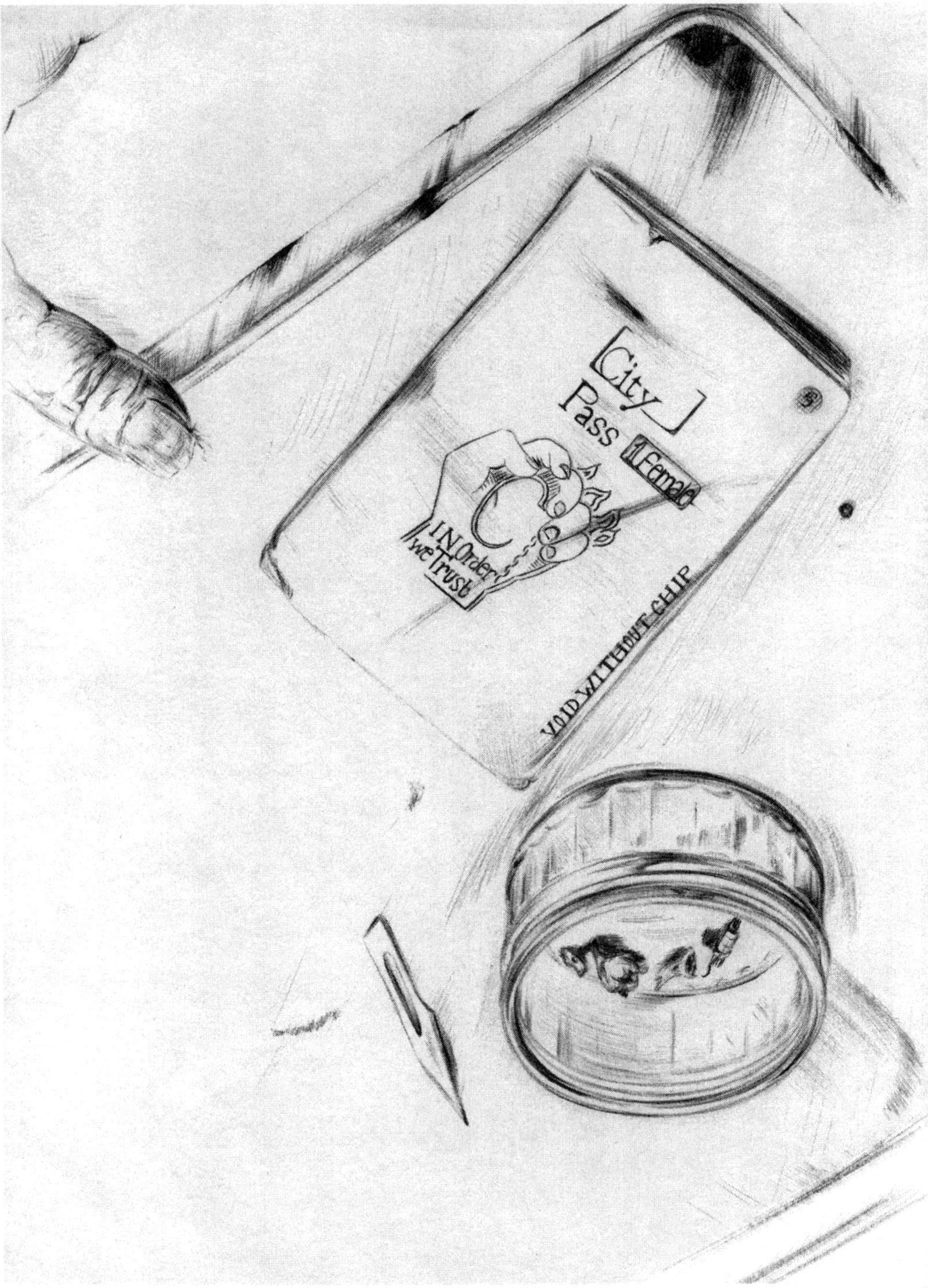
City
Pass
1 Female
IN Order
we Trust
VOID WITHOUT CHIP

and made some tea, rolled some weeds and then sat again. Katya also sat quietly, smoking. She smoked until finally she slept.

Katya stopped talking about The City and Kipling was kind enough to do the same but she still didn't want to go to Lykken Festen. Kipling begged her, worried about would happen to her, but Katya was fearless, knowing she had nothing to lose.

"I just want to go somewhere new, somewhere you haven't told me about. Maybe somewhere you haven't been, Kip?"

"Cheers Kat!" he laughed, and as he said it, she knew no offence had been taken.

"Where don't you go? Where can I start on my own?" she mused.

"I go everywhere though don't I? That's my job, I run things between places. You'd have to go really far, beyond the hills or round to the north side of The City, but I don't know what's there. There might be nothing."

"There can't be nothing and you can't have gone everywhere," she sighed.

"Well, some of the other smugglers reckon if you follow the wind and travel far far north that there is another festival clan up there, but they travel around to loose the hanger-ons. You could wait for them to come back but it might take weeks or months."

"That's so long Kip, I am only just getting the hang of this effort thing, you know!"

They smiled and smoked a while and Katya tried to imagine her future. She wanted to see it all. She wanted to join a traveling clan, but she might never find the clan who traveled around far far up north.

"Hey, what about The Circus? You've never been to the Circus. Isn't that supposed to be a place for people who have lost their faith?"

He was impressed that she'd remembered, surprised that she'd listened. Kipling had heard much about The Circus and it was true he had never been. He had never said so, but he feared The Circus. It was run by Smugglers, Fetchers and Crooks and was always swarming with Chip Hunters.

"I don't know about that Kat. It's more than a Circus. Some really dodgy stuff happens there."

"So what is it, too much competition?" she teased.

Kipling tapped his arm.

"I don't think it's safe for a boy like me."

"When you were trying to get me to go, you said it was supposed to be fun!"

"It is supposed to be fun, but it's dangerous for me to go there. It's always crawling with The Faithful because it's one of the few places any one can go to. The Faithful can't just roll up to a clan and be like, Oh hi! Thought I'd pop in for some tea!"

When the divide was called, The Order said The Faithful would be free but they were the least free people of all the lands. They giggled and spluttered, enjoying laughing together after so long.

"But seriously Katya, lots happens there, not just chip hunting. I heard they do transplants under the big top and you can buy babies and children there! Plus you're nearly of age, you wont have long to change your mind!"

"C'mon Kip, I can be tough! Remember when we first got here and we fought for the squat? I was pretty scrappy. I'm sure I can handle it. Anyway, a year's ages."

"The New World isn't like The Old World," Kipling warned, "The Circus isn't going to be pretty. I've met some of the performers. They're all piss-heads, stoners and cheats. The bearded lady is actually a man and the clowns can't juggle for gin!"

"So, you're basically saying, I can get stoned all day and get away with my rubbish juggling skills?"

They fell about, crumpled like the blankets they sat on, they chuckled together heartily until they could hardly breathe, knowing this might be the last long laugh they shared.

"Actually Katya, what was I thinking was that it sounds like you'll fit right in!"

PETER

.

WRITTEN BY JODIE DABER
ILLUSTRATED BY ANDREW WALTER

It's a paper avalanche and 5:00pm is his St Bernard. The muted clunk-a-thunk of the photocopier, the impenetrable spreadsheets, the terse emails from jumped-up shits too important to bother with pleasantries, the bland office banter – you up to anything tonight? What you having for your tea? What do you reckon about her off Corrie then? It's a constant, solid pressure, the kind that will either turn a man into a diamond or a smear of dust. And he thinks to himself, what the fuck did I do to deserve this?

It's 4:55pm when his boss looms, with his matronly hips and his short-sleeved shirt.

"Ah now Peter," his boss says, "it's about those figures. Could you just. . ."

So he misses the fast train and has to get the stopper that grinds though the stations of a thousand places he'll never visit. He walks down the carriages scanning for a Metro but it's too late, it's too late.

The stopper stops to let another train pass and Peter stares through the window into the scraplands that line the tracks, the bits of place that are neither here nor there, just unnamed woodlands and the backs of things. And there amongst the peeling birch Peter sees a man, inked and shirtless in the mossy light, a chicken clutched like bagpipes under one ham-hock arm. The train peels away and Peter cranes his neck but all he catches is the flick of the man's head and the flight of another as it arcs in a flurry of feathers and blood to land beak-down in the leaves.

She's already home when he gets back, wiping out the sink with her coat on. She's angry, he thinks. She only ever cleans to make a point.

"I've only just got in," is the first thing she says, and he closes his eyes for the shortest of rests before he replies.

"Hi there sweetheart, how was your day?" and the litany begins.

"Fucking weird, to be honest," he says when she finally asks him, "it's been a really weird day. I think I saw some guy in the woods on the train and he was just standing there with this chicken and then he fucking."

He stops and waves his fork.

"Probably imagined it," he says.

"Well if you will stay up until dickhead o'clock playing Call of fucking Duty then you will see strange things in the bushes," she says, scratching at her chin, but she's not so angry now she's eaten.

That night he's woken twice by a car backfiring in the street.

The next morning Peter's feeling pretty Peterish. He breakfasts on Red Bull and fags and goes to work feeling slightly less suicidal than usual. It doesn't last.

Lunchtime offers a brief respite from the petty demands of twats in ties. In the canteen, Peter picks up a tray and joins the shuffling queue. He opts for bangers as the best of a bad lot. The woman behind the counter globs on his beans and they keep the shape of her spoon, like little scoops of orange ice cream.

"Chips or mash?" she asks.

The mash is runny and bright white.

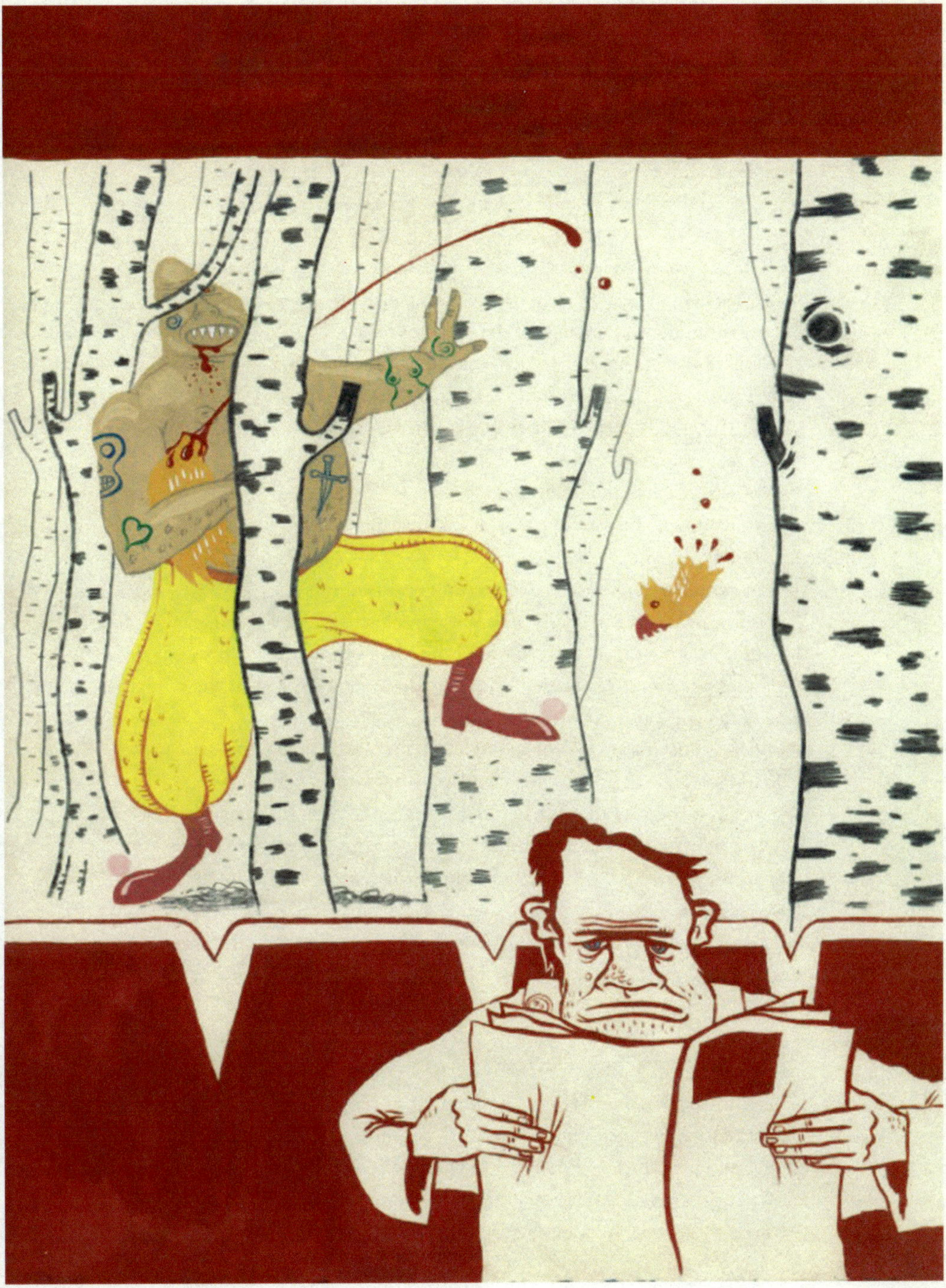

"Chips please," he says, and he's not looking at her, but somewhere just behind his eyes, when he looks back he sees popcorn piled all over his dinner, bouncing off the edges of his plate.

He looks up at the dinner lady and she holds his gaze. He looks back down at his dinner. It looks alright. Something thumps somewhere in his guts. He carries his tray past the lads from his office and finds a table on his own. Someone shouts.

"Ooooh, be like that then, Pedro!"

He sits down and picks up his fork. I always thought, he thinks, that something had to give.

But nothing happens on Wednesday and nothing happens on Thursday and then it's finally Friday evening, the longest possible time until more work. Peter's all de-mob as he pops into the office, so he picks her up a Topic and a six quid chardonnay, but then she texts to say she's off out with the girls.

There's nothing on except an old Mock the Week on Dave so he rolls himself a spliff and settles in. Idly he fingers his bellybutton, gouging out the bits of stuff he farms there. He rolls his harvest between finger and thumb but it feels strange, almost crispy on the outside and then sticky, or stickier than normal, anyway. He looks down at his fingers. They are stained. He can smell the stuff now, sweet and cloying, a scent as undeniably pink as his fingers. Candyfloss. I wonder if perhaps I should be frightened, he thinks, raising his hand to his mouth.

She doesn't get in until gone 4:00am and he's fast asleep. He surprises himself by not dreaming about anything.

On Saturday afternoon he stands in Topshop with carrier bags cutting into his palms. He looks for red noses on the mannequins, red tailcoats on the rails. He sees nothing and she doesn't let him go in Game.

She's scratching her chin again, he notices. Next to him on the

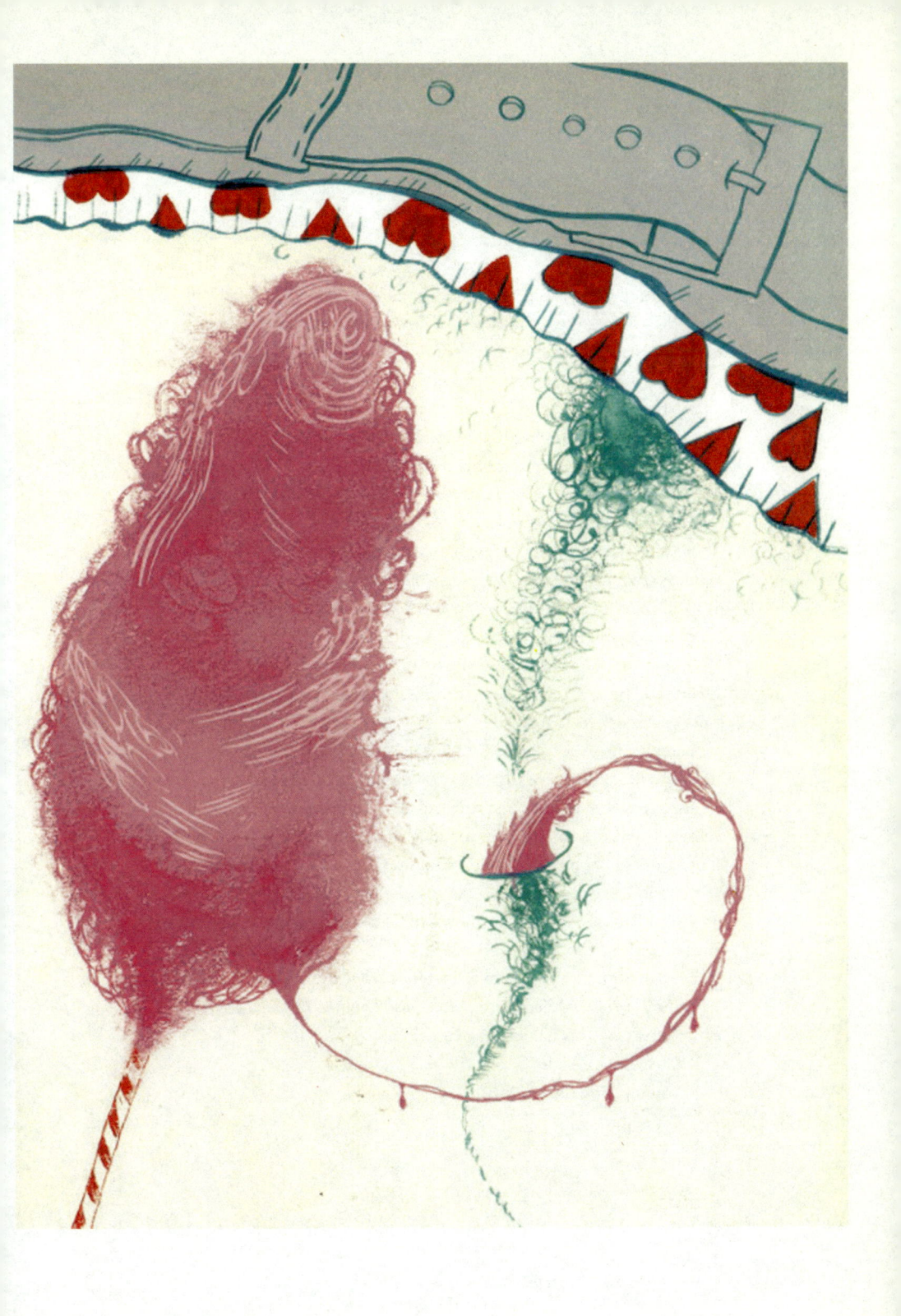

sofa, wearing his pyjamas, she holds a wine glass in one hand and with the other scrapes the soft spot just below her jaw. On the television Amanda Holden stares desperately into the stage lights to try and summon up some tears as another milksop moppet bleats out Pie Jesu.

"What's wrong with your chin?" he asks her.

"It's itchy," she replies, as though it were a stupid question.

She stops scratching, but only for a while.

"That fucking dog's finally stopped barking," she says, "I thought I was going to have to go round."

Next door's dog, a lumbering bolus of muscle and spit, had barked without stopping for weeks upon weeks, pausing only to eat and to shit and to rootle about its own crotch. It's owner mostly ignored it, every now and then screaming Tupac, shut the fuck up, will yer?

"*Finally*," Peter says, and picks up the remote 'cause it's the adverts and he likes to flick about during the breaks because he knows it pisses her off; little victories.

Later on he feels a bit frisky but she says she's not in the mood and anyway, *Sex and the City*'s on, so he goes to bed in a huff.

He can see next door's yard from the window on the landing. Sometimes he just stands there for ages, watching the dog go mental at people walking past the fence, or sauntering cats, or falling leaves, or the wind. Now when he looks out the dog's looking back, just standing there looking up at the window, at him. He looks behind himself without thinking and when he looks back at the dog it seems to make eye contact with him as it stands itself up, straight and tall on its hind legs, and begins to teeter in a drunken circle round the yard. Peter claps his hands like a little kid.

"What are you doing?" she shouts.

"Nothing," he says.

*

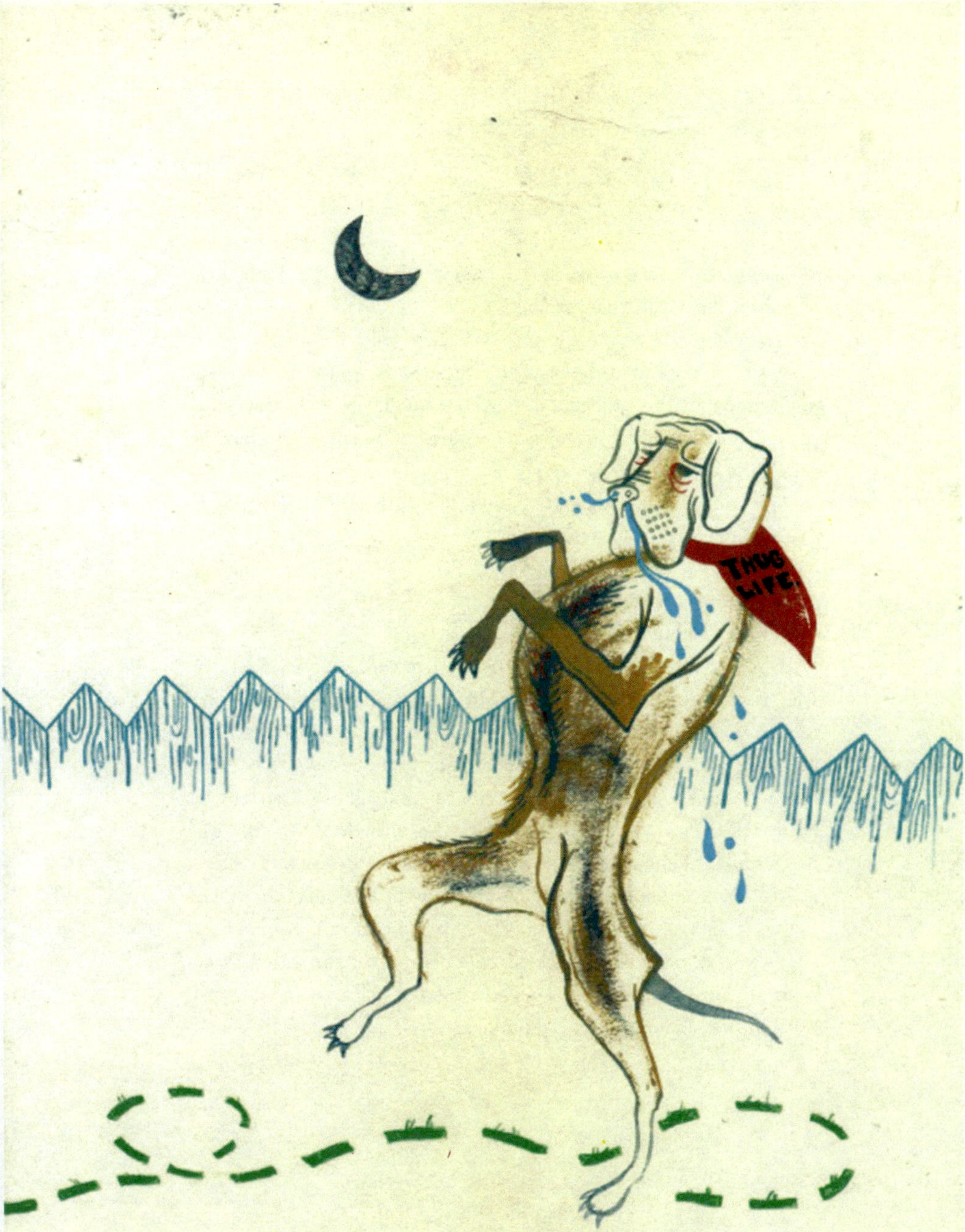
THUG LIFE.

On Sunday morning he walks in on her in the bathroom, sobbing as she blunts his Mach 3 on her chin.

To be honest, he's quite glad to go back to work on Monday, until he has his 1-2-1 and his boss starts banging on about missed targets and accountability and being more of a team player. Peter stares out of the window behind his boss, who starts talking about his lack of focus just as Peter sees the elephant.

"He can't help it," he shouts, "look!" and points out of the window.

His boss turns round to look.

"What?"

Peter points harder.

"Look, can't you see it, it's an," he stops.

Peter has never been to the circus. He's never seen a carnival. He went to the funfair on a date once, but they went on the waltzer one too many times and he was luridly sick on her shoes. He thinks for a moment. He thinks about his girlfriend and how she rolls away from him at night. He thinks about the credit card and all those red letters. He thinks about Lord Alan Sugar and another episode of The Apprentice. He thinks about his inbox and about Microsoft Excel. Then he doesn't think anymore, he just turns round and walks out of the office.

And then Peter blinks and he's in a birch wood, somewhere near a railway track. There's a chicken under his arm and through the pale trees he can see the stopper. He looks down at the bird and the bird looks at him. Peter opens his mouth.

FRAGMENTS OF
A STORM SUSPENDED
IN TIME

.

WRITTEN AND ILLUSTRATED BY
ZOE CATHERINE KENDALL

♥

Author's Note: This piece was written when I was age twenty-six on varied matters of living as I saw them then. It can be read as a collection of fractional texts, each housing their own fragment of meaning, as well as a series of anecdotes that overlap to tell a story. It's not a particularly unusual story and it's my hope that the commonalities will go a little way in making everyone feel a bit closer, all of us huddled together, comparing notes for the sake of better planning. . .

♦

W-o-r-d-s -w-o-r-d-s -w-o-r-d-s, sticky and enticing like your favourite fruit chew, sweet and gummy, you work them through to a slow lubrication of each syllable. That's where it begins. They shower from your tongue like soft rain, hail stones or dew, drip patiently like runny honey, each one with substance that you can get your teeth right into. Of the words you hear you can choose the ones you like, which to remember and which to repeat... Like life raining down we allow our thoughts to project through time, choosing the right words to define each passing moment. And boy do we fail, fail frequently in our definitions. I called it love but it was just play acting.

♣

When I was growing up I was a dancer. For ten years I learnt the moves, each class different; ballet, tap, jazz, modern and disco. Each style came with its own vernacular, words to describe the kinds of moves we were making. I learnt about discipline and precision from those lessons, I learnt that the body can become a vehicle for expression, and that each reflexion must be practised and refined. Each time we got a step wrong we would repeat it until we got it right. It's the same with all these definitions: rehearse them over and over.

Nowadays I feel as though I am holding onto a great wordy rope of time passing, a rope which thickens with each new experience, a rope that coarsens with emotion. I chase it down, marking the mile stones in a personal kind of chatter. There are times when I've ridden right past the important signs, stupidly eager. Finding yourself some place you never meant to be, everyone else around knowing that you don't belong 'there' before you do, that's hard. Some boundaries are just not meant to be crossed.

♠

A couple of summer's ago I had one of those sweeping whirlwind romances, though in retrospect it's probably more accurate to say 'I was in one' because otherwise I might run the risk of sounding as though I had some sort of control over the situation when really I didn't. A trip hazard you might say, he just sort of swooped in quick and low, one minute I was dancing and laughing with a friend and the next minute it was just him. I was at Visions Video Bar, a basement club on Kingsland Road, smoking cigarillos outside, ready for anything. Afterwards I told myself, it's not as though you can prepare for these things. . .

We burnt up in about two months, crazy love. So driven by hunger for each other, we gorged on far more than we could manage in the first few weeks and after that were left with nothing but rind and stones. It was too much. I remember this one particular occasion when I just lost it, all the sweet flavours had gone sour, he was apologising for being cruel and at the same time ripping me to shreds with his intentions: after that, pills and wine, a helicopter and hospital. I really lost it. Every syllable of sense was blown apart. It took me months to recover.

♥

Funny things, words, sometimes so easy to use, other times harder. Conversations can be very tricky. It depends on the associations, the expectations, all the big 'the's. . . before you know it you can find yourself overwhelmed by the whole apparent meaning. It has been known for a person to find themselves in a moment, mid-sentence, suddenly shouting, crying or making excuses, all the while thinking how on earth did I get here? I didn't mean to say those things, I don't even know what I meant! Just going through the motions.

"Wake up little girl, wake up!"

Some words echo, others reverberate or smart. It's often wise to forget those sounds, push them out of your mind before they get stuck. Then come the sticky moments, better than the imagined ones surely. I feel an urgency to really live, live through my thoughts, live right out of my head as if it were a hat I could don, exposing even those parts of myself that I don't like. It can be a shock sometimes, always good to have friends around. Mine are like a cloak, wrapping me up, so warm and embracing. You can wear friends out if you're not careful though and there are always a few who get away, lovers becoming strangers. I find that losing people, like losing things, can feel like you're coming apart at the seams.

◆

Recently I mended all the holes in my clothes, sewing together each section that had come apart, analysing what the apparent metaphor represented for my current state of mind. Until that moment I hadn't prioritised the maintenance of those garments but suddenly it seemed awfully important to stitch them up, all of the holes, the missing buttons and the hems. No longer would any sense of self neglect define these passing days. *I* would be in control of the times.

A worn out word is worse, limp and purged of any meaning, it just hangs in the air, a shadow of 'I love you', just an empty vessel, imposter. Can you sew words back together, string whole sentences up and out of the grave – has anyone ever tried? Sounds like a scene from an absurdist play, surely Beckett would have known the answer.

♣

Time changes things too, our perceptions mutate as we move from place to place, thought to idea. Time reins us in, fools us, mimics reality. I thought I loved a man before realising that I hardly knew him, tripped up for a moment by a racing embrace. . . all the while Time just looked on and laughed at my impatience. I won't do it again, I promise I will pay my dues. . .

I will pay glorious service to time – wow, what a phrase! It's something none of us can avoid. The future is something I look toward, firmly located here but with eyes ahead, this future of potential will help me to transcend the whims and fancies of the present moment. No amount of distraction will tear me from the path I'm on. Patience reveals strength, as does the admittance of weakness. But am I really that strong?

♠

jump!
high oh so very high
jump!
vert
unsympathetic
uncompromising
ATTENTION
cutting
woosh
HELP ME
HARD LINES
emphasis
punchy
PUNCTUATION
BLUNT
severe
bloody
FINAL
sick

Through weakness you will find yourself alone. Something about that sensation can send a person right up inside of themselves, isolating. We are proud people and do not like to admit our weaknesses, that isolates us even further. A new language is needed. Cher Godard, these are the places where I hurt. . .

Looking through a lens of the past, there have been times when I've experienced life in sepia. If you become too enshrined in a meaning that's been and gone, you'll find yourself on board another empty vessel. Old 'I love you's do not retain their original flavour. Instead, the memories taint and mock, time eluding the greatest among us as we remember. . .

Stop! That was the moment I chose to reclaim the present.
 "Everything in time," a lover once said to me.
 I liked this, it showed great promise. As it happened the promise it held leapt way beyond that relationship. I am still finding out what it means for me now. I've been gumming the words all this time and I'm gradually getting closer to the juicy bit. I can feel it coming, just over the horizon. . .

♥

My mother is the voice of society, my father also. My voice is that of the impertinent child always questioning, seeing fault in the arguments put forth. Twenty-six years and counting, occupied by thought. I am acutely aware of all the details of life as though I were swimming in an ocean of consciousness. Life is a storm and everyday a trial, every minute a transformation and every second a victory.

FRAGMENTS OF A STORM SUSPENDED IN TIME

Sometimes I am merely basic; walking, talking, eating, sleeping, washing and defecating. At other times I am transcendental in my thoughts and dreams. In between times I am creative; drawing, writing, painting and making mistakes. Mistakes are good, they facilitate learning, I didn't make enough when I was growing up so I am making a few extras now. I learn more from getting it wrong. All the big players do it.

◆

Many relationships are uncomfortable; my heart reverberates in my chest. I keep looking for meaning in cigarettes, it's not surprising I'm not getting anywhere fast. Speed, that's something too. A rush of adrenaline but where is it going to take you? Got to keep focusing on the road ahead, when your perspective is hindered you've got to refocus. Sometimes I get so bloody inspired by it all, a pedalling maniac aiming the wheel at visions of art and life. Head down, bounding toward oblivion, starved but ready to fill the void with meaning, ready to define it. . .

Sometimes it feels as though I can survive on nothing but my energy for this thing, carving out the grit and naming the different salts I find within it. Above all I want to keep learning, to keep discovering this life. It occurred to me whilst trying to fit the puzzle pieces together that perhaps this chaos first occurred when I tasted the metaphorical apple, acid trip, childhood spent worrying, crazy logic or none at all, you guys were always so freaking stressed out.

"Who bit your brother, your sister, was it you? Was it you!"

♣

I was cycling home on this one particular occasion, totally consumed by meditations on the efficiency of energy into movement, having just met a girl who was going to build a newer, faster bike than my current ride when this thought dawned on me, riding is like poetry in its purest form, a direct energy translation, poetry in motion.. . .. .

At that time I was always rushing from one day into the next, so busy impacting on life, conjuring up realities, my alchemy fearless, no boundaries to rein it in. I was sweeping out from an earlier pose, bold paint strokes that could take you right into the present second, giving life to hidden gestures, thinking that would evolve the heart.

And then, take off. On days spent alone, dreaming about alternative ways to live, I would imagine taking off on my bicycle and careening the lonely streets of this town as though it were a mind. This universal mind I was talking of was a boundless place, nothing off limits. And the more I challenged adopted conventions or concepts of the self, the more I willed this 'thing' into life. If at this stage the mutations of reality existed in thought only, I thought, let this be the first place to matter, the mind and its capacity to manifest reality. Ira Ryan, Richard Sachs and all the other legends in place.

♠

FRAGMENTS OF A STORM SUSPENDED IN TIME

DOWN!

Wheels spin, hands on bars, tracking, eyes gaze, fingers graze brakes, breaking in the vehicle, breaking in to life, sitting, bottom up, head down, fixed on a constantly changing point of view, elbows in, palms up, a mutation on the traditional riding position, we would ride alone, giddy warriors charging through dark nights and into beds across the cityscape, we were a group of individuals and dreamers, meeting on the road as passing ships alike in thought and belief, wandering silently, together in mind.

♥

After a night of lavish drinking I found myself in bed with the idea of you again. It can't have been consensual; the image just came flying through the door and into my head: throw me hard against the wall and rip out my heart as I lie before you. Honey, you are murdering me slowly. Honey, you are the best and worst of me. Honey, be careful. . . just the thought of you is killing me. . .

Can we beat this thing? All of us, somehow everyone all at once? We are sharing in this experience though we may be coming at it from different angles, the question being can we unify all of these perspectives? Let's get together, I think it might be the only way.

Last night I dreamt of you in various guises. Last night you visited me in my dreams. We are getting closer. This is really starting to happen. But baby, please don't hurt me. . .

♦

FRAGMENTS OF A STORM SUSPENDED IN TIME

I can be terribly sensitive like some kind of emotional medium. No feeling hides from these eyes. Already it feels as though I have lost so much. There have been times when I have wanted to cry out 'hold on to me, I am falling away from you, reality is peeling back and I'm afraid of the madness beyond, you've got to hold on, baby, hold on to me more tightly. . .' Apparently I know fear but it has never stopped me, perhaps that's the deal. Every time I've fallen, back up again to straighten out my dress, analysing the fall, knowing it, that's how I learn. And boy there have been some falls.

So much can hang on a single word. You. All the lovers the world over streamlined into one perfect version. It was just a name I liked to use, the point is it could have been anyone. A few faces flash up, yet none of them were quite *you*.

♣

Memories, they can really suck sometimes. It can be torture recalling those moments spent pining for something more. I was closer to it back then, the danger. Now I am older, supposedly wiser and still pining somewhat. I love taking sanctuary in the present moment. Now is enough. Sometimes I just sit and stare into space. Thought takes its toll, I can't always be in the midst of something tangibly fruitful but I do on occasion relish being in the midst of nothing, and that can really feel like enough. I can't describe the specifics of the state I enter into except to say that when it happens I often feel overwhelmed. A tired stupor of being, heavy lidded eyes drooping, mind on pause. Not every moment has to have a discernible flavour, sometimes just being is enough.

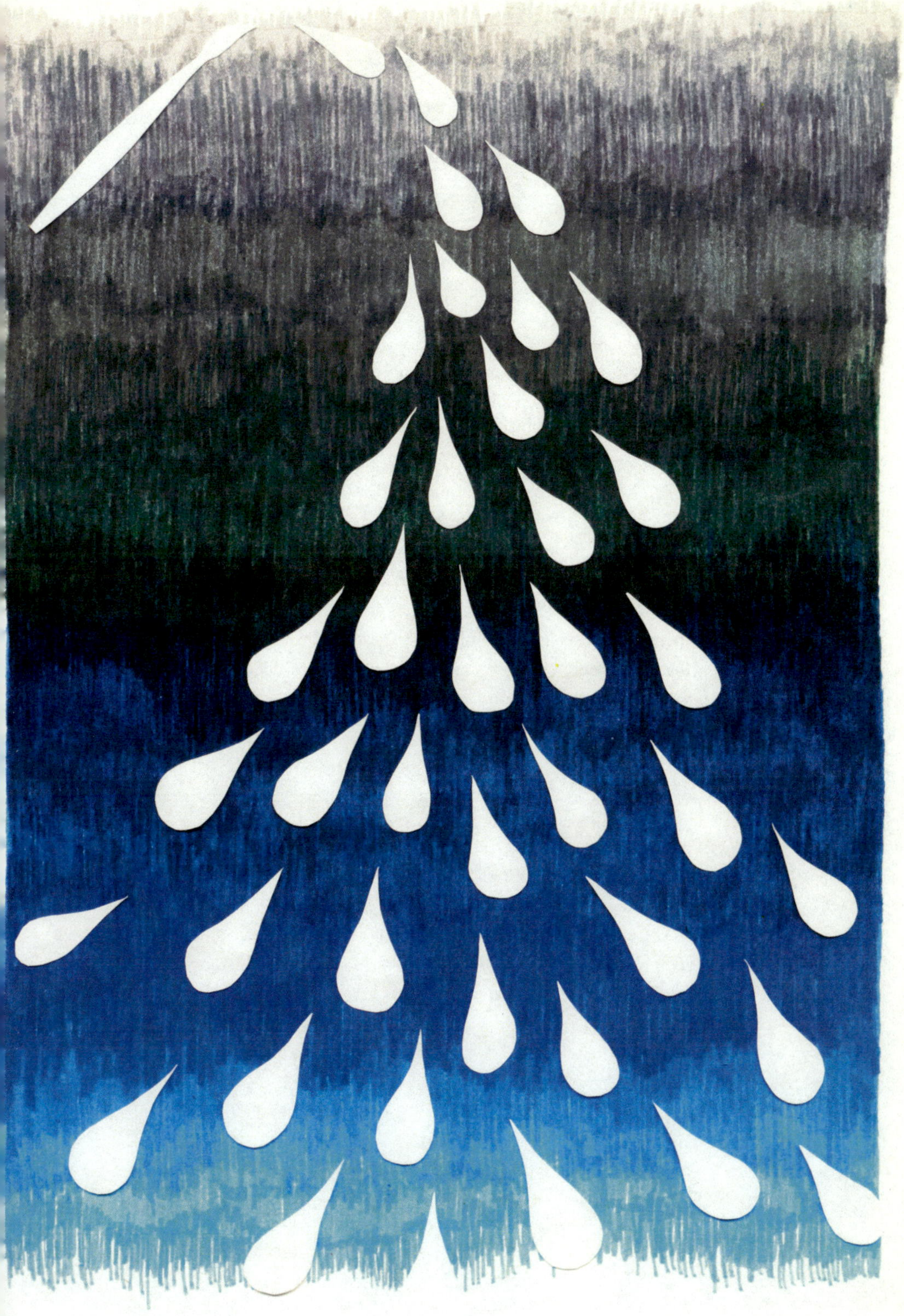

♠

At times my life has seemed more circus like than ever. On late nights, gathered in twos and threes, groups of us descend on the town, ready to tell tall tales to each other, polishing the ego with false hope of love whilst flexing the imagination into high spirits. Meeting and embracing those who enter into our path, we have become a real mix of young things barely knowing adulthood and others older bringing with them knowledge of war, broken hearts and abandon. Travelling together as a band of loveable rogues and idealists, we extend our dreams into space as a gymnast would his limbs but not always successfully. We have made London our playground, a soulless kingdom equally soulful as it brims full of what we've brought to it, a fork in the road where all four corners of the world collide. We're all so busy crashing and bumping into each other and just sometimes it works.

♥

I don't want to let it be defined by a sense of wanting more, my perception of all of this. What I have had has always been enough. The perpetual hum drum, motion that leads to nothing, a nothing wind blowing dreams apart, but has any of it moved me? All I know for sure is that I still have some way to go. God knows where I'll end up.

ADOLESCENCE—ADULTHOOD

HAUNTED BY

THE PERPETUAL

ROAR OF GRAVITY

.

WRITTEN BY SAM RAWLINGS
ILLUSTRATED BY JEANNIE PASKE

Not a sound to be heard,
a city without words
as she awoke beside he,
hearts pendulums, tides each side a single ocean.

Slender bodies two blades of grass,
upon the winds so they arose, so they swayed;
the dawn cloaked, a shroud of snow.
Yet still their barge smoked prophetically,
that evening's warmth beginning to temper
beneath a cold hue of plunging light.

Lips upon a cigarette she evoked
the orange sky now painting over ice,
that fevered rattle white as winter bone.
Both eyes below the gentle crush of hair
slowly she let rise a palm through the peace.

With twig like fingers her mast did anchor,
hand a signpost, bound in hope as any branch,
arm cast amongst the cascading seconds.

Haunted by the perpetual roar of gravity
a monument her silence, sombre limb.
Without time his pacing heart,
a scrawl his shade climbing London's walls;
and so it was the clock's hands did linger a while
longer than they had ever dared.

Our totem of stone and roots
a chest of earthen memories and crystal truths,
for a moment's sincerity declared
will pervade even the darkest despair.

Whereupon the sun sank,
sweeping its shadow across the city floor;
as if leaves that day's echoes falling,
peppering us all.

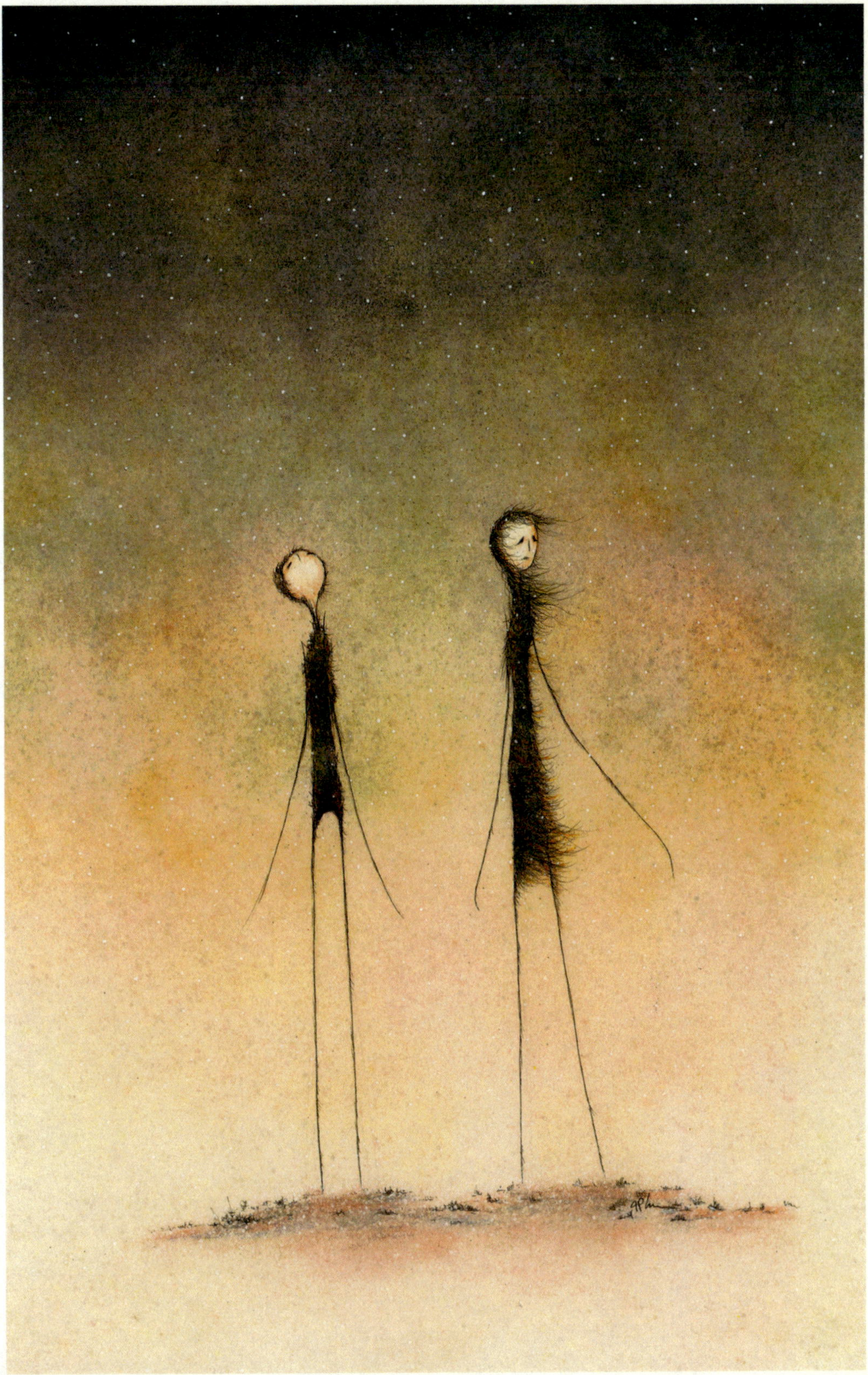

IF
ONLY
HE'D
KNOWN
.

WRITTEN BY MAT LLOYD
ILLUSTRATED BY JAMES KAMO

I.

If only he'd known
What he knew now
Before the snake
Slowly slithered off
Into the undergrowth.
He probably wouldn't
Have taken such
A large bite.

ADOLESCENCE—ADULTHOOD

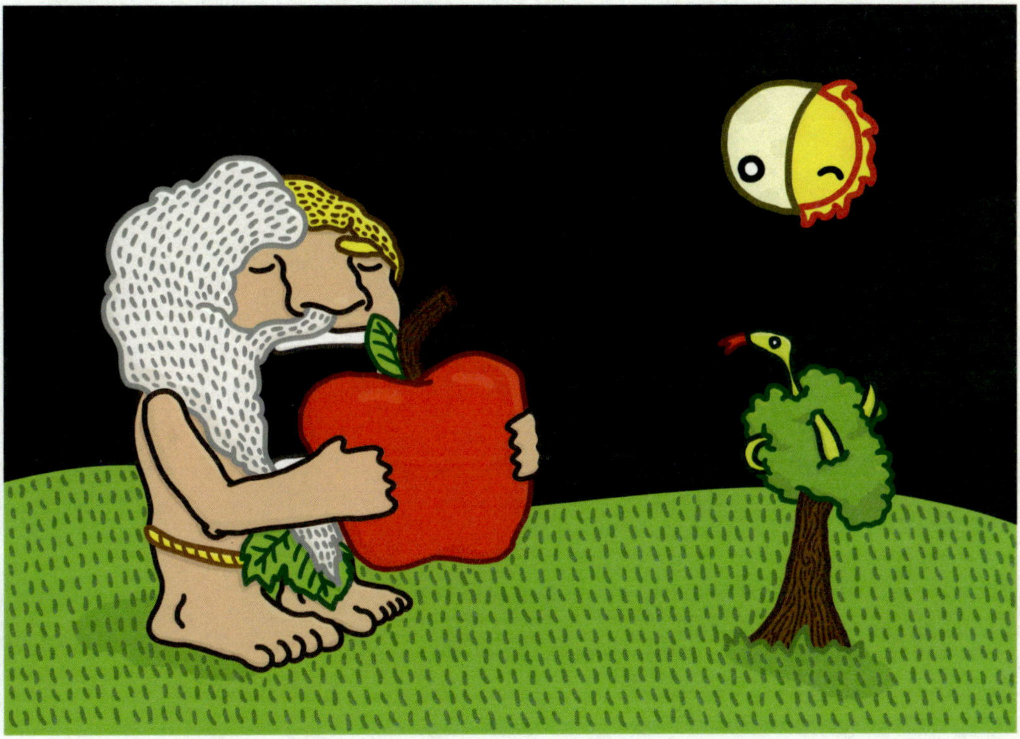

II.

Maybe just a small
Tiny taster sized bite.
Not a life affirming
All enlightening sized bite.
But now he knew.
Knew his future
Was in his naked hands
And he was scared.

III.

Scared that his future
Self would be disappointed.
Would look back with regret
At the choices he made.
Hang his head in shame
At the decisions
He decided to take.
Yet eager for growth
The apple was devoured.

ADOLESCENCE—ADULTHOOD

IV.

With each bite
A fleeting wave goodbye.
The path of blind
Discovery lost forever.
The hiss of the snake
Was a warning not heeded
"Eat and you shall grow
But never look back

For you shall be. . . a man"

IF ONLY HE'D KNOWN

VERTIGO

·

WRITTEN BY MUSA OKWONGA
ILLUSTRATED BY JAKE ELLIS

As a young boy I was scared of heights —
In other words, I was unprepared for life;
Thoughts of growing up had me throwing up,
Knew I'd never know enough; I was uneasy. . .
See, once you're getting tall, you're meant to get it all,
Be on the ball in life in general,
But there's no practice, or book of tactics:
Fact is, we just get one crack, and that's it. . .
There's no cheat guide, no pause, and no rewind,
No replays of those days at the seaside —
And you can't slow-motion your free time,
It's just fast-forward, each time . . .
Thank God to be an adult you don't need a licence
'Cause I'd have failed my test more than once or twice, and
Some nights when I'm sunk in the blackest of moods,
Wish I could pack up and jump back in the womb. . .
I'm six-foot two, and the view leaves me terrified;
I've got the vertigo, so I call up a friend of mine;
He's nervous, just had his first kid,
And tells me, yes, despite the stress it's worth it.
With his young family and all his high-hopes
Him and his wife are walking the tightrope. . .
It's easier, he has found
To stay top of the world if you don't look down.

ADOLESCENCE—ADULTHOOD

Fate and the human egg

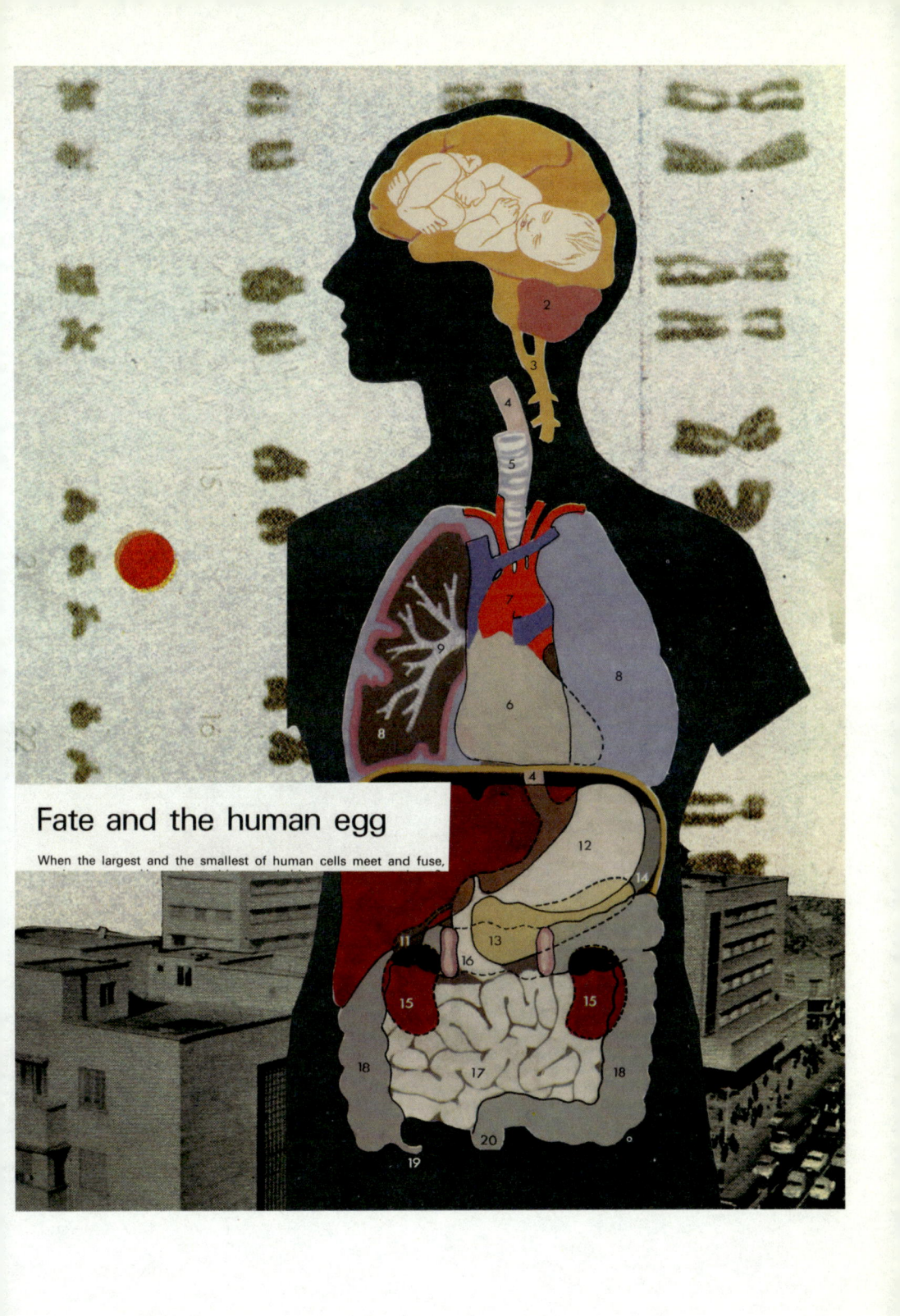

When the largest and the smallest of human cells meet and fuse,

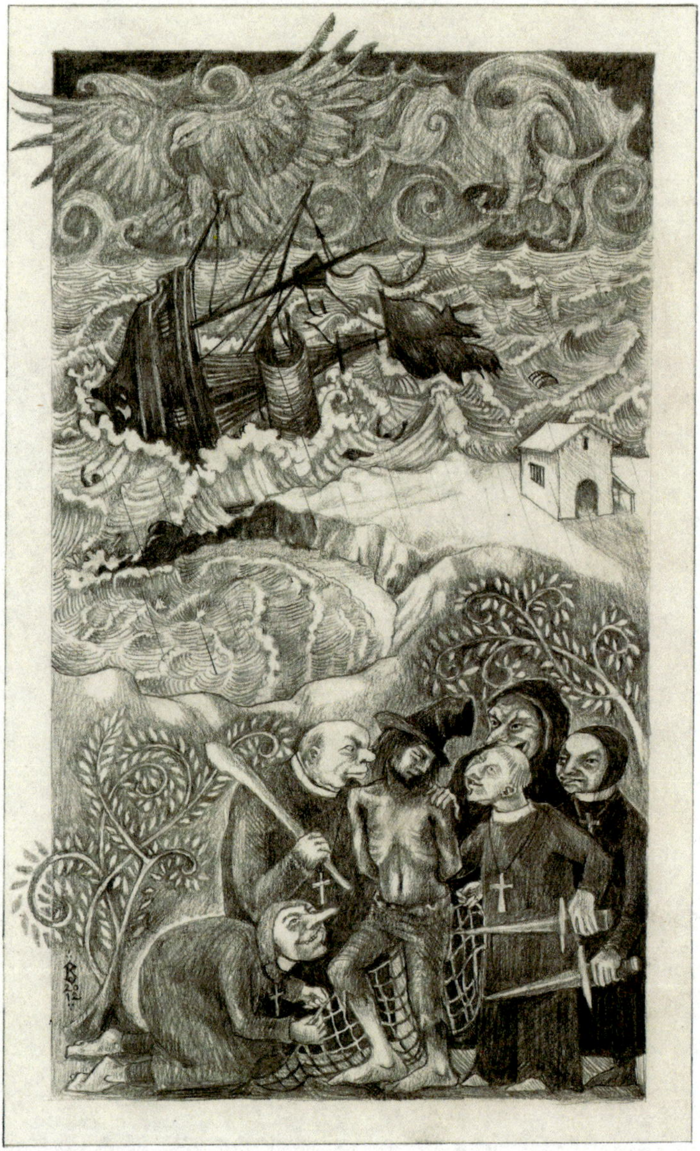

OLD AGE.

A storm brews from nowhere and
the ship whose arrival he feared
sinks off the coast . . .

*"The day my trial was to begin, there was a storm.
I watched it brew from nowhere, like the arrival of a whale
from the deep. Here's something: the ship sank.
She went down with stocks and stores and the judge and all twelve of the
jurymen sent to try me. The waves ate them like ship's crackers, without
delight or comment but only the necessity of sustenance. I watched them
sink. The sea closed over them like history."*

CENTRAL STORY

The Scrimstone Circus Gospel

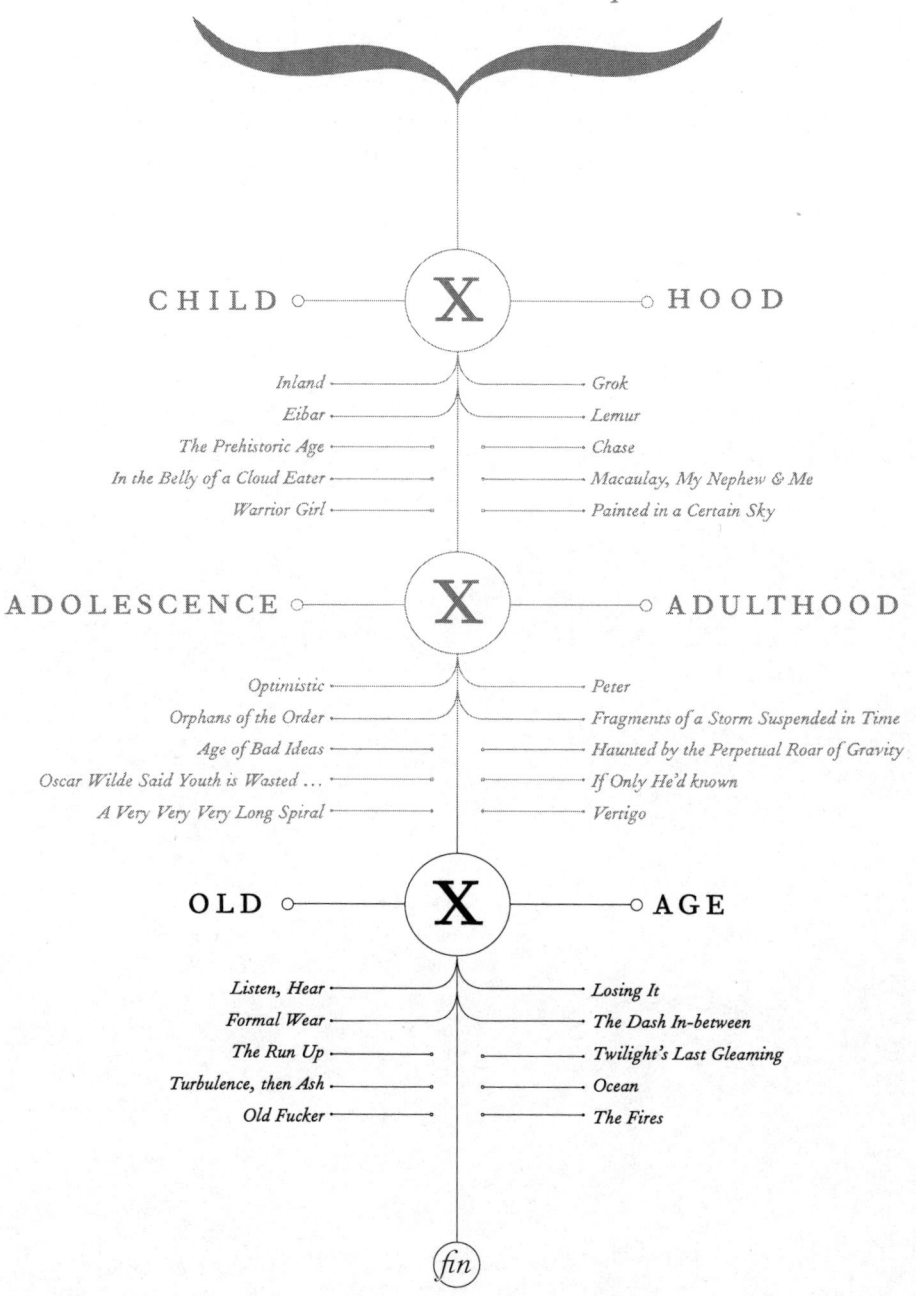

CHILD ⚬—— Ⓧ ——⚬ HOOD

Inland	Grok
Eibar	Lemur
The Prehistoric Age	Chase
In the Belly of a Cloud Eater	Macaulay, My Nephew & Me
Warrior Girl	Painted in a Certain Sky

ADOLESCENCE ⚬—— Ⓧ ——⚬ ADULTHOOD

Optimistic	Peter
Orphans of the Order	Fragments of a Storm Suspended in Time
Age of Bad Ideas	Haunted by the Perpetual Roar of Gravity
Oscar Wilde Said Youth is Wasted …	If Only He'd known
A Very Very Very Long Spiral	Vertigo

OLD ⚬—— Ⓧ ——⚬ AGE

Listen, Hear	Losing It
Formal Wear	The Dash In-between
The Run Up	Twilight's Last Gleaming
Turbulence, then Ash	Ocean
Old Fucker	The Fires

(fin)

THE RUN UP.

WRITTEN BY STACIE WITHERS
ILLUSTRATED BY ZOPHIEL WEBB

Mine has been a good life, a loud life, a live life.
I have stepped out, boldly, into oncoming traffic, with only my destination in view.
Foolish as it may have appeared, and I am aware it most definitely did, I threw myself, arms flailing
and dignity cast aside, into whatever new adventure seemed the richest.
Talked too much? Kept too quiet? Said the wrong thing at the wrong time to the wrong ear? Yes.
I am not weighed down by some silent list of 'I wishes', my humiliations all came with a reward.
I loved the unwise choices, the unwashed bodies; the unpolished edges.
My mistakes were victories in disguise.
Can you look at all the days that made you and see
all the different angles of perfect you couldn't make out at the time?
Each one stacked up beside you, something to lean on when tired feet need a rest.
Journeys are as exhausting as they are exciting, if you do them right.
But I have not travelled as far as I expected, though I covered much more ground,
I made it back to where I started each and every time, a little wiser, a little bruised,
but just as keen to go again, never really learned my lesson.
Hurt feelings, not always mine, were worth it all.
And standing at the edge of the end, out of time if not intention,
I'll fill as many days as I am given, although with what, I'd never promise.

TIME

Time takes the colour from memories, makes them all a shade of better,
the loves more sweet, the pain less sharp, the words more carefully picked.
It makes everything look the way you wish it had been,
or rather it fools you into believing it's what you wanted all along.

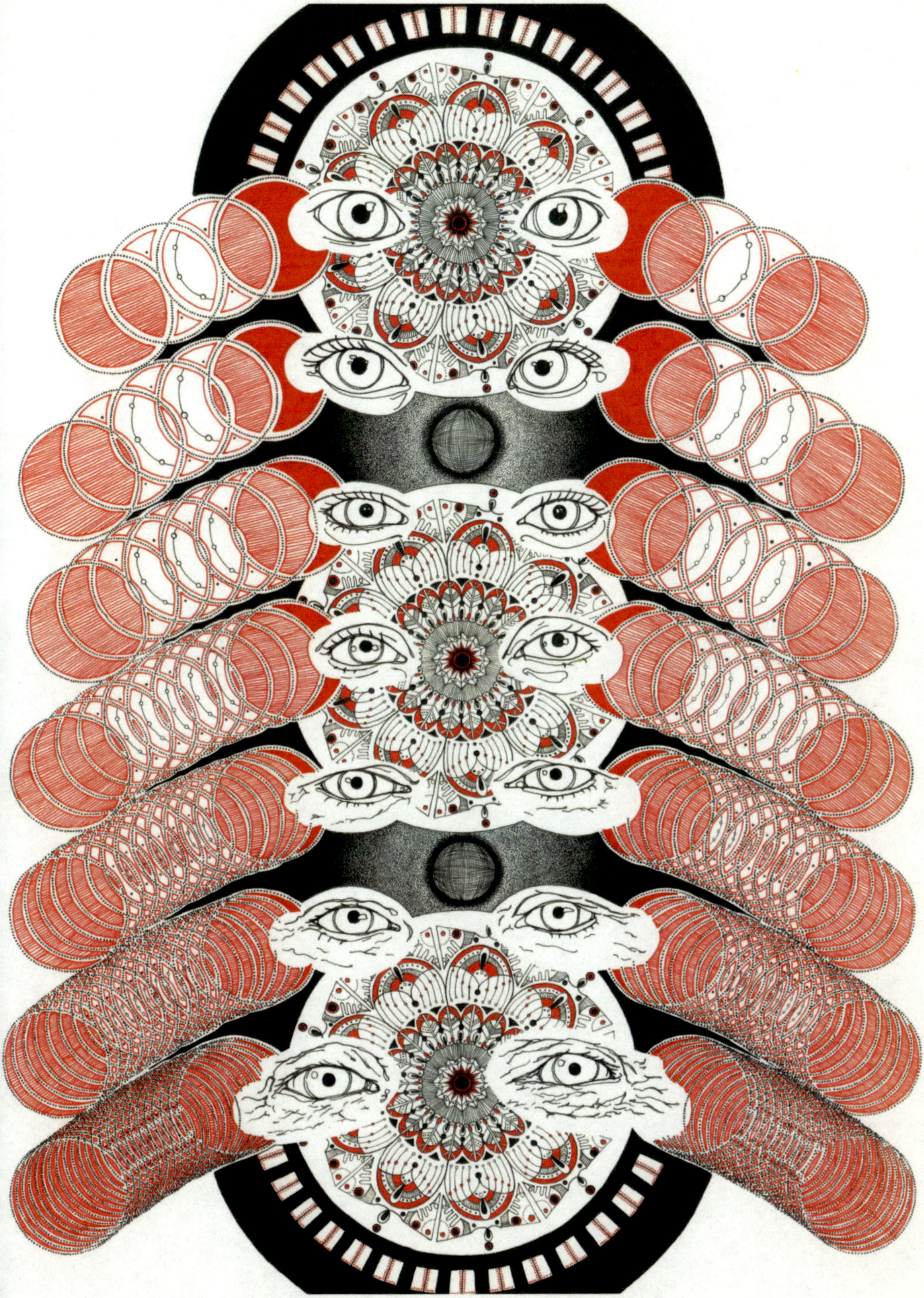

TURBULENCE, THEN ASH.

WRITTEN BY ADAM GREEN
ILLUSTRATED BY PAULA AFONSO

I am still gripped by thoughts of you
From time to time
A bangle on your arm, your dimple when you laughed
Darker ones too; your hands on someone else

I am lying on my sofa waiting
For these thoughts to lose their force, their turbulence
To be hollow, just leaves, ash breaking apart in the wind
Or like an anonymous car, passing me by in the street

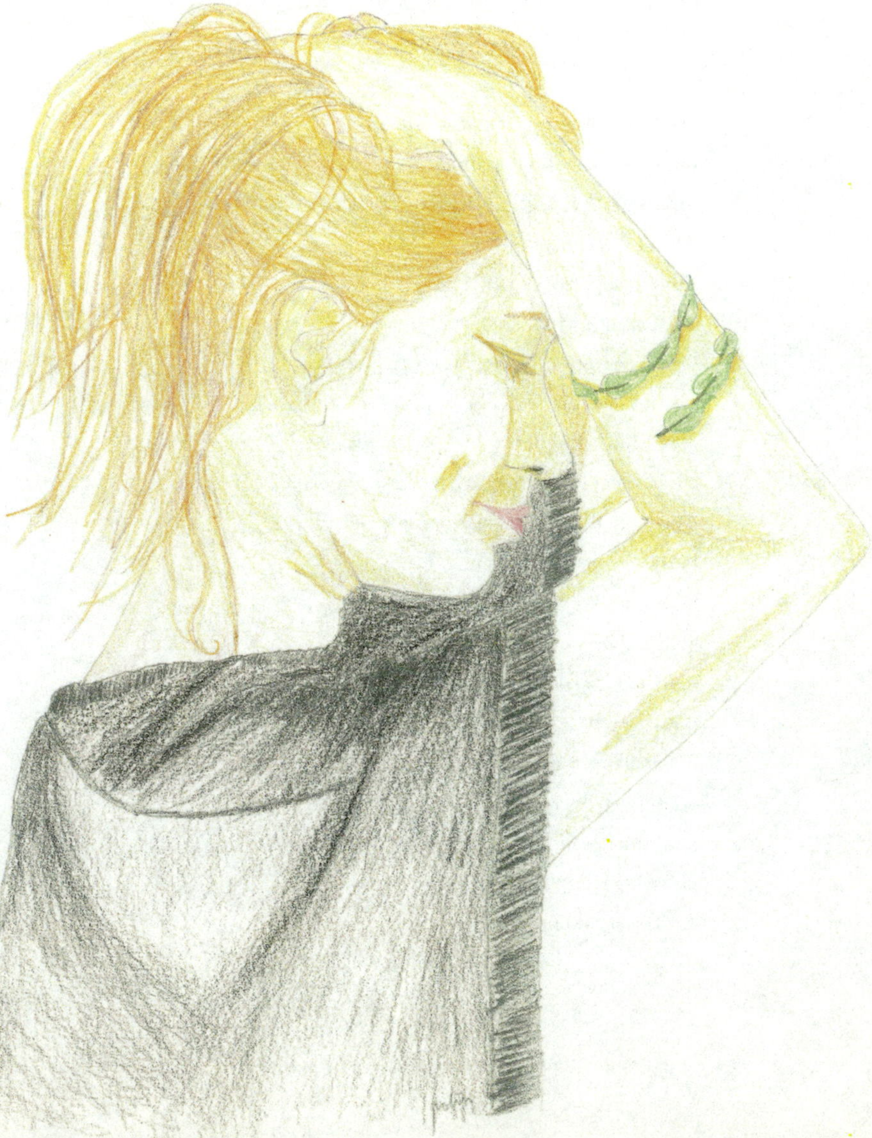

OLD FUCKER.

WRITTEN BY FRANCES K WOLFE
ILLUSTRATED BY DIEGO MALLO

I've been old for twenty odd years
Relaying back bone damage
Filling up jars with dry tears
That I never shed
Pillowcases full of prayers
That went unsaid
Don't pay attention to the rusty chants
From knees and elbows
Any old fuck will say
That's just how life goes
The only thing that raises up my neck hairs
Is the skin of my back
Hanging like crumpled linen
Saddled up on rickety chairs
And as I go round the roundabout
Back to where we all came from
I only ask for my memory
To stay strong
And for my fingertips to remember
How I traced the knots in her spine
And every lock in her body

OLD AGE

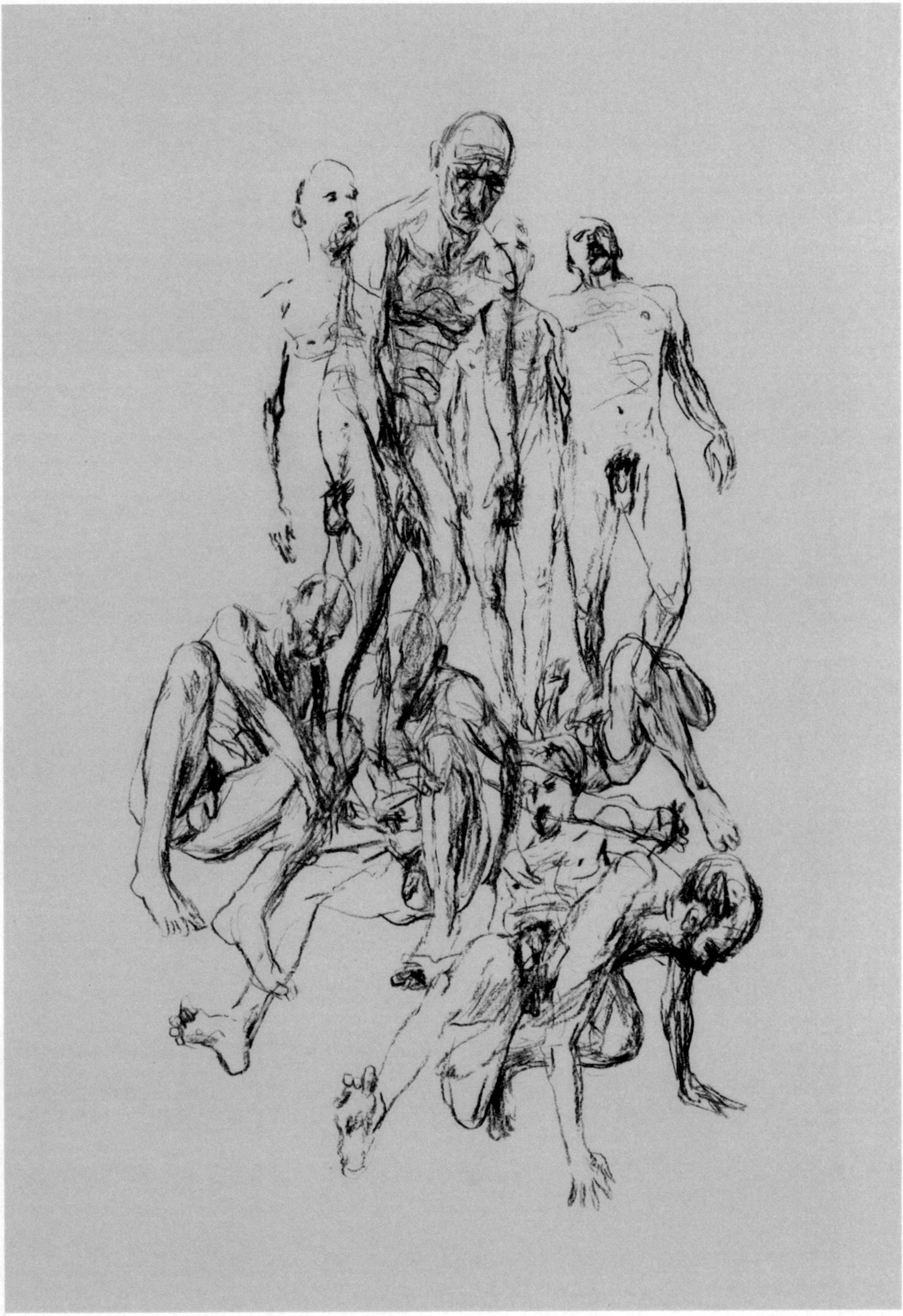

TIME

Found its key within mine
And I became old when she left our home
Checked myself into an island
To turn full moons alone
And now I'm on my last page
Slugging whiskey
Sour breath of ancient history
If only my demons were a dream
But for twenty odd years
There's been a bigger beast
Driving this machine
And age has made it worse
But they'll forgive me
When I'm hitch hiking in a hearse
And here comes the harbinger
And he's treading lightly
When he walks across my grave
I guess he'll have to fight me
But I'm not afraid of dying
I have been dead a few times before
This is just the final time
That I'll hit the floor.

LISTEN, HEAR.

WRITTEN BY VINCENT J PRINCE
ILLUSTRATED BY MATT BLACK

"**An**d you reckon you met this feller?"

Jack had managed, as he always did, to find another ear to bend – this time some portly imbecile, soused in cheap lager and even cheaper aftershave. At his age he knew it was difficult to get anyone to hear you, never mind *listen* to you. Drunks listened, even if it were just so they could take some fragmented facsimile of the tale told and pass it on, twisting the narrative so that Jack becomes the protagonist, and a mad one at that; the kind of second hand story that begins with, 'you never guess what this nutcase down the pub told me . . .'

"Aye;" Jack replied, his Yorkshire accent gently tempered through his years at sea, "I met him on occasion, words dripped from that man's mouth like honey."

"And this ship, with them who were after him, like, all't lot un 'em, dead?"

The younger man's face skewed with disbelief. His thick, gloopy accent an echo of what Jack's once was at his age, "some weird storm, yer reckon?"

"You can take it as gospel," Jack replied, staring wistfully at the ephemeral tumult, stirring within his recently poured pint glass.

"So this bloke then, what wer' his name, like?" the miscellaneous drunk questioned, as he nestled his elbow upon the bar, leaning, as drunks do, that bit too close of a proximity to Jack.

Jack drew his gaze from his drink and planted it on the man, his eyes performing a fleeting saccade as they scanned his face, before finally focussing upon the frog spawn spittle and peanut shrapnel that had gathered at the corners of his unsightly gob.

"God only knows," Jack replied, with a sincerity not generally applied to the phrase.

"Well what happened to him?"

"Damned if I know," again, the words spoken with an earnest that betrayed the flippancy usually ascribed to them.

The man groaned with effort as he removed his elbow from the bar to stand up straight, his face flush and rosy – partly because of the booze, and partly because his body's homeostatic system was labouring to maintain a stable temperature, inside a man with more insulation than most wall cavities. He fell silent as he pondered on the tale – the cognitive process clearly taking its toll, as it ploughed three furrows of confusion across his brow. After a few seconds of consideration he expelled a loud 'Psshhh' noise, like someone had pulled a plug out of his mouth and he was about to deflate, before announcing his conclusion:

"What a load of old bollocks! I'll tell yer what old lad, yer can't half spin a bloody yarn thee! Wait until I tell't lads this 'un!"

The greasy pig punctuated his disbelief with three clumsy slaps across Jack's back, with his clammy ham-hock hands, and let out an equally clumsy guffaw. This signalled that he'd had his fill of story time – for the time being, at least. He was ready to grope, shove, spit and shout his way into someone else's conversation, with all the tact and finesse of a ram-raid. Someone who no doubt wouldn't be as tolerant as what Jack was towards having what, for all intents and purposes, was a walking, talking butcher's shop window, draped in the heady scent of pissy urinal cake and turpentine, attempt to strike up a discourse – by way of sledge hammer.

People hear you, but they don't listen.

After a leisurely meander home, Jack inelegantly swung the door open into his modest bungalow-semi; the slight aluminium frame and frosted glass panels rattling against the stopper. On the very rare occasions that Jack had visitors, they found that the most immediate quality his house possessed was its distinct aroma – an overwhelming musk of damp and stale decay. He entered the house and slammed the door shut with the same finesse applied to its opening. Years of olfactory familiarity had made him blissfully ignorant to his humble abode's quaint, malodourous nuances.

The contents of his bungalow were spartan at best: to the right of the front door lay a dilapidated high-backed armchair; its brocade pattern threadbare in any area subject to frequent contact and its cushion pilfered from the superfluous two seat sofa – an item in a relatively decent state of repair by comparison. Opposite the armchair sat a 1983 Fergusson Vision Master, minus its remote control. A budgie cage hung in the corner; its resident long since departed to the great aviary in the sky, but Jack had neither the will nor the want to get rid of it. A sun-bleached Sun newspaper still adorned its floor; something about 'Argies' was just about visible from beneath the

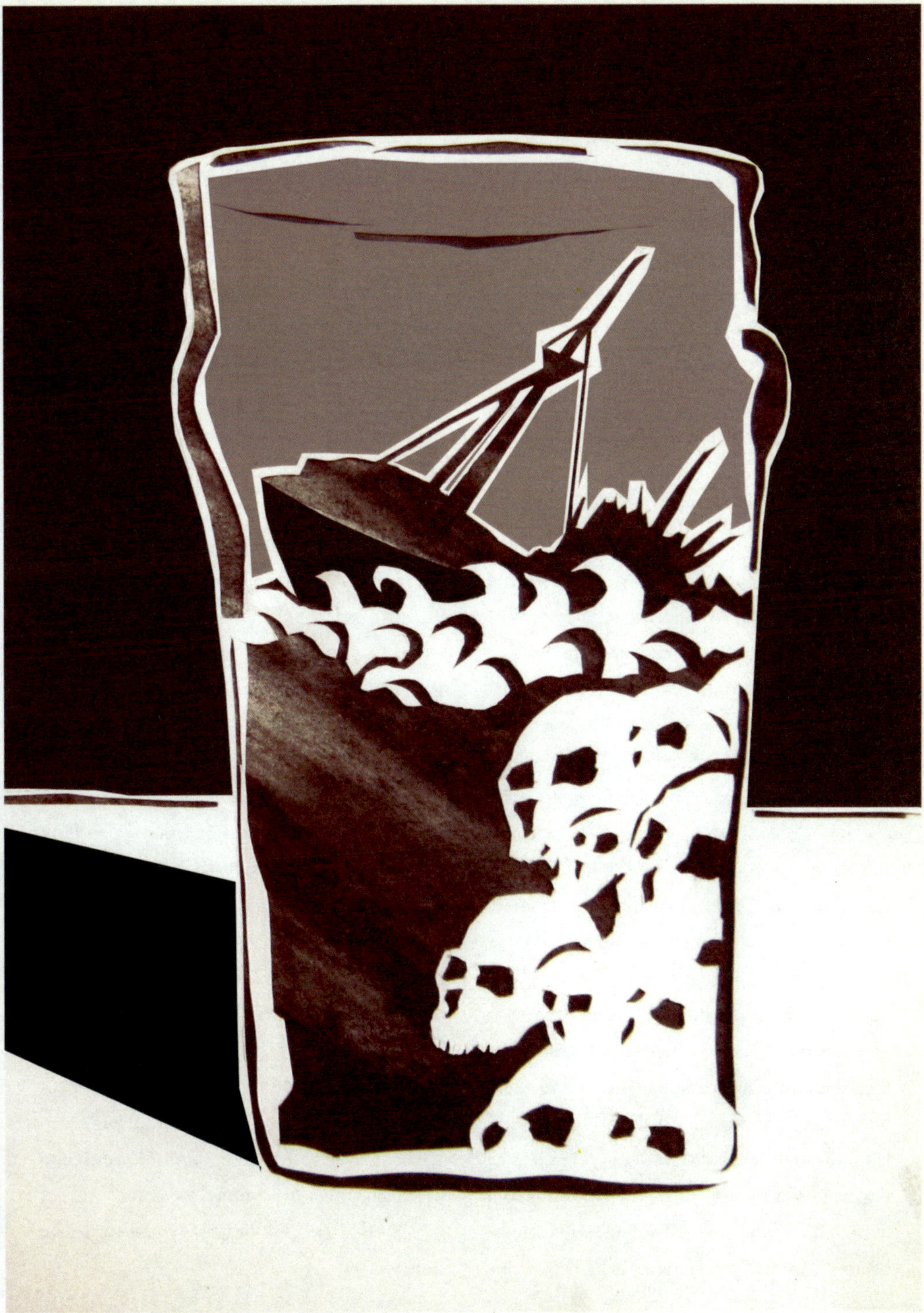

encrusted bird shit and Trill that still clung to it. Jack had slung the bird when its odour had begun to upset the delicate equilibrium established between all the other odours present in the house. Bird shit and Trill were among those odours, so the newspaper had remained.

As was customary when he'd had a few drinks, Jack neglected to lock the front door; instead he threw his keys into a cut glass bowl that sat upon a prosaic coffee table in the centre of the room. The table was a faux wood affair, with a plastic gold trim that was peeling in places, bearing the hazel-effect vinyl's dirty little secret – chipboard. He turned on the old Fergusson, which let out a plonk and a hiss of static as the cathode-ray tube fired up. He listlessly skipped through the four channels that would work, each button making a satisfying clunk-pop as it was seated in position, whilst evicting its neighbour. His whole philosophy on television was that, 'I can't find owt on't four channels I've got, why the hell would I want a hundred more?' – a mantra he frequently barked at anyone who wasn't listening.

His mantra reaffirmed, he turned off the television, which let out another plonk, hiss as its electrons became unenthused. Using his feet, Jack removed first his shoes, and then, with what little mobility he had with his toes, his socks, before cursing under his breath as he realised he'd have to cross the cold linoleum floor in the kitchen barefooted, to switch on the heating. As deftly as a man his age could, he hop-scotched across the frigid, waxy material, clicked on the heater, and hop-scotched back to the comfort of the thick piled carpet beneath his feet, his toes kneading the fibres for reassurance.

Jack stood in the centre of the living room and glared spitefully at his hands; each bearing witness to time's war of attrition, at the cellular level. His skin had long since began to resemble crumpled newspaper – grey and sallow, and peppered with the tell-tale stamp of age – liver spots: the stamp that grants you entry into a club you're never getting out of. He resented his hands. He could avoid looking into mirrors, and the rest of his body could be covered, but the sight of his hands was inevitable – unavoidable. He clenched his fists and put up his dukes, before throwing a few feeble, faux punches to the soundtrack of creaking joints – his limbs resembling the weary boughs of an old oak in a gale. Tiny eddies of dust swirled around his hands – fragments of his own body taunting what had bore them. Jesus – the ultimate betrayal, he thought, your own bloody body giving up on you. He moistened his thumb with his mouth and rubbed at the tattoo on the webbing between his thumb and index finger. What once was an anchor (albeit a shoddy one, even when it was fresh) was now no more than a greenish smear, bedimmed by age.

"Nothing's fucking permanent," he muttered, sourly.

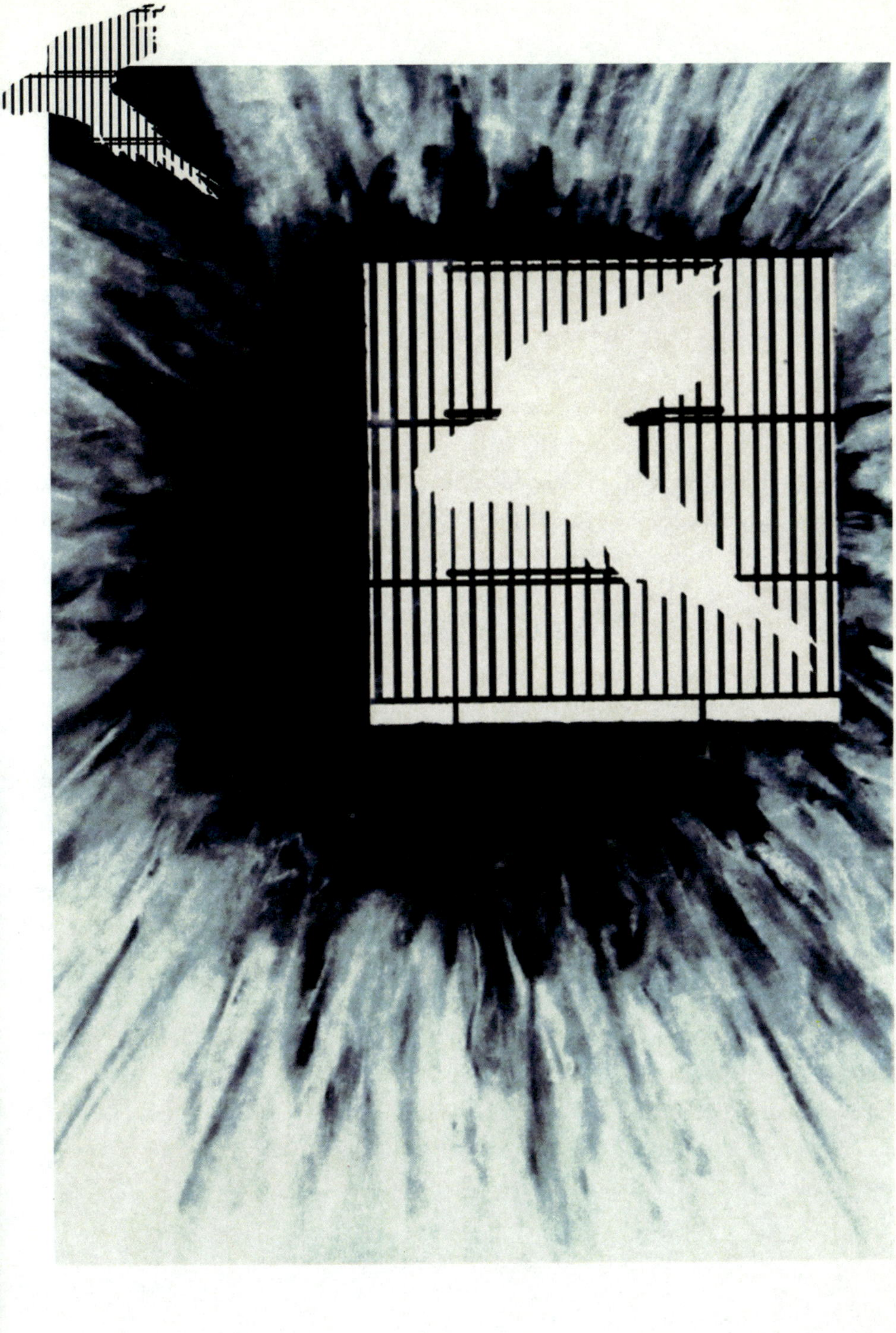

He idled reluctantly over to a mirror positioned above the mantle piece. It was an object that, whoever had decorated the house, had bought more for ornamental, rather than practical purposes. The fact that it wasn't particularly useful suited Jack just fine, as he didn't have much call to use it – a fact that was verified by the layers of dust caked upon the once gleaming shards, which protruded at all angles from the central, oval mirror. The central pane had a pre-etched template of dust from where Jack had previously run three fingers carelessly across the glass, in order to provide a modest window in which to view himself. Peering into it, he gazed at the grizzled face that stared back at him – framed by its own detritus. Straddling his face with his thumb and four fingers he drew his hand down, leaving a trail of wan skin behind it and inducing a rasping sound as three days of unshorn stubble ground against the calloused skin on his hands. Ergh, maybe it's us who betray *it*, with the booze and the cigs, the sleepless nights and the overindulgences. Perhaps it's retribution – cashing the cheque on a life misspent . . . Smarter men than you, have spent a lot longer than you've got left, thinking that one through lad, he reasoned.

Almost all of those he'd known, loathed, pitied, feared, cared for, and some he'd even loved – in his own way – had long since been committed to dirt. Jack took no solace in the assurances of scientific discovery; he'd borne witness to the birth of the modern age, an age when the inexplicable is explained and in terms that he didn't understand. They say happiness is relative, but it wasn't related to Jack, not these days anyway.

He slumped into the armchair, his form aligning perfectly with the dog-eared patches beneath. Staring at the peeling wallpaper, given a sickly, nicotine hue through years of contact with tobacco smoke, he never heard the front door. Despite the fact that there was no inelegant rattle of aluminium and frosted glass on *this* entrance, he already knew He was behind him.

"Hello Jack, it's been a while," hissed the snake-oil voice, the words dripping from His mouth like honey.

Jack's eye-line never faltered from its focus upon a miscellaneous tan patch on the flyblown, jaundiced wallpaper. He inhaled deeply, his nostrils widening at the fresh, briny tang cutting through the previously fetid air, before exhaling a sigh, tainted with relief, and responding.

"Aye, yer certainly took yer fuckin' time."

"And yet here I am, Jack, it's time to tell your last tale . . ." the mellifluous voice replied, each viscous syllable oozing like molasses, ". . . I'm listening."

OLD AGE

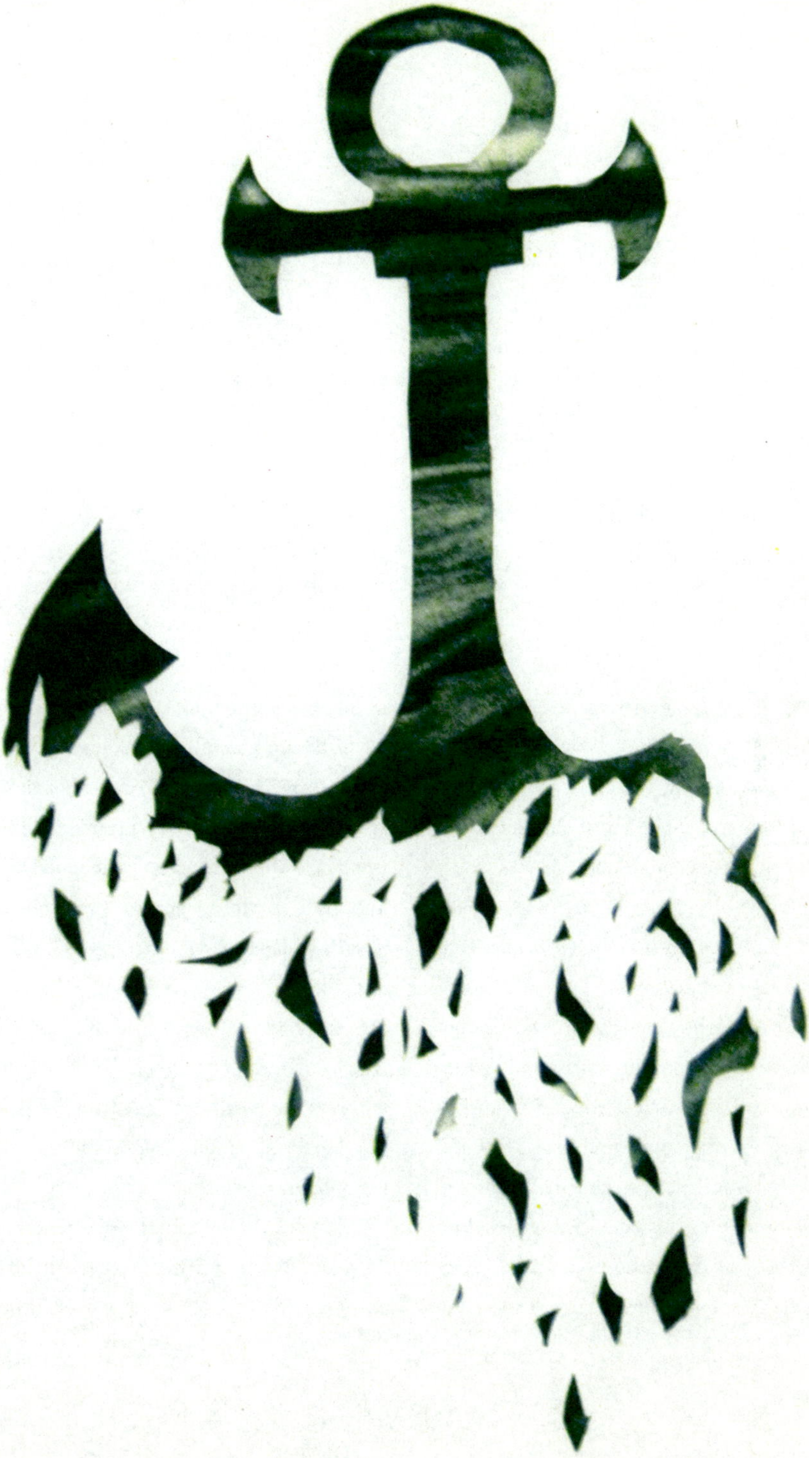

FORMAL WEAR.

WRITTEN BY RUPERT J MUNCK
ILLUSTRATED BY MINA MILK

'How far away the stars seem,
and how far is our first kiss, and ah, how old my heart.'
William Butler Yeats

Time called in sick. Benedict's throat choked dry. Naturally, having no known causes, he hunkered forward, caged his fingers across his face and began to weep. Black. He was black: hands – face – chest and, having woken each morn of the last sixty-two years white, was somewhat taken aback.

Outside April showered against the glazing.

A single bulb, tempering with all the anticipation of a collapsing star, brooded an unspoken light about the bathroom. Benedict – still naked, still old, still black – remained crumpled on the ceramic tiles; his back straightened up from the heel of the bathtub and a hot flush broiling up his spinal column. He ran his vision along the length of his arm. His glare quivered vacantly upon the back of his hands. Light from above him dripped onto his rich black skin. A gleam, a glisten – mimetic glint of sun upon an Italian lake, firstly quenched his pores and then filtered back at him; reluctantly absorbed. He took a moment to incline his head and allowed a smile to flatten across his face. He reached over for some double-quilted toilet tissue, dried his sunken brown eyes and emptied the Northern Line from his nose. He surveyed the remnants upon the tissue. Even his phlegm was black.

Silence: the word subsided to the sound of Tabitha's Audi TT yawning up the driveway. Benedict froze – stopped, still, his eyes blossomed with fear. Quickly unpeeling himself from the ceramic tiles, he darted into the hallway to be greeted by his wife's silhouette on the porch wavering through the stain glassed semicircle upon the top of the door. Straining each nerve ending – stooped, poised – Benedict glued himself in an anticipated stance as he watched Tabitha jangle about for the correct key. A myriad of thoughts: shock – fear – divorce, stumbled through his mind. She might think of me as an intruder, a burglar, rapist, she won't recognise me, panicked Benedict. She would surely attack me. Who wouldn't?

The front door opened.

Entering, Tabitha took one look at the elderly Afro-Caribbean man before her, who just happened to also be utterly naked, ready to pounce on her at any second and, quite casually, in her own time, turned to her right, removed her slightly damp Macintosh and placed her gingham patterned brolly in the bottom of the hat stand.

"Tabs! Tabs!" Benedict spat, rushing towards her outstretching his arms, "It's me, it's me... Look what's happened; I'm black!"

Tabitha bridled as if Benedict had the breath of a math's teacher, flapping him away with her tan lamb nappa driving gloves.

Benedict paused, and then steadied.

He took half a step back. Lowering his confusion into the suggestion of a frown, he studied her pupils: no expansion, no contraction, nothing of the sort.

"Tabs?" he exclaimed again, this time calmer with a frequency of scrutiny. "You *can* see what has happened to me can't you? Look! Look!" he frothed, fervently thrusting his upturned palms into her squawk like features. "My skin's gone all black."

Stepping toe-to-toe, not before perching her gaunt designer glasses on the end of her nose, Tabitha looked him up and down then walked a lap slowly around his body, peering forensically into each crease of his paunches. She stopped in front of him. Lowering her eyes upon him she fished out her bottom lip and shrugged.

"Hmm ... not bad."

"Not bad –"

"Indeed ... not bad. Now run along and put some clothes on," she further communicated with a flick of her driving gloves. "The neighbours shouldn't have to bear witness to you scampering around naked."

"Neighbours?"

"Yes, run along."

"Tabs, I'm fucking black!"

"Don't. Swear. Benedict – it's unbecoming."

"Sorry."

"That's quite alright."

"///"

Benedict dropped his head and scuttled back into the bathroom to fetch his clothes. Half-dressed, he hurriedly appeared in the sitting room.

"Aren't you shocked?"

FORMAL WEAR

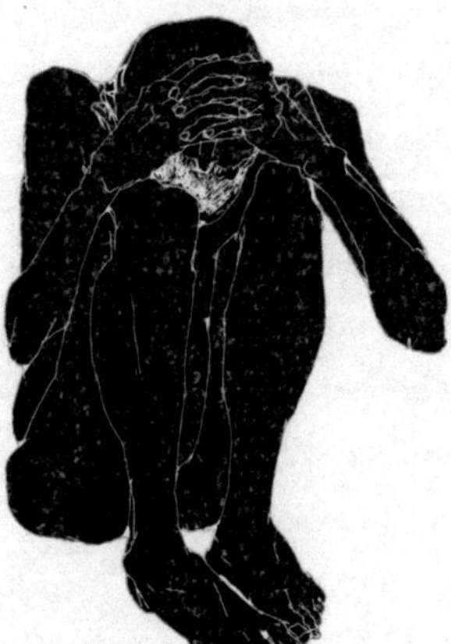

Tabitha laboured a look up from her Blackberry. She squashed her eyes and indulged in a flicker of her head.

"What *are* you prattling on about Ben?"

Benedict thrust his outstretched hands an inch from her face.

"This!"

"As I said before, it's come out rather well don't you think?"

"What?"

"Your new skin. I might add it's patchy in points, especially around the buttock region, but overall the pills have done as advertised and you get the desired effect."

"Skin? Patchy? Pills?" Benedict took a step forward and welcomed the cotton filling at the back of his throat that suppressed his desire to raise his voice. "What . . . what are you on about?"

"Well you haven't quite finished the program yet so you're going to be patchy in parts."

"You mean you . . . *you* had something to do with this?"

"Of course . . . What do you think? You brushed past someone on the tube? or are the dietary repercussions after your impulse last Tuesday to shop somewhere *other* than Waitrose? It was a week program darling. I've been slipping the pills in your wine with supper."

Benedict's face tumbled. His entire body wrinkled like a pricked balloon onto the Chesterfield sofa next to Tabitha. He put his hands on his head, pinching his thumb and forefinger upon each side of his temple. His chest contracted. Lips cracked dry. Slowly he turned round to Tabitha who had begun tapping away on her Blackberry.

"Why?"

"Hmm?"

"Why Tabitha? Why!" he pressed curtly.

She looked up from her smart phone. "Why what? Oh . . . black's back darling. Thought you'd like it. You're always saying how much you like Miles Gillespie or Dizzy whatever his name is. I just wanted to surprise you."

"Black's back? *Sur*prise me?" Benedict mouthed to himself, lumbering his body forward; suddenly paralysed with rage.

Unable to look at Tabitha (or himself) he tossed his vision indiscriminately around the sitting room of the Highgate house the pair of them had owned for the last twenty years. Save a few books — Frege, Proust, Voltaire — a few decorative items he'd never quite had the gall to call antiques and a small painting that might well of considered itself Post-Impressionist, the entire contents — style, decoration — were entirely Tabitha's. Even Betty the dog, a chocolate — male — Labradoodle was hers.

They had met formally in middle school: a draconian system, now superseded by larger primaries designed to numb the anticipation of puberty. Informally, both being from the same fishing town on the Sussex coast, birthdays months apart, the pair of them used to jest that they would have passed each other and exchange smiles in their buggies whilst being wheeled around the local Woolworths. Since this smile, or supposition of a smile, ribbons of time had spooled out together across Brighton, New-York, Manchester and Paris to finally unravel in London, in which Tabitha worked as a brand manager for Fan-Ni, an established Couturier who had recently branched out to handbags and Benedict a professor of Mathematical Logic at Kings College. He remembered Tabitha before she had chosen to iron out the truths of time; so slender, strong yet subtle – her face once floated with a counter-culture buoyancy when even the mere suggestion of a smile would crack warmth across her face. This was before the surgery.

Benedict turned slowly back to Tabitha. His only reaction, in a vain attempt to comprehend the situation and to anoint some frustration, was to arch his right eyebrow and slowly shake his head.

"Is it permanent?"

"Is what?"

"This! This!"

"Oh of course darling. Cost me a pretty penny I might add."

"But I'm too old to be black. What will my students say? And Olive, what will our daughter think of me?"

"Oh . . ." Tabitha's tone lengthened as if speaking solely to the dog. "You're never too old to be black."

She tittered to herself, eyes down still on the phone, now arbitrarily rubbing the back of his shoulders.

"In fact, that happens to be one of their advertising slogans."

Benedict started palpitating and expanded his glare upon his wife.

"Don't frown Benji darling, you'll only deepen your lines."

Benedict was far too riled to question as to how she knew he was frowning.

"But . . . *I've, we've*, got your dinner party *thing* tonight. What am I supposed to do? I can't go like this!"

Tabitha put her Blackberry to one side and finally looked Benedict directly in the eye.

"Don't talk such nonsense; it's black tie darling."

*

Outside there was rain no more. Although it was but 6:00pm, the night had begun to fall; hard. At this moment the hired help, an agreeable looking student with a chrysanthemum of curly blonde hair, came into the drawing room to announce dinner was served. The clutch of guests – politics, fashion, art – all draped in a pursed expression that denoted a perpetual nod of agreement, surveyed each other's reactions, placed their aperitifs on the nearest lace coasters and began to trickle into the dining room. Benedict remained seated in an inchoate state

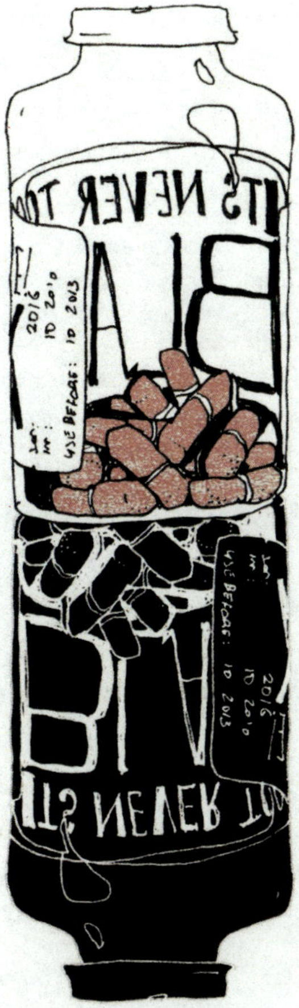
ITS NEVER TO

gazing vacantly at the notes of light tinkering from the chandelier. He set aside his gin and water, drew a Gauloise cigarette (a recent lapse) to his lips, and sparked it with the froth of a Swan match. Since arriving at the party not a word had been spoken about his new blackness. Nothing. Behind his eyes it occurred to him that a new haircut or high-street tailoring would have caused more of a stir. He agreed with himself that he'd calmed since his initial reaction and, moreover, was inclined to believe his wife's suggestion that he looked slightly younger and less like himself. She assured him this was a positive. Naturally he agreed. Benedict despised confrontation.

"Has anyone seen the recent Munck play showing the National?" announced Francis Franco across the table from behind a pair of horn-rim spectacles (a mere prop since having his eyes zapped) and pewter green bowtie.

"Absolute bollocks!" guffed Clark, a paunch solicitor that had acquired the standing amongst his peers of a rare butterfly due to his devotion to cravats.

"Bollocks? The *Standard*'s critic noted that it was..."

"Balderdash."

"Balderdash?"

Clark lent into the table. The wobble of his chin would have typically taken a moment to catch up with the rest of his expression; if he hadn't recently had it hovered from under him.

"If you think *that* kind of louche... all bums and buggary is suitable for National, then I can ensure you; it's not. I mean... what gives him the eligibility to write about class? The man's utterly classless."

"Clueless," added Pandora.

"Clueless/classless – the pair are mutually exclusive my darling."

Benedict shifted in his seat.

He surveyed the diners' reactions. They all seemed to agree with Clark's examination. Although, undertook any reactive expression attached with the least possible fuss. Benedict had seen the play in question: 'Aye! Aye! Capt'n' and felt it a triumph of social satire.

"I thought it substantial, open handed and extremely enjoyable," he felt impelled to meek to his fellow guests.

Benedict's thoughts were passed over with silence. Usually, being from academic stock, (albeit philosophical) his opinions on such matters were nearly always entertained at length. Tabitha shot him a frozen look from across the table. Benedict put this down to her most recent Botox injection. The rest of the diners inclined their heads, coddling slow nods as if preparing to pat a child on the head after performing a bumbled soliloquy from 'Troilus and Cressida.' Almost immediately Benedict could feel himself blushing. He was unsure if this was visible. He retreated back into himself and looked down at his hands resting upon the table. His skin winked back at him.

By the time the main course arrived –

OLD AGE

fresh calf's liver — not a whisper, uttering or even suggestion had been made about his new skin. He looked up at Tabitha. She was sat at the other end of the table draped over Brian. Lypo, tummy tuck — albeit utterly ineffective — Brian was a former broker that liked cars. He liked cars that went *broom*. The cars that went *broom* the loudest he liked the bestest. These were the bestest because they were the fastest. Ferrari were his most favourite of cars that went *broom* the loudest and had owned one once before the crash. Now he collected all of the necessary paraphernalia — key ring, driving shoes, driving mat, branded jacket/baseball cap — everything apart from an actual Ferrari. Nowadays he drove a Ford Mondeo 2.5i Titanium X and, twice weekly, took Tabitha for a spin at the Kings Cross Premier Inn.

Benedict remained quieted.

By the time of dessert — fresh lemon sorbet — he felt himself becoming subsumed in agitation. Mind, he was quite at home with agitation, and seldom unaccustomed to being ignored, more so amongst Tabitha's friends. However, in regards to his recent pigmented circumstance he wondered as to why no-one had thought to ask him why he was suddenly black. They had met him before, on umpteen occasions a few of them. So why the silence? He was half-tempted to broach the subject himself. Not even Tabitha — still gazing endlessly into the gleam of Brian's chemical peel — had thought to mention it to anyone.

"So Benedict," chewed James, a once serviceman who drunk like a pike, smoked like a kipper and claimed (only when broached of course) at the age of fifty-one, fifty-two, his hair was just naturally *that* black: "How's work going?"

"Fine, fine . . ."

"And Olive . . . how's she?"

"Completing her post-graduate at Durham."

"Splendid, and the new suit?"

"Suit?" Benedict almost choked on his sorbet.

"Yes — suit. Tabs tells me it's Fan-NI's new Brut collection."

Benedict looked down at his navy suit.

"Oh . . . yes, um Tabitha picked it out."

James hollowed his cheeks to further extenuate last season's implants and nodded.

"Well it looks like a good cut. It works well with your shirt," he replied, before turning away to a more suitable conversation.

Benedict looked over to Tabitha.

A pang of frustration obliged him to leave the table. He half excused himself, only for the sentence to flop into a coda of mumbling embarrassment. He turned down the hallway and headed for the conservatory. He flopped onto a wicker chair. A silver moonlight illuminated through the window. He lumbered forward. A cigarette and then another was promptly swallowed. Scratching his beard, he informed himself of the current state of his skin.

(1) The law of identity: 'Whatever is, is.'

Yup — still black. Benedict couldn't understand it. He'd yet himself come to grips with the phenomena, however, why so ignored, brushed under the carpet, utterly unspoken? Was it that laissez faire a procedure it had attenuated to Logician's reflection of Metaphysics? Benedict scratched away at his skin as if an unwanted tattoo. He was not that vain as to want to be noticed. The middle or centre of anything — attention, ground, politics — brought him over all queasy. But he was black. Had polite society nothing to say of this? Not of temporality, or something for the weekend. Thanks to his loving wife, it was permanent. If his dinner guests had cared to notice, or at least ask, they would know this. Why was this doomed to silence?

Benedict, now as irked as he could get, felt the urge to storm in there and shout this across the table at the top of his voice. But didn't. Of course he didn't. It was Benedict. Instead, still lurched forward, he began to knead the furrows of his brow with the angle of his index finger. Maybe he was just being boring old Benedict? It occurred to himself. Or the guests were just *that* British? Perhaps he was the one that was not of a normal mind and infinitely changing ones appearance was as normal as brushing ones teeth? Something stirred in his memory that when Tabs had had her first (of four) facelifts, it was passed over unspoken. Not one of her friends mentioned it. Nor he. He wouldn't dare.

He lent back into the small of the chair and edged his fingers into the nape of his neck. From the entrance of the conservatory, still flushed with conversation, Brie Muffin wafted in — silken, oriental print — with a regal face of low-comedy. He'd met her once before but doubted she'd have remembered, especially not now. She perched herself next to Benedict and drew a lean Vogue cigarette complete with silver holder to her lips. Benedict brought the back of his hand to his nose. Her drip of Chanel No.5 did little to mask the odious cling of divorce that lamented from her pores.

"Are you *hyah* for what I think you're *hyah* for?"

'///'

"Your colours," she traced a circle around her face, "Where are they from?" Brie snapped pedagogically.

"Sussex."

Whilst the muscles around her visage visibly struggled with the capacity to mull this over, she sparked her Vogue with a Sterling lighter and leant in closer.

"I slept with a negro man once," she rasped into his right ear through a fist of blue smoke, cleavaging her silicone towards him.

As only Benedict could do, he slowly turned to his right, wrapped his lip around the top of his gum and tossed her a row of teeth. He looked down to his knee. A tall, translucent hand, encrusted with diamonds and visceral veins, had found its way onto his knee.

OLD AGE

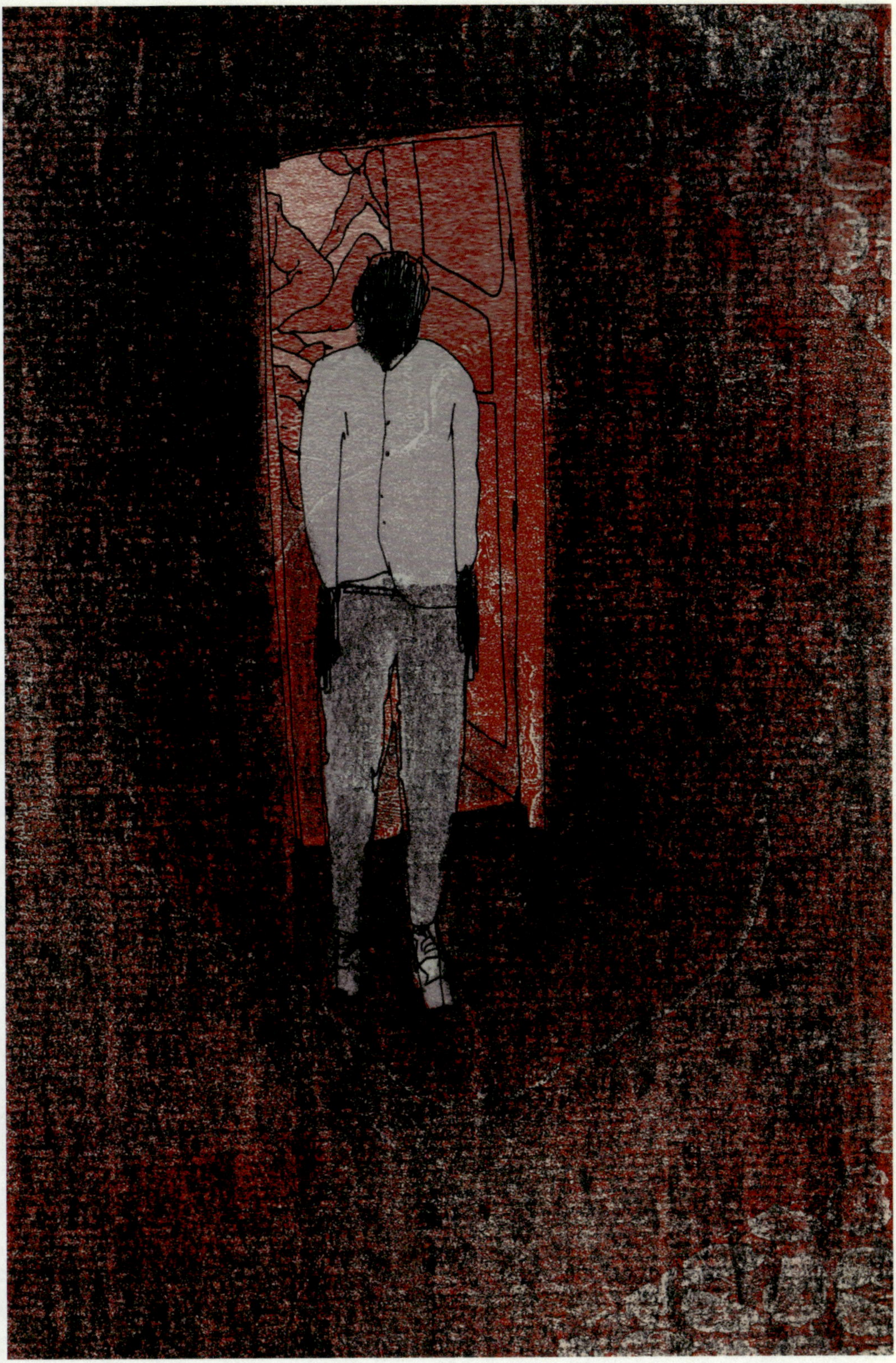

"He was in the Merchant Navy and had a penchant for tying me up."

"Well, I bet he knew some good knots."

Brie lowered her eyes and wrinkled her nose back at Benedict.

"That's none of your concern," she pursed, flicking her ashen hair and turning her back.

Benedict found himself stuck in an absence of motion, halfway between sitting and hunching. Slowly, Brie turned herself back round to face him.

"Samson, *yes* Samson Samsonroy," she indulged through a rather too gluttonous inhalation of her cigarette, "He had lips like rubber buoys and the yokes of his eyes fried when he climaxed."

Benedict's body faintly reclined into the chair.

"It run aground," she exhaled, "the vessel he manned. Somewhere owff the coast of . . . oh, where was it . . . ? I forget where now. But I remember him well." She shrugged. "Well apart from the obvious, it was, well . . . Samson . . . the Negro chap, he didn't have a birthday. Or rather, had never known when he was born. Poor man had no conception of time."

Benedict's expression responded with a faint doubt.

"Yes – I thought it rather queer too."

Brie's tone trailed off in reverie. She turned, flicked a crook of ash into a crystal tray and then turned back to Benedict. Her eyes suddenly curdled. Closer – closer still, she moved in.

"As you know it's *true* what they say."

She nodded suggestively towards Benedict's crotch. Benedict edged away into his shoulders.

"Really – I thought black was slimming?"

Brie thought about this for a moment and then laughed, flirtatiously padding Benedict gently away.

"So . . . I best, I've been I here for some time, so . . ."

"Oh, yes – quite. I'll just finish this," nodding to her cigarette, "and catch you up."

Benedict rose from his seat and made his way back towards the dining room.

"Oh, they've already begun."

"Begun?"

The moons' reflection glistened back off the white of her recently bleached teeth.

"Yes darling, started without you I'm afraid."

Benedict shrugged this off and exited the conservatory.

Through the gleaming parquet floors, passed oval tables hosting framed family moments on the slopes of Val d'Isère, along through the loom of taxidermy and into the hallway, he turned the handle to enter the lounge. It was locked. He rattled at it to open. He pressed his ear against the oak door. Bach – he could make out Bach's 'Air on a G String' and movements from within. He knocked thrice. After an agitated wait, the door was unlocked and Clark's po-face peered through the crack.

"Yes?"

"Hi... erm... can I come in?"

Clark guffawed something into the barrel of his chest and then turned his back to Benedict, leaving the door ajar. Benedict entered to a dim level of lighting reflecting off an unscrupulous amount of writhing, jiggling, rubbing, sweating, naked flesh. The air was dour. A stench of high blood pressure slapped about the room. He squished his eyes and pressed them towards each darkened corner. Bit down on his tongue and then the inside of his mouth. Groan, after eddying groan — he stepped delicately over the pairs of bodies until he located Tabitha in a corner. She was on top of Brian, otherwise engaged. Benedict looked down upon her, the pair too absorbed to notice him. His eyes were drawn to the moles on her cheek dipping in and out of the light. Moles he knew better than the mottle of liver spots on the back of his hand, streets of Paris and Vienna Circle. Moles he'd first traced with his finger before his nineteenth birthday. Moles he'd rested his lips against daily. Moles he'd over the years helped plucked thick sprouting hairs from. Moles he'd named. Moles he'd despised. Moles he'd loved. Moles that were questionably her last remaining original feature. For some reason, they'd all merged into one. One throbbing expansion of blackness; close, weighty — like a duvet of thunderous cloud that beds seamlessly across the night with the specific intention of a weekend lie in. It was starting to envelop him. Devour him like a dream upon a Kansas barn. He had to leave. Turning on his heels, removing his dinner jacket, he allowed it to fall onto the carpet and strolled out of the door. If he was more lucid he'd have blamed the nausea ripping through his nervous system faster than Napoleon from Egypt for his presbyopic darkness. But he wasn't lucid. Black.

Only black.

FORMAL WEAR

LOSING IT.

WRITTEN BY CHARLIE COTTRELL
ILLUSTRATED BY DAN PRESCOTT

Viewed from far away, John Saunders' walk to the library through sheeting rain, bathed in the glow of streetlamp light, had a romantic, old-movie quality. He wore a hat. That could be it. Few older men still wore hats. It gave him a Cary Grant look. Up close the romance died. John's shoes flicked water from the street which soaked into the legs of his trousers and crept up the fabric until it stuck to his shin bones and made them clammy and itchy.

He carried a leather briefcase, though it made him look more awkward than anything. The case contained a notepad and a photograph. It did not contain the one document he needed to forego this whole meeting. If it had, he would have been enjoying the rainstorm from the comfort of his living room with the radio on and the familiar weight of his old dog, Lupin, on his slippered feet.

Inside the library the committee were waiting for him. Since they worked in the library and hadn't had to wade through the rain they looked altogether more tidy, John noticed. There were more of them too. Marianne Carr, the committee leader, was already sitting in the centre seat of five. They were arranged in a line along the back wall of the carpeted area used for children's story time. One chair was placed facing them. John suspected this was for him.

He stood in the doorway, finding comfort in the distracting task of peeling off the layers of damp outerwear, scarf, hat, gloves. Then his hands were too full to take off his coat and he was suddenly awkward again. A cropped-haired girl, the library assistant, came over to him, she was smiling.

"Would you like a cup of tea?" she asked, helping him with his coat and leading him to the cloakroom, "it looks bloody horrible out there."

"Thank you," said John, shoving the scarf and gloves into the pockets of his coat, now hung up neatly thanks to the administrations of the cropped haired girl.

He balanced his hat on the same hook. Rain cascaded to the floor leaving a guilty puddle beneath his things.

Without being shown to it, John sat himself down in the lone seat. The girl brought him his tea. In a babble of small talk and sing-songy voices the rest of the committee took their seats. Women. All of them. It was easy to see that women made John nervous. As she gave her rival a visual pat-down, Marianne concluded that his mother must have been nothing short of formidable. She pictured a lifetime of awkward bachelordom and utter failure with the opposite sex. John sat on his chair, clutching at the handle of his briefcase.

"Thank you for coming Mr Saunders," Marianne began.

The other women fell silent.

"I'm sure we all want to settle this matter before it becomes unpleasant."

John nodded. The women stared; Marianne hardest of all. For all her soft wavy hair and dainty pearls, it was clear she would be no easy foe. She kept John fixed in her eye-line. It was impossible to look back at her. He shifted in his seat and did a little cough. His seat was a hard wooden type, such as you find in schools. For a man of nearly eighty years, it was not at all comfortable.

"You've been part of this library for more than a year now Mr Saunders. We've all come to know you," the other women nodded, "and I hope you would think we've been more to you than just staff. I hope you'd think of us as friends."

John looked at the panel, every one of whom he would cross the road rather than be caught in conversation with.

"Janet helped you with the internet that time . . ." Marianne went on.

John had no idea who Janet was but he remembered a gruelling thirty minutes when he'd come in for an Agatha Christie and been coerced into sitting at a computer while one of the cardigan wearing women told him why, absolutely, he had to send email. John had no idea what email was.

". . . and I've felt we had a special connection. So. I'm sure you will want to be reasonable."

Time slowed down. At a loss for anything to say, John opened the document case and took out the photograph. It was a yellowed image of a weighty old book, biblical in its austerity.

"The thing is . . ." he began.

Marianne looked at the picture.

"Oh, I see how you want to play this," she said, "straight to business is it? Alright then.

Here's business. That book is worth fifty-thousand pounds. Give us fifty-thousand pounds and it's yours. Otherwise it's going to auction."

"I don't have fifty-thousand pounds," said John.

"Then I cannot see why we are still having these conversations," laughed Marianne, "the terms seem more than clear!"

John looked at the photograph again. He had never so much as touched the book. But he had seen it a hundred times.

"Excuse me, Mrs Carr," he said, with a small voice, "but the book is mine."

Marianne laughed as though a wonderful joke had just been shared.

"Mr Saunders. I'm so very sorry."

She didn't sound sorry, John thought.

"If that is the case then please, do show me your Receipt of Loan and I'll give it back to you this instant. In fact, I'll carry it to your house myself! Just show me the receipt and the book is yours. Is it in your bag, is it?"

"No."

"I'm sorry, is it in the bag? Just hand it on over . . ."

John was upset. Awkward.

"No Mrs Carr, you know full well I don't have the receipt."

Marianne's eyes bugged.

"But Mr Saunders, if you don't have the receipt how on Earth can you claim the book is yours?"

"I think my mother lost the Receipt."

"I see. Because as I understand it, your mother donated the book to the library as one of its great benefactors."

"I don't think that's correct."

"Otherwise surely she wouldn't have misplaced such a valuable thing as the Receipt of Loan? I can't say I'm fortunate enough to have many valuable items in my possession, but if I were I'm sure I'd take very good care of them!" laughed Marianne again; that odd, unpleasant laugh.

John looked at the photograph again. Changing tack, Marianne closed her eyes, threw up her hands and sighed. Her body slumped slightly, her perfect posture faltered and she hung her head.

"Mr Saunders," she said, shaking her head slowly, sadly, "John, why do you *hate* the library?"

The other women looked to their leader, then to John, open mouthed. Aghast, John was stumped.

"I don't hate the library," he stuttered, "it's a very nice library."

"Then why, oh why, are you determined to shut us down?"

The lady to the left of Marianne (was she Janet?) put her hand on Marianne's shoulder and stared at John accusatorially.

"I'm not!"

"Without funds the library will close. Without that book, there are no funds. It seems to me that is exactly what you want to do."

"I don't. I don't, but . . ."

"But what John?"

Marianne's vigour seemed replenished.

"Why must you absolutely have this book? Now, after all these decades, why must *you* have it?"

"Because the book is my great-grandfather," said John.

He could tell everyone in the room wanted to laugh. He looked down at his hands, to the picture of the book he had never touched, the book that contained the life story of a man he'd never met, the cover that looked like old aged leather and was embossed with the words, 'The Skine of Simon Horcroft'.

John didn't want to laugh at all.

"I don't have any family Mrs Carr. I haven't for a long time, and, well, as much as I don't care to admit it, I find it difficult to remember things these days."

John went on.

"I barely remember my mother Mrs Key."

The other ladies began to squirm.

"I have some photographs, that's true, but sometimes, sometimes I look at those and it takes me a moment or two to remember who it is I'm looking at."

The teacup shook in John's hand. The cropped haired girl was at his side. She took the cup from him, letting her hand rest on his for just a second. John coughed, and continued.

"So you see, I thought that, if I had the book, I'd at least have something I could read. Even if I forget again, I can read it again and then . . ."

John risked a look at the panel of ladies.

"Then I suppose I will always have an idea of who I am."

It was Marianne's time to shift in her chair.

*

John was not long home when he was startled by a knock at the door; behind it stood the cropped-haired young woman from the library.

"Hello," she said, "It's me."

John stood in the doorway as though dumbstruck.

"Kirsty," she said, touching her hand to her chest.

John nodded.

"May I come in?"

Without waiting for an answer she walked past him into the house. John found her crouched on the floor with Lupin on his back getting a vigorous belly rub, his paws twitching and a big doggy smile on his face.

"I've brought you your hat," said Kirsty.

She pointed to a carrier bag on the floor by her feet.

"Thank you," said John, "do you know, I hadn't even missed it? I've worn it every day for sixty years."

"But to be honest, that was just a crappy excuse to come over. The book. That big old one. I can get you to it."

LOSING IT

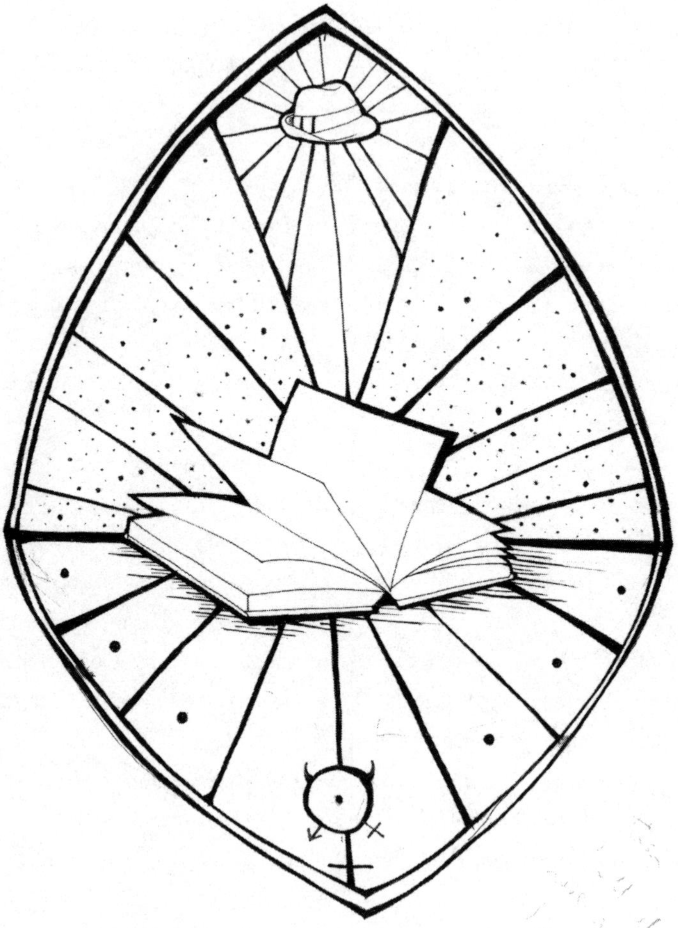

"Steal it?" asked John.

"Are you fucking mad?" said Kirsty, the words left her mouth and landed with as much impact as a slap to his face.

"Excuse me. Thank you for my hat, but . . ."

"Look Mr Saunders. I like you. You seem like a nice old man. Not nice enough for me to risk going to jail for maybe, but you're better than that other lot. I've worked with those old bitches for two years and they don't deserve jack shit. They'll sell that book and never look back. The least I can do is let you have a go at it. We could photocopy it or something."

"But your job? We'd be breaking in."

"Fuck my job. The library's going down the pan. They all are. How much do you think they need to keep it open? It's a shit ton more than fifty grand. The way I see it, I'm fucked anyway. And it sounded like it meant something to you . . . the book or whatever?"

"It's my great-grandfather," said John.

It sounded a little better the second time.

"Right, so listen up, because I've got a plan."

*

Wednesday evening was bridge night. It always had been. It always would be. It involved some light food, heavy gin consumption and bitchy card playing with Marianne. Wednesday evening was also fire drill night. This was a much less interesting affair that involved checking the fire alarms and sensors in every room, dummy-running the rare-books evacuation process and sealing off each individual fire zone before cataloguing every step then setting everything back as it was. At very best it was a two hour job and the bane of every library worker's life, that was, until Kirsty arrived and was gifted the dubious duty of fire marshal.

On Wednesday evening, at 6:02pm, chattering ferociously, Marianne and the ladies left the library; only the occasional clink of their makeup compacts against concealed gin bottles hinting at the revelries ahead.

Kirsty waited. She had told John to stay in the café across the road until he saw the ladies pile into Marianne's car and leave. This would give them three hours with the book before she would have to bring the master keys back to a drunken Marianne. It wasn't a lot of time, but enough to make a start. She had a Dictaphone and a notepad with her. Photocopying would have been easier but something told her that two-hundred year old bindings and a crappy old Canon would not mix.

6:15pm came and went. 6:30pm. At 6:45pm Kirsty began the fire drill, angry, worried and rushing, so that by the time her car pulled up at John's it was 9:30pm and she was sweating like an ox.

"What happened to you?" she cried, as John opened the door, "I waited nearly an hour for you. I thought you'd been hit by a bus."

John looked at her.

"Can I help you?" he said.

He sounded nervous.

"You *could* have helped me by showing up at the library three hours ago," said Kirsty, fluffing up her pixie cut that was now plastered to her forehead.

John looked into the house.

"The library. Oh dear. Are my books overdue? I'm sorry. I sometimes forget things you see. Let me look now..."

"What are you wittering on about?" said Kirsty, "we made a plan..." and then her brain kicked in.

"John, it's me. From the library."

"Delphine?"

"Close enough. Come on, make me a cup of tea and I'll walk you through it."

*

Seven days later, despite several intervening calls, Kirsty was taking no chances. Once she'd bid adieu to Marianne and co. she got in her car, drove to John's house and brought him back to the library. Once he was safely installed in the rare books archive she began to relax. John was less assured.

"Put these on," she said, handing him some lint-free gloves.

He slid his fingers into each hole with diligence, like a surgeon preparing for theatre.

Kirsty lifted down the huge tome and placed it onto a plinth. It smelt as old as time, musky, sweet and ancient. John's hand hovered over the cover as if afraid to touch it.

"Is this the first time you've actually seen this thing?" Kirsty asked.

John nodded.

"We'll I hope your Latin's shit hot. It's no easy read," she said.

"Latin?" asked John.

"Yeah, the whole bloody thing's in Latin. What did you think it'd be in? It's bloody old."

John looked down at the book. He traced his fingers over the embossing that told of its jackets' sinister origin.

"Oh fuck off, don't tell me you don't read Latin?"

Kirsty sighed.

"I thought it was mother tongue to you old farts?"

"Sometimes I forget..."

"Cut that crap," said Kirsty, "names you can forget, Latin endures."

She left the room. A moment later she came back with a Latin dictionary.

"I'm good, but I'm not that good," she said.

John smiled.

With gloved hands, she opened the book to its first page. Passages spilled out across the paper in a cursive hand that swooped and twisted, one word into another. Muddied row upon muddied row of inked lines lay heavy against each of the opaque pages. Kirsty clicked on the Dictaphone and began to read.

"In this, the year of our lord, 1763, we are jury and judge convened to sit over the trial of Simon Horcroft, the accused. Against him are spoken charges of crimes against God and the heavens, against law and his fellow man; of devilry, sorcery and murder of the most foul degrees..."

Kirsty stopped.

"Sounds like a fun fellow," she said, "are you sure you're up for this?"

"I suspected he wasn't an angel," John smiled.

Over the next hour Kirsty uncovered the origins of the book's protagonist while John sat in a chair, his eyes closed, taking it in. A birth into poverty; a family of rogues, petty thieves and itinerants; a catalogue of misdemeanors that seemed to begin as soon as he was old enough to stand on two feet; circus scams, pickpocketing, childhood scraps that grew up into bar-brawls; illegal boxing bouts and an accidental homicide.

After an hour it was time to return to the fire drill. Kirsty rushed through each process and panting, she came back to the archive to collect John. The room was empty. Her first thought was that the book would be gone, but no, there it was, on its plinth. She pulled on her gloves and retuned it to its place in the stacks.

She found John a few minutes later standing in the cloakroom next to the peg where she had hung his hat and his coat after the last committee meeting. He looked confused. Kirsty felt a pull in her chest.

"Come on you old bugger," she said, "let's get you home before you bust us both."

*

They fell into an easy pattern. Every Wednesday Kirsty would wave off the women, rush to her car, pick up John and rush back to the library. Then she'd read for an hour, rush to complete her fire checks, drop John home and deliver the library keys to an unsuspecting, gin-tinged, Marianne. Progress through the book was slow, not least since John's slips in memory often required a recap that ate into every precious minute they had.

"I don't think you want us to get through this," Kirsty joked with the old man. "I think your so called-memory loss is your way of keeping me hanging on."

John would smile. Kirsty suspected she was half-right. She never heard him mention any other friends. Either they had died or moved away, or he had simply forgotten them. She suspected she was his only companion, and truth be told, he was probably hers.

*

LOSING IT

The book itself was fascinating. Even with the fits and starts of her broken Latin and paraphrasing to save time, Kirsty managed to uncover a story of a man who, if the case for the prosecution was true, had been such an unsavoury character it was impossible to imagine any characteristics had been inherited by his aging, awkward progeny.

"You can't cheat fate, John," she said, "listen to this. Your old man had been up for murder before. Says here he was accused of killing and robbing two young girls and only escaped his trial because the judge and jury were shipwrecked in a storm. Lucky fuck. They reckoned he'd used his black arts to kill them off."

She paused and looked at her friend.

"That's not a family hobby is it?"

John chuckled.

Kirsty translated straight from the text.

"'Pity be on him who turns in the face of goodness and the will of God to align with the evil one, for his delights are short lived and the Lord's vengeance eternal. Better for that man, that his mother rip him early from her cursed womb and throw his infant flesh to the dogs of the street . . .' He was a bit Marmite, your Great-grandad."

*

One Wednesday Kirsty arrived at John's house and beeped the horn twice, their secret code. When he didn't emerge she beeped again. Then she parked up and went to knock on his door.

John's face appeared, poking out from behind a curtain. Kirsty waved at him. A little while later the front door opened.

"Come on you old bastard," Kirsty chirped, "I want to find out what horrors your creepy old grandad's been up to."

John stood looking at her, one hand on the door frame, the other holding the latch. He looked terrified.

"John? What's happened?"

Kirsty stepped toward him. Next moment he'd slammed the door but Kirsty was quicker and wedged her booted foot in the jam.

"John? What's going on? It's me, Kirtsy, or Delphine, or whatever you want to call me. Let me in, Please?"

She could feel all the old man's feeble energy trying to push the door closed. He started to cry. Kirsty eased his hand off the latch; she put her own on his shoulder and led him into the house.

The smell hit her the instant she entered the building.

"Oh God, John, what happened?"

John stood, rooted to the spot, weeping. Kirsty advanced through the living room and to the sitting room, sniffing cautiously, trying to locate the origin of the stench. In the kitchen she found it: Lupin, long dead, was decaying in his basket. Kirsty retched.

"When did the dog die?" she asked John.

He wouldn't answer.

"Jesus Christ," She muttered, and headed back to the kitchen to deal with the mess.

She buried the dog in the garden, in a hole as deep as she could manage to dig before that evening's darkness fell. Lupin went into his grave, basket and all. When the deed was done Kirsty returned to John. He was still sitting in the dark, in the living room where she'd left him.

"I've buried him," she said.

"Yes," said John.

He smiled.

"The dog," said Kirsty, "I buried the dog."

"I have a dog?" said John.

Kirsty sat in her car and thumped the steering wheel. Angry tears streamed down her face, huge choking sobs shook her body. When she was calm enough to drive she turned toward Marianne's and returned the unused keys.

*

Next Saturday afternoon, dressed in tennis whites and on her way to the club, Marianne ran into Kirsty on her doorstep.

"So sorry Marianne, I know you're on your way out but I need the library keys," Kirsty explained, "I can't find my fucking pill anywhere. I must have left it in the loos last night."

Marianne winced at Kirsty's language and wondered why she'd ever, ever hired the girl.

"I wouldn't ask Marianne, only, I've got a date tonight and when it comes to condoms he's not the most reliable."

It was enough. Marianne dropped the keys into Kirsty's hand and with a shudder, breezed past her into the car and away.

Half an hour later Kirsty dropped the keys back through Marianne's door. From there she drove directly to work where she used her set of newly cut copies to slip into the library and liberate the skin-bound book.

"Put the kettle on old man," she said when she arrived at John's house, "it's going to be a fucking long one."

It was a race against time, against Marianne, against John's memory; against death. Hour after hour Kirsty translated, surmised and recorded from the ancient book. She recorded to tape after tape. John, in turn, labelled and catalogued each one; placing them in a wooden box that he kept by the cassette player which Kirsty had given him. When he fell asleep in his chair Kirsty read on and labelled the tapes herself. Through Sunday she read until in the early hours of Monday morning they reached the trial proper.

"The defendant claimed to know nothing of the contents of the chest," Kirsty read,

LOSING IT

"though it had been found in his own home, the home where he lived and had lived with his wife and his children, from where he had conducted the business of sorcery; a deed which he has also denied. But we have heard from witnesses in the dozens who watched him conjure daemons, expel spirits into animals and converse with the dead. People of good character have vouched this, as you have heard. So it should be clear to all who love reason that the chest was indeed in the possession of the defendant, and as such, that the contents therin are also of his making and doing.

"The alderman who discovered the chest described its contents as the most heinous, Godless and wicked stuff that man should ever witness. From out of the chest came a stench too powerful to mask, a stench that would bring forth sickness in even the strongest of men. When he forced the lock, the alderman saw at once what he recognised to be a small hand, a hand such as could only belong to a child. On further inspection, such as was dutifully demanded of him, the alderman concluded that there was no arm, nor body attached to the hand, but that the part was alone and severed from the body it had once belonged to. Furthermore, the alderman saw that there were other hands in the chest; other parts too: feet, fingers, ears, the lips and nose part, all severed and heaped upon each other inside the chest. He says that the parts were roughly cut and that some were scored with knife marks, marks such as you might see when blood-letting a fever patient. Hair was in the chest and other parts too, and all these parts were small so as to indicate that they were from the bodies of children; some smaller still, from infants. When asked what he suspected this was, the witness of the alderman was certain as to say that it was the action of a devil worshipper. The parts, he told, were gifts to the devil. When asked if there was anything more, the alderman recorded that parts of these looked to have been marked with teeth. It was as though they had, in fact, been gnawed upon and eaten."

Kirsty paused. John was awake.

"We don't have to read this bit," she said.

John nodded for her to continue.

"On inspection of the house more parts were found, bones too, all small bones such as are the bones of children. These had been hidden and concealed underneath floorboards and in cupboards; more still in the yard, in wooden boxes and under animal skins. As the bones were uncovered the defendant was said to have laughed and called upon Satan. His wife did laugh and his wicked children too, all maddened on their sin laughed . . . and let it be noted, that while we sit here in this trial and while these deeds of grave monstrousness are related, let it be noted that all the while the defendants sat and smiled.

"The coroner report has stated that, in the bones they have found, he could identify more than twenty complete children's bodies and

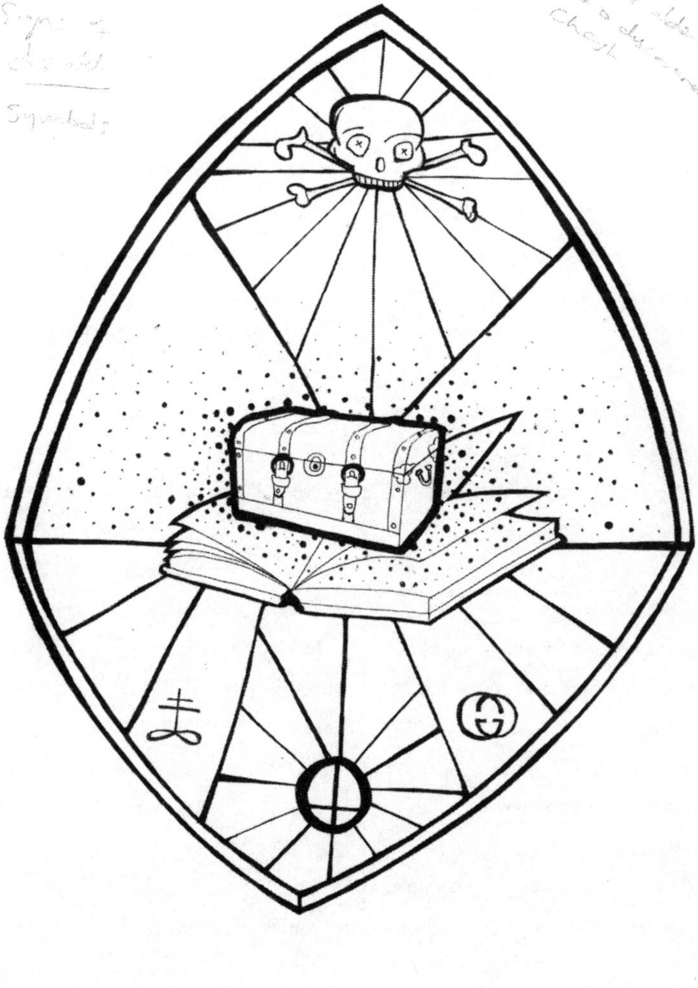

also some parts of other bodies. His conclusion: that these children had been tortured and subject to injury which is beyond the reach of Christian salvation."

Kirsty closed the book and hit stop on the Dictaphone.

"We're done," she said, "agreed?"

The sun was beginning to rise.

"I have to get this back to the library before Marianne gets in anyway."

"I'll come with you," said John, "it's not safe for a young woman alone at this time of night."

Kirsty looked at her withered bodyguard.

"Come on then, Rocky," she said, "get a fucking wiggle on."

They entered the library in darkness, Kirsty leading the way, bearing the weight of the book. John followed behind her, carrying her oversized floral handbag.

"Stay here," she said, leaving him in the safety of the cloakroom.

John's eyes were wide and white in the darkness. After weeks of cursing his dementia Kirsty was desperate for it to kick in now. She hoped with all her heart that next time she saw him he would have forgotten everything she'd read.

She took the hideous tome and crept to the rare books archive. Not until it was slotted back into the gaping space in the stacks and the door locked did she finally feel at ease. Then she and John exited the library and left the past behind them.

*

A phone call ripped Kirsty from her sleep. She had been in bed less than four hours.

"Get here now," screamed Marianne.

Police tape cordoned off the area around the library. Kirsty slipped underneath it and went inside. Marianne was stood at the lending desk talking to an officer, her face puce. When she caught sight of Kirsty her eyes bulged from her head.

"Her!" she yelled, "ask her!"

The book was gone. There were no signs of a break in. Kirsty reached into her handbag, into her purse. The copied keys had been taken.

Kirsty drove at break-neck speed to John's house and banged on the door. She bent down and shouted through the letterbox. The door swung open as she leaned against it. Inside, not a trace of the man remained. Kirsty's brain raced as she tried to find excuses but her gut told her everything. He had stripped the house of furniture, fittings, anything that could have carried a fingerprint. He and the book had vanished.

A plume of smoke rose from the garden, from where, over Lupin's grave, a pile of books and clothes and a Cary Grant-style hat were consumed by the flames of a bonfire.

air
fire
water
earth

esoteric sigils
death

THE DASH IN-BETWEEN.

WRITTEN BY CLAIRE FLETCHER
ILLUSTRATED BY TIM GREAVES

The final story woven by the greatest storyteller I have ever known began in the last days of his life. As a child I had revelled in the stories told by my grandfather, tales of extraordinary experience, intricate in detail and enveloped in magic. With my youth, I would listen intently to this unfeasibly old man. Words dripped from his mouth as he spoke, splashing colour on the walls around us, sailing my mind's eye to places and people I had never seen. I felt incredulous that these stories had come from his actual life. Despite the hardship he had encountered, of which I had been told about by my parents, and despite the horror of war he had experienced, his tales were always bursting with wonder and daring. He would laugh his toothless and musical belly laugh and it would echo like my child's voice under a wishing bridge. I could hear his strength as I sat there listening, and it enthralled me. It was as if he never began or finished a story, the words were on his tongue as soon as we met and they carried on in his eyes even after I kissed him goodbye. Like the tunes he would hum under his breath as he worked, there was no 'Once upon a time', there was never a 'The End'. The magic of his words streamed into my own childhood stories, my play, the imaginings of my far away future which I felt to fill with the same sense of wonder as I did each passing moment. I yearned to experience all that would come my way. I was a fearless child, and as I looked at his wrinkled skin, his toothless grin and his shiny eyes, it felt like I had forever.

Yet as I grew, the world began to swallow me whole and eventually I sank. I was consumed by a wholly different world to that of my childhood; a world so small, so tight and full of habit. Hope no longer filled my eyes with wonder. Gone was the elasticity of days, the possibility of chance, replaced by the sense of an impending future, of my movements being slowed, as if under water. I built bridges from each moment to find the next, I no longer felt a smile spread from my stomach. I no longer saw my grandfather. He now belonged to the past and to the future, as did I.

Unbeknown to me, time marched to its own tune. My limbs lengthened and my eyes became fixed, I didn't give a thought to where my grandfather's stories were going now that my ears had stopped listening. My life had become a set of trials I needed to work through; dates, deadlines, duty.

So I received the message of his shortening days on that cold, pale morning in the same way I received all calls of duty in my adult life. I was to visit him, to pay my respects, to say my goodbyes, to do what was expected.

I began my journey back to the place of my family. It took me a full day to come within reach of my grandfather's house. The hours were growing smaller and the sun had fully lowered. I came to my place of rest for that evening, a lodge house run by a kindly gentleman, and after carrying out my evening's ablutions I fell to a long sleep.

*

Upon waking, washing and breakfasting, I prepared myself for the final part of my journey. I caught sight of myself in the hallway mirror as I put on my coat. My reflection brought to mind our photos that had decorated the walls of my grandfather's house throughout my childhood. Staring at the face staring back at me, I wondered whether he would even recognise me. I had been told that my grandfather's memory had forsaken him and that he now lived in the one room of his house, and that he had taken to guarding it, almost as if it was the last outpost of the present. He could become confused, angry, he would shout into the air as if throwing stones at the sky. I swallowed hard upon remembering this and continued out towards the house of my past.

Surrounded and chilled by this new day's pale morning light, I set off. As I drew nearer, the roads were lined with trees taller than I remembered, their leaves few; the ones left, breathing the last of the oxygen in the cold air. I shivered and pulled my coat tighter around me. Birds sang their song in the tall branches, a familiar melody which brought back to me the memory of when, small in my clothes, I would wander the lanes whistling back to them. I felt my stomach warmly vibrate and forced my eyes back forward. Watching my breath as I travelled, I saw great plumes form in front of my opened mouth. Through my

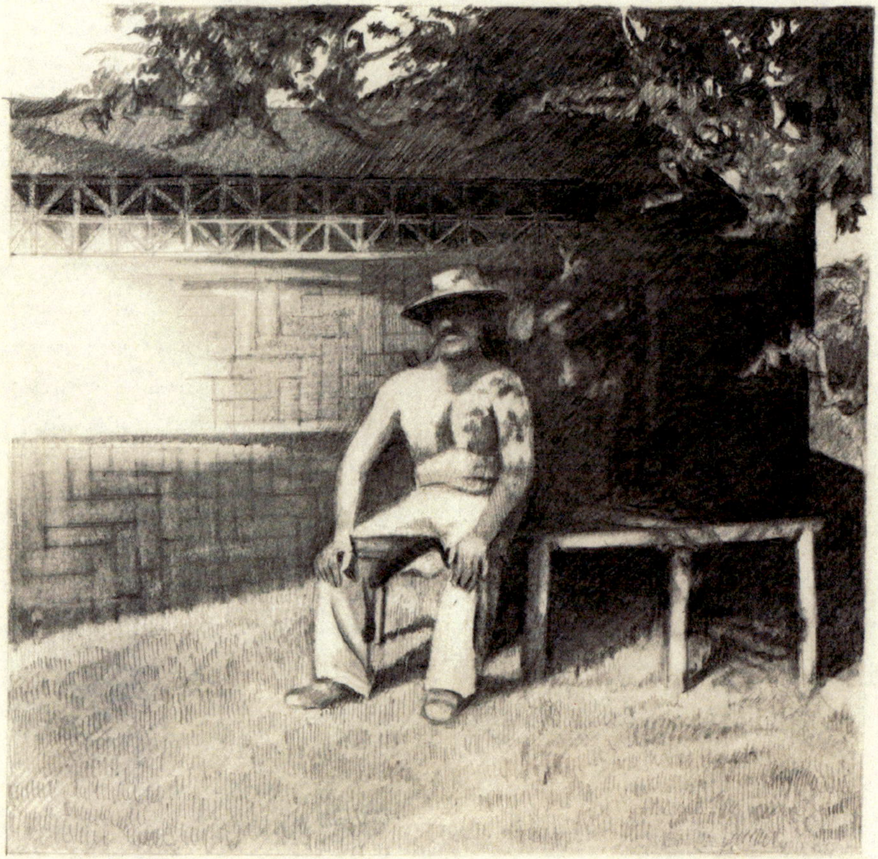

narrowed eyes I saw the boundary road of my childhood world. It was the furthest place where I, chest full of my own daring, would brave to go. As I walked down the lane I looked across the green and yellow fields that spread away from me on both sides, their colours made misty in the winter's air. As I looked, wisps of memory started to rise from the ground, as did the steam from my lips and they began dancing before my eyes, stinging them as they did so. It felt strange that these were happenings I was once inside of and I dwelt on the disconnected feeling of remembering them from the outside, as if they were stories I had long forgotten.

I arrived at the door of my grandfather's house and knocked. My eyes trailed the familiar lines in the wooden door and I waited. A smiling face met me as the door creaked open. It beckoned me inside. As I stood in the hallway the old musty smell of the walls began to rise through me. It reminded me of burying my head into my grandfather's shoulder as I hugged him, curled up small on his lap. I felt my vision swim. The kindly face returned and introduced herself as Jean, my grandfather's nurse. I smiled and upon naming myself she exclaimed that he had been long awaiting my arrival.

She took me through to my grandfather's living room. My eyes turned the corner behind the door as she left and there was my grandfather, stood leaning over a makeshift bed next to the fireplace.

"Hello Granddad," I said.

"Yes, hello," came his crackled reply without his looking up.

His frail hands worked as he stooped. I looked at the bed and saw that placed all over its surface were small piles of meticulously folded clothes. As I watched from the doorway he took a jumper from one neat pile and spread it flat in an empty space on the bed. He then began to delicately fold it. He stretched out the empty limbs and bent them, he then folded the middle and placed it on the top of another pile. He pulled back his arms and snorted in approval, before straightening his back to look at me. I looked at him. His dewy eyes shone through his thick rimmed glasses which now seemed so large on his pallid and fragile face. His once rotund paunch of a belly, which seemed only kept in by the braces that used to stretch aside it, had disappeared and his braces seemed to dangle, forlorn for a long lost friend. I smiled weakly as I pecked a kiss on his cheek. He turned his head toward his chair and his body dutifully followed slowly behind. I stood there as he began to shuffle over to it. He sat down in a crumble. I hastened over to the sofa positioned opposite and awkwardly took up the situation of my childhood, facing him and the wall behind him. I felt my eyes widen as they once did, and it hurt. There remained on the wall the echoes of the years, decorated with photos and pictures of my family at various times in our lives, frozen droplets in time. My stomach felt warm. I asked him how he felt.

"Can't complain," came his reply.

Jean returned with tea. As she placed the tray down with a jangle and ruffled a cushion for my grandfather, I glanced around the room. Every one of my grandfather's things seemed to have been placed with great care and precision. My eyes followed the rows of ornaments and picture frames in particular positions, even the well wishing cards were sited specifically in a symmetrical pattern on the mantelpiece. On noticing my observation, Jean spoke.

"Yes, your granddad does like his things just so. This is his cabin. He likes to keep it ship shape."

I hummed a response; his beloved navy. She left and my eyes fell to the mantelpiece. It was full of my grandfather's favourite story books. I smiled, got up and walked over to it. My fingers trailed over the tops of the books and came to rest on a familiar burnt orange cover. Although mostly my grandfather used to tell me stories, 'The Scrimstone Circus Gospel' was one of the stories that he used to read to me. I picked it up and turned to face my grandfather.

"I remember this one Granddad."

He was staring out the window, he seemed far away. I followed his gaze and my eyes were enveloped in the ashen afternoon sky. I took my seat again and began leafing through the book. Then I came to it; the ship wreck. Warm bubbles filled my chest as I recollected how my grandfather would diverge from this point in the story. Hurried on by my youth, excited to hear of danger, I would urge him to tell me of how he sailed on two ships that sank in the war. Before I knew it, I was reading:

"The day my trial was to begin, there was a storm. I watched it brew from nowhere. Like the arrival of a whale from the deep. Here's something: the ship sank. She went down with stocks and stores and the judge and all twelve of the jurymen sent to try me. The waves ate them like ship's crackers, without delight or comment but only the necessity of sustenance. I watched them sink. The sea closed over them like history."

I looked up. A tear had added to the dew in my grandfather's eye. I felt gravity in his breathing.

"Time . . ." he began, and in an exhalation he continued, ". . . suddenly I have become my own history. The ship coming won't sink before it gets to me this time . . ." he trailed off, eyes sad.

I could tell he was tired. The book slid from my hands and on to my lap. He was still staring out the window. I felt water gather at the bottom of my eyes and then Jean came back with a blanket.

"He's tired today deary," she said with

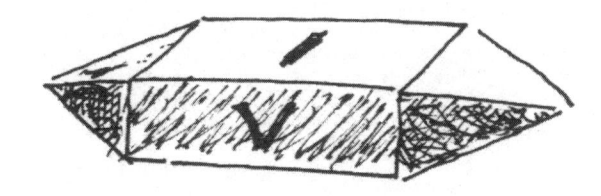

concern, "I think he needs to sleep now," and leaning to feel his wrist pulse she looked at her watch.

My grandfather closed his eyes.

"I'll show you to the bedroom," she said as she stood up and I followed her upstairs.

"He'll sleep 'til morning now my love," said Jean, as I laid to rest my travelling bag in the bottom of the wardrobe, "it's not one of his good days."

The following hours of that day fell away from me as I headed outside and wandered the lanes of my childhood. Although tentative at first, the tide of the past was too strong and I was immersed in the fjords of memory around every corner. My sturdy present shrank, I felt returned to a wide eyed state and washes of hope and possibility flooded back into my body. With my senses swimming in the past, it was nightfall when I returned to the house. The silence of the countryside hummed in my ears and I stepped back through the front door. I walked slowly into the still space of the hallway. I stood looking. The room had not changed a bit. My grandfather moved all around, his life beat met my eyes as I looked one by one at the beautiful wooden things he had carved and made with his hands. I felt that same sense of wonder fill my eyes as I ran my hands over the polished wood, over the spinning wheel and three legged chair, the rocking horse, the tables. As a child I couldn't understand how it was possible that he had made these things. They seemed so perfect, as though they had sprung into existence. My thoughts were mixing with the smooth wood under my fingers and I stopped and sighed. I felt uneasy to see how time had petrified him, so animated he had been when I was a child. I came to the mirror and felt a jolt of alarm tingle down my spine as I saw my reflection. I had my granddad's eyes. But who was this person looking back at me? It was as though I hadn't seen myself before. Shivering, I looked away and began to climb the stairs to bed.

I awoke to a loud commotion coming from down stairs. I dressed myself and followed the noise. As I came into the hallway I saw Jean hustle through the closing door carrying a tray of medicines and a glass of water.

"Oh, good morning dear. Your granddad had a very bad night. He has an infection and we've had to put him on oxygen and a drip."

She placed the tray down on a side table. I asked if I could go in and see him.

"Give him a little time, he was quite upset but the drip will make him feel more comfortable soon. Get yourself washed and I'll make you a little breakfast."

I dutifully nodded, thanked her and returned upstairs to carry out her instructions.

I sat in the kitchen eating my breakfast next to the window, through which the winter's sun streamed. It was a perfect winter's day, the sun was held in a pure blue sky. I smiled as I remembered that most of my childhood visits to see granddad had taken place on days like these. Bundled up in warm clothing we'd walk the fields. Eyes wide and laughing, our breath warm in our throats and turning to steam as it met the cold air. Then, as the day was dying, we'd return to the house and huddle around the fire, its warmth prickling our skin as we thawed. There we would stay in our warmed cocoon until darkness fell. I would listen intently as my granddad wove stories, painting pictures in my eyes, his full and mischievous laugh making me giggle, until my eyes fell heavily and I would have to be carried to bed. Jean's footsteps broke my reverie.

"You can go in and see him when you like my love, he's comfortable now and he's asking for you. I've called your father to let him know and the rest of the family will be coming tomorrow."

I must have looked shocked as she placed her hand on mine. I felt the warmth of her skin on mine replace the cold air of the room and her voice softly continued.

"You know he's strong your granddad, he'll wait for them."

My granddad was in bed when I walked through the door. He was lying down with tubes running from his nose and arm.

"Morning Granddad," I said, softly.

He smiled slowly and beckoned me to sit on the chair next to his bed. I sat. I took his hand in mine. It felt so cold. He lay still with that same far away look in his eyes.

"Tell me your stories," he asked breathlessly.

My mind raced. I dutifully opened my mouth as if to begin, but I felt no words come. Instead I felt a dry, burning sensation close up my throat and I swallowed deeply. Tears sprang to my eyes and I felt a cold, heavy weight of emptiness flood my chest. Breathing hard, I let go of his hand and jumped up. I walked over to the window and starred out, my eyes searching disbelievingly. As my vision settled I saw that the winter's mist still clung to the fields and blurred my vision of the horizon. I had nothing to tell, nothing to offer him. The cold sun shone through my emptiness, white light revealing to me my barren self. I stood there and implored my mind to divulge meaning to me. Silence. I felt the cold white light fill my senses and steady my breathing. I returned to my chair, defeated I sank into it.

I sat with him all of that day, spooning his food, adjusting his pillows, reading stories from his favourite books. Just as the day's light was dimming through the window, I reached over to flatten his crumpled hair. His eyes caught mine, suddenly focussed. I breathed in.

"Are you scared Granddad..?" I asked him, quietly.

"No," he whispered, as fearlessly as I always remember him, eyes at once shiny and determined. "On my gravestone will be my birth date, my death date and a dash in-between. We all would do best to remember that dash in-between..." his voice trailed off, coughing.

He lay his head back down on his pillow and I breathed out. I felt my scalp prickle with heat. The time for him to sleep had come. I went to pull the curtains closed and he whispered weakly.

"No, leave them."

I pulled his blanket up around his arms and kissed his grey forehead.

"The dash in-between," I whispered.

My granddad slipped into a coma under the dark of the sky that night. The next morning my family arrived and we stayed at his bedside all day. Throughout the hushed conversations, Jean monitored his drip feed and vital signs regularly.

"He's not long now," she whispered to me.

The night time came again and the room was bathed in alabaster. We were all ushered to our beds and the house fell from concerned quiet into the silence of stone. My granddad passed away that night. In the morning I saw a room of sad eyes before me as I sat in my granddad's chair. My hands became warm as I rubbed them on the chair arms and I felt a smile flood through my body with the knowing that his hands had rested there so many times.

The stories of my granddad's life were told one by one at his funeral. Many I had heard him

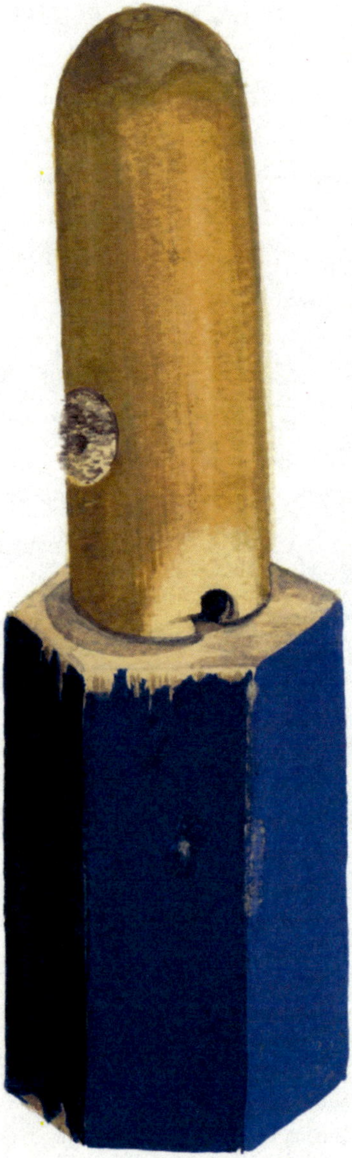

tell before, some I hadn't. I felt the lifting of a stone's weight slowly leave my chest. A sense of lightness spread through me, for I realised that I was listening to them in just the same way as I had done in my childhood. This sense had been warming in my stomach those last few days. The heat had risen into my throat. Each tear expanded into the hope from each story as it fell down my cheek. The past flooded through me and I knew; it was my time now, my dash in-between.

Looking up, with my granddad's eyes as my own, I saw the sky half open with hope.

TWILIGHT'S LAST GLEAMING.

WRITTEN BY ALEXANDER ASPINALL
ILLUSTRATED BY TOM HARRIS

Twilight's last gleaming;
Deep blue echoes of what we knew,
With no twinkle for regret,
Knowing days were spent with you.

OCEAN.

WRITTEN BY SORANA SANTOS
ILLUSTRATED BY KAITLIN BECKETT

When from that depth where I revealed this life, my crest,
And from that vantage point there I discerned that hymn,

An echo tumbled slowly and I was undressed,
Disrobed, my nakedness fixed its concern with Him.

And follow . . . how I followed! Like the rocket's tail!
Sparkling, effervescent, down, as sterns did sing,

That sailor who could catch the wind without a sail,
In tides that drew us under and spurned us within.

The storms that broke the surface when our currents crossed,
The nights I drew back deepest – when I learned to swim –

Forged a stronger wave from out those lowest troughs,
That left no stone unturned that was not turned for Him.

Yet shallow! How so shallow are His ripples cast?
The depths at which He coasts have been adjourned by Him.

OLD AGE

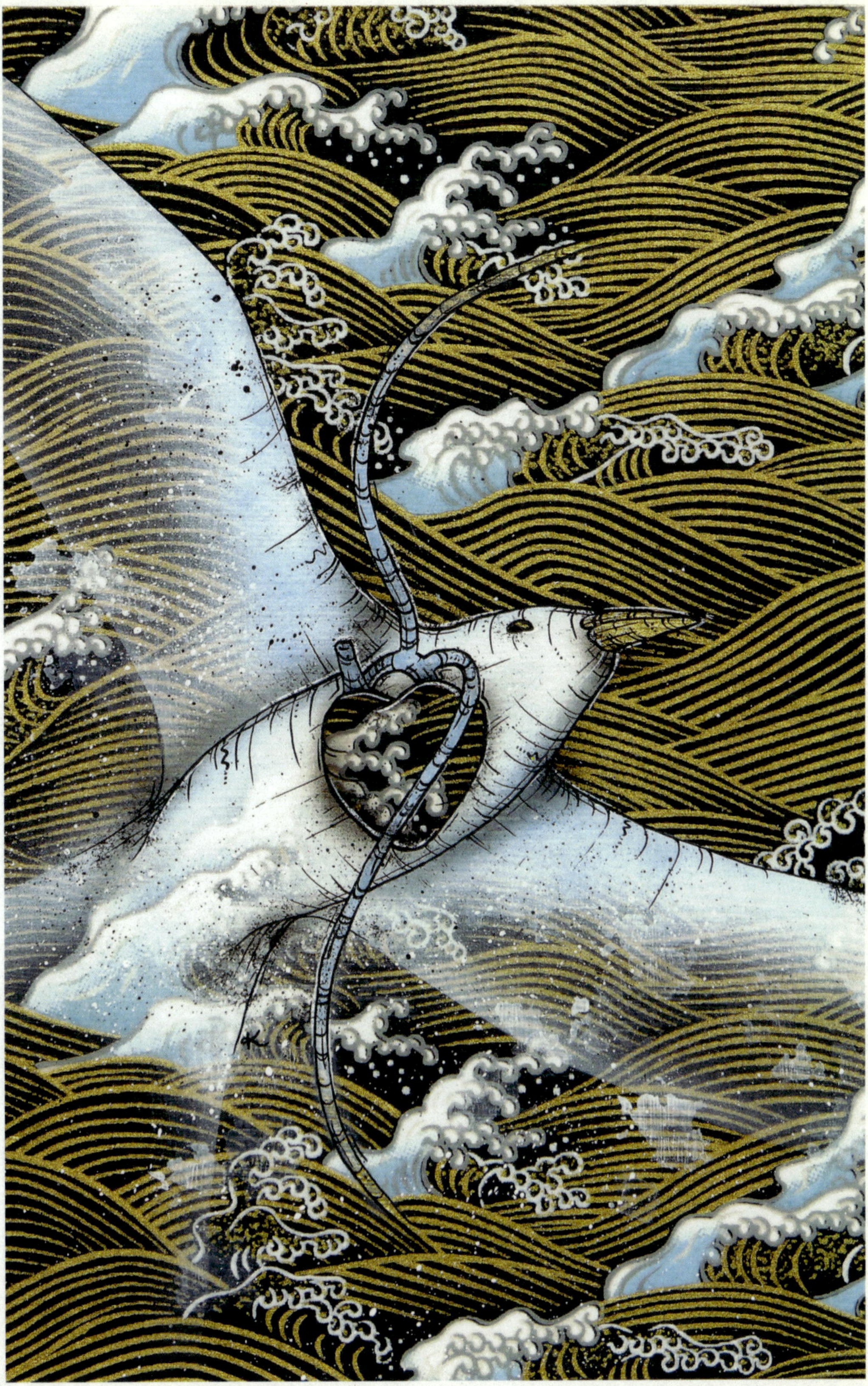

That is not His mascot that sits atop His mast,
Now I, a vessel, have been overturned by Him.

To sink with shadows to the depths, or reappear?
No blaze of glory roared that did not burn for Him.

But I am – and so exist – as salt and tears,
In ebbing and in flow I only yearn for Him.

So wallow . . . how I wallowed in those haunted pools,
Whilst seagulls swooped and swerved and sang nocturnes for Him,

And I lapped softly at the rocks for molecules,
Of that wave broken too soon, once more to turn to Him.

Not consecrated with the wearing of a ring,
But celebrated with the sacred urn and hymn,

When seers stargaze to the depths of the ocean,
And mariners cast good eyes on Saturnine rings,

And even swallows fly that they may mate and thaw,
And man makes miracles that show us worm with limb,

Yet never was there wave that could remain ashore,
And broken now, once more, I will return to Him.

OLD AGE

THE FIRES.

WRITTEN BY LIZ ADAMS
ILLUSTRATED BY DANIEL CHIDGEY

Age of buildings & the new wash of flames
that guzzles them brick is not so unlike
the human body then all matter corroding the fire
is unstoppable reaching across dreams
in this city we love love love. Sob
in the next room — old car in the drive
paint burning off to leave a white skeleton
helicopter sirens twirl up from
clouds cough cough to the stars this night
hugging the buildings at first light.

OLD AGE

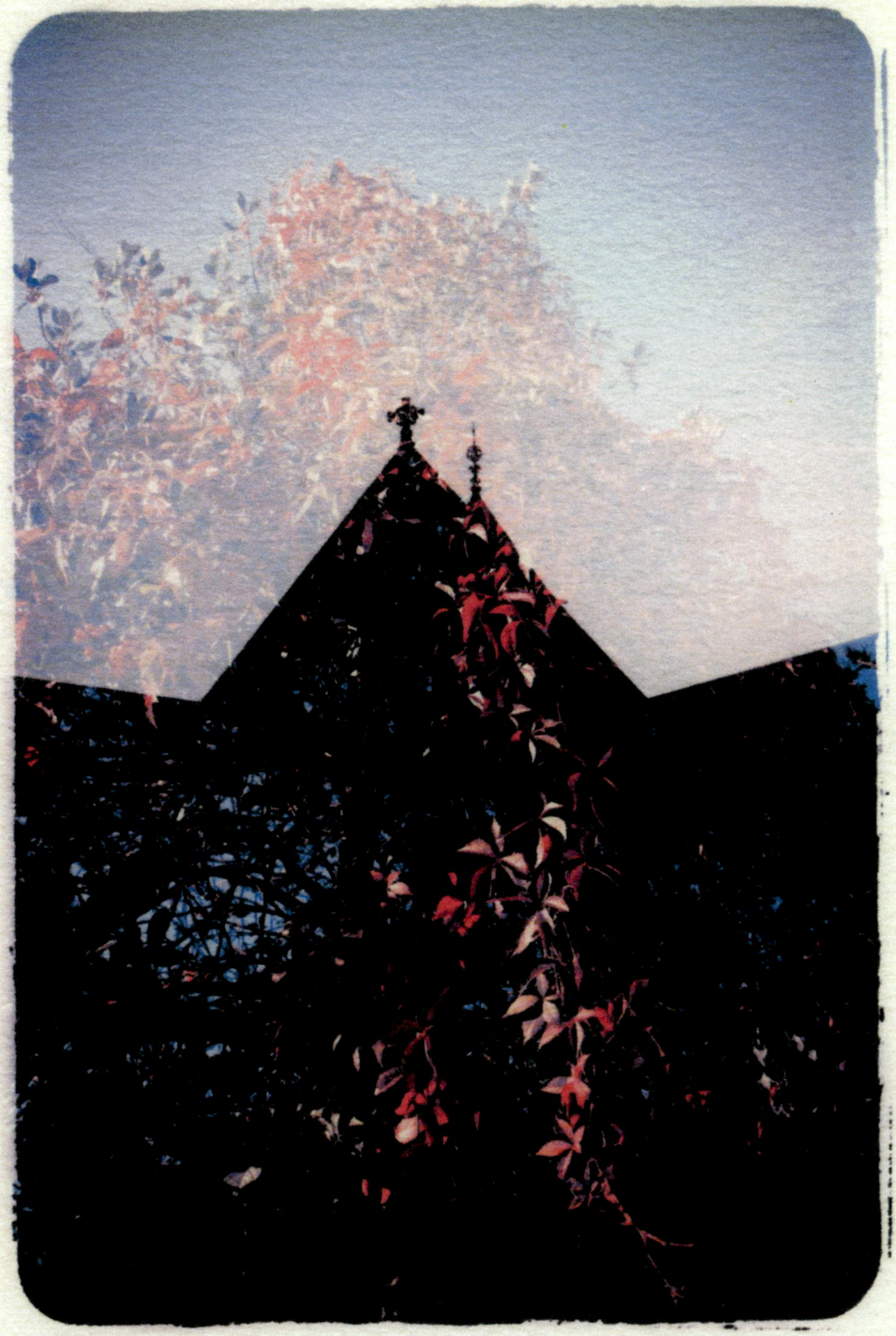

BIOGRAPHIES OF CONTRIBUTORS.

TOM HIRONS

Tom Hirons is a storyteller and acupuncturist living on the edge of Dartmoor. He also makes masks, as Smickelgrim, and leads occasional wilderness rites of passage groups. Sometimes, he writes it down. His written work also appears in issues of Earthlines and Dark Mountain.

RIMA STAINES

Rima Staines is an artist using paint, wood, word, music, animation, clock-making, puppetry and story to attempt to build a gate through the hedge that grows along the boundary between this world and that. Her gate-building has been a lifelong pursuit, and she hopes to have perhaps propped aside even one spiked loop of bramble (leaving a chink just big enough for a mud-kneeling, trusting eye to glimpse the beauty there beyond), before she goes through herself.

Rima was born in London in 1979 to a family of artists and has always been stubborn about living the things that make her heart sing. She travelled for a year and a day in a hand-built wooden house on wheels to a village on the edge of Dartmoor where she now lives in an old cottage on top of a hill with her beloved, Tom Hirons, and their otherworldly lurcher.

Rima's inspirations are too innumerable to name, but a selection from the bottomless list might include the world and language of folktale; the faces of the people who pass her on the street; the folk music and art of Old Europe and beyond; peasant and nomadic living; magics of every feather; wilderness and plant-lore; the margins of thought, experience, community and spirituality; and the beauty in otherness.

Crumbs fall from Rima's threadbare coat pockets as she travels, and can be found collected here (intothehermitage.blogspot.com), where you may join the caravan. Otherwise you can wander through the rooms of her Hermitage (the-hermitage.org.uk), buy from her emporium (the-hermitage.etsy.com), or peer, bewildered, at her timepieces (onceuponoclock.com).

HANNAH STEPHENSON

Hannah Stephenson is a poet, editor, instructor, and singer-songwriter living in Columbus, Ohio. Hannah earned her MA in English from The Ohio State University in 2006, and her poems have appeared recently in places like: Contrary, MAYDAY, qarrtsiluni, Huffington Post, The Nervous Breakdown, and Fiddleblack. She is the founder of Paging Columbus!, a literary arts monthly event series. You can visit her daily poetry site, The Storialist, at www.thestorialist.com.

PAUL BLOOM

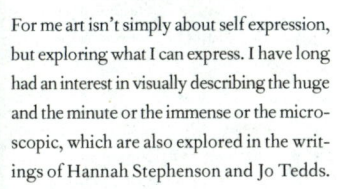

For me art isn't simply about self expression, but exploring what I can express. I have long had an interest in visually describing the huge and the minute or the immense or the microscopic, which are also explored in the writings of Hannah Stephenson and Jo Tedds.

As individuals we experience extremes in our lives and through our interactions with people and nature we discover, adapt and learn. Hannah Stephenson's poem is personal and intimate, whilst Joanne Tedds' short story depicts a few solitary experiences in a wider bleak world.

A long time ago I set about producing work inspired by 'The realization of an event'. I was fascinated by exploring the descriptive movements in art; kinetic art, and the ways that movement can 'mime' certain emotions and ideas (literal movement or representation). I was particularly interested in the notion that a single monumental but personal event could be captured and described in this way. So I built kinetic sculpture and kinetic jewellery, using moving parts and translucency to hide then reveal hidden events, almost like a burlesque dance. My working drawings planned out these pieces, but I soon found an inherent hidden aspect to drawings which goes beyond sculptural depiction, revealing moments of mystery and drama. A drawing can show a particular moment in time, caught in the middle of an event, questioning 'what could happen or what has happened'.

My drawings are intended as both beautiful and sinister, and often in good humour. They are unsettling, mysterious and distorted, as are our dreams. I use Biro which is a mundane every day tool that can achieve a high level of contrast and subtlety, far beyond its logographical design.

Paul Graduated from an MA in silversmithing at London Guild Hall in 2002. He has been a designer/maker since 1995, and a teacher since 2003.

ELIZA GREGORY

Beverley-born musician and writer, Eliza Gregory, lives in London. Fresh from school in York, she migrated south and cut her teeth as a musician (vocals/bass/guitar) in UK DIY hardcore, doom and metal bands, before entering education at Kellogg and Ruskin Colleges, Oxford.

2011-12 saw a hiatus from music to complete an MA at Goldsmiths College with a focus on poetry. Projects over the past year included writing in collaboration with the Royal Philharmonic Society, curating noise and poetry nights at V22 for This is DIY collective, work published in the latest (26th) Highgate Poets anthology, releasing a record with Necro Deathmort on Distraction Records, and moonlighting with various other bands both live and on record.

Eliza has written numerous songs, short stories and poems and is currently completing several volumes of poetry and music. All of which are to be published/released as part of disparate projects over the course of 2013.

STACIE WITHERS

Stacie Withers began writing so she could be like her idol, Lynda Day. When this showed itself to be the pipe dream it had been all along, she switched to poetry, because it's good for the digestion. Stacie says she writes, mainly, so she doesn't have to talk to people. After studying Creative Writing at BSU, where she wrote for and edited the now discontinued 'Pegasus' zine, and went on to complete post graduate studies in Library Management at Northumbria University, which indulged her twin passions for libraries and promoting open access to literature. Her work often focuses on themes of decay and the passage of time, although her experiences of motherhood have also influenced her work over recent years, and she explores the implications of each of these ideas within her poetry and short fiction. She has written articles for various online publications and is also author of a 'mummy blog', focusing on her experiences parenting a child with ASD. She lives in the Wiltshire countryside and eats far too many biscuits.

CLAUD FORSBREY

Born 1987, Claud is a multi-disciplinary artist and designer, with a Fine Art Degree from the University for the Creative Arts.

Her work is predominantly pattern based, geometrically inspired and influenced mainly by the indigenous cultures of South America, Egypt, and tribal Africa.

She is additionally inspired by fashion, nature, art deco, and astronomy. Her art has simultaneously been described as semi-figurative and semi-abstract; it is always striking, and she has a playful way of using colours, which – whilst often reminiscent of childhood and innocence – also suggest a mature understanding of the wider world.

"When I draw, I never think – I just draw; for me it's like meditation. The end product is nearly always a result of what I've absorbed, without realising."

All Claud's pieces are hand drawn, and sometimes collaged together on computer. Her work has been exhibited at the Milkwood Gallery in Cardiff, on a Trans-Siberian moving exhibition between Moscow and Beijing, and at Latitude Festival.

She has also featured in publications such as *Yuck n' Yum*, *Rojo & Garabato*, and *Blanket*. Commissions for design include LeJu (jewellery company) where she produced illustrations for lasering onto jewellery, Supersweet online illustrations, and The Russian East London nightclub exterior mural.

Check out Claud's stuff at: http://claudforsbrey.tumblr.com/

RAHIMA FITZWILLIAM HALL

Currently living in Brixton, South London, Rahima can sometimes be found writing poetry, fiction and non-fiction. While she writes she is playfully exploring the relationships between nature, place, people, and contemporary society as well as our relationship to language itself. Her work has been previously described as enigmatic, perceptive, still, and naively powerful.

In the past Rahima has been a stand-up poet at various London venues and events and co-founded stand-up poetry collective 'Littlest Birds', which hosted collaborative performance nights such as 'A Poem That Isn't a Poem But is a Poem' at the Poetry Cafe.

Rahima has several writing projects in development including a collection of reflections on her childhood in Jeddah Saudi Arabia, an enquiry into the role of 'story' in our current social and economic circumstances and continued collaboration with the Lazy Gramophone collective.

TOM HARRIS

Tom left his degree in Animation with a 2:2, which is fine. However, bereft of the facilities of college and armed only with what was at best a useless computer, some three years later Tom reached an epiphany. He realised that staring blankly at a screen while you waited for the technology to work its ever more protracted 'magic' was just too tedious, a bit like waiting for Chris Tarrant to reveal an answer on Millionaire. Plus his PC had developed the lifespan of a Fruit Fly.

So Tom turned off his computer for the last time and, like many others before him, picked up the closest thing he could find to alleviate the boredom from the chasm of time that opened up in front of him: A Biro and a scrap of A4. An outpouring of visual diarrhoea was unleashed.

As Tom himself puts it, in a slightly related way:

"I remember in one CDT lesson at school drawing a small picture of a kettle in the corner of my exercise book with my Biro and it looked quite good."

Anyway, since then Tom has turned his hand to illustration. He has produced various pieces for us here at Lazy Gramophone, as well as work for the likes of Scroobius Pip, Marmaduke Dando, Woon and King John along with countless gig posters around London. In January 2008 Tom produced an installation at The Macbeth Gallery in which he white-wallpapered the entire gallery and invited members of the public to come and scrawl whatever they liked on the walls, so elevating the art of toilet wall graffiti to gallery status. Tom continues to champion the universal art of the doodle.

SAM RAWLINGS

Books have always fascinated me. I began to develop my own writing through the study of poetry. My poems have since appeared in a number of literary magazines such as Fire, Obsessed with Pipe Work and Harlequin. After university I went on to co-found Lazy Gramophone. It was during this period that I published my first book, Circle Time. Lazy Gramophone led me to appreciate the value of collaboration. I have since invested a lot of time and energy in editing two large collaborative projects; The Book of Apertures, and this one, Time, which you are holding in your hands. Storytelling seems now to have become the main focus of my work. I have published numerous stories, both within The Book of Apertures and Time, as well as within the Lazy Gramophone Shorts series. A limited edition print run of my apocalyptic short story Echoes of Dawn remains on sale in the Lazy Gramophone Shop. As for the present; well, I grow increasingly obsessed by the building of worlds and particularly enjoy stories that contain an element of magic as well as a good deal of adventure. My current work-in-progress reflects a fondness for these things. I hope to release it one day soon – The End.

CARL LAURENCE

"C Laurence is one of those humble mysteries that burrows underground, yet remains distinctly visible to the knowable eye and mind. His drawings offer an intense period of time where all its fruits of labour and strategic problem solving becomes fuzzy, slowly revealing the perfect recipe to a well-baked tangent cake. Improvising, rendering tones and transforming stories into pictures becomes all too possible when his imagination engages like a newly recruited space cadet on too much sugar intake on board a big ass spaceship . . . Being an abstract and dedicated trooper of LazyG, he plays ball with illustration and its writers, continuing as a destined MVP on the shortlist for doing something significant in this world before finally up and moving to planet Saturn . . . with brains to another dimension, constant hemorrhaging of realistic tendencies, it's in his black and white world where love is made between a mechanical pencil and a sheet of paper, minus the implication of colour blindness."

Luther Feathersby. Godfather of Critique.

Laurence's pastimes have known to include, mowing the grass, sniffing door handles, dogs ears, fascinations between the floor and wall, kung-fu films, overproof rum, soap, raves, romance, green tea, and getting high on creosote. Carl Laurence is actually a female 57 year old accountant with 7 children, 12 border terriers and too much time on her hands.

Log on, Find her and Like him on facebook at: http://www.facebook.com/Carl l laurence .... NOW!!

MEGAN LEONIE HALL

Thank you for reading my ramblings. I think language and words are extraordinarily powerful tools for illuminating all the in-between bits, the spillages and intangibles of being alive; emotional, physical, psychological, metaphysical. Meaning is subjective. And when it's done, it doesn't belong to you anymore. Verbal alchemy is getting kicks from distilling chaotic, hot vapour into dense, oral liquor. Flavours and effects vary. If we drink the same drink at the same time then we're thinking the same think at the same time.

Welcome to my worlds. I'm grateful for your time :)

BRYN HALL

Yew, wasson!?

My name's Bryn 'Byrd' Hall. I dwell in the deepest, darkest corner of South West Cornwall. I work as a Freelance Illustrator and as a passionate surfer, naturally I stumbled into the 'Surf-Art' category.

My work is inspired by the ocean. I try to express the freedom and beauty I find when out in the water, looking back at the world. I have worked for local and multi-national brands, mainly Surf companies such as Oxbow Europe, Blue Lava and Nordic Surfers Magazine. With a constantly evolving style, I'm ever ready to try new methods and techniques in whatever design orientated worlds that open up to me. I hope you like my work as much as I enjoy making it! Cheersy

GUY J JACKSON

Guy J. Jackson

Currently living in Los Angeles, Guy J Jackson is a writer, performer, and movie-maker, and he can be somewhat found online at http://www.youtube.com/user/guyjjackson. BBC sound engineer Robin The Fog collaborated with Guy on their recent storytelling album "Notes On Cow Life", downloadable via http://thefogsignals.com

JUDE MELLING

@JCMelon aka Jude Melling, an unprofessional illustrator, comic artist and writer based in London.

He has an artblog: http://judemelon.blogspot.com/

BIOGRAPHIES OF CONTRIBUTORS · 266

LIZ ADAMS

Liz Adams is a poet and writer. Her first collection of poems, *Green Dobermans*, was published in 2011 by Lazy Gramophone Press. She has an MA in Creative Writing from the University of East Anglia, and her work has been published or is forthcoming in *Iota Fiction*, *The Frogmore Papers*, *morphrog* and *Stand*. Liz completed the MRes in Humanities and Cultural Studies at the London Consortium in 2011; her work there considered the emotion of envy in William Blake's *Vala or The Four Zoas* through an application of colour theory. She was part of the Voiceworks project 2010-2011 which comprises of poets from Birkbeck's Contemporary Poetics Research Centre, and musicians from the Guildhall School of Music & Drama. For the project she wrote the lyrics to a protest song against the government's spending cuts which was sung at the Wigmore Hall. She has also worked in collaboration with dancers at The Place (London).

MADDIE JOYCE

I'm an English las, born and bred on the South Coast, nestled away in the countryside. I've always had a massive appreciation for the ocean, the way it's constantly changing, adorning our coastlines with wildlife and unimaginable beauty. Drawing for me, is a way to express my inner child without getting weird looks. It keeps me positive and my mind healthy, it's definitely feel-good food for the soul. There is so much art in surfing and the lifestyle that surrounds it, from the sport itself to the adventure, which ultimately go hand in hand. It's where my heart is and the pen just follows.

www.maddiejoyceart.blogspot.com
www.themagicbuscollective.com

INUA ELLAMS

Inua Ellams was born in Jos, Plateau State, Nigeria in 1984. He works as a poet, playwright, performer. Under the moniker 'phaze' he also works as a graphic designer/artist. He has five books published including *Thirteen Fairy Negro Tales* (Poetry, Flipped Eye, 2005) *The 14th Tale* (Play, Flipped Eye, 2009) and *Untitled* (Poetry & Play, Oberon, 2010). His poems were included in anthologies: *Generation Txt* (Penned in the Margins, 2006), *City State* (Penned in the Margins, 2009), *The Salt Book of Younger Poets* (Salt, 2011). His second pamphlet *Candy Coated Unicorns and Converse All Stars* came out in November 2011.

MARIA DRUMMEY

I do not have my own website, most of the words are still in my head... when inspiration strikes, either on a train, just before sleep, or listening to a beautiful piece of music or enjoying a wonderful illustration, if I am lucky enough, I have a pen and some paper or a scrappy old notebook and can let the words pour out and capture them on the page. I tend to find that the best poems, stories and the beginnings of stories are the ones that flash into your mind when you don't have that pen and paper (the essential artists tools), and like the magical mist on a lake, they are frozen in time and perfection all too briefly, admired and longed for just for a moment and they evaporate before dawn. One of these days, those elusive words I am so happy to even think of, will find the pen and paper and I will jot them down and hopefully you will enjoy the reading of them.

EMMA DAY

I love analogue photography, the smell of chemicals, the darkroom. I love being experimental with photography, anything film and polaroid based always appeals to me. For me photography is about sharing your experiences and preserving memories. It allows me to question reality.

WILLIAM KHERBEK

William Kherbek: Multi-instrumentalist, living on the margins of our technological society; intermittently tolerated. So things are improving. Denizen of Bethnal Green. Has performed at the Zabludowicz Collection, Barbican Arts Centre, and Paradise Row. Poetry published in Orbis and anthologised by Friary Road House Editions. He gets older every day.

VINCENT GILLAN

My name is Vincent Gillan and I'm eighteen. I take pictures of my friends and things I see.

KIRSTY ALISON
Bio Image by Gaynor Perry

Kirsty Allison is a Londoner and started writing for fashion magazines as a teenager whilst presenting late-night trash TV, pursuing print journalism for Dazed, Vogue, The Sunday Times, NME, The Guardian and many more. In the 90s she had a DJ band with Irvine Welsh and a residency at Ibiza's Manumission, which led to producing radio with the BBC, where she won a Sony Award. She produced the award-winning film, Tantric Tourists in 2011, shot on the road in India by Alexander Snelling/Slack Alice Films, and supports the writing of her first novel with styling, creative direction and lecturing. She has a rusty camper van and a puppy (which, will have drowned its cuteness in the fountain of youth by the time you read this).

"Kirsty Allison combines the cerebral with the carnival." The Sunday Times Style Magazine

www.kirstyallison.com

LOLA DUPRE

Born 1982 – Algeria. In early 2012 Lola moved to a new studio in the south of France near Avignon. Previously she worked from the Chateau studios and then the Chalet studios in Glasgow, Scotland. Lola grew up in Algeria, Paris and London before moving to Glasgow where she has produced the majority of her work to date. Highly fractured and complex, her collage work represents her fascination with detail, the normal and the abnormal. Lola Dupre works with portraiture, editorial, commission based projects and collaborates with other visual artists. She is currently working with photographers on several upcoming editorial projects, a clash of art and fashion. Lola Dupre works exclusively with paper, scissors and PVA glue, her collage work is sometimes mistaken for digital manipulation but her work has always been grounded in traditional media. Her inspiration however includes the modern photoshopped collage, as well as people, nature and the work of her peers and accomplices. In 2011 Lola exhibited works in Los Angeles (Phoneboothgallery, CES FA), San Francisco (FFDG), Glasgow (Collins Gallery) and Tokyo (Vacant).

LAURA DOCKRILL

'Everyone's falling for Laura Dockrill'
VOGUE.

Not only author and illustrator of Mistakes In The Background, Ugly Shy Girl and Echoes, Laura also resurrects her words on the stage performing poetry spanning festivals to bookshops; including London Literary Festival, Big Chill, E4 Udderbelly, Latitude, Kosmopolis in Barcelona and Domino festival in Brussels. Named one of the top ten literary talents by The Times and one of the top twenty hot faces to watch by ELLE magazine,

Laura continues to stir up the literary universe with her passionate, contemporary and imaginative way with words. She has performed her work on Woman's Hour, The Huw Stephens show, The Jo Whiley show, The Verb, Newsnight, BBC Breakfast and each of the BBC's respective radio channels 1-6.

Having recently joined the advisory panel at The Ministry Of Stories, Laura is currently writing a sitcom, creating a series of bespoke artwork pieces and writing a piece of work for a new BBC radio show.

NIKKI PINDER

Nikki Pinder is an Illustrator and Designer based in Cheshire. At age four she tried to fly with books as wings; in later years she turned to illustration and other kinds of artwork. Obsessed with drawing, differing textures, details and making new things from old, Nikki takes inspiration from nature and often works outdoors, creating new imagined landscapes and creatures with ink and pen. Nikki has worked on many collaborative projects, most recently creating illustrations for popular art-collective The House of Fairy Tales, designing the front cover of CALM Magazine, illustrating t-shirts and shoes for Acupuncture, and designing a travelogue book and stickers for 'The Wonder Lands' area of 'End of the Road Festival'.

Nikki is currently dreaming up adventures for self-created characters 'Mr. Moostashio' and 'The Shadow Catcher'; these will appear soon in two self-published picture books. Robots, flowers, antique books, mechanical constructions and photography inspire Nikki's energetic and engaging artwork. With several successful UK exhibitions under her belt, Nikki is currently creating new artwork for a solo show which will take place in Becnicks Wonder-Emporium, Chester, beginning in June 2012. Nikki studied Illustration and Graphic Design at Nottingham Trent University where she graduated with First Class Honours.

WILL CONWAY

Will lives and writes in London. He has just had a shower and is thinking about cutting his hair. He has a collection of short stories called Tastes of Ink published by Lazy Gramophone and is always up to something.

LEE HOLLAND

Lee Holland is an artist/illustrator currently based in Stoke on Trent.

Holland's work is bold, sometimes grotesque and often deals with content from the darker side of the human experience (seen in his 2008 project – 'Isolation' – where he trapped himself in a room for one hundred hours to draw deprivation from first-hand experience). Perhaps paradoxically his work also makes reference to popular culture and politics (seen in works such as Syrian Media Ban, sinking sun and Diplomatic car) and often transcends the gap between fine art, illustration and cartoon.

Holland's work has appeared in various exhibitions at venues of note such as The V&A and The Candid Arts Cafe.

Clients include: H&M, Future Cinema, APN, ArtBelow and The Staffordshire press.

JO TEDDS

Since transitioning from the stage to the page, Jo has been experimenting with genre and style; attempting to address how memories can change with time and specifically how people can be the authors of their own past and each others. Jo is currently working on a collection of short stories – Subject to Change, which she hopes to publish in the near future.

JODIE DABER

I live in the North and I like meat and adjectives.

ANDREW WALTER

Andrew Walter is an illustrator/wannabe printmaker based in Wood Green and Southwark. His life is lived mostly in a soporific bubble of literature, heavy metal, horror films and role-playing games, a bubble which is occasionally punctured by the flinty reality of creating artwork and crushingly monotonous day jobs wherein the public ritually castigate him for money. He wishes people would stop telling him his work would 'look really good on a Wacom tablet, yeah?' and believes not all motion is progress. He is trying to incorporate more colour into his work.

ZOE CATHERINE KENDALL

London based interdisciplinary artist, writer and jewellery designer Zoe Catherine Kendall is busy inserting herself into the gaps between varied definitions. After graduating from a Jewellery Design BA at Central Saint Martins in 2007, Kendall went on to launch her own jewellery brand which has been represented by several independent galleries and larger shops in around London including Kabiri, Selfridges, The Last Tuesday Society and Johnny Rocket.

However, unsatisfied with being introduced by friends as a Jeweller, in 2010 Kendall began her own blog as a place to think and write about the inseparable processes of living and making art. Shortly afterwards she was invited to write the artist blog for Run Riot. This was to become the perfect opportunity for her to combine her distinctive styles of visual art with her use of the written word, allowing her the freedom to construct cross genre pieces which she broadly describes as treatments of existence. This alongside reviews and interviews of artists and figures whose work inspired her practice.

Her current body of work explores various mediums of expression including spoken and written word, illustration, painting, moving image, performance, installation, book and diary art, momento making, collected paraphernalia and body adornment. Kendall believes that by allowing herself a freedom in her forms of expression, the diverse methodologies she calls upon to voice her ideas will merge together, forming a whole story from their fragmentary parts. These fragments she says, are a much more authentic reflection of the thought process and ultimately result in a more immersive experience for her audience.

She says of her work 'personal living experiences inspire my practice, often autobiographical but never self-serving, I seek to illuminate those invisible spaces between people, action, emotion, thought and idea. Themes include a treatment of existence and consciousness, psychotherapy and play, states of mind and the self as emotional medium for wider society. I challenge my audience by making public thoughts often confined to more private contexts as a form of societal therapy. I use my life as a single twenty-something female living alone in London as a platform to begin, depicting what might otherwise be an invisible, individual struggle which is in fact shared by many.'

Zoe is a member of arts collective and independent publisher Lazy Gramophone and a member of Fabelist Artists' and Writers' Collective.

JEANNIE PASKE

Jeannie Paske is a self-taught artist who combines watercolor, charcoal, pastel, powdered pigments and ink to form richly textured illustrations of thoughtful monsters and peculiar creatures. In 2006 she established 'Obsolete World' as a place her various creations could call home. She is a big fan of philosophy mixed with humor, and strives to convey hope and introspection, as well as curiosity in her work. Obsolete World art can be found in shops and galleries throughout the United States. Jeannie currently resides in Portland, Oregon and is working on a book of illustrated short stories.

MAT LLOYD

Once referred to as "an angry middle finger to poetry purists", Mat has mellowed in the last couple of years but he is still a staunch supporter of taking poetry to the unconverted.

An avid writer from a young age, Mat was inspired by his early love of rap music, but it wasn't until a local open mic night in 2005 that he first took to the stage as a Performance Poet. Frustrated at the misconception that poetry was the preserve of the pretentious and arrogant, he moved his performances to London. With an easy and accessible style he quickly established himself.

Having performed in venues the length and breadth of the country, Mat's hard work and determination has won an unconventional audience, appreciative of his anarchic approach to poetry, an approach which helped him to win Nathan Penlington's 'Poetry Idol', and progress to the final of the Hammer and Tongues national Slam Competition.

Appearing in film festivals and educational programs from Canada to Russia, Mat's video work reaches a global audience. His first video poem 'Suicide Note: Bank Manager Lament' was adopted by the UK's Consumer Action Group, and 'Blokes,' his first collaboration with Illustrator Matt Frodsham, won the Best Film prize at the ShortCuts Film Festival, going on to be used by the Charity CALM. Their second collaboration received an 'Editor's Choice Award' on VIMEO, and was featured in magazines throughout Europe and the US finally ending up on the shortlist for a 'Left Field Award.' Mat's latest video, a joint piece with cinematographer Marc Webb titled 'This City' has led him to work with composer Stuart Hancock on a project for the Barbican.

Mat's unique and exciting poetic style has given him the chance to work with a number of educational authorities who use his poems both in the UK and further afield. Programs like TrueTube, an award-winning website for schools that provides videos, lesson plans & assembly scripts for RE, PSHE and Citizenship at Key Stages 3/4 use Mat to captive young people with his poetry and videos.

Mat's second collection 'Extended Play' is due out later this year. As well as continuing to write, he is the 'Team Manager' for Discipline Skateboards and is currently lurking somewhere in the south...

JAMES KAMO

Name: James Kamo
Stance: Regular
Home Town: Irvine, California
Favorite Foods: Stuff from Tesco, Asda, Wagamama's, and Pret A Manger.
Favorite Color: Blue
Current Location: USA and Sleeps in a Tent
Education: London College of Fashion + University College Falmouth
Random: I broke my leg jet skiing

MUSA OKWONGA

Musa Okwonga is a poet and sportswriter. A qualified City lawyer, he is the author of two books, A Cultured Left Foot and Will You Manage?, the first of which was nominated for the William Hill Sports Book of the Year Award. He has written for the New York Times and The Independent, and has been a regular guest on the BBC Radio 4 Today Programme and the BBC World Service. He is one half of The King's Will, an exciting new electronica act, whose work has been featured and acclaimed in January 2012 by BBC6Music, Xfm, Knowledge Magazine and The Sunday Times.

JAKE ELLIS

Jake Ellis is a man with 1950s hair. He is utterly unqualified to call himself an artist. He makes pictures out of bits of other pictures, usually with fragments of text. He likes them and hopes you do too.

He is also uncomfortable referring to himself in the third person, but accepts that it's probably necessary at times.

ZOPHIEL WEBB

Hi, I am Zophiel Webb and I draw pictures. I grew up in Croydon and graduated from the now non-existent Byam Shaw School of Art. At university I realised how much I enjoyed drawing over and above everything else. It means everything to me and feels as though I couldn't exist if I could never draw again.

I like to produce images, mostly portraits, which look as though they're printed but when you concentrate you can see it's been created by hand. The portraits usually feature a mandala in the background that has different significance in each drawing. There's normally an excruciating level of detail that I'll try and fit in so you have to get really close to see what's happening. The people I choose to draw in this way have normally had a significant impact on my life in one way or another.

I also make what I call "Bookassettes" which is a mixtape disguised as a book. I make these to give away and it consists of a mixtape, tracklist, collages and trinkets, all hidden in the hollowed out book. Music and literature have always had a huge influence on my work and this I felt was a way of combining it all. I've given them out to people that I felt I wanted to give something back to.

There are obviously many other things I think about drawing and ideas I've been mulling over for years but these are things that will happen in the future. Right now I'm happy drawing random folks and listening to music and working at a record store, but I do long for a day when I'll get the chance to expand my illustrative horizons.
www.zophielwebb.com

ADAM GREEN

Adam Green is a writer and musician from London. His debut novel Satsuma Sunmover, which includes illustrations by Carl Laurence, was published by Lazy Gramophone Press and long-listed for the Dylan Thomas Prize for Young Writers. His band Blue Swerver released its first album, The Art of Collapsing, on Modify the Van Records in 2008. He sporadically performs spoken word renditions of his prose in various subterranean locales.

PAULA AFONSO

My name is Paula Afonso. I was born in 1976 in a small town in Galicia, in Spain. Some of my first drawings still exist within the cookbook of my mother . . . When I moved to the city to study at college, I began to draw more continuously. Although I do not illustrate professionally, still I like to draw and colour without any specific reason; I think it just relaxes and entertains me. I draw quotidian things around me: home furniture, building, scissors, a spoon, the views I have from my window, people traveling with me on a train, people sitting waiting in a cafe. If you look in my bag you will always find a notebook, a pencil or a colour with which to draw. I just think to myself, draw and enjoy!

FRANCES K WOLFE

Frances K Wolfe is a twenty-six year old writer, photographer and artist from London. She began working for magazines in 2009, as a journalist, then eventually a features editor but was fired unceremoniously after refusing to write what she may or may not have described as, "frilly, cupcake baking, pro-gossip culture propaganda bullshit," and has never tried to restart her journalistic career; much to the relief of the publishing industry. She recently graduated from the Royal Court Theatre's Young Writer's Programme. She likes the music of Karl Blake, cigarettes and wine. She dislikes baking, knitting and necrosis of the flesh.

You can read more at www.franceskwolfe.com or follow her at twitter.com/franceskwolfe.

DIEGO MALLO

Diego Mallo is a visual artist and illustrator currently living and working between Barcelona and London.

As a passionate devotee of the absurd, the unexpected and of the random situations of daily occurrence, he likes to dig deep without mercy into the human soul, into the dubious values of our society, and the paradoxes of contemporary reality.

Depicting situations that are uncomfortable, irritating or surprising to look at, Mallo seeks an emotional impact.

Interdisciplinary experimentation keeps him alive. Diego Mallo flourishes on diversity and considers contemporary dance, music and cinema a great source of inspiration.

VINCENT J PRINCE

Infamous drunk, notorious public nuisance and vitriolic vernacular vandal – Vincent J Prince has been stuffing his readers' peepers with an erratic concoction, ranging from the profoundly profane, to the pensively poetic, for some five odd years now. Constantly courting controversy (and usually a hangover), Vincent's eclectic catalogue spans poetry, fiction and a rather oblique optique upon life itself. Genetically predisposed to find it nigh on impossible to finish anything; VJP roosts upon a nest of half-baked theories, part-scrawled manuscripts and the odd bread crust. If you see him in the street, DO NOT approach him; he is likely armed with a pen and almost certainly sozzled.

MATT BLACK

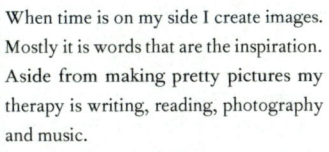

When time is on my side I create images. Mostly it is words that are the inspiration. Aside from making pretty pictures my therapy is writing, reading, photography and music.

I am currently training to be a Teacher of Art and live with my wife and children near Oxford.

RUPERT J MUNCK

Rupert conscientiously objects to biographies.

MINA MILK

I was born in Russia, now I live in London and Moscow. I did economics for a bit, now doing illustration and visual arts. Exhibiting in the UK, Russia, Spain, France, USA; doing commercial projects that include diesel, snob mag, dreamers united etc. As for inspiration, I do have a keen interest in traditional printmaking, patterns and animals; also I'm collecting sculls and travel memories.

CHARLIE COTTRELL

Charlie finds it difficult to form habits. She's tried loads of times: exercise, telephoning her parents, watching TV shows. Nothing sticks. Once in a while she'll sit down in a Caffe Nero and start putting down some strings of words that sometimes weave themselves into stories. The results are something like what you'll find here.

In between times Charlie is an Editor working with some of the biggest companies and charities in the world, helping them to tell their stories too. A member of Corvoisier Future 500, Charlie recently presented a trend forecast on the Future of Food; a subject she thinks is the most important story of all.

CLAIRE FLETCHER

Since childhood I have used writing as a way to elucidate and explore the feelings and events that awe, baffle and inspire me. Writing helps me to search and bridge the space in-between the world I know and the world I am exploring. It is one of the ways that I make meaning from my experiences. I am a collaborator in Lazy Gramophone's *The Book of Apertures* and *The Time Project*.

TIM GREAVES

Born in 1979, Hitchin, UK. Lives and works in Berlin, Germany.
BA Fine Art, University of Newcastle, Newcastle upon Tyne, UK.
Post Graduate Diploma Fine Art, Chelsea College of Art, London, UK.

SOLO EXHIBITIONS

2011
Jalousien, Praterstrasse 48, Berlin, Germany.

2009
This Twilight Could be Right, Kotti-shop, Berlin, Germany.

SELECTED GROUP EXHIBITIONS

2012
The Nail, The Colours, The Mast Kotti-shop, Berlin, Germany.
Availabilism, Superfluo, Padua, Italy.
Omnia Mea Mecum Porto, Kotti-shop, Berlin, Germany.

2011
My Own Private Leitkultur, Parkhaus Projects, Berlin Germany.
This is what happens with that kind of thing,
Historischen Gewölbekeller, Spandau, Germany.

2010
Over and Over, Forgotten Bar, Berlin, Germany.
From the nipple never satisfied,
Nadania Idriss Contemporary, Berlin, Germany.
The Knot, Parcul Carol I, Bucharest, Romania.
Reduxdelux, Parkhaus Projects, Berlin Germany.
The Knot, Marianneplatz, Berlin, Germany.

Circlework, Parkhaus Projects, Berlin
Germany.

WORKSHOPS / COLLABORATIONS

2010

Transform, Deutschbank, Unter den Linden, Berlin.
Quartier fuer Vielflieger Workshop, Kottishop, Berlin.
Kinder-Arkiv-Workshop, A-maze-ing, Marianneplatz, Berlin, Germany.

2009

Kinder-Drawing-Workshops, Kotti-Shop, Berlin, Germany.
Speed Draw Dating, Kotti-Shop, Berlin, Germany.
Slidebar, Kotti-Shop, Berlin, Germany.

2008

Enter the Diarama: The Life-Size 3D Drawing Workshop, Extrapool, Nijmegen, Netherlands.

Archidrawww, Raumerweiterungshalle, Berlin, Germany.
Zzzine-Making Sessions Pt. 1-3, Raumerweiterungshalle, Berlin, Germany.

ALEXANDER ASPINALL

Alexander Aspinall is a writer and digital editor.

He can often be found writing stories that might include other places, normal people or magic dogs, and things like rain, spiders, breakfasts, sleeping and delusion.

He lives in London.

SORANA SANTOS

London-based award-winner and multi-instrumentalist, Sorana, set her heart on going to Music College in early childhood, and subsequently gave up what seemed to be the ideal record and management deal to follow her dream and take up a place studying Composition at The Guildhall School of Music and Drama.

A lifetime music-collector and music obsessive extraordinaire, there was rarely a day that went by without her playing the piano, composing and singing for hours on end, after which she would do homework whilst taping and cataloguing John Peel sessions.

"It was always very clear to me that I was going to be a musician; there was never any doubt of that. My teacher would ask me to learn a piece and I'd go off and learn the entire book. I also went to extreme lengths to buy music and get to gigs, saving the pound coins I got for lunch to buy CD's with, and pawning the CD's I'd learned to get to gigs. In sixth form I had a job in an art shop that paid cash, which I'd blow at the record shop on the way home. I'd end up having to drink tap water when I went out with my friends at the weekend, but it was a no-brainer really."

During her time at The Guildhall, Sorana found herself founding, composing for and managing various contemporary orchestras, whilst establishing herself as an in-demand arranger and session musician.

Upon graduating, Sorana was poised to accept funding to study Electroacoustics at City University when a spell of labyrinthitis had her intermittently housebound for long stretches of time.

"I couldn't work consistently and had an awful lot of time to think. For a long time I'd had the feeling that something was missing from my work, but I couldn't fathom what it was. Then I remembered and looked through this old box of letters, poems, stories, and little books I'd lovingly written over the years, and realised that working with words was what was missing. Getting ill became my good fortune."

Soon after, Sorana found herself being asked for pieces by Lazy Gramophone Press, who have continued to support and promote her work. At the same time, Sorana has established herself as a well-respected musician, composing and performing extensively for both major and independent labels, artists, and publishers, film and theatre directors, as well as releasing three self-produced EP's and writing for The Guardian.

2013 will see the completion of her fourth EP *Our Lady of Sorrows*, a portrait of women's solitude, and will also mark the publication of her first book *Posthumous: Poems Through the Concept of Contemporary Music* and essay in literary journal, Agenda Poetry.

"At the moment, a lot of my inspiration is derived from uniting the unsettling aspects of the worlds of psychoanalysis, religion, myths, and nature, with Eastern structures that are atypical to Western art... and, of course, the darker areas of my own life."

KAITLIN BECKETT

A collection of curious beasts of the sea, air, land and subconscious; painted and drawn with airbrush, dip pen and stained fingers, lovingly embellished with iridescent pigments and metal leaf. Kaitlin is originally from New Zealand and is currently living and working in Melbourne, Australia. She has exhibited in and her works have been collected in Australia, New Zealand, the US and the UK.

"Since childhood I have had a love for the fantastic and the imaginary – I enjoy depicting the real and the unreal together, biomechanical juxtapositions, the unusual engaged with the everyday. The natural world, odd dreams, cryptozoology, literature and science fiction inspire me; and attachments, disguises, viscera and machinery are recurring themes in my bestiary. My characters invoke a sense of pathos, unease or humour, and I like to encourage others to invent their own narrative around my creatures."

DANIEL CHIDGEY

Founding member of Lazy Gramophone, master printer, covering digital, letterpress and Giclee. Photographer, designer and generally appreciative of all visual media. Born 1982 and still breathing.

DAN PRESCOTT

Dirty draws.

Get in touch at info@couperstreet.com

ABOUT LAZY GRAMOPHONE PRESS.

"A handsomely produced book (The Book of Apertures)."
Philip Pullman

"I love Lazy Gramophone, you're doing terrific work."
Terri Windling

"In a time when publishers are taking fewer and fewer risks on unknown writers, Lazy Gramophone are to be applauded for giving their collective a chance to shine."
Litro Magazine

"A wonderful environment of ideas and imaginings – The Lazy Gramophone group as a collective have demonstrated a remarkable and inspiring ethos throughout and their willingness to provide a means of expression is second to none."
Amelias Magazine

Lazy Gramophone was established in 2003 with the aim of helping independent artists, writers and musicians gain exposure and showcase their work.

www.lazygramophone.com, designed by Ben Chidgey, was the initial platform from which these works were projected into the world. To this day the website is constantly being developed, establishing www.lazygramophone.com as one of the most prominent creative platforms in the UK.

> *"Lazy Gramophone places a strong focus on collaboration. By encouraging artists and writers to work together and support each other, we hope to establish a sustainable creative platform upon which each member will have the opportunity and the resources, to not only create their own work but also to reach a wide audience once it has been completed."*
>
> Sam Rawlings, Co-founder Lazy Gramophone

Since 2006, 'Lazy Gramophone Presents . . .' has hosted regular live events and small day-long festivals at The Macbeth, The Miller and at The Luminaire (all central London). These events have included music, spoken word, theatre, film, art displays, fashion shows and comedy. Throughout all of these activities, 'Lazy Gramophone Presents . . .' has remained dedicated to supporting and developing artists and groups from the UK and London. Among others, 'Lazy Gramophone Presents . . .' events have featured Dan Le Sac Vs Scroobius Pip (Sunday Best), Paloma Faith (Epic), Lucky Elephant (Sunday Best), Kate Tempest (Ted Hughes award for innovation in poetry) and Inua Ellams (National Theatre). Lazy Gramophone are proud to have instigated charity events in aid of Cancer Research UK and C.A.L.M: The Campaign Against Living Miserably.

> *"During each creative project, we work closely with the artists and the writers involved, listening to their ideas and then proceeding with absolute care and with our full attention to the smallest of details; our focus remaining at all times on creating the work we love."*
>
> Danny Chidgey, Co-founder Lazy Gramophone

Art has always been an integral part of Lazy Gramophone and since the beginning of 2008, Lazy Gramophone Artists has been coordinating and collaborating with artists in the curation of gallery shows, displaying both up-and-coming and more established artists' work. In the past, Lazy Gramophone Artists has also been fortunate enough to have gained the support of London's The Hospital Club. The club has exhibited and made available for sale, the work of artists from the Lazy Gramophone Artists cooperative. The artists featured were Tom Harris, Garry Milne and Dan Prescott, whose piece 'Quentin Armstrong' was also featured on the front cover of its members' magazine. Further success in 2009 saw two more of the cooperative's artists, Dan Prescott and Matt Black, commissioned to contribute work for 'Love in the Sky', the Institute of Contemporary Arts' inaugural charity exhibition, auction and global competition launch. The event took place in June 2009 at the ICA. Further artistic developments have seen Lazy Gramophone establish a partnership with Rooms Uncovered Magazine. Rooms Magazine is an independent and open organisation based in London. Their main objective is to facilitate better connections between the art community and the wider public. Lazy Gramophone has also been represented at the Art Below art fair at the Candid arts trust in January 2012.

> *"Lazy Gramophone is a strong supporter of independent shops and markets. We have made many strong and valuable links with stores both inside and outside of London. If you want to find a Lazy Gramophone item, then we encourage you to explore your local shops and markets."*
> Philip Levine, Co-founder Lazy Gramophone

The Lazy Gramophone Press department remains focused primarily upon the publication and distribution of books. Lazy Gramophone Press was established in 2006, and on 1st May of that year, published Adam Green's debut novel, Satsuma Sun-mover. The novel went on

ABOUT LAZY GRAMOPHONE PRESS

to be long-listed for The Dylan Thomas Prize for literature. Lazy Gramophone Press then went on to publish Sam Rawlings' poetry collection Circle Time, 2007, and a limited edition of his short story book Echoes of Dawn, 2008, as well as a series of handmade illustrated poetry booklets featuring collaborations between artists and writers. Lazy Gramophone Press's first large scale collaborative project, The Book of Apertures, was published in 2010: containing fifteen short stories and nine poems by fourteen different writers, exhibiting forty-one pieces of original artwork by nine different artists, The Book of Apertures represents a series of explorations into the enigmatic nature of life, as viewed through each contributors personal aperture. Building upon this success, Will Conway's short story collection, Tastes of Ink, was published in April of 2011. This was closely followed by Liz Adam's poety book, Green Dobermans, which was published in September of the same year. All of these works are available via the Lazy Gramophone shop: www.lazygramophone.com/shop.

"By sharing in this way we hope to inspire each other as well as those around us, to draw a diverse audience and so help to illuminate the work of alternative artists and writers everywhere."
Dan Prescott, Co-founder Lazy Gramophone